Deceit
Book #1 in The Gallows Hill Trilogy

Katelyn Taylor

Copyright

Published by Katelyn Taylor

Deceit is a work of fiction. Names, characters, incidents, and places are used fictitiously. Any resemblance to real people or events is coincidental.

Deceit Copyright © 2024 by Katelyn Taylor

All rights reserved.

Playlist

Everybody Wants To Rules The World by Lorde
Natural by Imagine Dragons
Graveyard by Halsey
Ocean Eyes by Billie Eilish
RUNRUNRUN by Dutch Melrose
Uprising by Muse
Him & I (with Halsey) by G-Eazy
Legends Are Made by Sam Tinnesz
Which Witch by Florence+The Machine

Trigger Warning

As always, please protect yourself and your mental health when opening a new book. Some of the triggers included in this book are, but not limited to:
Violence, Explicit Language, Explicit Sexual Scenes, Forced Medical Intervention (BC), Bullying, Cheating (Not on the FMC) Spanking, Graphic Torture, Dismemberment, Sharing, Branding

Dedication

To the spooky babes who want an extra three helpings of cock, this one is definitely for you.

Prologue

Welcome to Gallows Hill University.
The history of Salem, Massachusetts is not what we are known for, it is who we are.
Born in the ashes of evil, a society was formed, impassioned to protect the righteous and holy from the vengeance of the sentenced and their descendants.
Prove your loyalty, and you shall be given the world. Betray our trust, our secrets and our sacrifices and you will follow the path of the wicked; charred and beneath the dirt.
We look forward to your membership and cooperation.

Chapter One
Skyla

"I'm taking the airwrap as a sign of protest!" I shout down the hallway.

My aunt Steph shouts back to me as she makes her way down the hall.

"The hell you are! That was my birthday present *from* you," she laughs before peeking inside the doorway.

Her blonde hair is only a few shades darker than my own and her eyes aren't the same as mine or my mom's. Instead of the deep emerald green I inherited, she got my grandfather's hazel eyes that look absolutely mesmerizing against her creamy skin.

"What can I say, I have excellent taste," I tease before my smile slowly dims.

I turn away from her, bending down as I rifle through the bathroom cabinets, knowing I've grabbed everything that is mine. I just don't have it in me to turn around and let her witness me fall apart for the ninth time this morning alone.

She bends down beside me, rubbing a soothing hand up and down my back. It helps a little, balming the hurt from what comes next, the only way a parent should be able to. Aunt Steph is so much more than that, though. She isn't my biological mom, but she might as well be in every sense of the word.

I was three when my mom passed away. Boating accident, I guess. Though I only have one or two hazy memories of her, Steph tells me stories about her often. Steph was her younger sister and to her, my mom hung the moon.

When it was time for me to start boarding school here in London my father had no qualms about sending me away without a single friend, family or even parting look. Aunt Steph wouldn't allow it, though. She was somehow able to convince him to allow her to move with me.

From three-years-old to nineteen, I've lived in this flat just down the road from my school. All of my friends are here, my memories. Every Christmas and birthday started around this brick fireplace and every batch of diet breaking cookies were baked in this kitchen. The flat was nothing compared to the mansion that awaited me back home in Massachusetts, or what most kids were living in when they were on break here in London, but it was ours and it breaks me that I have to leave it all behind.

"You'll visit often, it'll be okay." Steph smiles through watery tears.

I swallow roughly, shaking my head as I speak.

"Why won't you just come with me? Please? All you ever do is complain about England anyways, 'It's too cold, it's too busy. The beer is warm, and the food is weird,'" I say, in my best imitation of her whining.

She rolls her eyes but pushes my shoulder to the side with a smirk.

"I do not sound like that."

"You most certainly do," I laugh.

Smiling sadly, she shakes her head.

"We've talked about this, Sky. I just got that new job at the firm.

I've worked really hard to get here, I don't want to throw that away."

I knew I was being selfish by wanting her to come with me, but who can blame me? It's like I'm losing a parent all over again, one I actually remember.

A sharp knock comes from the front door, sending my stomach plummeting before we share a look. Without a word, we move into the living room where my half a dozen bags are packed. My entire life being stuffed into a luggage set, destined for its new home at Gallows Hill University.

It was always the plan that once I graduated I would attend there, I just didn't realize how fast everything would go by. Maybe I'd feel less devastated by it all if my father and I were closer or friendly in any meaning of the word.

He's not a cruel man, he's just...aloof. Unbothered by pretty much anything that doesn't have to do with his precious company or the stock market. It's how he made his grand fortune, and he loves them like one would love a child, or more so in our case.

Now, I know I sound like the typical dramatic nineteen-year-old with daddy issues, but who could blame me? The man only shows up once a year, every year, on my birthday. He takes me to dinner, makes uncomfortable small talk about my studies and then he's gone the same night. I didn't understand it as a kid, I didn't get why he didn't want to spend time with me, why he didn't love me like the other kid's parents did. Eventually, I accepted it and now, I'm indifferent altogether.

Obviously, indifference isn't a fantastic feeling when I'm going to be living with the man. Maybe this will be what we need to have a functioning relationship, though I'm not holding my breath.

Steph opens the front door, and two men that I recognize as my father's personal security step inside before he files in after them. I've asked him a few times why he never goes anywhere without them, it's not like he's the president or anything, he's never answered, though. Either he doesn't want to answer, or he doesn't feel I'm worthy of the wasted breath, either way I stopped my interest in really anything to do with him a long time ago.

"Stephanie," he says, in a superior tone as he lifts his chin to her.

"Henry," she responds, in a tone that is equally respectful but holds a touch of contempt.

He doesn't appear to hear it or doesn't care before he faces me, his eyes raking over me like he's looking for a single hair out of place. He won't find one, though. I know how he is. The man takes OCD to a new level and appearance is everything to Henry Parris.

My white shorts come down to my mid-thigh and my pin-striped dress shirt is tucked into them. There isn't a wrinkle out of place on this balmy London day, my hair perfectly smoothed and straightened.

I stand still, awaiting his evaluation to be complete when he finishes with a satisfied nod and a stoic face.

"The plane is waiting," he says, turning on his heel and walking out the door, his security carrying my bags as they follow after him.

A ripple of defiance stirs inside of me and though I know it will implode my life itself, I want nothing more than to tell him to leave without me. That I have no intention of getting on that plane and will proceed to live my life the way I and only I desire. Of course, I don't say or do any of that. Like the good daughter I am, I keep my mouth shut, lower my head and walk out the door after him. I only stop for half a moment, turning and hugging Steph with everything I have. She holds me tighter, whispering that she will call soon, and I hold onto that, desperately.

I don't know exactly what awaits me back in Salem, but I know it won't be nearly as wonderful as the life I've lived here.

We are in the air, slicing through the early morning sky like a hot knife through butter when my father sets down his phone, his signature gaudy silver ring glinting in the light as he looks up at me across from the coffee table between our chairs.

"You're getting married."

I don't think I hear him correctly, so I wait for him to continue whatever sentence he was actually trying to say. He doesn't say a word, though. Instead, he just stares at me like I'm the one who is supposed to respond.

"I beg your pardon?" I ask, in the most demure voice I can muster.

"You're engaged to be married. The date has been set, June twenty-third."

I blink at him slowly, doing my best to keep my tone light and my question simple.

"And, who am I expected to marry?"

"Asher Putnam."

"Who is that?" I practically scoff, biting my tongue as soon as I do.

The impartial mask he was wearing slips away as he narrows his eyes at me.

"Your fiancé. That's all you need to know."

Well, I've already upset him. Might as well bring it home.

"I'm too young to get married. I'm only nineteen. I *just* turned nineteen. I can't get married, especially to a man I haven't even met."

"I'm aware, Skyla, which is exactly why you will spend as much time with him during your time at Gallows Hill. I've arranged your schedules to coincide as much as possible, and his father has ensured he will stay on campus so that you two can get to know one another."

I pause at that.

"Wait, I'm not staying at the house?"

He rolls his eyes like I'm being stupid.

"Of course not. You will be staying in a dorm, same as all of the other students."

"I just assumed that because Aunt Steph and I—"

"The only reason I allowed you to live off-campus was because of Stephanie's insistence and my disinterest over the subject. However, Gallows Hill University is my alma mater, all eyes will be on the both of us and it is crucial that we do not disappoint," he says, his meaning clear.

That *you* don't disappoint. Henry Parris could never disappoint anyone, he's perfect. I'm the daughter he's practically hidden away since birth.

I've done enough research on Gallows Hill to know that it is an elitist school. Invitation only and it churns out some of the most influential and important people to America's society over the last three-hundred-years. Two presidents, five governors, one tech mogul and countless prestigious judges, lawyers, scientists and doctors. All circling back to this university. It's the best of the best and I have to go there. No, *get* to.

"I won't disappoint you," I promise, lowering my eyes as a form of respect that he seems to enjoy.

He nods, reaching his palm out and patting the back of my hand twice.

"Good. Be the respectable young woman you were raised to be, get to know your fiancé and trust no one else. The Putnam men are good people. They will protect you."

Nodding my head, I turn to look out the window. I assume he means Asher's father as well, since this is very clearly an arranged marriage. I don't know why I'm so surprised. He has hinted at the idea of an arranged marriage for quite some time. I just always thought he was joking or at least I had hoped. The man doesn't have a joking bone in his body, though, so this is really on me.

My cage must look so pretty to others on the outside, all gilded and shiny. Make no mistake, though, bars are bars. I'll never be free to make my own choices, to live my own life. My fate was sealed the moment I was born, and my birth certificate signed with the last name Parris.

I've talked with Steph about it for years, spoke about running away, begged her to come with me. Each time I did though, her face would pale, and she made me promise I would never say those things again, that I would never do those things. If it wasn't for her, for fear of never seeing her again and maybe for fear of what my father would do to her if I did disobey him, I'd have been gone a long time ago.

So instead, here I am flying away from the only home I have ever truly known, to an unknown man and an unknown place.

I'm thrilled.

Chapter Two
Skyla

I stayed at my father's home last night when we landed, but first thing the next morning, my bags were packed in the car and I was being chauffeured across the city to my new home. As soon as we arrived something rippled through me. It wasn't necessarily fear. It was almost something... foreboding. A feeling of being unwelcomed. Then again, that could just be my unease with this entire situation.

The campus is breathtaking, though. Large grand buildings that look more like cathedrals than university buildings line either side of the courtyard. Large pillars stand on either side of each entrance, an obvious display of wealth and history. My eyes skate up the sharp peaks and steep rooflines of my dorm building, practically black stained glass windows adorning each ridgeline.

My father assured me that Asher would be waiting in my dorm to welcome me and introduce himself. I can't lie that as I stand in the elevator, watching as each level lights up, my anxiety ratchets. What will he be like? Is he kind? Does he want to be in this engagement or is he being forced like I am?

When the elevator reaches the last floor, level seven, I step out of it and walk until I find my room. The door is wider than others and it's at the very corner of the hallway. Taking out the keycard that my father gave me this morning at breakfast, I wave it against the card reader much like a hotel before pushing it open.

My eyes widen and my mouth drops at the sight before me. I expected your average dorm room with a few extra amenities inside. After all, my father went here, as well as my mother and aunt Steph. She told me a lot about the school, how it was grand in ways other schools could never be. I assumed she meant the historic gothic architecture of the buildings outside that more closely resemble a castle, or maybe the sprawling land it sits on that seems to go for miles. I had no idea she was talking about plush leather couches, full kitchens and what looks to be an en suite to my left.

I also didn't expect to walk into my new dorm and find a naked woman bent over a queen sized bed as a man's bare ass thrusts into her savagely. The noises she's making has me shifting uncomfortably as he slaps the side of her ass and continues. I'm not a prude by any means, but I'd also be lying if I said I was experienced. Being forced to attend an all-girls boarding school and not being allowed out of an adult's supervision at all times made the whole engaging with the men thing virtually impossible.

The girl turns her head to look around the man, giving me a satisfied grin that makes my stomach turn. I spin on my heel as I head for the door. Obviously I was given the wrong room number. I'm stopped in my tracks almost immediately though, when a deep voice calls out to me.

"Where are you going?"

I don't turn around, continuing to stare at the doorway as I speak.

"Sorry. I must have the wrong room. I'm Skyla Parris."

I hear a deep groan and a breathy whimper come from behind me and I take another step to leave when he speaks again.

"Stay," he practically commands. "You," he says, as I glance behind me only to find him staring at the girl beneath him. "Get dressed and get the fuck out of here."

She does as he says happily, smiling the entire time she slips on her dress and heels. Running a hand through her hair, she leans in to press a kiss to his lips, but he easily dodges her, gripping her arm in his hand as he escorts her to the open doorway, slamming the door in her face.

Wow, harsh.

His pants are securely fastened by now, and his forehead is dotted with small beads of sweat as he turns to look at me. His short dark brown hair and matching brown eyes are nearly the same color, his sharp jawline looking like it was carved from marble.

I watch as his full pink lips twist up into a scowl as he speaks.

"Why are you staring at me?"

I startle at his question, fastening my eyes to the floor as I respond.

"I'm sorry."

He doesn't say anything for a moment before he begins circling me, much like a predator does to his prey.

"So, you're the Parris princess."

I frown at that, my eyes tracking him as he continues to slowly circle me.

"What? I'm not a princess. I'm—"

"You are on this campus, Princess, and I'm the king."

Tilting my head to the side, my face pinches in confusion.

"So, on this campus, I'm your daughter?"

He pauses for a moment before his face is slashed with irritation.

"Fucking smartass. My father told me you were a good girl. Quiet, obedient. Guess he was wrong."

His father? So this must be—

"Asher?" I question.

"Is that a question?" He asks with a lifted eyebrow.

My eyes roam over him, his wide shoulders and lean muscles a stark contrast from who I expected. I'm not really sure what I was expecting, but it definitely wasn't...him. His smug attitude is really starting to irritate me though, and before I can stop myself, I speak.

"Disappointed more so. What can you do? Life is full of them," I shrug.

Fire rages in his chocolate brown eyes before he reaches into his pocket, throwing a jewelry box at my chest. I make no move to catch it, allowing it to fall to the ground as he sneers.

"Put it on and don't take it off," before he's storming out of my room, slamming the door shut with a shake that rattles the walls around me.

Irritation rises inside of me, before I close my eyes and let out a ragged breath. And that is the guy that I'm supposed to be marrying in less than nine months? What an asshole.

***

After my bags are brought up to me and my things are unpacked, I get a call from the nurse's office.

"Can you please come down this evening so we can go over your medical records?" a soft voice asks through the phone.

"Oh, of course. How do I get there from the Parris dormitory?" I ask, internally cringing that my father felt it necessary to have an entire dorm named after himself. Then again, it could be my grand-father's doing, or maybe my great-grandfather. Supposedly, Parris's have been attending Gallows Hill since the college first opened back in the early seventeenth-century.

"Just head through the main courtyard and it's the building straight ahead. You can't miss it."

I nod to myself as I speak.

"I'll head there now."

"See you soon."

I hang up and grab my purse and key card, making sure to throw my phone in for good measure as I trek across campus. The sun hasn't quite set yet and it's actually fairly quiet. Tomorrow is the first day of classes and according to my father, move-in day was officially last week so everyone is undoubtedly turned in for the night.

When I get to the main building, I see a sign saying 'nurse' with an arrow on it. I follow the hallway all the way to the end before stopping at a full on ER, at least that's what it looks like. Dozens of beds, several nursing staff and medical supplies as far as the eye can see.

One guy is sitting on a bed, football uniform caked with mud and his bloodied nose stuffed with gauze. His eyes track me curiously, as if I was a newly discovered species. A cherubic looking nurse smiles at me as she makes her way over.

"Miss Parris?" she questions.

I give her a polite smile and nod as she escorts me to a bed, pulling the privacy curtain before she fires up the computer at the station. We are going through all the routine questions like my date of birth, history of illnesses or surgeries when she catches me off guard.

"Are you sexually active?"

I blink at her for several seconds.

"Do you really need to know that?"

She gives me a sympathetic smile as she nods.

"University policy."

I stare at her for several more seconds, before I gently shake my head. She smiles at that, like being a virgin is something to be proud of, before she quickly types away on her keyboard. Then she rifles through a medical cabinet, grabbing a needle and other supplies.

"What is that?" I ask.

"Birth control," she says easily, as she begins readying the syringe.

"Uhm, no thank you. I'm good."

"It's not optional, sweetie. Every student is tested for STDs when they return from each break and every female student is given birth control each quarter."

"Even if I'm not having sex?" I ask dubiously, instantly regretting it when she gives me a pinched look like I'm irritating her.

"Yes," she says, before she gestures to my arm. "Roll up your sleeve, please."

I want to argue more, she's literally forcing me to get birth control and submit to an STD panel? This is ridiculous. I don't even have sex. I got a lengthy lecture from my father about the very subject, which was as uncomfortable as it sounds. He told me that it was of the utmost importance that I was a virgin before Asher and my ceremony. I didn't argue with my father at the time, but after meeting Asher, I have to say, I have some complaints.

Slowly, I roll up my sleeve and she makes quick work of giving me the shot. It only hurts for a moment and soon she's bandaging my arm before she runs the STD panel, which is a hell of a lot more invasive. I guess it keeps their precious children from getting pregnant or catching diseases. It is still a college, despite its impeccable education and really what else is there to do at college except go to class and have sex?

I've thought about what it would be like to lose my virginity a thousand times, but not once did I ever picture myself losing it to an asshole like Asher. Apparently he can have sex with whoever he wants, but of course as the woman I have to stay pure and chaste for our arrangement.

What a bunch of bullshit.

Chapter Three
Skyla

The next day, I slip on a white sleeveless pantsuit with an off-the-shoulder camel coat that hits just at my knees. I decide to leave my hair for the day, only throwing in a few curls for volume before I expertly apply my makeup until I look effortlessly flawless. This is the bare minimum in my father's eyes.

I already know that nearly everything I do here will get back to him. My health records, who I'm seen chatting with, my grades– I have no doubt my father will be getting regular reports of it all. So, as much as I'm more than slightly disappointed this won't be the college experience I was hoping for, it's not all that unexpected.

Unlocking my phone, I pull up my schedule again, trying to correlate it with the map posted in the middle of the courtyard. I feel myself staring at it for an embarrassing amount of time before a figure comes up beside me. A girl, with a knowing smirk and beautiful red hair, stares at me before she speaks.

"You're Skyla Parris, right?"

I frown at that. "Yes, have we met?"

"No," she laughs. "I'm Maggie Bartlett."

I shake her hand as I nod.

"Sorry, how did you know my name? It's a big campus and it's a little odd," I say with a guarded laugh.

Maggie shakes her head. "It may look like a big campus, but the student population is small, and we all grew up together. You're the first new face that's come around in a long time."

"Really?" I ask, extremely envious at the moment that all these students have the advantage of knowing each other, while I'm stuck being the new fish in the tank.

She nods her head, gesturing towards the sign.

"I'm assuming you're lost? C'mon. I'll show you around," she smiles.

Relief flutters through me as I throw an irritated farewell look to the useless map, before I hand my phone over to Maggie. Her eyes flicker across it before she smiles and nods.

"Perfect. We have history up first together. Let's go," she says as she starts practically booking it across campus. Thank god I didn't opt for heels today.

Finally, we come to a door that Maggie opens for me before sweeping her arm out in a grand way that makes me laugh.

"Thank you," I smile, as I step inside the lecture hall.

It isn't nearly as large as I expected, with only five rows of seating available in three sections. That doesn't mean that just like the rest of this school, it isn't drenched in opulence. The ceiling is high and arched sharply, continuing with those seventeenth-century themes that seem to have been embalmed in this city and especially in this university.

My eyes move across the room, looking up at one of the black stained windows, or maybe it's closer to a grey color. The intricate patterns and designs on each vary. Some have religious crosses, while others are too hard to make out from down here. Several large chandeliers decorate the ceiling, surprisingly bright for how old they appear.

I expect her to ditch me now, obviously not owing me a single thing as she goes in search of her friends. Instead, she loops her arm through mine, walking me towards the middle back of the room before plopping down into a seat. I give her a cautionary look, making sure it's okay that I sit before she looks at me strangely and nods.

Setting down my bag, I slide into the seat and adjust my posture, always making sure to be presentable and attentive. That was one of the first lessons I learned back in London, first impressions are everything. It's how you set yourself up for the world, and the way everyone will always perceive you.

"Why are you sitting like that?" Maggie asks.

I tuck my folded hands into my lap as I turn to her with a raised brow.

"Sitting like what?"

She mimics my posture, sticking her nose in the air as she does.

"All prim and proper, there is no one of importance around here. You're fine, relax."

I go to tell her she's clearly never met my father, that he would argue that there is always someone of importance on the horizon. However, I can't help but test the theory slightly, relaxing just a bit into the chair, instantly feeling a sense of relief as I do.

Maggie's smile is playing at her mouth as she watches me before shaking her head and laughing.

"We'll have to work on that."

I smile and shrug my shoulders. "So, do you have any siblings?"

Her smile strains and her eyes squint slightly as she shrugs.

"Not blood."

I wait for her to elaborate, but she doesn't. I think that's the end of the conversation when she continues.

"Stepsister. Total cunt."

I grimace at that. "My condolences."

She laughs and nods when a smooth voice practically croons from above me.

"Well, hello."

My eyes go up and up and up, until they land on a guy with blond hair, bright green eyes and a blinding white smile. His skin is perfectly tanned, like he spent all summer outside. His white polo shirt and tan slacks make him look like every bit the trust fund baby he no doubt is. I can't deny a fluttering that runs through me, as his eyes obviously rake over me like I'm a five course feast before him.

"Hello," I smile politely, doing my best to keep my tone even under this man's stare .

"What's your name, babygirl?"

"Skyla Parris, and you?" I ask, with an outstretched hand.

He takes my hand in his, practically dwarfing it. He wraps his other hand around mine, lifting my knuckles to his lips as he does. A strange look passes across his face when he hears my name, before his grin widens as if that were even possible.

"Liam Walcott," he says, pressing a chaste kiss to my hand.

Maggie makes a gagging sound as she scoffs at Liam.

"Could you be any more desperate, Walcott?"

He turns his head to the side slightly to make eye contact with Maggie before he smirks.

"Aw, you scared I'm gonna swipe your girl out from under you, Bartlett?"

She gives him a challenging look, draping her arm over my shoulder and hauling me into her side.

"Not in the slightest."

Liam bites his lower lip, a flash of silver catching my eyes as his tongue traces over his lip before it's gone in the next minute.

"Fuck, please tell me I can watch?" he practically groans.

Maggie chokes out a laugh as she shakes her head.

"Not on your fucking life."

I watch as Liam's playful smile falls, quickly replaced with a sad frown, akin to when you deny a puppy a treat. His shoulders slump dramatically, as he practically mopes off down several rows before plopping into a seat haphazardly.

I can't help but give Maggie a confused look and she's quick to explain.

"That's Liam Walcott, Gallows Hill's resident flirt. I've heard he's slept with almost every single willing girl on the entire campus. All have nothing but glowing reviews, I guess."

"You guess? So you aren't one to fall under his spell?" I tease.

She snorts, squeezing her hold on me a little tighter.

"Definitely not, he doesn't have the right plumbing for me."

My eyebrows dip at that, as she stares at me in what seems like waiting before she speaks again.

"I prefer women," she hedges.

Oh, well now I feel slow.

"Well, how could you not? We're beautiful and we don't smell half as bad as men," I shrug.

She tosses her head back and laughs, her beautiful hair tipping back with her.

"Exactly, but unfortunately for me, you seem to be far more interested in men than women."

Her words register but I'm still curiously staring at Liam, or well, the back of his head. He's animatedly talking to a guy next to him and they are both smiling and laughing. His laugh is practically infectious, and I can't help but smile in the wake of it.

Feeling a set of eyes on me, I turn to see Maggie staring at me with an amused grin.

"What?" I ask.

"Nothing, you just proved my point," she laughs. "But, if you ever get sick of these men, let me know. I eat pussy way better than all of them put together," she says, with a wink that makes me laugh.

In an all-girls boarding school, it was actually pretty rare not to hook up with one of your friends. I was about the only one actually, and it wasn't because I didn't think women were stunning and kind and all around wonderful. It also definitely wasn't because I didn't have needs, because virgin or not, my battery operated boyfriend was practically a staple in my life.

I just never got that rush of excitement, the tingles and the butterflies when I looked at a girl. A friend of mine kissed me once, and though it was nice, it didn't do anything for me.

Aside from her, I've honestly only been kissed one other time. I was at a friend's birthday party and her cousin cornered me against the side of the house when no one was looking. He was cute enough, but he drooled a bit too much and definitely used way too much tongue. I've been a bit traumatized since that event.

A lankier guy with auburn hair takes a seat in front of me, setting all of his things out on the desk in what looks like a perfected system when Maggie smiles.

"Hey, Andrew."

He turns around, giving her a smile before his eyes stop on me. They take me in for a moment, before his cheeks begin to pink up.

"Hi," he rasps softly.

"Hello," I smile, causing his blush to deepen before he quickly turns around.

I watch as Maggie does her best to contain her laughter, before she whispers into my ear.

"Andrew Hutchinson. He's very sweet and super shy as you can see."

Nodding at that, I smile as the teacher walks in and introduces himself, beginning the class with the syllabus for the semester.

As soon as class is over, Maggie and I file out together. Liam is just ahead of us and I watch as he meets up with a tall brown haired man. It only takes a second to place my fiancé and disgust fills me as I see him tuck two girls beneath his arms, one of whom was the naked girl from my room. Liam does the same, taking two beautiful girls under his arms, as he gives them a smile as bright as the sun. They both seem to melt under it, and I honestly can't blame them.

Asher's eyes land on me, irritation filling them as he sneers and turns away abruptly. The naked girl, because that's what I'm going to call her, casts me a venomous look. She snuggles into him further, as if he wasn't holding another girl under his other arm while they walk away.

Liam turns to see what has Asher running for the hills, and when his eyes land on me he grins mischievously before tossing me a wink and following after him. Maggie rolls her eyes at them, before looking over my shoulder at my phone.

"What do you have next?"

"Looks like I don't have anything until eleven," I say.

"Ugh, lucky bitch. Give me your phone," she says as she takes it out of my hand, quickly tapping the screen before handing it back to me. "K, I gave you my number. Text me at lunch and we can go grab something!"

With that she's off, practically speed walking again. I wave goodbye and turn to my left. I haven't been over here yet but no time to get lost like the present, right?

I make my way through a building of classrooms before it leads me to a separate building just outside of it. Curiosity gets the better of me and I step inside, a heavenly smell filling my senses and wrapping around me like a warm blanket. The distinctive smell of chlorine and wet pavement lingers in the air. The deeper I move down the hallway, the more intense the scent becomes.

Before I know what I'm doing, I'm pushing the door in front of me open, revealing an Olympic regulation sized swimming pool. There is a large set of bleachers to the left of the pool, and I can see the door that leads to the locker rooms off to the right.

My eyes come back to the water, so crisp and blue. I would do almost anything to slip under the surface right now, to sit on the bottom and just forget everything for a little while.

Swimming has always been my passion. As a young kid, Aunt Steph put me into lessons, and I was in our school pool as much as humanly possible. I even made the mistake of mentioning my passion to my dad. I told him how when I grew up, I wanted to be an Olympian. I wanted to swim and swim until my body gave out, for the rest of my life. He didn't like me having such a strong passion for something that wasn't in his realm of interests. He quickly made Aunt Steph discontinue the lessons and had my school ban me from the pool.

The last time I had been near one was at my friend Marissa's house. She had an indoor pool, and on the weekends I would spend hours upon hours in it. It was never quite the same though.

I look to my left and right, before I set down my bag and slip off my shoes. Quickly, I move across the room, rolling up my wide legged pants up to my knees before sitting on the edge of the pool. As soon as my toes hit that crisp water, pleasure rolls through me and I tilt my head back, closing my eyes as my feet slowly glide through it.

I'm not sure how long I'm sitting there, enjoying the feeling of the water wrapping around every inch of submerged flesh when I get the feeling that someone is watching me. My eyes fly open, looking up to see a man staring at me. He's tall, at least 6'3", his shoulders are wide, and his waist tapered. He's wearing a black polo shirt with the school's crest on it and a pair of almost charcoal dress pants.

His deep brown hair is not buzzed, but not long either. It's the perfect length, where he has just enough room to style it a bit in the front. Those eyes are what get me though. He has these piercing blue eyes that are practically the same color as the pool.

My eyes come down to his sharp jawline, a smattering of stubble covering it as his perfectly pink lips dip into a frown. Quickly, I flick my gaze back up to his eyes to find them shadowed with confliction.

"Pool is closed," he says sternly, a rough gravel to his voice as he speaks.

Fear of being in trouble rips through me, as I quickly pull my legs out of the pool and go to stand.

"Oh, sorry. Sorry. I just...I'm new and I found this and—"

He walks over to me and holds his hand up to stop me from talking, which I appreciate because I didn't really have anything to follow up with. His eyes trace over me, assessing, before he kicks off his shoes and socks. Taking a seat a few feet away from me at the edge. He rolls up his pant legs, much like I did before slipping his toned calves into the water.

I watch him carefully as I return my legs to the water. He stares out at the pool silently and I do the same, a sort of comfortability settling in the air as we just...exist.

I find myself stealing a glance in his direction and when I do, I find that he's already staring at me.

"I'm Skyla," I say, feeling the need to say *something*.

He watches me for several seconds, before he dips his head in what looks like a greeting.

"Coach Ronan."

"Coach?" I ask. "Swim coach?"

He nods his head, but doesn't speak for a moment. "Do you swim competitively?"

I open my mouth to respond before I stop short, curious on how much I could reveal to this man and if it would make its way back to my father. He doesn't seem to have the persona that some of the other staff possess. He's a little more...solemn, jaded maybe. I suppose that could work in my favor either way.

"No." I answer, choosing the safer, more honest route.

His eyes don't relent though, burrowing into me like he knows there's more to it. How would he know? I have no clue.

"Why do you ask?" I question, mainly to get his intense stare off me.

"The way you looked when you put your feet in the water, it was like you were at peace. As if you were coming home. Only real swimmers, true athletes, get a look like that."

My head tilts curiously.

"You saw me come in?"

He gestures his head towards another door that I didn't see from around the corner.

"There are cameras in my office to keep an eye on the pool, make sure no little shits vandalize the place or something."

I lean my head back, spotting at least two cameras instantly. Nodding to myself, I look back out at the water.

"It's really beautiful, don't you think?" I ask.

He looks at me for several seconds before looking out at the water.

"Extremely."

His eyes cut back to me, and I can physically feel my cheeks flush. I wish I could will them to stop, but it's impossible. His gaze is so serious, so focused, and completely trained on me. If I were to guess, I would say he looks to be at least in his late twenties, maybe early thirties. Definitely too old for me to be sitting here blushing over.

When my jerk of a fiancé flashes to the forefront of my mind though, I figure what's the harm in a little inappropriate flirting, right?

"Do you swim competitively?" I ask with a small smirk, mirroring his words from before.

I don't know why, but something about that makes him give me half of a smile. Just half of it is breathtaking, I can't imagine the whole thing hitting you at full force.

"Not anymore."

His smile slowly fades as that same look of confliction passes over his face. The nosy part of me wants to pry, but the respectable part of me knows better than to pick at what's obviously a sore subject. So I stay silent, enjoying the crisp water on my toes and the gorgeous man before my eyes. Not the worst way to spend a morning.

We sit there for another few minutes in comfortable silence, before my alarm goes off, reminding me that my next class is starting soon. I give a wanting look out to the pool before I sigh.

"I have to get going," I say with a sad smile.

He's up and out of the pool in a flash, coming to my side and offering me his hand. I give him a brief look before I accept his gesture, sliding my palm into his as he wraps his fingers around my wrist. Butterflies race from the start of our contact all the way to my toes. It's a feeling that has me gasping softly, as he easily helps hoist me out of the water and onto my feet.

I stumble for a moment and he catches me easily, stabilizing my hips with his palms as he looks down at me. The tension is palpable and so thick I can hardly breathe over it. Not that I mind at all.

I practically hold my breath as his eyes slowly roam over my face, starting with my eyes before going down my cheeks over to my mouth and up the other side. When he's finished, those bright pools of blue stare back at me, his fingers tensing for half of a second before he quickly drops his hands and takes a small step back. All of the building tension slips away, fading into the air between us as he clears his throat.

"Sorry," he says roughly, like it's hard for him to speak.

Giving him a soft smile, I shake my head.

"Thank you," I say before I move past him, slipping on my socks and shoes and grabbing my purse.

I could just head out the door, it's right in front of me. Instead, I turn to face him and give him the barest of smiles as I speak softly.

"Thanks for letting me stay for a bit. I...I needed it."

He dips his head in acknowledgement but doesn't say anything, so with a small wave, I slip out the door. I head in the direction of my next class, wherever it actually is, all the while thinking of two bright blue eyes the entire way.

Chapter Four
Skyla

The rest of my day went by surprisingly well. Maggie and I met for lunch. She ended up taking us to this really cool hole in the wall sandwich shop that had to die for chili cheese fries. I had never tried them before. Carbs were practically banned at my school in London, which is a disgusting rule, I know. Oh my god, though. Change my freaking life– delicious. I could gain twenty pounds for all I care, as long as I can have an infinite supply of those fries.

Once I was in for the night, I called Steph and we talked for a few hours. I told her about my 'lovely' fiancé as well as Maggie. I even mentioned the pool that I had found on campus. Conveniently, I did leave out the whole sexy swim coach part. I'm not sure why I didn't tell her, we tell each other everything. Maybe I didn't tell her because honestly, there was nothing to tell. God, he was so hot though.

I set my alarm for a few hours before my first class today, because ever since yesterday I've only had one thing on my mind. I slip into my swimsuit, grabbing my cap and goggles before throwing on a t-shirt and baggy sweatpants. If my father saw me looking like this, out in public no less, I think he would die of a heart attack. I refuse to get all done up only to submerge myself under water, though.

The way to the pool from my dorm is actually pretty straightforward, and I get there in minutes. The sun still hasn't risen, and the courtyard is quiet as I sneak inside the building. Crossing my fingers that the door is unlocked, my heart does a happy little flip when I pull the door and it gives way to my hand.

I make my way through the hall before pulling open the door to the pool. I'm smiling to myself, excited to have the pool to myself, except I'm not the only one here. There is somebody already in the pool. I can't tell who it is, not like I really know anyone here anyways. All I can see is a back covered in what looks like tattoos. They stretch down the length of both of his arms and his back, stopping just above his swimsuit.

His moves are so fluid, so graceful. He practically glides through the water like he's a part of it, as if it was as easy as simply existing. He's making the breaststroke look that easy at least, as he rises up and down from the water, taking only enough breath to push him one more stroke. I have to admit that he's incredibly fast as well, I'm dumbstruck just watching him go.

Suddenly he stops, ripping off his goggles as he levels me with a stare that feels capable of incinerating me right here, right now.

"The pool is closed," he practically snarls.

My head jerks back, as if his words physically struck me before I raise an unimpressed eyebrow at him.

"Doesn't look closed."

"It is. You can't be in here," he bites out.

God, this man is absolutely infuriated. Like my proximity offends him on a cellular level, and he's two seconds from decimating everything and everyone near him.

Unfortunately for him, he's not even close to one of the most intimidating men I've ever met, and the worst thing I could do is show weakness in front of someone like him. So, I don't.

I keep my eyes on him the entire time I set my bag to the floor before taking off my sweatpants and shirt. I don't even break our stare as I pull my cap out. Somehow, I magically keep my eyes in his direction, as I bend over to tuck every piece of hair inside and slip my goggles on before I stand up again.

His nostrils are flared, and his mouth pulled up into an ugly sneer that doesn't do anything for how surprisingly good looking he is.

Seriously, what is it about this college? I don't think I've seen a single bad looking man or woman since I've gotten here. Genetic lottery or something? I'm definitely not complaining, I just wish some, or most, of them had better attitudes to compliment those good looks.

I walk past him, keeping my head high and not having a care in the world that he's watching me as I do a perfect dive into the opposite side of the pool. Instead of doing a warm-up lap or jumping straight into a workout, I dive down until my belly scrapes against the bottom before I cross my legs and sit.

It doesn't matter that I can't physically breathe down here, metaphorically, emotionally, spiritually, whatever you want to call it, I finally have breath poured into my lungs. A soft peace falls over me, and the stillness of the water heals something inside me that I'm not sure is even broken.

I've missed this. So much.

Sadly, my lungs begin to burn, and I feel the warning signs that I need to return to the surface for air, but I'm so desperate for this peace that I want just another second or two.

Unfortunately the next thing I know, two strong arms are wrapping around me, hauling me to the surface. When we break through, I inhale a greedy breath, allowing my chest to heave as my breathing begins to normalize.

Once it does, I'm furious. I spin around to face my 'savior' splashing a large amount of water into his face. His goggles are still off and I get him right in the eye. I wish I could be sorry, but I'm not.

He winces, rubbing at his eyes, before he levels me with a murderous look.

"What is your problem!? Why did you grab me?" I snap.

His gaze becomes almost crazed.

"What the fuck is wrong with you? You trying kill yourself down there?"

I roll my eyes at him.

"Did it look like I was trying to kill myself? No. I was just taking a moment. I was about to come up for air."

"Whatever you say, Siren," he scoffs.

I frown at that and am about to ask him what he means by Siren, when something catches me off guard. His eyes are so grey they look like slabs of slate. They're a perfect combination between dark and light grey. I've never seen anything like it in my life.

God, what is it with me and noticing everyone's eyes? Do I have an eye fetish? Is that a thing? I think it might be.

Some of the anger begins to fade in them as I continue to stare at him before he looks away, practically shoving out of the water as fast as he can. He easily lifts himself out of the pool and onto the concrete walkway, grabbing a towel and a duffel bag in the corner, as he heads for the locker rooms.

Shaking my head, I begin with some warm-up laps before I line up on one end. Though I was never given the chance to actually compete, me and some of the girls at my school and in my swim club would race. It made it all the more fun, having someone push you, someone to compare yourself to and setting new goals to strive for.

I look up at the clock, waiting for the hand to hit twelve before I begin. I've always been a fan of the butterfly stroke. Though it is arguably one of the most challenging strokes, it's the most fun in my opinion. If I could have competed, this is definitely what I would have chosen.

My arms glide through the water and my shoulders burn as I bring my head up to the surface, gasping in a breath before doing it again and again. My legs are burning as they fight to continue propelling me. God, it's been a while that's for sure. Like riding a bike though, it starts to come back to me. I can feel each stroke getting more fluid, more synchronized as I make it to the end of the pool, flip and do it all the way back.

As soon as I surface, my head whips around to see my time—sixty-eight seconds. Damn. I mean, it's not bad but it's not great. When I was an avid swimmer, I was comfortably under fifty-nine seconds when doing the butterfly 100 meter.

"You again," a deep voice rumbles from across the pool, forcing my eyes to land on the figure above.

Coach Ronan is wearing basketball shorts today and a sleeveless tank top. His forehead is dotted with sweat, and it looks like he just got done with a run if his shoes are anything to go off of.

I don't say anything, mainly because I'm not sure what to make of his statement. He let me stay yesterday. Was that just a one-time thing? Did he not want me to come back again? I really hope it isn't the latter.

He stares at me for several seconds, looking up at the clock before his eyes come back down to me.

"100?" he questions.

I nod quietly as he lifts the bottom of his shirt to wipe off the sweat from his forehead, gifting me with the view of gorgeously toned abs.

When he drops the material, I can't lie that I'm disappointed. Would it be so bad of me to tell him that he missed a spot?

"What was your time?" Ronan pants, taking a slow controlled breath, forcing his chest to settle.

Embarrassment nips at me, he's a swim coach for an elite college. I'm sure he has swimmers that are cutting my time by ten seconds at least. He continues staring at me as if he won't accept my silence, though.

"Sixty-eight," I say softly, lowering my head so I don't see the disappointment on his face. God, I hate being a disappointment. Chalking it up to whatever kind of mommy-daddy abandonment issues you want, I hate being in trouble and I hate being a letdown. Like, to an absolute extreme.

"When was the last time you trained?" he asks, his tone curious with no judgment.

I glance up to him carefully before I shrug.

"Five years."

His eyebrows knit together. "You haven't swam in five years?"

"No, I have," I say. "Just not in a serious sense. Not outside of doing laps in my friend's pool."

"Well, shit. With a time like that and virtually no training in over five years, that's impressive."

"Really?" I ask. "What are your other girls' times?"

He shakes his head. "We only have a men's team."

My face screws up at that as I take off my goggles, tossing them to the side as he slowly starts walking towards me.

"Why?"

He shrugs, choosing not to fully answer which I find odd. His steps take him all the way up to me, crouching down so he's closer to my eye level as he speaks.

"You should start training again. You could be really good."

I can't stop the smile that spreads across my face, even if I try. I do try to bite it back, but it's no use.

"Why are you trying to hide your smile?" he asks, that half smile of his own tugging at his lips.

"I've just never heard that before. It's nice," I say softly, cringing at how insecure I sound.

His hand reaches out to my cheek, cupping it tentatively, like he's giving me space to pull away. Yeah, like that'll happen. I lean into his touch and his thumb pulls at my lip, freeing it from my teeth.

"You should hear it more."

There was nothing I could do, no way it could have been prevented. My smile turns megawatt, as I grin up at this deliriously good looking older man, cupping my face tenderly and giving me all the words I've longed to hear from anyone before.

We stay like that for several seconds, just staring at one another before I speak.

"Are all teachers as caring as you?"

Something flickers behind his eyes as he lowers his voice, still holding my face as he does.

"If any of them are to you, you let me know."

With that, he pulls away, standing up to his full height as he turns on his heel. I don't let him go that easily, though. I lift myself out of the pool, climbing to my feet before I start after him.

"What's that supposed to mean?" I ask.

He continues walking for several steps and then he pauses, causing me to bump into his back before he turns to face me.

"It means, if a teacher is looking at you the way I am, you should definitely report them."

My stomach flips at his words as I look up at him curiously, doing my best to keep my tone light.

"Doesn't that mean I should report you?" I test.

He shrugs.

"You could, but I'm a coach, not a teacher."

"Is there a difference?"

"Definitely," he nods.

I let out a laugh at that as I nod.

"I'm not sure my father would see things that way."

"I don't know, I can be a pretty charming guy," he says with a smirk.

"Oh, I don't doubt that. Regardless, you're definitely too old to be flirting with students, Coach."

"Who said I was flirting?" he asks, that flirtatious smile speaking volumes.

I got the vibes a little bit yesterday, but I wasn't sure if I was making it up in my head or not. Now I know, without a doubt, I was absolutely not making it up and I don't even want to question it. So, I take a step closer to him, brushing my chest against his in a way that makes him skip a breath, before he looks down at me. His eyes flick over his shoulder as if he were checking to make sure no one was coming, before he turns back to face me.

"Me," I smile.

"Yeah? You, Miss..."

He trails off, waiting for me to fill in my last name no doubt.

"Parris," I fill in.

His teasing smirk drops in a moment and his eyes widening as he takes a quick step away from me, like my touch has burned him. It takes him a moment to seemingly compose himself, before he straightens his posture and slips on a mask of indifference.

"Your name is Skyla Parris?"

I frown at his lightning quick change of character as I nod.

"Yes, is something wrong with that?"

He shakes his head once.

"No, I just didn't realize. You're engaged to Asher Putnam."

I roll my eyes at the reminder.

"Does everyone on this campus know that?"

"Yes," he answers quickly, so quickly it makes me take a second look at him. Really? Why on earth would it be everyone's business? I've only been here two days. Unless arranged marriages are extremely common around here, it wouldn't surprise me if they were. Or maybe this arrangement has been set in stone for a lot longer than I'm thinking. That, I really wouldn't be surprised about.

"Well, if I'm honest, I don't have much interest in marrying him. He's an ass and has nothing but disdain for me. I don't know why my father thought we would ever work out."

"Working out doesn't matter, committing to your arrangement is all anyone will care about," Ronan says.

"Well, what if I'm unhappy? What if it would make me unhappy to marry him? I humored my father out of respect, but I can't marry a man that can hardly stand the sight of me."

"Doesn't matter," he says briskly.

"It does to me," I counter.

Ronan looks away for a moment before he speaks, keeping his eyes fixated on the wall as he does.

"Happiness is just a fairy tale dream. Even if you think you have it, think you can taste it, you'll wake up soon enough and it will fade from your mind, until you can't remember it at all."

There is something so strong in his words, so truthful. Like he knows this pain firsthand. It breaks my heart. First, to hear someone be so cynical about something as simple as happiness. Second, to be so obviously crushed under the heel of life's boot that you've accepted a future devoid of happiness.

"I hope not," I say softly.

He swings his gaze back to me, a disbelieving look in his eye.

"You hope not?"

I nod. "In the lack of happiness or light, or anything relatively good, there is always hope. It's always sitting there, idly by, ready for you to take it. You just have to be brave enough to."

Ronan doesn't say anything, and honestly, I don't know what else there is to say. So with a small shrug, I walk past him, grabbing my things and head back to my dorm before the sun comes up.

Chapter Five
Asher

I'm sleeping, or at least trying to, but some annoying fuck keeps pounding on the door. Finally, having enough of it I drag myself out of bed, hopping over the passed out girl beside me before I open the door. I expect it to be Liam, he's about the only obnoxious fucker out there that would have the balls to bang on my door so early in the morning.

To my surprise, it isn't my best friend but instead, my uncle. He looks down at me, sneering as he looks away.

"Christ. Can you at least have the decency to get dressed before you open the door?"

"Why should I care? You're entering my space." I shrug as I leave the door open, strolling back inside unapologetically naked, before I jump over the girl beside me and land on the bed.

She rolls over sleepily, looking up at me like I'm her whole fucking world when she notices we have company. Glancing up at him, she pales as she scrambles to cover herself.

"C-coach Ronan! Sorry, I was just going," she says, wrapping herself up in my blanket as she quickly grabs her discarded dress and stripper heels before scurrying out of the room.

Ronan shakes his head at me in what looks like disappointment. Then again, I think that's just his face. He's disappointed in most shit nowadays.

"Dude, you're engaged now. You can't be doing this shit," Ronan chastises.

I choke out a laugh as I shake my head and throw my arms over my head.

"I can do whatever the fuck I want, and we both know that."

He levels me with an unimpressed look.

"Within reason, Asher. Your dad is not going to like it if he hears you're publicly making a fool out of your fiancée, out of your arrangement. You have to be more discreet."

I roll my eyes, even if he has a point. Father doesn't care what I do, just like I don't give a fuck what he does. What he does care about is power and perception, if I threaten either of those for him... maybe Ronan has a very good point. I just wish I had it in me to care.

"Put some fucking underwear on at least," Ronan grumbles as he looks down at me, shaking his head before rifling through my drawers.

He grabs a pair of boxers and throws them at me before looking out the window. I roll my eyes but slip them on.

"There, happy?" I ask, as I lean back against my bed.

"Hardly," he says flatly, as he sits in one of the recliners across from me.

I snort at that. We have the same bleak and dark sense of humor about life and the future. He's more like a brother than an uncle to me and it's not just because we are only ten years apart. We both hold a deep resentment for our last name and what it means to be a Putnam, the responsibilities we are bound to from birth. Though we know there's no way out of it but through it, it's nice to bitch about it with someone who gets it.

"So, what's your fiancée like?" Ronan asks after a minute or so.

I scrunch up my face before I shrug.

"She's hot. Seems a bit too prudish, but I'm sure I can fuck it out of her one day. Definitely not who I would have chosen."

Ronan makes a face, before looking towards the wall and shaking his head before looking back at me.

"Who would you have chosen?" he asks.

"Does it matter? We both know I don't get jack shit say in all of this."

He shrugs as I mull over his question. No one comes to mind, honestly. There are plenty who come to mind under the hell fucking no category. My phone chimes beside my pillow and I unlock it to see it's the president of the hell fucking no club.

Bridgette Brenton is the most annoying fuck I've ever dealt with. I took her virginity about three years ago and she still chases after me like a bitch in heat. I swear to god, I could tell the woman to jump into a lake of fire and she would do it, gladly. Sometimes I feel something close to empathy for her. She truly believes that one day I'll wake up and realize I've always loved her, when the truth is, I can hardly stand her. The only reason I keep her on the rotation is because she sucks dick like a goddamn porn star.

She does come in handy for things other girls wouldn't be willing to do as well, like greet my fiancé butt ass naked while getting fucked on her bed. I smirk to myself when I think about the shocked look on the Princess' face. I could have sworn I saw a touch of arousal in those crazy deep green eyes, but it was probably wishful thinking.

We don't get lucky enough to marry women that will meet all of our needs. We get matched with the respectable kind, the ones who will produce as many heirs as we want and will stay silent all their lives. Looks like Henry Parris did a good job of providing that, considering the Princess seems about as subservient as they come. Probably what comes from being hidden away from our world for the last sixteen years.

Ronan is the only member of an Elder family that has made it unscathed thus far. He was engaged when he graduated from Gallows Hill like every man typically is, but he was able to slither his way out of it.

Lucky fucker.

Unfortunately for me, they decided I needed to be betrothed earlier than most. Usually arrangements aren't even made until after graduation, and most of the time you get a little say in who, at least a few top choices. Not me though.

"I've heard she's a nice girl," Ronan says, assumingly talking about the Princess again.

"I'm sure she is. Gonna suck for her when she figures out I'm not a nice guy."

"You sure she doesn't already know that?" Ronan asks with a dubious look.

I grin at him. "If she doesn't now, she will soon."

It's Saturday morning and I'm sitting on the cement steps of the courtyard with Liam and some especially clingy women when a fuming blonde tornado comes tearing up to me.

"What the hell is this!" she seethes as she throws a crumpled up piece of paper at my head.

I don't flinch, allowing it to hit me and roll to the floor. I don't need to look to know what it is.

"Looks like a note," I draw out casually.

Smoke practically billows out of her ears, as her fists clench at her sides and her arms shake. I've got to say, I'm a little surprised. Maybe she isn't as subservient as I assumed she was. I have to admit, this makes things a lot more fun.

Margret Bartlett comes up beside her, pulling her arm slightly like she's trying to get her to back down. Margret may be a rebel by her mother's standards for preferring the company of women, but she knows better than to cross me. Looks like she's trying to convince her new bestie of the same ideals. My *fiancé* doesn't appear to be in a wavering mood, though.

Liam reaches down, the little shit unable to help himself from stirring the pot, as he un-wrinkles it and begins reading it out loud.

"To my dearest fiancée, I hope your dreams are as wet as your pillow."

He grins before looking at me, his eyes searching mine as he shakes his head.

"You didn't."

I shrug casually, doing my best to bite back a smile.

"Don't know what you're talking about."

A cackle erupts from him as he jumps to his feet, his laughter escalating until he's practically in tears. The princess sends him a fierce look that only quiets him down some, before one of the girls besides me asks, "What did he do?"

I turn to look at Skyla, curious if she has the guts to admit what she woke up to this morning. Of course she doesn't though. Too proud with that iron clenched jaw, not allowing a single weakness to show.

Alright, I'll do the honors for her.

"I left her a little....morning delight on her pillow this morning."

It takes the slow women around me several seconds before realization hits them. They all begin hysterically laughing and Liam starts up once again. Swear to god, the guy is like a goddamn hyena.

My eyes don't leave the princess as the laughter grows, her hardened exterior softening with each passing second. A tear even slips out of the corner of her eye, before she discreetly banishes it away. Damn, she's not nearly as tough as I was anticipating. That's a shame for her. She won't last two months at Gallows Hill. Then again, maybe that could work in my favor.

With a withering glance– that I'll be honest, would shrivel most men's balls right up– her and Margret turn on their heels as they head back to the dorms. No doubt, they are hell bent on getting out of here before too many people join in. Guess she'll probably be upset when she finds out that the picture of the note, the cum soaked pillow and her drooling face was mass sent to every student enrolled.

Oops.

Chapter Six
Skyla

"Do you want to go somewhere? We can go anywhere you want," Maggie offers, as we make it away from the pack of assholes and closer to the dorms.

I shake my head as I continue walking past my dorm, heading for the end of campus.

"I just want to be alone. Thanks, Mags," I say with a miserable smile.

She frowns at me, but nods as she stops walking with me. I can feel her eyes watching as I walk through the large black gates and past the parking lot. Honestly though, I don't know where I'm going.

Technically, I don't have my license. I learned how to drive in London, but I haven't even been here long enough to attempt to get one. There is no way I'm calling my father. If he finds out about this it'll be my head, I'm sure of it.

I guess I could call a rideshare or something, but walking is the best way to clear my mind. I don't really know where I'm going, but my feet just keep carrying me further and further away from campus, which is really all I need right now.

Three or four miles in, my feet begin to ache and I end up stopping outside a bar and grill. Hopefully, I won't run into anyone that knows me or my face here. Maggie showed me the picture, that's actually what woke me up. Her hurried knocks at my door, followed by the humiliating photo of me asleep, drool coming out of my mouth beside my cum stained pillow and Asher's lovely note.

To say it's been a terrible start to the day would be an understatement.

When I step inside, I notice the restaurant is significantly darker than I expect it to be. It takes my eyes a moment to adjust when a familiar figure comes from what looks like the bathrooms, nearly knocking me over in the process. His hands quickly stabilize me, his bright blue eyes pinning me in place as he looks at me.

At first, surprise is written all over his face. Then, concern covers his features as his eyes flick over me.

"What's wrong?" Ronan asks.

I do my best to smile, shaking my head as if everything was right as rain, but he isn't buying it.

"Your mascara is all over your face, Skyla."

Panicked, I reach my hand up touching my wet cheek and internally curse. Well, this is just wonderful. I've been parading myself all over Salem looking as broken as I feel right now.

Ronan's hand slips to my lower back as he gestures to a corner booth in the back. Wordlessly, I follow him as he stops by the bar top, grabbing a glass of water and a few napkins. He dunks the napkins in water before handing them to me. I hesitate to take them for a moment.

"I don't have any makeup with me to re-do it."

He frowns. "So?"

"So, everyone will see my bare face. They'll think I'm some hot-mess girl who doesn't care about her appearance."

"And black tear-streaks don't say that?"

My lips smash against each other, his point more than taken as I grab the napkins from him. I pull out my phone, turn on the selfie camera and cringe when I see myself. God, this is humiliating.

Slowly, I scrub away every scrap of makeup left on my skin. When I'm done, I set the makeup coated napkins on the counter before I lower my face. Maybe, if no one sees me, it won't be that bad. They won't notice my dark circles or how my cheeks are always a little more red than the rest of my face, and hopefully they'll miss the scar here and there from good old hormonal acne.

"Why are you so worried about not wearing any makeup? You weren't in the pool?" Ronan asks.

"It's different. I wasn't supposed to see anyone in the pool, this is public. Anyone could see me and—"

"And?" he interrupts.

I shrug. "Judge. Talk."

"So, if you would have known I was going to be in the pool, you would have put on makeup? Despite having your face submerged for a significant amount of time?"

I think about that for half a second before I have my answer. Would I have much rather preferred having my metaphorical war paint on when dealing with the grumpy tattooed swimmer and the unfairly hot swim coach? Absolutely.

I nod. "They make waterproof makeup for a reason."

Ronan doesn't seem impressed by my answer though, instead just shaking his head as he reaches for the beer sitting on the table, lifting it to his lips and taking a healthy sip before setting it down.

"You don't need that shit anyways," he grumbles, almost to himself more than anything.

"Makeup?" I laugh. "I definitely do."

"No," he says seriously, his eyes ensnaring me as he speaks. "You don't."

Something inside of me twists at his words, and I find it difficult to swallow for a moment before I nod.

"So, what's wrong?"

"Hm?" I ask.

"You were crying, obviously. Why?"

The reminder of this morning hits me in full effect, and just like that, I'm furious all over again.

"My lovely fiancé just decided my Saturday needed to start off with a heavy dose of public humiliation."

His brows knit together at that.

"What do you mean?"

I bite my lip and turn my head away, refusing to go into detail. It's bad enough that without a doubt, the whole school is literally laughing in my face right now. I don't need it from the staff as well. I feel a thumb press against the side of my chin, gently turning my face back to him, as he leans across the table a little more and watches me intently.

"What did he do?"

Something about the way he is looking at me, the way he is touching me, is forcing all of my walls to drop simultaneously. So, with a shaky hand, I pass my phone to him. It's open to the personalized message I got from Asher this morning, along with the photo.

Ronan removes his hand from my chin, before looking down at the phone. His jaw ticks, as he stares at it for longer than I'd care before he looks back up at me.

"I'll take care of this."

I shake my head. "Please don't, it will only egg him on. For whatever reason, he's trying to make my life miserable, despite me wanting nothing more to do with this situation than him. Feeding into it only gives him the attention and control he's clearly so desperate for."

He stares at me, seemingly speechless for several seconds before he speaks.

"You're a hell of a lot more intuitive than your meek demeanor portrays."

I shrug. "You notice a lot when you stay quiet."

Ronan nods and is about to say something when the waitress comes up beside him and smiles.

"Anything else I can get for you, Mr. Putnam?"

Any pleasantries on my face die in a fiery burn as my eyes swing to his face. He gives her a scathing look like she outed him, which she did, before brushing her off.

"Putnam? Please don't tell me you're Asher's father," I balk.

Oh my god. If I've been, not so secretly, flirting with my fiancé's dad and having him flirt back with me, I will die. I swear.

He shakes his head. "Of course not. I'd have been ten when I had him."

"So, what? You're his brother?" I guess.

"Uncle," he corrects.

Awesome.

I move to slide out of the booth while grabbing my phone, when his hand reaches for my wrist, holding me back half a step.

"It's not what you're thinking."

I let out a hollow laugh as I peer down at him.

"Really? It seems as though you were being kind to me to gain my trust. Worming your way past my defenses, to do god knows what, either at the bidding of my fiancé or maybe even his father. Hell, maybe for your own vendetta. Either way, I would very much appreciate it if you would take your hand off of me."

He lets me go instantly, and I take a step away from him when he speaks.

"I didn't know who you were at first."

I pause, casting a disbelieving eyebrow towards him.

"How? Everyone on this bloody campus seems to have known who I am, from the moment I arrived."

Ronan shrugs, his eyes on mine as he continues.

"Do I seem like the type of man to keep up with the latest gossip?"

No, but still.

"You do seem to know enough."

"Just enough," he agrees.

Something in his words rings true, as ignorant as it might be of me to believe, I decide having an ally through this mess might not be such a bad thing. Flirting is most definitely off the table now. Damnit. He was the only blip of light apart from Maggie, in this school and this town.

"Okay," I say, taking a seat in front of him. "If you really don't mean any harm, then tell me what I can do to handle Asher. What can I do to make sure he never humiliates me like this again?"

He's silent for a moment, his body language unwavering and I go to stand yet again. Of course he's not going to turn on his own nephew. Not even if he thinks it'll buy him brownie points with the young college student he was most definitely interested in, at least at first.

"Ignore him," Ronan says. "I know it's probably not the revenge you want, but Asher is just like his dad. He feeds on attention and power, the more you give him, the more insufferable he becomes. He may spiral from lack of attention, but him coming for you and you not reacting is like attacking a dead animal. It becomes boring after a while."

He's right, that's not what I wanted to hear, but it is what I suspected. Asher seems to have every bit the arrogance and controlling nature that my father possesses. So though he's, in a sense, a new enemy, this is an old game. One I've been playing my whole life.

I nod. "I haven't met him before– your brother. What's he like?"

Ronan's jaw tenses and he takes several seconds before speaking.

"Didn't I just tell you?"

"You told me the downsides of his personality. Are you really telling me that's all there is to him? To both of them? You're the only good Putnam man around?"

I say that last part teasingly and he seems to pick up on it, a self-deprecating laugh escaping him before he shakes his head.

"Who said I was any good?"

"Fair. You were trying to coerce a nineteen-year-old student," I agree.

His jaw drops and he looks outraged.

"I did no such thing," he defends.

"You would have in a heartbeat," I challenge with a laugh and a 'don't lie to me' look.

He opens his mouth to argue before he snaps it shut, shaking his head as if he were trying to hide his smile before his blue eyes peek up at me.

"I'm not sure how much coercion you would have taken, Miss Parris."

True.

I don't agree, obviously. Instead, I shrug my shoulders as I look across the bar.

"Do you want something?" he asks.

"What do they have?" I ask.

"Food, beer, liquor," he rattles off sarcastically.

I roll my eyes at him, but don't hide my smile.

"Well, since I'm only of legal age for one of the three, I will stick with food."

"You're in Salem now, Skyla. You can have whatever you want," he says with an easy shrug, as he takes another drink of his beer.

"Surely the drinking laws aren't different here?" I scoff.

"They are when your last name is Parris, soon to be Putnam."

I laugh at him, because he must be kidding, but I decide to test his little theory. I catch the waitress's eye and she walks over to us with a smile.

"Can I get something for you, hun?"

"Could I please get a chicken salad and a glass of pinot grigio?"

Her eyes briefly flick to Ronan, as if she were asking him for permission before he gives her a quick nod. She smiles brightly at me and nods before walking back to the computer to ring up the order. I watch her go, completely bewildered. I won't lie, that was something I was disappointed about when I was forced to move back to the US. The drinking age in London is eighteen. I had just started being able to order a glass of wine at lunch or dinner with Aunt Steph when I was forced to move back here and now have to wait another two years before being able to do that again. Though apparently, not in Salem.

I'm not sure I understand this city yet. It's not that small and yet, it's as if everyone knows everyone or at least everyone is connected to each other in a way. It's an odd dynamic that I'm still trying to wrap my head around.

My food and wine arrive in the next few minutes and Ronan gets another beer. We spend the next hour or so just talking about anything and everything. I told him about my time in boarding school, my Aunt Steph and my love of swimming. He told me how he went to Gallows Hill University himself and actually went on to join Team USA in the Olympics. He placed Bronze in the freestyle 100 meter two games in a row.

I was floored with that bit of information. I was about to start drilling him with question after question, but a sad look flickered across his face when the topic was brought up so I thought it was best to let it lie.

When we're done, Ronan hands the waitress his card.

"Let me cover my share," I say, earning a disapproving look from him as he continues holding his card out for the waitress.

I move my hand away from my wallet, lowering my head softly.

"Thank you," I say with a small smile.

"Good girl," he murmurs, causing a flutter to run through me.

There has been absolutely no flirting or sexual tension *until* this very moment. Obviously, him being a swim coach and over thirteen years older than me was enough of a no-no. Add in that I'm engaged and it's really inappropriate. Sprinkle in the fact that he is my fiancé's uncle. Yeah, it's a hard no. Unfortunately.

Neither one of us speaks, our eyes locked on one another before I force myself to look away. My eyes land on his hand, something familiar catching my eye.

"Hey, that looks just like my dad's ring," I say, leaning over to take a closer look at it.

He stiffens as soon as my fingers touch the cool metal. A cursive letter B is embossed on the front of the silver ring, with similar Latin script carved around it.

I look up at him expecting him to say something, but I only find Ronan staring at me intently, his jaw tight and eyes focused.

I let his hand go and he seems to relax almost immediately, which I can't lie, kind of bugs me. Is my touch really that off putting? That repulsive?

Clearing his throat once, he gestures towards the door, and I nod my head. Silently yielding to whatever get out of this moment free card he wants to use.

"Where did you park?" Ronan asks, as we step out into the parking lot.

I cringe softly as I shake my head.

"I walked here."

"You walked?" he scoffs. He looks down at me, towering over me by nearly a foot before he shakes his head.

"C'mon," he says as he hits his key fob, unlocking a sleek, black BMW.

I don't follow him, weighing my options. I probably shouldn't ride with him. Having lunch with him was bad enough, right? Then again, my feet are practically begging me to say yes because I can't imagine walking another fifty steps, let alone miles.

"Please," Ronan adds from the side of the car. "It will make me feel better to know you aren't wandering the streets alone."

The soft tone in comparison to his normally rugged voice is enough to sway me, and I nod my agreement as I move towards him. He holds open the passenger door for me and I dip my head in thanks before sliding inside. The plush leather seats are like butter, and I sink into them as Ronan shuts my door and walks around to his side.

When he starts the car, he pauses for a moment staring at me for half a beat longer than I'd expect.

"What?" I ask, suddenly feeling self-conscious as I smooth down my hair with my hands and wipe under my eyes. Did I miss some makeup? Is my hair now also feeling the wrath of the hot-mess express I am on the inside?

"Nothing," he says with a shake of his head, before firing up the car and backing out of the parking spot.

Chapter Seven
Ronan

You will not touch her thigh. You will not touch her thigh. You will not touch her thigh.

My grip on the steering wheel is practically punishing as we make our way back to campus. This was a bad idea. I didn't like the thought of leaving her there stranded, but I'm reconsidering my decision now.

The fresh smell of oranges, vanilla and something uniquely her practically fills my car and makes it fucking impossible to focus on anything other than the girl next to me. She's wearing a plaid skirt and a ribbed sweater. Though her thighs are covered with a pair of black tights, it doesn't make me want to grab her soft flesh any less.

I don't know what the fuck is going on with me, and I don't know how to stop it. I don't flirt with students, I don't even entertain the idea, ever. She is not even close to the first student to try to gain my attention, but she sure as shit is the first that's succeeded. Fuck, she has more than just my attention.

From the moment I saw her step through my doors, I was frozen in place. I watched her for ten minutes at least, peacefully swinging her legs in the water, mesmerized by the patterns her skin cut through the pool. My pool. Okay, it's not my pool but I'm the one that paid for the school to put it in during my sophomore year, so it's basically mine.

When I finally decided I needed to stop being a fucking creep and abandon the cameras, I had a million scenarios flickering through my mind. I was hopeful that she was a new teacher, an employee of some kind, fucking anything. Obviously I knew none of those could be possible. She was very clearly a student, and I did my best to come off abrasive and rough. A feat that is normally just my personality. It was hard to stay that way with her, though.

Before I knew it, she was leaving and I was desperate to keep her there for as long as I could. I couldn't even remember the last time I felt so...calm.

The next time that I saw her, I promised myself I'd put some distance between us, maintain a professional boundary with her. I couldn't be caught lusting after a student, especially not one from Gallows Hill. All the women are spoken for, either now or will be soon. Inserting myself would not only create problems now, but it could be the end of my life if I wasn't careful enough.

Well, that plan was shot to hell when I watched her body glide through the water as if that was where she truly belonged. She moved like the water brought her peace and a little sense in this world. I never related to someone more than in that moment.

I was tempted to say to hell with all the rights and wrongs in the world, lay her down right there and bury myself inside her. We could talk later. We could worry later. All I knew was there was something about this woman that I needed, that I craved.

Unfortunately for me, the worst tword that could possibly spill from her lips did in the next moment– Parris. She's my nephews fucking fiancée. How about that coincidence.

I struggled to push her from my mind over the last few days. It drove me even crazier when I'd get to the pool extra early each morning and she wasn't there. I decided I wasn't going to wait around today and went to my favorite bar in town. The beer is cold, people leave me alone and my brother doesn't have any spies in there that are *too* loyal to him.

Then, she just had to show up.

Out of all the restaurants in Salem, she had to come into mine.

I can't fucking believe Asher. No, I can, but fuck I'm pissed. I'm going to tear his ass apart and then, his father no doubt, will do the same. I actually hope for his sake that my brother doesn't find out about this. A disrespect like this, against his own betrothed? Christ, I don't think he realizes how badly he's just fucked up.

"What dorm are you in?" I ask.

"Parris," she says softly, her meek voice practically crooning into my ear.

Goddamn, I don't think I've ever heard a sound as sweet as her voice before. I want nothing more than to listen to her pant and shout my name from now until the end of time. As slyly as I'm able, I adjust myself so that she doesn't see the way she affects me. I'm fucking gross. If you take a step back and look at the situation before us, I'm a gross predatory man and I fucking hate it.

The way she looks up at me with those big green eyes though, it doesn't make this thing feel gross. She looks at me like she wants me more than I want her, which I know is impossible. Fuck. This girl has been in the states for less than a week and she's already consuming practically every thought of mine. This is bad, bad, fucking bad.

I pull up to the entrance near her dorm, braking with a harsh stop before I throw the car into park. I have to physically bite my tongue so I don't do something stupid, like offer to walk her to her room. That's a temptation I know I couldn't resist, her bed only fifteen-feet from me...fuck that. I'd cave in a heartbeat and not only would I burn in hell for it, I'd be signing my own death certificate in the process.

"Thank you," she says softly as she shifts in the seat, her sweet voice begging me to look at her. I can't, though. I keep my eyes forward and my hands firmly on the steering wheel as I give her a jerky nod.

I can feel her eyes on me for several seconds, but I know better than to look. It doesn't make it feel any better when a soft sigh of disappointment escapes her, and she pushes open the car door before slipping out of it.

My car stays parked as I watch each graceful step she takes through those wrought iron gates. It's an odd thing, seeing such a light soul walk into such a dark place. She won't be that way for long, not here. A part of me is actually saddened by that fact. That someone will taint her innocence, her fire. If Asher has it his way, I'm sure he'll stomp it right out before their wedding day can even come, and I really fucking hate that.

A buzzing comes from the center console and I groan to myself, wiping my hand down my face before answering.

"Hello," I answer.

"Ronan," my brother greets curtly. "Where are you?"

"At the university, about to head home."

"Perfect. Annie Williams will be meeting you there at seven o'clock sharp."

Fucking hell. I'm so sick of this. Ever since everything happened years ago, he's been hell bent on marrying me off, like I'm his prized pig or something. I've repeatedly expressed my disinterest, but he's not really a man that you say no to.

Then again, Annie Williams is a beautiful woman, an appropriate woman. Maybe all I need is a night full of debauchery, with anyone that isn't Skyla Parris. Who knows, if I like Annie enough, maybe I'll marry her to get my brother off my back. And have something to distract me from the fact that my nephew will be marrying the first woman, in a very long time, who has captured my attention.

"Fine," I agree, as I put the car in drive and take off.

"Really?" he asks, a heavy tone of surprise in his voice.

"Well, I don't have a choice, do I?" I ask.

"No, no you don't. I just expected you to put up more of a fight."

"Not today, big brother. I'm not in the mood."

I hang up without a word, not giving a fuck if it pisses him off. He has bigger things to concern himself with, and the fact that I'm submitting to his wishes means I'm as good as off the hook. For now.

Chapter Eight
Asher

The damp musty odor of the tunnel permeates my nose instantly. A familiar and unwelcome feeling settles inside my stomach, turning and tightening its grip on me much like it did as a child. The stone walls at my sides feel as if they are closing in already, and I just got here. You can hardly see a hand in front of your face, the only light guiding us being the dim glow of the lit torches lining either side of the walls every six feet exactly.

I make sure not to let my discomfort show in the slightest as I raise my head high, pushing my shoulders back and stride through the ancient tunnel as if I own it. I mean, I do. We are on University property. My family owns everything here. Hell, we own everything, everywhere. I suppose that's the one and only perk of the Putnam name.

Liam lazily trails behind me, his fingers moving across his screen like lightning. Yours would too if you had four regular hookups, three situationships and a handful of girls and guys on the line, waiting to be reeled in. My boy has options, just like all of us, the problem is he can never just choose one. He can't make decisions to save his life, so instead of picking one or two he picks them all.

As long as he wraps it up, I don't see an issue. He does need to hide where he parks his car though, since it gets keyed about every other week. Hell hath no fury like a scorned woman. He hasn't had any of the guys he's been with flip out quite like the women, *yet*. Not sure if it's a personality thing or if that shit is something only a psycho female brain can come up with.

Once we make our way further into the tunnel and take the left turn, Liam pockets his phone, instantly acting casual as we come in sight of the first guard. Oh, and when I say acts casual, I mean he begins bouncing on his feet while attempting to touch the ceiling as he runs and jumps high over and over again. You'd think a tunnel beginning underneath the school church and leading out into the forest wouldn't have very high ceilings, but for whatever reason, they are nearly ten feet tall.

When the original Brethren were building this tunnel system, they really spared no expense or cut a single corner. At least, not by 1696 standards.

In the next moment, we see Alexander Booth just ahead as usual. His family isn't one of the Elders, but they are a part of the Brethren. It's bad luck though, because when you join the Brethren without Elder blood in your veins you are offered the life of your dreams, but it comes at a price. For instance, Booth's price is that he is the Elder's resident bitch-boy.

He comes down here and lights the tunnel for the Elders and the Legacies. He is also the attendance taker if you will, though this is the closest he will ever get to being inside of that room. He's never even seen past the door he keeps. If he did, I have no doubt my father would gouge out his eyes in an attempt to eviscerate the image from his mind. Then again, he'd probably take his tongue too for good measure, should he ever try to speak of what he sees.

To my knowledge, he's always been a faithful servant– dutiful and silent. Just as he should be. Wordlessly, he flips open the leather bound book before him. It only gets bigger and bigger as time goes on, since the Elders insist on using the original log book to maintain tradition.

I reach into my slacks pocket, grabbing my pocket-knife before flicking the blade open and pricking the end of my finger. When that first drop of crimson appears, I press my pointer finger to the blank line, where I quickly sign my name and the date before handing my knife to Liam. He quickly does the same, logging his attendance as well.

There are a lot of traditions and practices we still participate in that are weird as fuck. This one, for instance. The scripted writing across the top of the page, a clear direction as to why we do what we do. *Witches bleed black.*

Obviously, it's far less about eradicating witches and far more about multiplying our power, wealth and reach nowadays. Even so, we all cut our fingers to make sure we bleed red. Weird as fuck, but it's been practically the norm since I was first brought down here as a young boy.

Booth nods at us, dipping his head in respect as we move past him and push on the stone wall. In appearance it is just another part of the wall, but the twenty-second brick up from the floor is loose, so when you push it in just right—

Before I can finish my thought, the wall gives way, just enough for one person to slide through at a time. Liam is quick to shut the door behind himself as we step into the waiting room, at least that's what I call it. Though you'd expect the Brethren to have a more refined space for their elite, that isn't the case down here. Up above is where we flaunt our wealth and status, where we indulge in our every desire. Down here, we are just as they were before us. At least, that's the horse shit my father has been peddling down my throat since I was old enough to understand how different our family was.

Vincent Griggs is already here, standing in the corner so he can watch everyone as usual. The guy is a fucking creep, and has been ever since his parents died. He got even worse after his Bond Brother died. As a Legacy, when we're thirteen, we are assigned a Bond Brother. He is, for all intents and purposes, an extension of ourselves. You do everything with each other as kids, so that it strengthens your bond as adults. I'm just glad I was matched with Liam. We had been best friends since birth and if I would have had to have been Brothers with someone like Griggs, I think I would have gladly offered myself as well.

His eyes come to mine and Liam's instantly, a sneer pulling at his lips as the grey in his eyes flash like a knife. We are similar in build, and if I had to take him on there is a good chance I would win. Then again, because his family was who they were and because of what they did for the Brethren, maybe not. Either way it doesn't matter, every family here, including Liam's, will one day submit to me. It's my birthright.

Thomas Preston and Andrew Hutchinson step into the room next, closely followed by Jeremy Stroughton and Dane Lewis. They all acknowledge everyone in the room with a simple nod before taking seats around the room. We've timed it well, and don't have to wait long before the wall in front of us shifts revealing yet another hidden door to the main room.

Ronan steps out, eyes scanning to make sure all of us are here. His job, to the Brethren, is essentially the Legacy guardian. Until we are officially inducted into the Brethren, he's basically our babysitter.

He gives us a silent nod as we all stand and begin slipping through the door, one by one, before it's snapped shut behind us.

Chapter Nine
Skyla

Professor Corwin is droning on and on about the colonial era, and no offense, I couldn't be less interested. I learned a completely different history syllabus growing up in the UK. So I probably should be paying attention, but as nice as he is, listening to him lecturing is practically mind numbing.

I do my best to avoid Liam's flirty eyes, but it's proving to be more difficult than I predicted seeing as he took the empty seat to my right while Maggie is on my left. I have absolutely no interest in conversing with the neanderthal, though. It's very obvious he's just one of Asher's henchmen, the lead henchman in fact. Every time I look at him, I think about the way he reveled in my public humiliation. No amount of pretty blond hair or eyelashes for miles can make up for that. Not to me at least.

My eyes flick down to the scratch paper I've been doodling on, that same heart crest imprinted in my mind. When I woke up this morning, someone had slipped an envelope under my door. Inside of it was a silver necklace with a heart shaped pendant. This wasn't just a normal heart, though. It had thorns and wire wrapped around it that looked to be bleeding. Accompanying it was a piece of paper with a single sentence.

Sometimes the most precious things hurt the most.

Obviously it's some kind of weird scare tactic from Asher, as if the lovely little photo wasn't enough. I don't know what his game is and I don't care. I threw the entire thing straight in the trash and didn't mention it to anyone. I won't let him have the satisfaction of me even acknowledging his efforts.

When class is over Maggie and I stand up, pushing past Liam as we walk down the stairs. I'm applying Ronan's advice and ignoring Asher, as well as all of his associates. If it bothers the king, I have no doubt it bothers the servants just the same.

I'm in such a rush to get out of the classroom that as soon as I step out into the courtyard I barrel into someone, forcing them to stumble a step or two before they face me.

"Watch it," he practically snarls.

It only takes me a moment to place him as the tattooed guy from the pool. I haven't seen him around campus, and I haven't been back to the pool since that day. Despite how much I already miss it.

"It was an accident, Griggs," Maggie snaps right back.

His hate filled eyes flick from me to her, before coming back to me. He dismisses us with a shake of his head, before he's storming off across campus.

"Who is that?" I ask Maggie.

"Him? That's Vincent Griggs. Total loner and a complete jerk off."

Yeah, I could tell.

"Why do you call everyone by their last name?" I ask as I walk her to her class, since I have a gap in my schedule for a few hours.

"What do you mean?" she asks.

"Anytime you talk to people you call them by their last name, almost in a derogatory way. Why?"

She is quiet for a moment before she speaks.

"Heritage is really important around here. It's ingrained in us. Some families are good, some not so much."

"Well, that's just life right? Are there literal family rivalries here or something?"

Maggie shakes her head as we round the corner of the building and step inside.

"Not at all. We are all on the same team. It's just complicated. I don't know– hard to explain. If you would have grown up here, you would know these things," she sings lightly before laughing.

"Yeah, sorry. I didn't have much say in that."

She rolls her eyes and pulls me in for a quick hug.

"Yeah, yeah. Excuses, excuses. K, see you at lunch," she says before slipping into her class.

I wave goodbye as I begin heading back to my dorm until my creative writing class, which I absolutely despise by the way.

After classes are done for the day, Maggie and I are heading to the parking lot when Liam comes jogging up. He steps in front of us in an attempt to stop our movement, but I give him an unimpressed look as I continue walking.

He grins at me like he expected nothing less before he begins jogging backwards, keeping his eyes on me.

"Hey, babygirl. Where you going?"

"None of your business," I cut.

"Aw come on, don't be like that. It was funny. If it would have happened to me, you would have been laughing."

"No, I wouldn't have. It was cruel and undeserving. I most definitely wouldn't participate in the public humiliation of others because I was so desperate to be accepted by my peers," I snap back at him.

His teasing smile falls, and he stops in his tracks as he nods solemnly.

"You're right. I'm sorry, it was a dick move."

My eyes narrow in suspicion for a moment, searching his face for something teasing or disingenuous. But I come up empty.

"It was," I say carefully.

"Can I make it up to you?" he asks.

I raise an eyebrow. "Probably not, I've been known to hold a grudge."

A laugh escapes him as he smirks.

"I'll bet. There's a party tonight, be my date?"

Now I'm the one that laughs, causing his smirk to drop and a confused look to knit his brows together.

"Absolutely not," I snicker, as Maggie gives me a side eye before chuckling to herself.

"Why not?" Liam asks, obviously deeply offended.

"I don't need a reason. No is a complete sentence," I say, as my laughter dies down with a shake of my head.

I brush past him, looping my arm with Maggie's to take her with me. Liam quickly jogs after us, grating on my nerves as he speaks.

"Fine, don't be my date but at least come. There will be drinks, dancing. I've been told I'm quite the dancer," he says as he takes a step to the side, practically humping the air as he does.

I'm not sure if he's trying to look like an idiot, but either way he's succeeding. I can't help but let a laugh slip out at his expense as I shake my head, when Maggie speaks up.

"Bonfire?" she asks.

His eyes flick to her before he smiles and nods.

"You in, Bartlett?"

"As long as you stop dancing, Walcott," she laughs.

His body stops instantly as he snickers.

"Done. I'll see you ladies tonight," he says with a saucy wink in my direction, before he saunters off back to campus.

I look over to Maggie with wide eyes as I shake my head.

"We aren't actually going, right?"

She rolls her eyes at me and smirks.

"Of course we are."

Chapter Ten
Skyla

I've decided to wear a pair of dark blue jeans and a dark grey wrapped sweater since we are going to be outside. It's comfortable but practical, and it's about the most casual outfit I own besides leggings and a tank top, which is obviously not an option.

Maggie said she would meet me at my dorm, and we could walk together. Sure enough, a steady knock comes from my door seconds after I smear my nude colored lip gloss on.

I run a hand through my barrel curls as I open the door. Maggie's wide smile dies on her lips as soon as she sees me. She's gone a little edgier, wearing ripped black jeans and a Lynyrd Skynyrd crop top with some combat boots.

Maggie's eyes roam over me, judgment clear in them as she shakes her head.

"Babe, what the hell are you wearing? It's a bonfire, not a Lamaze class."

I frown at her as I look down at my sweater.

"What do you mean? I like this sweater."

"My grandma likes that sweater," she deadpans. "You have a banging body. Why are you hiding it?" she asks.

I cross my arms over my chest uncomfortably before shrugging softly. A sympathetic look crosses her face before she nods.

"Sorry, I'm being a bitch. You look beautiful."

I don't quite believe her, but I don't get time to argue before she's pulling me out of the room by my arm. The door shuts with a resounding thud and my heart sinks.

"Maggie, my phone was inside and my key! How am I supposed to get back in?"

She waves me off as she continues pulling me down the hallway, like I'm a pet on its way to be neutered.

"It's fine. You can crash with me. Let's just go already!"

I roll my eyes at her carefree attitude as we step inside the elevator, whooshing down to the bottom floor in no time. Apparently, it's a back to school tradition to hold a huge bonfire at the edge of campus. I wasn't able to determine if it was sanctioned by the school or not, my guess is obviously that it's not.

My suede knee-high boots cover the distance across campus, and soon a flicker of fire can be seen from afar. It gets larger and larger the closer we get, until we come right up to it and see it's nearly twenty-feet high and ten-feet wide. Several guys wearing Gallows Hill football t-shirts are laughing, fueling the fire more and more with wooden pallets. Dozens of people are gathered around singing, dancing and laughing to the music coming from a huge speaker in the corner.

There are several kegs to the side, and nearly everyone has a drink in their hand. I glance at Maggie uneasily and she rolls her eyes before pulling me over to an empty area near the fire, shaking her hips to the beat. Her hands rest on mine, physically forcing me to move along to the beat as well. I can't help but laugh before I finally stop fighting her, moving to the upbeat R&B song.

She grabs a beer out of some guy's hand, winking at him as his shoulders slump and he walks back over to the keg where he got his drink.

"Who was that?" I ask.

"My neighbor, he's too nice to say no to me," she says in my ear over the thumping music.

"Maybe he likes you."

She snorts and shakes her head.

"I fucked around with his sister last summer. He knows he's definitely not my type."

I can't help but laugh at that. She's so unapologetically her, it's amazing. The comfortability she has in her own skin is something I admire deeply. I wish I could be as strong and proud in just *one* thing, as she seems to be in everything.

When the song changes, to something a little slower and more seductive, I watch as Maggie sets her eyes on a girl behind me. She gives her a sultry smirk before moving past me, grabbing her hips as she begins dancing again. The girl looks a little caught off guard, almost like she wants to push her away. The lust is apparent in her eyes though, even from over here and she quickly succumbs to my friend's charm.

I genuinely think it's Maggie's mission to switch every straight woman on campus, at least for a night.

Laughing at my amazingly sexual friend I turn to step away from the fire, already sweating from the direct heat. Maybe a sweater actually wasn't the best idea for a bonfire. I'm moving through a crowd of people when a familiar face pops-up in front of me. Her sleek black hair and bright blue eyes are nearly unforgettable, as well as the mental image of her naked body lying on my bed with Asher on top of her.

"Hey! You're Skyla, right?" she slurs slightly, swaying a bit as she holds her drink a little higher like it will somehow counter her center of gravity.

I nod, but don't say anything, and that's okay because her drunken rambling continues.

"I'm Bridgetteee," she exaggerates, before giggling to herself. "We met earlier this week."

I give her a tight smile as I nod again. "I remember, you were bent over my bed."

She snickers at that, covering her mouth as she nods.

"Sorry about that. You know how it is, when Asher Putnam asks you to jump, you fling yourself right off the bridge."

I actually can't relate to that statement, at all. I'm not sure I would willingly do a single thing for Asher Putnam. I give her a polite nod but take a step to the side, ready to be done with whatever this is. Her hand whips out, those long nails digging into my forearm as she holds me back.

"Wait, I wanted to say I'm sorry and hopefully we can start fresh. I swear, I'm not the bitch I seem to be. I just like him," she says softly, a hint of vulnerability peeking through the drunken haze.

I shrug at that. "Well, you can have him. Honestly, I have zero interest."

She laughs, like I just told the most hilarious joke, before she stares at me like I've grown a second head. It looks like she's about to say something before she shakes her head.

"Have you been to the spot yet?"

"The spot?" I question with a shake of my head.

She rolls her eyes before practically squealing. "Oh my godddd. C'mon. You have to come check it out, it's like a tradition for new students."

I frown at that and look over my shoulder to see Maggie making out with the girl she was just dancing with. Damn, she moves fast.

Bridgette's hold on me is practically iron clad and her coordination isn't all that bad considering we are walking through grass and she's wearing heels, obviously drunk off her ass. We quickly round a corner behind a building before coming up to an iron gate. There is a sign above it that says, 'Gallows Hill Cemetery'.

A chill runs down my spine as we cross the threshold, goose-bumps immediately erupting over my skin. My feet begin to drag, suddenly not as willing to follow this drunk girl into a wooded cemetery.

"Where are we going?" I ask.

"I told yous," she slurs. "The spot!"

I want to shake her stupid drunk self and tell her she didn't answer my question, as we weave around the graves surrounding us. My eyes catch on a few of the dates from the headstones.

1692, 1693, 1695.

My god, these graves have been here for over three hundred years. Part of me is completely fascinated that this cemetery is so old, especially considering its nearly immaculate condition. A bigger part of me is completely creeped out by the fact that the college has a three-hundred-year-old cemetery on campus.

We walk a little further before I see a tiny bright red light in the middle of the darkness, at least that's what it looks like. As we get closer my eyes adjust, and I realize it's the end of a cigarette. The owner of said cigarette is instantly recognizable, and I don't even try to hide my irritation.

"What are you doing out here, Princess?" Asher draws out lazily, taking a large inhale as Liam smiles at me beside him.

"She was showing me the spot," I say as Bridgette pulls us to a stop, giving Asher unashamed goo-goo eyes.

Asher nods, as he pushes off the headstone he was leaning up against, unfolding himself to his full height as he looks at the ground in front of him. He pulls the cigarette from his mouth and grabs a beer bottle from the floor, twisting the cap open before he speaks.

"Looks like you found it."

I frown at that, looking down at what I can now tell is an empty grave. It looks to be the size for a coffin, but appears to have been dug years ago based on the dirt and surrounding grass. Asher closes the distance between us, stopping inches before me as he rests his free hand on my shoulder.

"Wha—"

My words are cut off as Asher shoves my shoulder– hard. The ground literally slips out from underneath my feet as my body falls right into the hole, landing with a rough smack into the dirt. Cackling comes from above, and I have to push the dirt away from my eyes to look up and see Bridgette smiling down at me with an evil smirk.

Asher is laughing hysterically, and Liam is chuckling to himself lightly.

"What the hell?" I shout, before forcing myself to my feet. A twinge comes from my left ankle that leads me to believe it's at least sprained. Great.

The soft ground beneath me sinks, practically swallowing my shoes as I stand. I try to grip the edge of the grass and pull myself up, but I can't even reach. This thing is at least ten-feet deep, equal amounts of irritation and panic fill me.

"Get me out of here!" I demand.

"Nah, I think you are right where you belong, but I'm not a total monster. Let me get you something to drink," Asher says before standing over me, tipping his beer bottle upside-down. The cold sticky liquid hits my hair first, streaming down my face and my back as he empties the entirety of its contents over me.

I squeal at the feeling, doing my best to protect myself with my hands before Asher tosses the bottle into the grave with me. I don't even have it in me to be humiliated right now. Instead, I'm just pissed.

"You asshole! Get me out of here, right now!"

He looks down at me, sneering as he wraps an arm around an eager and actually very sober looking Bridgette.

Nice acting, little bitch.

"Pass."

I watch as he begins walking away, before glancing to see Liam still standing there, a frown tugging his full pink lips.

"Ash, we aren't leaving her all night, right?" he asks, hesitance in his voice. "There's a shit ton of coyotes, man."

Asher looks over his shoulder at his friend, shrugging nonchalantly.

"They can have her."

Anger burns inside me and right now, I've never wished anyone would be struck dead by lightning more than him. His little groupie right along with him.

"Liam," I ask, hoping I can appeal to the humanity in him that is obviously trying to poke through. "Please," I whisper softly, allowing the deep-seated fear inside me to bleed through.

He grimaces as he looks at me, before looking over to see Asher watching him carefully. Liam gives me an almost pained look, before he shakes his head and begins walking away with Asher and Bridgette.

Fuck!

"Liam!" I shout desperately. "Please! Asher! Get your asses back here! You can't leave me out here! Help! Someone help me!" I scream.

I hear Bridgette cackle again and it becomes more faint with each step away from me that they take.

Shit. Shit. Shit.

I reevaluate the dirt walls surrounding me, digging the toes of my boots into the side in hopes I can make footholds of sorts. Unfortunately, the ground is practically rock-hard, and my efforts are completely useless. My ankle twinges in pain again, forcing me to grimace. Fuck.

A cold chill sweeps through the air, forcing me to shiver.

At least a half an hour goes by as I try and try to get out of this stupid hole, all attempts completely failed. A howl suddenly sounds out in the night sky, followed by more than I can count.

Liam's words about coyotes come to mind and my stomach turns. I've never seen one before, but it's related to a wolf and that's enough information for me.

My hands quickly scramble against the dirt wall, digging my fingers in as deep as I can to try and at least get closer to the top. As soon as I'm able to get a firm grip though, I realize how truly screwed I am. All that I'm doing at this point is burying more dirt beneath my nails.

In the next moment a noise comes from my left, all of the breath from my lungs being sucked right out as I hear another.

"Hello? Is someone there?" I ask, only to be met with silence.

The sound of a twig snapping on my right has my head snapping in that direction, but I can't see anything.

Shit. Shit. Shit.

I'm not a baby when it comes to scary things. I can watch horror movies and I have no problem with the dark but I'm trapped, in an abandoned grave, in a practically ancient cemetery, where there are definitely coyotes coming in my direction. Tell me you wouldn't be ready to throw up right now.

"Hello?" I call out again, my voice quaking this time as I begin to spiral into a full-blown panic.

Ghosts aren't real, right? Just because this cemetery is over three-hundred-years-old doesn't mean that it's haunted. Even if there were ghosts out here, it's not like they can materialize enough to snap twigs and actually make noise....right?

One more sound comes from just a few feet to the left of me. I practically jump out of my skin as my heart sinks and my voice shouts. In the next moment, a pair of black boots comes into view before two legs crouch down to look at me.

My eyes trace over the black clothed man, surprised when I see that it's Vincent Griggs, staring down at me like I'm an insect he found underneath his boot.

"Vincent?" I question, half disbelieving but also half in relief. "Can you help me out? Please?"

He doesn't respond, instead, just choosing to stare at me. My relief quickly begins to shrivel inside, replaced with the acceptance that I will probably live out my remaining moments in this grave, before I'm killed by hypothermia, coyotes, three-hundred-year-old ghosts or maybe even Vincent himself.

We end up just staring at each other for what feels like minutes, suspended in time. My mind races with what I can use to defend myself. I think I saw a rock half buried in the wall to my right. Maybe if I can pull it out, it would give me some sort of fighting chance. Go out swinging and all that.

Slowly, Vincent's tattooed hand reaches down into the grave, extending his fingers to me. I hesitate for only a moment or two, before I greedily accept his help, practically scrambling to latch onto his arm as he begins pulling me up. Pushing my feet into the dirt wall I try my best to ease the burden, but it doesn't seem to be much of a task for him. He practically yanks me up and out of the grave, without so much as a strained muscle.

I land on the wet grass with a thump and quickly roll onto my back before standing up.

"Thank you! Thank you so much! I thought I was going to freaking die out here," I say, the building tears beginning to let loose as I throw my arms around him.

He immediately tenses beneath me for a moment or two, before roughly shoving me. I right myself before I fall again, and I look up to see him staring at me, with that same angry look he seems to always have ingrained in his features. I open my mouth, to say what? I'm not sure, but I don't get the chance before he turns and begins stalking deeper into the cemetery, without a single word.

What the hell?

Part of me wants to ask what his deal is, but another chill runs through the air sending goosebumps down my arms. I decide to hell with it, as I practically sprint out of the graveyard. As soon as I pass through the gates, that foreboding fear deep in the pit of my stomach eases, as if I was officially out of danger or something.

As I limp my way back towards the party, I find it alive and well. My eyes scan over the crowd in search of Maggie, but I come up short. Seriously? Not only did she not realize I was gone, but she left me too? Rationally, I hope she is looking for me or maybe assumed I decided to leave early, but irrationally I'm pissed that I was trapped in that grave for nearly an hour.

Screw this, I'm out of here. I begin making my way towards my dorm, craving nothing more than a warm shower and my bed. On the negative side, I'm cold, beer soaked and caked with dirt and mud. On the positive side...nope, all negatives. This night sucks.

Chapter Eleven
Skyla

My teeth are practically chattering together as I wrap my arms around myself, walking as quickly as I can just for the sake of trying to warm-up. It only took me another twenty-feet of walking to realize that I'm still locked out of my dorm.

When I pass by the pool, I pause. I doubt it's unlocked, but it's worth a shot. At least they have showers.

Please, please, please.

I repeat the word over and over again, hoping and praying the door will give, but all my hopes are dashed in an instant when I pull, only to be met with locked resistance. Damn.

I turn on my heel, heading to I don't even know where, when I hear the door open behind me and a deep voice rasping my name.

"Skyla?"

My head whips around, locking eyes with a dripping wet Ronan. He's wearing a t-shirt that is soaking by the second and a pair of grey sweatpants.

"Are you okay?" he asks as he leans against the door, keeping it propped open as he does.

"Yeah, I'm fine."

He frowns at me. "You're wet, dirty, and bleeding."

I look down to see my palms are cut open, a small drip of blood coming from my right hand before splashing onto the light grey pavement. When did that happen?

"C'mon," he says, with a nod inside the building.

He doesn't have to tell me twice. I rush inside, slipping past him and into the warm hallway. A shiver runs through me as the heat pricks my skin. I feel a large hand rest against my lower back and turn to see Ronan nodding to me.

"Let's go clean you up."

I shakily nod as I begin walking. He guides me easily, not removing his hand from my back the entire time.

When we are in his office he gestures to the empty seat across from his desk, before he crouches down and begins rifling through a cabinet. In no time he's pulling out a first aid kit, taking out a few alcohol wipes as he kneels before me.

His large hands tenderly take my own away from my lap, holding them out to him palms up before he speaks.

"This probably won't feel great."

He takes the wipe and runs it across my cut. I sink my teeth into my lip as I cringe. God, it's way deeper than I even thought. How did I not notice until now? How did I not feel how much it stings until now?

"You won't need stitches," he says softly, almost to himself.

His strokes are careful, but thorough, as he brushes away chunks of dirt and blood. Eventually it stops hurting, instead of focusing on my hand, I stare at the gentle giant before me.

Not a word is spoken between us as he dutifully cleans my hands, bandaging them up as soon as he's finished. I move to pull my hands away, but he stops me, tightening his grip as my eyes come to his. Those deep blue eyes staring at me intently, practically pinning me in place.

"What happened?" he asks.

I swallow roughly, before I shake my head and let out a bitter laugh.

"Asher."

His eyes narrow at me.

"Explain."

Turning my head away, I shake my head, too tired and honestly too defeated to get into it right now. I just want this night to be over.

He doesn't seem to accept my silence, holding his gaze on me and seemingly waiting me out. I don't give in, though and he lets out a rough breath before he stands.

"C'mon. You can shower in the locker room."

He moves to a cabinet to the side, pulling out a few small bottles and what looks like a shirt and a pair of sweatpants before he walks through his office door. I follow after him as he leads me just outside the locker room, pausing at the entrance as he hands me the mini bottles of shampoo and bodywash, along with a black Gallows Hill shirt and sweats.

"Towels are in there. The door is locked so you don't have to worry about anyone coming in. Make sure you keep your bandages dry."

"How am I supposed to do that when washing my hair?" I question.

He rolls his lips together for several seconds, that signature stoic look on his face.

"Do you need me to do it?"

A thrill runs through me, the thought of those strong fingers running through my hair. The warm water running against my skin—

"Clothed, obviously. Your clothes could use a rinse anyways," he adds.

Disappointment pangs through me, though I don't know why. It's not like him washing my hair is going to lead to us sleeping together. He's not going to strip away my virginity right here and now, nor would I want him to. Right? Right.

I nod. "That would be great. Thank you."

He dips his head and I slowly make my way inside the locker room. They only have one, probably because there is only a men's swim team so there is no need for a women's locker room.

The perimeter of the room is surrounded by lockers, the middle has several benches and a line of showers. I step up to the first one, turning the water on for a moment as I allow it to heat up. Once it's warm enough, I take a step into the spray, practically melting into the warmth despite the heavy soaked feeling of my sweater and jeans against my skin.

I let the water run through my hair, trying to resist the temptation to run my fingers through it as my makeup begins washing away. God, what is it with Ronan seeing me without makeup? Either bad timing or something more cruel. He's probably seen me barefaced more in this last week than my father has seen me from puberty up, which I guess isn't saying much.

He takes a step towards me, squirting a small amount of shampoo into his hands, gesturing for me to turn around. I do as he says, allowing the spray to run down my front as his hands begin lathering my hair. At first, his movements are rough and jerky and I wince as he yanks on my hair. Soon, though, his fingers reach deeper, slowly beginning to massage my scalp. I let out a pleasured groan that has his movements pausing. Damn it. That's what I get for opening my mouth, I ruin a perfectly good thing.

To my surprise, he continues a moment later. I do my best to stay quiet as his fingers work through every single strand of hair. I'm practically putty in his hands as he washes the beer and dirt from my hair, replacing the smell with something fresh and a touch masculine. You won't hear me complaining, though.

"Rinse," he rasps roughly. I turn around to face him, keeping my eyes locked on his as I lean my head back under the water.

Only a second or two passes before he closes the distance between us, leaning over me as his hands massage my scalp a bit more, rubbing out all the shampoo as he does. I feel his breath against my neck and when he looks from my hair to me, my stomach flips. Without meaning to, I feel my teeth sink into my lower lip, pulling on it slightly. Ronan's eyes snap down, watching me with rapt attention. I don't know how long we stay like that before he's shaking his head and ripping away, like touching me physically burns him.

"Go ahead and dry off. I'll walk you back to your room once you're dressed," he says, practically jogging out of the locker room before I can even tell him I can't get into my room.

I stand there for several seconds, allowing the water to pour over me for just a little bit longer before I shut the shower off. Quickly, I peel off my soaked clothes, tossing them on the ground before slipping on the shirt and sweatshirt. They are both at least five sizes too big for me, so I end up rolling the sweatpants several times and tying the shirt off into a crop top.

Wrapping my clothes up with the towel, I walk out of the bathroom to find Ronan leaning up against the wall. He pushes away from it quickly, as his eyes rake over me for only half a second before he looks to the floor roughly.

"Let's go."

"I don't have my key, I left it inside my room."

He nods before moving into his office, grabbing out a key card. "Master key," he explains.

I frown at that.

"I'm not sure I like the idea that people have access to my room whenever they want."

"Not people, just me and the dean."

My head tilts to the side at that.

"Why you? The dean and the swim coach? Seems like a strange combination."

His jaw tightens as he gives me a look of irritation.

"Is that how you say thank you?"

"No," I answer flatly, causing him to let out a gruff laugh. Or maybe it was a bothered huff. Either way, he scrubs his hand against his jaw and shakes his head.

With that, he heads for the door. I follow right behind him as we leave the pool, shutting the lights off as we go before stepping outside. The crisp night air instantly bites at my wet head, and I shiver the entire way until we make it to the Parris dorm.

As soon as we get there, Ronan smashes the elevator button like it has personally offended him before stepping to the side. When the elevator opens, he makes a sweeping motion with his hand as I step inside. He follows in after me, and soon the doors are opening again once we've reached my floor.

We walk down the hall until we're outside my door. I point at it in silent communication and Ronan waves his key card over it, forcing the locking mechanism to whir on command before I push it open. Instead of just walking inside I turn to look at him, so many words, yet none at all resting on the tip of my tongue.

He doesn't wait around for me to say anything, though. Instead, he turns, moving to the elevator before hitting the button once more. His blue eyes turn to mine as he speaks softly, just before the doors open.

"Good night."

"Night," I say, my voice being cut off midway as he steps inside the elevator, the doors shutting right behind him.

My head is pounding, and I'm not sure I've been so ready for a week to be over in all my life as I step inside my dorm. I don't bother turning a light on. Instead, I numbly walk over to my bed, pausing when I see a white rose and a note on my bedside table. I squint at it, my eyes trying to adjust to the darkness with only a stream of moonlight illuminating the room.

The note is scribbled in messy handwriting, and I already know exactly who it's from.

Welcome to Gallows Hill.

My lip curls up in disgust, as I shake my head and crumple up the note, tossing the rose and it into the trash. I don't know why he is so hell bent on harassing me. I have literally done nothing to him, other than exist. Is he mad that I'm marrying him? Well, same here.

Fucking asshole.

Chapter Twelve
Skyla

I woke up the next morning to my phone ringing. I blink my eyes blearily as I pat around for my phone, glancing at the screen quickly. I immediately sit up right, clearing my throat as I run my fingers through my hair, as if he could almost judge my appearance straight through the phone.

"Good morning, Father," I say in my most polite tone.

"Your presence is required tonight at Putnam manor."

My mouth pulls into a grimace and my shoulders slump.

"Is it really necessary?" I ask, letting it slip out before I can stop it.

He is silent for several seconds, either out of shock that I would even slightly question him or in anger and he wants me to squirm in punishment. Either way, I'm on edge when his icy voice rumbles through the phone.

"If I say so, then it is. Be there, accompanied by your fiancée at seven o'clock sharp," he says, ending the phone call immediately after.

A text message from an unknown number comes through, causing me to roll my eyes as I read it.

Unknown: We have to go to a party at my dad's house. Wear something nice and stuffy like you normally do and don't forget the ring.

My eyes lock on the black box, hiding the massive diamond ring inside. I haven't been sheltered by life's luxuries by any means, but the thing is downright massive. It's a beautiful cushion cut with encrusted smaller diamonds wrapping around the band. Maybe, if it had been given to me by someone I love, someone that loves me, it would be more special. Instead, it's more like a noose, tightening around my neck with each impending day.

Since it's Saturday, there are no classes today and I take full advantage of staying in bed extra-long, catching up on some schoolwork. I even tried to sneak into the pool, but unfortunately for me, it was locked. When I waited for Ronan to come open the door much like last night, I was met with disappointment.

My mind flicks to the handsome, inappropriately too old and clearly off limits man. I don't think it's all in my head, I think he feels it too. I swear he was about to kiss me in the shower last night, or at least he wanted to. I know I sure as hell wanted him to.

Is it really so bad to lust after your fiancé's uncle, if said fiancé is a grade A asshole? Maybe, but I can't seem to stop myself all the same.

I spend the day working on my English lit paper and some homework for history until I can hardly see straight. Thankfully, after a ridiculously late lunch, it's time to start getting ready. I'm just, honestly looking forward to getting this night over as soon as possible.

Due to the time of the event and my inferring of how similarly these people live their lives to my father, I decide a sophisticated dress is the perfect option for tonight. I decided on a black floor-length gown. One sleeve is full-length, ending just at my wrist while the other side is strapless. It does have a thigh slit that goes up to stop a few inches below my hip, but the overall modesty of the top makes it an even balance. That's what I told myself when I bought it, at least. We will see if my father has a conniption when he sees me in it.

I accompany the gown with a modest pair of black heels and pearl teardrop earrings, sliding on the gaudy diamond ring last. I almost cringe at it knowing my fate is sealed, all because of this five-carat gem.

A text message comes through in the next moment.

Asshole Fiancé: Outside. Hurry up or I'll leave you.

And they say chivalry is dead.

Rolling my eyes, I grab my black clutch and put my things inside, going out of my way to remember my room key before I leave. As soon as I step outside my dorm building, I notice a black Maserati parked in the walkway, literally. He's parked cockeyed and blocking the main entrance of the building. It's the type of arrogance that says, I'm too lazy to park in the parking lot and walk like a normal person.

When I get closer to the car the door opens, swinging up instead of out. Tucking the long skirt of the dress behind myself, I slide into the leather seat easily before the door comes back down, officially locking me inside.

Asher is in the driver's seat, his brown hair perfectly styled, not a strand of hair out of place while wearing a crisp black Armani suit. He looks like he stepped right out of a magazine and I'm not sure how to feel about it. On one hand, I wish he would be as ugly on the outside as he clearly is on the inside. On the other hand, if I have to marry anyone at least it's someone who is pleasing to the eye I suppose.

His eyes rake over me, an unimpressed sneer pulling at his lips before he puts the car into drive and takes off down the walkway. Granted, there are no pedestrians right now, but what if there were! He'd run them over dead and not lose a wink of sleep, I'll bet.

As we speed down the road I scoff to myself, smoothing out my slick bun in the side mirror as he turns at a light. I don't have time to brace myself and I smash my face against the window before shooting him a lethal glare.

"What is your problem?" I ask.

"Currently, you," he snaps curtly, as he sails down the road.

"Okay, can we drop the bullshit at least for tonight? Please. I don't know what your dad is like, but my dad is expecting us to be loving and affectionate towards one another."

"You always do what daddy tells you?" Asher asks, with an unimpressed brow.

"Always, as I'm sure you know. He's a hard man to say no to and before you judge me, you're the one in the monkey suit picking me up at my door. If I had to guess, I'd say you're just as trapped as I am."

He lets out a hollow laugh, shaking his head as he turns away from me.

"You and I are nothing alike."

I nod in agreement on that when my eyes snag on something. A perfectly shaped red pair of lips are pressed against his neck, just barely visible past his collar.

"Seriously? You couldn't even wash off your whore's lipstick before you picked me up?" I scoff.

Asher looks in the rear view mirror, turning his head so he can see his neck before he shrugs. He is clearly unbothered.

"Someone's gotta suck my dick and I know it's not gonna be you."

Embarrassment flushes through me at his callousness and I grit my teeth together before speaking.

"Let me out."

He keeps driving, blatantly ignoring me and I lose it. I take my clutch and begin smacking his arm with it, shouting over and over again.

"Let me out! Let me out! Let me out!"

"Ow, fuck! Stop," he snaps, as he tries to continue driving while holding back my arms.

In desperation, I do the only thing I can, and I sink my teeth into his wrist. He lets out a rough curse and yanks his arm away from me before whipping the wheel to the side. We pull over with a screech as he turns to face me, a wild look of rage in his eyes.

"Get the fuck out!"

"Gladly," I shout with a toss of my hands, pushing my way out of the car and onto the pavement in the next second.

I'm barely out of the car before he takes off, the door slowly lowering as he speeds down the road. Good freaking riddance. Letting out an irritated breath, I shake my head before looking around. Damnit. I don't know where I am, and I don't know where I'm going. Even if I order a ride, it's not like my driver is going to know where Putnam Manor is.

My heels begin clicking against the paved road as the sun dips low, bathing the city in darkness. I'm not sure what direction to head in but straight seems like a good bet, at least for now. Maybe I'll just call my father. He won't be happy, but maybe he'll take his anger out on the one that rightfully deserves it— my manwhore fiancé.

Several cars pass me by, veering uncomfortably close before one slows down altogether. A rush of fear pangs through my body as I subtly look over my shoulder. The passenger window rolls down before a familiar voice calls out to me.

"Skyla?"

My head whips around to see Ronan watching me with a pinched look. In the next moment, he's shutting off his car and jogging around the front of it to stand beside me. His eyes roam over me from head to toe, heat licking at my skin in their wake. When his blue eyes settle on me, they're practically on fire. I watch as he closes them, squeezing hard, before seemingly shaking off whatever he's thinking as he looks at me with concern.

"What are you doing out here?"

I roll my eyes and shake my head.

"Asher took off."

"He just left you," Ronan asks sharply, blinking slowly like he can't be hearing me right.

"To be fair, I told him to let me out when I saw the smeared lipstick on his neck," I shrug, with a defeated sigh.

Ronan doesn't say anything again before I speak.

"It's an arranged marriage, obviously we don't love or even like each other, but I have a problem with arriving at an event on the arm of my supposed fiancé, who is donning another woman's lip shade. It's disrespectful and embarrassing. It looks like I'm not enough to hold a man's attention. I just—"

A large hand cups my own, his thumb brushing against my knuckles before stopping on the ginormous rock on my left hand.

"You're more than enough. Asher is rebelling and taking it out on you. It's not fair but I hope you know it's not personal."

For some reason, his words help a little, I guess. Maybe I'm too much of a people-pleaser, hardwired to crave the acceptance of those around me. I'm sure my life would be easier if I didn't care what anyone thought of me. I'm still working on that part.

"C'mon, we're going to be late," he says, as he rests his hand on my lower back, ushering me towards his car.

I nod and accept the gesture before sliding inside. The familiar scent of leather and something musky and delicious wraps around me as he slides into the driver's seat. He gives me a small, almost reassuring smile before taking off down the road.

"Did Asher prepare you?" Ronan asks after a minute or so.

"Prepare me for what?"

"Tonight."

I shrug, shaking my head in response. Ronan nods, his knuckles tightening slightly as he speaks.

"As I'm sure you've noticed, Salem is...different. We have a hierarchy of sorts and Asher's dad is at the top."

"Does that mean you are too?" I question.

He shakes his head. "It doesn't quite work like that. It's like the royal family. It's always going to be the king and the heir that's of the most importance, yeah?"

I nod.

"My brother can be...challenging, and first impressions are everything. Be respectful but silent. Only speak when spoken to and don't seem too interesting."

"Why not?" I say, with a raised brow.

Ronan's eyes come to my own, a hollowed look entering them as he speaks.

"Because he loves people who are interesting."

Something about the way he says that sends a chill down my spine. My head moves up and down in acceptance as we ride the rest of the way in silence.

When we arrive, we pull up a long paved driveway, surrounded by large bushy trees. The front gate has the name Putnam carved into it, like it has been here for generations before Ronan parks in the looped driveway. A valet hurries over to us, taking the keys as Ronan opens my door for me and takes my hand to help me out.

"Thank you," I say, as he dips his head and releases my hand.

A figure leans up against the large stone column outside the grand staircase, a lit cigarette in his fingers as we close the distance between us and him. When Ronan speaks, I'm taken back by the pure anger in his tone.

"What the fuck is the matter with you?" he snarls. "You leave your fiancée stranded on the side of the road?"

Asher rolls his eyes, taking a long drag of his cigarette as he does.

"It's not my fucking fault. She wanted to get out. What was I supposed to do, drag her ass back kicking and screaming?"

"No," Ronan snaps, smacking the cigarette out of his hand and crushing it beneath his heel. "You're not going to lay a goddamn finger on her unless she has given verbal permission."

Once again, Asher's eyes roll to the back of his head as he pushes away from his uncle.

"Whatever."

Ronan is fast to stop Asher, clasping his shoulder tightly as he speaks.

"I'm serious, Asher. I can only protect you for so long. With..." he pauses for a moment, his eyes coming to me before he continues in a more hushed tone. "Everything, aligning the way it is, you have to be better."

"Maybe, I'm tired of it," Asher draws out.

"You don't get to be, and you know that. So throw your little fit later. When you're here, you are respectful, you will display an insurmountable level of couth and you won't fight with your *fiancée*."

Ronan grits that last word out, like it tastes bitter on his tongue before he looks at the both of us. He nods, asking if we are good, before he straightens his suit jacket and begins his ascent up the stairs. Asher and I don't move an inch, though. We are both staring at each other, not talking, not moving before he blows out a breath and wipes a hand down his face.

"C'mon," he says, almost defeatedly. "We're already late."

Chapter Thirteen
Skyla

I quietly follow Asher up the front steps of his father's mansion. When we get to the top, we're greeted with two large doors that are at least fifteen-feet tall. They appear to be hand carved wood and are absolutely stunning. I wait for Asher to push the doors open, or maybe I should? I steal a glance to see him staring at them blankly, like if he tries hard enough he could suddenly become invisible and slip away. It's the most vulnerable I've seen him, his cocky 'I rule the world' aura gone, and not the least bit sorely missed. Still, it is a little odd to see him so off.

He closes his eyes, letting out a near silent breath before offering his arm for me. I slip my hand through the crook of his elbow, allowing it to rest as he pushes one of the doors open. Immediately, we are greeted with the sound of classical music playing throughout the mansion, accompanied by nearly one-hundred people all donned in striking suits and luxurious gowns.

Familiar faces are recognized everywhere. My eyes roam around the room before landing on Liam, his cheesy smile looking a lot more plastic than usual as he speaks with an older man and woman. In the corner I see Vincent sulking, which is no surprise there, but he is wearing a nice tuxedo so that's definitely a shift from his typical punk style. I even see Andrew from my history class. He's with a kind looking couple and making small talk with a few men when his eyes catch mine. His cheeks pink up as he looks at me and gives a discreet wave, before turning back to the man in front of him.

Unfortunately, the next person my eyes land on is my father who looks unbelievably irritated.

Lovely.

Asher smoothly walks us towards him, a man in front of him turning to face us with a slow smile.

"Ah, you've finally arrived," the man says, his mouth moving in a way that makes my skin crawl.

Asher is practically a carbon copy of him, just twenty-five years younger. There is something else about him though, something that turns my stomach and tells me to flee far and fast. Unfortunately I can't, instead staying perfectly silent as Asher speaks.

"Apologies for our tardiness, father. You know how women can be about being ready on time."

I shoot him a side-eye that I hope burns him to his core while my father's face pinches up in disgust as he steps closer to me, a dangerous air surrounding us as he does. Asher's dad just laughs though, turning to face me as his eyes take in every inch of me. It's an uncomfortable feeling, and I want more than anything to squirm under his gaze. I resist though, doing my best to keep my head held high and a demure smile on my face.

"It's a pleasure to meet you, sir," I say with a nod.

He holds out his hand to me and I hesitate for a moment, until I feel a sharp pinch come from my side. I know it's my father and I know what he's saying.

Let him take your hand, do not embarrass me.

I slip my palm into his as he lifts it up to his mouth, before he presses his lips against my knuckles and smiles as he speaks.

"Please, call me Christopher. After all, we are going to be family."

I give him a soft smile and wiggle my fingers in an attempt to pull my hand away, but he doesn't seem ready to allow that to happen.

"You're even more beautiful than your pictures," Christopher muses, almost to himself.

My smile doesn't slip as I nod my head once more.

"Thank you. Your home is lovely. When was it crafted? Mid-eighteenth century?" I ask.

"Early," he says, something like interest flickering in his eyes as he tilts his head to the side. "How could you tell?"

"The architecture reminds me a lot of this home back in London. It was built in 1705, but I assumed being across the pond it would take a little longer for similar influences to reach here."

Christopher's smile curls, practically taking over his entire face as he speaks.

"Salem has been blessed with the finest craftsmen for some time. Have you made it down to the town museum? I'm sure you'd find it absolutely fascinating."

History was never my passion, by a long shot, but that doesn't mean I don't appreciate a beautifully built home. In my opinion, I found the way of life in England from the seventeenth to twentieth century much more interesting than America's, but maybe I'm biased because that's all I was taught for practically my whole life.

"I have not. I'll have to do that."

"Asher will take you soon."

Christopher smiles with a cutting look to his son.

Asher nods dutifully, a lot like the way I do with my father as he speaks.

"I'd be honored."

"Wonderful," Christopher says, before finally releasing my hand.

He begins talking with Asher about his grades and I tune out slightly, allowing myself to people-watch. I stop on Maggie, or at least I think it's Maggie. No way is my all black, all the time edgy, friend wearing a Pepto Bismol pink dress. Her red hair clashing with the dress as hard as her fake grin is cracking.

A good looking man and woman are on either side of her, introducing her to a handsome guy around our age. I think I have economics with him, actually. His name is Seth or Sean, something like that. He leans in, pressing his lips to her cheek in a greeting kiss and I don't miss the way she practically cringes. Oh no, are her parents trying to set her up? With a man, no less? Do they not know? No, they have to know. She wears it loud and proud.

My brows furrow and I take a half of a step to move towards her when her eyes catch mine, subtly shaking her head as if to call me off. I frown but nod, turning back to see my father and Christopher deep in discussion. Their eyes swing to Asher, seemingly sizing him up, before Ronan steps into the group.

"Excuse me, brother. I wonder if I might show Skyla the gardens."

Christopher grins, like it's the best idea he's ever heard before he nods.

"Excellent idea, Ronan. Thank you."

I watch as Christopher turns away from me brushing me off dismissively before he begins speaking to Asher in hushed tones, my father sending me a withering glance before he's listening and speaking as well.

I take a few steps with Ronan, before my feet slow as curiosity gets the best of me. I want to stay and listen to what they're saying. Based on Asher's face, it doesn't look good. A warm strong hand is pushing me forward, though.

"Keep moving, face forward," Ronan says as he continues walking, practically dragging me along with him.

I do as he says, turning around as we weave through the large home. A few people greet Ronan, but he's quick to dismiss them until we make it out to a balcony at the back of the house. My breath is nearly stolen when I see a maze of rose bushes expanding over a large chunk of the backyard. You can see just the tip of what looks to be a large fountain, before everything else is hidden in the privacy of the bushes.

Ronan's hold on me continues as he ushers us down the stairs and to the front of the maze. We enter wordlessly and he doesn't speak until we take our first turn.

"Are you okay?"

My brows dip at that, my heels slightly sinking into the grass as we walk.

"Yes, why?"

"I told you not to be interesting."

I look up at him as I shake my head.

"I wasn't."

"You were, I could see it in his eyes. He's intrigued by you already and that's not a good thing."

Shrugging, I take the left turn in front of us first, moving us deeper and deeper into the garden.

"Well, I don't know what to say. He seems...nice enough."

Ronan stops in his tracks, his face stoic and unmoving as he speaks.

"No, he doesn't."

I smile sadly, shaking my head as I continue walking.

"No, he doesn't."

His steps continue after me, and we don't speak again until we stop in front of the fountain. I move over to the ledge, sitting down on it before turning to watch the water flow. Ronan takes a seat beside me, his eyes on me the entire time.

My gaze moves from the fountain to him, watching as his forearms rest against his thighs.

"So, what's this party for anyways?" I ask.

His eyebrows furrow at that as he tilts his head to the side.

"No one told you?"

I shake my head.

"This is your engagement party."

My stomach flips and irritation rolls through me. Wow, should I honestly expect anything different? This entire arrangement has been absurd from the start. I wouldn't be surprised if I went out to breakfast one morning and stumbled into my wedding. Apparently, I'm not important enough to be filled in on little details like this.

We're silent for several seconds before Ronan speaks.

"He doesn't deserve you. He never should have left you like that tonight and shouldn't be treating you like he has."

I shrug, breaking eye contact with those hypnotic blue eyes as I stare out into the laurel greens and pops of color woven between them.

"When my father told me I was betrothed, I didn't anticipate meeting the love of my life or anything, but I'll be honest, I expected to be treated with the minimum amount of respect," I laugh bitterly, shaking my head as I do.

His palm slips underneath my chin, tilting my head to face him as he cups my face tenderly.

"You deserve so much more than that. You deserve... everything."

I smile sadly, sinking into his touch.

"Even if I did, I'm not sure that's in the cards for me."

Ronan's eyes flick back and forth between my own before they move down to my lips. I feel myself moving closer to him, inch by inch, and he doesn't stop me. In fact, when I'm just a hair's breadth away from him, his grip on me tightens before he closes the remaining distance between us.

All at once it's like fireworks and ecstasy tearing through my body, as his pillowy soft lips press against my own. His hand adjusts, forcing my head to tilt back and he takes full advantage of the new position, deepening the kiss as his tongue swipes against mine. I can't help but moan against him, my hands blindly reaching for him.

With each stroke of his tongue my pussy begins pulsing. Before I know it, I'm being lifted up and over him, settling down on top of his lap. My thighs easily straddle him and the slit in my dress allows me a lot more freedom than other dresses would.

I whimper when I feel his hard cock rub against my quickly dampening panties. Ronan's hands grip my hips, guiding my movements as he begins grinding me against him. Soon I don't need his guidance though, as I continue to lose myself in our kiss and use his body exactly how I want, how I need.

He breaks away from our kiss, cursing roughly as he speaks into my neck.

"Christ baby, you're fucking soaking my pants."

"I'm sorry," I pant as I continue my movements, angling myself so my clit is perfectly stimulated against his cock.

"Don't be," he practically growls. "It's so hot. Ride me, baby. Make that pretty little pussy come all over my suit."

I feel myself spasm as I increase my motions, another moan slipping out of my mouth. Ronan cups the back of my head with one hand, crushing our lips together once more. His other hand grabs my ass, forcing me to grind against him harder and faster. Just when I think it can't possibly feel better than this, I see white. Literally, my vision flashes and for a moment I'm completely blind.

Pleasure rips through my body like a hurricane, and the only saving grace in containing my screams is Ronan's tongue that is currently tangled around mine. That euphoric feeling pricks against every inch of my skin, all the way from the top of my head to the tips of my toes. I can hardly even catch my breath as our movements stop and he slowly pulls away from me, lust clouding his normally bright blue eyes.

Confliction passes across his face, and he opens his mouth to say something before we hear the sound of the door open from the balcony. We both still before I quickly scramble off his lap. Ronan goes to stand, quickly wiping at his mouth to remove my smeared lipstick. I lean over to look into the reflection of the fountain, using it as a makeshift mirror, as I clean up my makeup and reapply some more lipstick.

When I'm finished Ronan is watching me with a look that is significantly colder than before. I go to open my mouth and ask him what that was about? What does it mean? What happens next? But I don't get the chance.

"You should get back to the party. You've been gone for too long. After all, you're the guest of honor."

Hurt stabs through me that he's very clearly trying to brush me off, but I don't let it show. Instead, I raise my head a little higher. Stridding back in the direction that we came from, not giving a damn if I get lost in the process.

Surprisingly, I make it out of the gardens easily enough as I slip inside the party. The noise is overwhelming with sounds of music, laughter and the clinking of glasses in cheers. My eyes land on Bridgette and a few of her friends. I've already had a less than stellar day and I'd rather not have an encounter with them.

There is a door to my left and I quickly dip inside before they can see me. I glance over my shoulder relieved when no one follows after me, until I hear a breathy moan. My head whips around, meeting the eyes of Liam. He's leaning up against a large kitchen island with his hands braced against the counter, pants around his ankles and not one, but two mouths latched around his cock.

For a moment, I'm frozen in place. A woman in the caterer's outfit is on her knees beside a man in a matching outfit. I can't tell who is enjoying themselves more. All three of them look to be having the best time. My eyes come up to Liam only to find him watching me with a knowing smirk, before his eyes roll into the back of his head. He drops a hand to the man's head, pushing on it encouragingly before doing the same to the woman.

For some reason, instead of being embarrassed and ashamed of walking in on such a private moment, I'm incredibly turned on. A part of me wonders how long I could stay here and just watch them. According to Liam's smile, I'd probably guess the entire time.

Logic wins though, when I consider what my father would do if he found me in here. If anyone found me here, they'd assume I was part of this. The rumor mill would run rampant. So, I quickly turn on my heel, not giving them a backwards glance, as I slip back out to the party.

Chapter Fourteen
Asher

"Thursday– the usual time. Ensure Liam is with you," my father says, his eyes flicking carefully from side-to-side.

Always listening, always watching.

I dip my head in respect, knowing better than to speak unless asked a direction question. In the next moment, a figure moving through the crowd catches my eye. Skyla is walking towards us with a myriad of emotions on her face. I look back to see both our fathers watching her carefully, before sharing a look as they glance back to me.

"You're dismissed," my father says.

Nodding my head, I quickly step away from them and turn to start walking towards Skyla. I'm not sure why he's willing to cut us loose in the middle of our own engagement party, but I don't really care. I feel a hand grab my arm and I look down to see Bridgette holding it, batting her eyes up at me like that shit is actually going to work on me. I sneer at her, shaking her off my arm as I close the distance between me and my fiancée.

I stop her in her tracks, grabbing her elbow and weaving her through people as we make our way to the front door. I'm practically speed-walking and I can tell she's having a hard time keeping up.

"Asher. What the hell?" she whispers in a hushed tone.

"We're leaving."

"Leaving?" she questions.

I nod as we step around Liam's parents. I give them a winning smile and they smile back approvingly before casting disappointing looks at their son. He doesn't shrink under their gaze. Instead he tunes them out, focusing his eyes on the princess in my grip. A flirtatious smile spreads across his face before he gives her a sly wink. I grit my jaw in irritation, he's such a fucking flirt.

We move further through the party, almost making it all the way to the door when someone steps in front of us.

"Giselle?" he practically gasps, his mouth open and eyes wide as he stares directly at Skyla.

I raise a confused eyebrow in his direction. Looks like someone's getting off well with the open bar.

"Um, no. I'm Skyla," she smiles politely, a guarded look in her deep green eyes.

The man who I now can place as Clark Lewis nods, closing his eyes for a moment before opening them back up and smiling at her.

"My apologies. Your mother, you look so incredibly like her. It's amazing, actually."

Skyla's face softens, and I see her eyes begin to slightly water as she takes a small step towards him, lowering her voice as she asks.

"Really?"

He nods. "Undoubtedly. You're practically her twin."

"So, you knew her well? What was she like? Do you have any memories of her? I was so young when she pass—"

"Sorry Mr. Lewis, my fiancée and I are needing to get home. I hope to see you again soon," I cut in, thoroughly bored with this little stroll down memory lane.

Skyla delivers me a hurt look before she masks it, giving him a polite smile. He smiles back at her in a sad way, before he steps to the side, allowing us to pass.

"Where are we going?" Skyla asks, while the Valet goes to fetch my car.

"Back to campus."

"Why?"

"We were dismissed," I say stiffly.

Her brows furrow. "Why?"

I roll my eyes, before facing her just as the car pulls up.

"Who knows, but I'm not going to snub a get out of jail free card, and neither should you. Know one thing about this place, Princess. If they give you an out at any point, you take it with both hands and run like hell."

Before she can respond I'm practically dragging her to the car, opening the door and pushing her in before slamming the door shut. Look at me, being all gentlemanly and shit.

When I make my way around to the driver's seat I put the car in gear and take off almost immediately. We drive in silence for a few moments, and I relish in the peace. Until she decides it's a good idea to open her mouth again.

"That man back there. You knew him?" she asks.

I nod as I hit my blinker and take a turn.

"I know everyone."

"How?" she counters.

I frown at that. "What do you mean how?"

"How do you know everyone? How does everyone know you? I looked it up, there are close to forty-four-thousand people in Salem, Massachusetts. How on earth do you know everyone? How do they know you? Know me?"

I contemplate on how much to tell her. According to the Elders, I shouldn't tell her anything. Women were never meant to be involved, and if they ever became so, they didn't live long after.

That thought isn't nearly as terrifying as it should be, but rather enticing. No future bride, means no future wedding.

Fuck it.

"I don't know everyone, just those that matter. Those that are connected to The Brethren."

"The Brethren?" she questions slowly. "What the hell is that?"

"A group of families, with common history and goals for the future."

She's silent for a moment, before she practically guffaws at me. "A cult?"

Amusement plays on my lips. If only the Elders could hear her say such an egregious thing. She'd have her tongue cut out before she could even take her next breath. Now there is an idea, if I can't get out of a wife, maybe one that can't talk wouldn't be so bad. Though, I'm sure I'd miss that tongue for other purposes eventually.

I don't respond, curious if I let that little idea fester and bloom what will come of it. Hopefully, something that benefits me.

"Every family at Gallows Hill University is connected to The Brethren. Why do you think the college is invitation only?" I ask, taking my eyes from the road to give her a 'duh' look.

Understanding comes to her, and she nods.

"And my father? He's a part of this...society?" she hedges.

There we go, that's a little more accurate.

I nod my head as I turn to pull into the parking lot outside of her dorm.

"Does everyone on campus know, except me?"

I park the car and nod.

"All of us grew up together. The same elementary, middle and high schools. Same sports teams or other activities."

"Why was I excluded? Why was I sent away then?"

I roll my lips together, knowing this is a secret I can't share. So instead, I just continue.

"The Brethren believe in keeping our future lineage clean from outsiders, hence why most will end up in arranged marriages. Usually arrangements aren't made until after graduation, but ours was expedited."

"Why?" she asks, leaning towards me like she's desperate for any morsel I'll give her.

I wish I could give her this one, but I've been wondering the same myself.

When she realizes I'm not going to answer, she lets out a soft irritated breath before leaning back into her seat. She stares out the window, solemnly speaking as she does.

"So, what does this all mean for me? My future? Are you saying I'll never truly be free from my father? Even after we marry?"

I shake my head. "Freedom is an illusion, Princess. This place," I say, gesturing around at the grand gothic buildings surrounding us. "It's all smoke and mirrors. Beautiful on the outside, captivating, promising life's biggest riches and rewards. Everything comes at a price, though."

"What price will I have to pay?" she asks.

My eyes come to her, flicking back and forth between her pretty green ones.

"You'll have to wait and see."

She nods at that, looking down at her hands in her lap before she speaks again.

"Thank you, for telling me. You didn't have to, I don't think anyone else would have."

I'm shocked she's thanking me, this isn't what we do. We hate each other, that's what I know. That's what I'm comfortable with. I don't know what to do with her...her gratitude. So, I try to dismiss it.

"No one else would have, because they don't want to see you wind up dead," I say bluntly, making it clear that I have no such qualms.

To my surprise, she doesn't wince or glare. She doesn't look hurt in the slightest. Instead, she nods like I've said something well thought out and reasoned.

"I appreciate the honesty. I can't see the knife coming for my back if my eyes are facing forward."

True.

"You can't stop a knife just because you are looking at it," I counter.

She shrugs. "You're probably right, but at least I won't be the naïve girl that never saw it coming."

I wouldn't say I'm impressed, but I am a bit taken back. She's smarter than I anticipated, more aware. Just because she's been kept in the dark over the last fourteen years, doesn't mean she isn't sharp. Sharper than I expected.

"So, can we call a truce or something?" she asks.

I furrow my brows at that.

"Why would we do that?"

"Well, you don't want to marry me and I definitely don't want to marry you," she laughs hollowly with a shake of her head.

Irritation fills me, what the fuck is that supposed to mean? I've been the Brethren's most eligible bachelor my entire life. I had three dates to prom, because women wouldn't stop throwing themselves at me. The day my betrothal was announced, dozens of women sobbed . Why the fuck doesn't she want to marry me?

"So," she continues, "until we can find a way out of this god awful impending marriage, maybe we could at least be cordial to each other?"

"There is no way out," I say stoically.

She shrugs. "Then maybe we can be amicable roommates."

I narrow my eyes at her, waiting for the but, some type of condition or clause. She seems to be done speaking, though.

"Sure," I say hesitantly, noting the pleased smile that upticks her full lips before she opens the car door.

It swings upward and she smoothly slides out of the seat with her clutch in hand. She doesn't say goodbye, doesn't invite me up to her room and she doesn't even try to make a move on me. Not like I would have allowed any of those things to happen. Right? Yeah, no.

She's still the enemy. I want the fuck out of this god awful match. Though she has a wet dream body and a mouth I'd love to sink into, there are plenty of women willing, ready and already dripping for me.

I close the door, stealing one more glance, as the Princess happily walks herself to her dorm, completely unaware of the predators surrounding her in the dark. A good guy would walk her to her dorm and make sure she got there safely. Too bad there isn't a good guy around.

I step inside my dorm, tossing my keys onto the counter when I see Liam is sitting on the overstuffed bean bag chair in the corner, scrolling on his phone.

"Hey," I say as I walk in, kicking off my shoes before grabbing some clothes from my dresser. I fucking hate suits, and I can't wait to get the fuck out of it.

Liam, the weird little fucker he is, loves getting dressed up. Sometimes, it'll be a Tuesday and he'll dress up just because it's 'fun'. Sometimes, I swear to god, I don't know why I'm friends with him.

"Got my dick sucked in the kitchen while the appetizers were being made," he says casually, as his thumb continues sliding across the screen.

"Congratulations. Guy or girl this time?" I drawl sarcastically, not giving a fuck about how he got off.

He looks up from his phone and grins.

"Both."

I let out a short chuckle as I move into the bathroom, starting up the shower before sliding inside. Liam is very proudly bisexual, at least when his parents aren't around. They're already disappointed in him enough, and The Brethren are very...traditional. They treat anyone who isn't their singular version of perfect, like absolute crap. It's fucking bullshit but unfortunately, it's the society we were born into, trapped into.

He doesn't seem to have an interest in dating men, though. He says he just likes to get topped every once in a while, which was more information than I needed, but he's an oversharer. He identifies as Bisexual Heteromantic or something like that.

My shower is quick, and I throw on a pair of black sweats and a band t-shirt before I come out. Liam still hasn't moved from his seat and when I plop down onto my bed, I turn on a movie.

"What took you so long to get back? I left after you," he says.

"Had to drive my wife-to-be home," I drawl out sarcastically.

Liam snickers but shakes his head.

"Man, I don't know why you're so pissed about marrying her. She's easily the hottest fucking woman that's ever set foot on this campus. I'd stick my hand in a blender just to eat that ass once," he says, with a groan and bite of his lip.

I can't help but laugh.

"Shut the fuck up. You have to beat men and women off with a stick on campus alone. Forget going out in public with you. You're not hard-up for some ass."

"Nah, but I've never seen a better ass than hers."

I raise an unimpressed eyebrow at him.

"You been eye fucking my wife?"

"Fiancée," he corrects, "and fuck yes I have. She's fucking delectable man. You need to stop the douchebag routine and benefit from this arrangement. A beautiful virgin cunt, promised to you and only you? Sign me the fuck up."

He has a point. Something in me doesn't like the idea, though. It's easier to demonize her in my mind. Safer that way. I've always played it safe, played it smart, and I always will. A girl isn't going to change that, I'll slit her throat myself before I let her.

Chapter Fifteen
Ronan

I'm walking through campus, cutting through the courtyard when I hear a familiar laugh. It's an airy sound that instantly has my heart hammering in my chest. My head whips up, landing on the woman I haven't been able to shake from my thoughts since the moment I met her. The woman that I haven't been able to stop obsessing over since I found out what her lips taste like.

It's been over a week since I kissed my nephew's fiancée in the gardens. Though I should feel bad about it, I'm just disappointed. Disappointed that it can't happen again, disappointed that she's going to marry Asher one day. I'm just...disappointed.

Skyla is walking with the Bartlett girl, Margret I think, and they are both cracking up laughing. Her smile is wide and so carefree, it stirs something inside me. I feel my steps faltering as I turn to face her fully. Of course, she doesn't see me but that's okay. I see her and fuck, I think she gets more beautiful every time I do.

They start walking closer to me and I'm about to turn to head back to my office when a guy steps in front of them, forcing Skyla to crash into him. He catches her easily, smiling down at her in a way that makes me want to break his fucking jaw.

I recognize him as Will Stroughton's son. Little prick is who he is, and one of the Legacies I'm in charge of watching over.

"Whoa, sorry about that," he smiles down at Skyla, as if him stepping in front of her was a total accident.

Jackass.

"It's fine," Skyla smiles, her eyes skimming over him for longer than I'd appreciate before she pulls out of his grasp. Stroughton doesn't let up though as he takes another step, erasing the space she put between them.

"I'm Jeremy, what's your name?" he smiles down at her.

"Skyla."

"I'm Maggie in case you were wondering, Stroughton," her friend scoffs.

Jeremy laughs and looks at Maggie.

"Hey, Bartlett."

His attention quickly shifts back to Skyla.

"Are you doing anything tonight?"

I frown as she tilts her head in interest.

"Not really, why?"

"I was hoping you'd do me the honor of letting me take you out."

Skyla grins, a smile that pisses me the fuck off. A smile that is obviously only reserved for me, or at least it should be.

"I'm not sure that would be such a good idea. Doesn't the whole me being engaged thing kind of make me off limits?"

Jeremy's head moves down to her bare hand before he winks.

"I don't see a ring."

She laughs at that. "You know what, sure. Why not?"

"Yeah?" he grins.

Skyla nods, causing my blood to turn boiling hot as he winks at her and makes plans to pick her up at seven tonight. When he walks away, I start moving towards her. I couldn't stop myself if I wanted to and before I know it, I'm barreling right into her.

My hand reaches out, gripping the crook of her elbow as I wordlessly pull her down the courtyard and into the pool building, not giving a fuck about the confused look on her friend's face.

"Ow! What the hell, Ronan?" she whispers vehemently.

I don't speak though. I continue pulling her down the hallway, past the pool and into my office. I release her roughly as soon as we are inside and slam the door shut, before bracing my arms on either side of the door. She stands there silently, thank fuck, because I don't even know how to control my breathing right now.

Eventually she speaks, and it sets me right the fuck off.

"Ronan, what the hell was that?"

I spin on my heel, eating up the distance between us, my eyes widening with rage. She takes a few startling steps backwards, before her ass bumps against my desk. I cage her in, forcing her to not place a single toe away from me as I speak.

"You agreed to go out with him," I fume.

Her brows dip before realization dawns on her perfect face.

"Were you watching me?"

"Fuck yes I was. How can I not? You're everywhere. In my pool, my school, my bar, my brother's home, my fucking head!" I snap.

Her frown softens a bit at that, as well as her voice.

"I didn't think anyone would care. Asher obviously doesn't and—"

"I do. I care, a whole fucking lot," I snarl.

Skyla's softened tone fades, as irritation passes across her face.

"You're the one who pulled away. I haven't seen or heard from you since you told me to go back to the party in the gardens. You got me off, shut down, and pushed me away. What part of that was supposed to make me think you even wanted to look in my direction again, let alone care if I go on a date with some guy?"

"You know exactly why I care," I grit between clenched teeth.

Her pissed off expression falls away, as lust flickers in her eyes before they come down to my mouth.

"Say it," she whispers.

"What?"

"Say it," she says, those green eyes practically punching me straight in the gut as they look at me. "Please."

My body tenses at her soft plea, and consequences be damned. I can't control my next actions. My hand grips the base of her neck, smashing her mouth against my own. It's as if she was prepared for it, though. Her arms wrap around my neck, as her tongue tangles with mine. Just the feel of her has my cock throbbing, but right now more than anything I need to taste her.

I slip my hands beneath her legs, lifting her up and onto my desk before pushing up her skirt. She lays down instantly, but her legs aren't parted. I look up to see her face drenched in want, but a timid energy emanating from her.

"What's wrong, baby?"

"I've never had anyone..." She clears her throat, but doesn't go on.

I can't help but let the shit eating grin on my face spread so wide it practically hurts.

"Are you telling me, I'll be the first person to taste this sweet pussy?"

Her teeth sink into her lower lip as she nods.

"Is that okay with you?" I ask.

"Yes, god yes. I'm just...nervous, I guess. I don't know. Now I feel dumb," she says, covering her face with her hands, forcing me to let out a soft chuckle.

My palms skim up her smooth legs, pausing on her knees as I speak.

"Don't feel dumb, baby. It's okay to feel nervous. If you want me to stop, just say so."

She nods, a steadiness seeming to take over as her legs slowly fall open. I keep my eyes on her until I feel her legs fully part. My eyes come down to see a tiny pair of white cotton panties covering her bald pussy. The material gets thinner and thinner until it's just a string.

"I didn't expect you to be the thong wearing type, baby," I murmur, as I lower my head between her legs, inhaling her scent, before gripping the fabric with my teeth.

I make slow work of pulling them off her, making sure to give her plenty of time to change her mind and back out. Though I know it would be the hardest fucking thing I've ever had to do. If I have to walk away from her spread open like this for me, I'd do it for her in a heartbeat.

When I reach her ankles with her panties still between my teeth, I pull them down and off before gripping the damp fabric in my hand. I lift it to my nose, inhaling deeply, as I let out a groan.

"Goddamnit, baby. You smell like fucking heaven. I'm gonna fucking devour this pussy."

She squirms on my desk, papers rustling beneath her, before I pocket her panties and lower myself to her legs. I begin peppering light kisses on the inside of her thighs, inching up higher and higher until I reach the apex of her legs. Her pussy is practically dripping on this morning's memo, and I can't hold myself back any longer.

My tongue flicks out, running a long swipe through her, catching every drop of her I can manage as she bucks against the desk.

"Oh my god!" she moans. "Do that again."

I do as she asks, running my tongue through her. Forcing her moans and gasps to increase when I pause on her clit, swirling my tongue around it before I begin sucking on it.

"Ronan, Ronan, Ronan," she chants, her fingers digging into the back of my head. She forces me closer until I'm practically suffocating in her pussy. My fucking favorite.

I begin flicking my tongue against her clit rapidly and am about to slip a finger inside of her when she shutters, a scream so loud tearing from her mouth that I have to lift my hand up and cover it. Her screams of pleasure are miraculously heard through my palm, as her body shakes and jerks against the desk. Shit, that was easier than I anticipated.

When her orgasm subsides I pull my mouth away from her, pressing one more kiss against her delectable pussy before looking up to her. My hand moves from her mouth, pushing back her hair from her face. She's wearing a delirious expression, like she's practically drunk.

I stand up to my full height, towering over her as she smiles up at me, my fingers continuing to tangle through her silky strands.

"Are you okay?" I ask.

She nods softly, leaning into my touch. I can't help but smile down at her, before I blow out a breath and shake my head.

"Fuck. I really shouldn't have done that," I say.

Her smile slips away, a frown taking its place.

"Let me guess, this is the part where you say it can never happen again?"

"Fuck no," I laugh. "We're gonna do that again, and more, a lot. As long as you're comfortable with it."

"Oh," she smiles, a deep blush settling into her porcelain cheeks.

I lift my free hand up to cup her face, smiling down at her as I speak.

"But, we have to be careful. No one can know anything, for all of our sakes. You understand that, right?"

She nods slowly but doesn't speak. I lean forward, pressing a kiss to her forehead before I whisper against her skin.

"Meet me here tonight. Seven o'clock. I'll take care of the cameras."

When I pull away, she's watching me with a small grin.

"Is it a coincidence that you want me to meet you at the exact time I'm supposed to go on a date?"

"Absolutely not."

Chapter Sixteen
Skyla

I feel bad that I'm standing up Jeremy. Really, I do. He seemed nice in a very flirty, obviously just checking out the new meat, kind of way. Clearly, I don't feel bad enough not to do it, because I feel myself practically running to the pool building at 6:58PM.

My bag is over my shoulder, packed with my suit, cap and goggles just in case we actually do swim. Though, I can't lie, I really hope we don't just swim. I've never had an orgasm stimulated by anyone other than myself until Ronan. I already feel like an addict, desperate for more. I mean, I suppose there was that thing in the gardens at Putnam Manor, but I feel like I stimulated that and he held me as I did, so it's different.

I've been taught my whole life that my virginity is something to be treasured, protected. It makes more sense now as I realize my father has had plans to marry me off from conception. Of course my virginity is so valuable, it's a selling point, and if the buyer is Asher then I would gladly give it away to practically anyone else. Though I admit, sleeping with Ronan would hardly be a compromise on my part, the man looks like a Greek god and he tongue fucks like one too.

I go to grab the door to the pool when it pushes open. I can't help but smile as it does, butterflies racing through my chest. However, they quickly wither and die when it's not Ronan in front of me, but Vincent. His slate grey eyes are practically incinerating me where I stand, before his lip lifts into a sneer.

"Fucking the coach?"

I pale at his words momentarily, doing my best to brush him off as I roll my eyes.

"Don't be disgusting."

His face turns thunderous as he takes a step closer, our chests brushing against each other as he looks down at me.

"Don't lie to me," he grits out quietly. "I saw you two in the gardens. I see the way he watches you."

Keeping my expressions composed, I lift an unimpressed eyebrow as I tilt my head to the side.

"Well, if you see all of that it must mean you're watching me too."

His steely mask seems to falter for a moment, something akin to surprise, before it's back in place.

"Don't flatter yourself. I was having a smoke and couldn't help but notice the predator luring the young naïve girl to a private location."

My eyes narrow at him. "I'm not naïve."

"That's just what I'd expect you to say," he says, his deep voice grating on my nerves.

My jaw is clenched before irritation practically consumes me.

"You're an asshole!"

He shrugs, pushing past me without another word. I wrap my hand around the door handle, looking over my shoulder to see Vincent stride out into the courtyard without a care in the world. I can't help but watch him with narrowed eyes before I pull the door open again, storming inside.

I collide with a hard chest, and a familiar musky scent fills my senses as I look up to see Ronan smiling down at me.

"Hey," he smiles easily, before his brows knit together. "What's wrong?"

The concern in his voice stirs something in me. I allow my irritation towards Vincent to melt away as I stare up at this ridiculously good looking man before me.

"Nothing, I'm good," I smile.

His hands come up to either side of my face, cupping my cheeks gently as his eyes flick across my face, as if he can find the truth from a single look.

"I don't believe you. Is it my little shit nephew? Do I need to kick his ass?" he asks.

I can't help but laugh.

"No, but could you anyway? I think it would do him some good."

"For my girl? Anything."

"Your girl?" I ask teasingly. "That seems a little fast, Coach Ronan," I tease.

"On the contrary, Miss Parris. I think it's just right. That is, unless you let any man off the street eat your pussy until you come all over his face or ride his lap until you soak his pants?."

I'm proud that I don't blush at his words. Instead, I keep my teasing smirk in place and look up like I'm thinking it over.

"Well, not *every* man."

His eyes narrow as he shakes his head, before smashing his lips against mine. It's a kiss that starts out sweet and teasing, but with a swipe of his tongue something changes between us.

Suddenly his grip on me tightens, the air thickens, and our kisses become frantic. A rush I've never felt before rips through me as his mouth moves across my cheek and down my neck, sucking on the sensitive skin behind my ear. I gasp at the feeling as I tilt my head back, granting him easier access as his hands begin roaming down my body.

My heart is practically beating out of my chest with each touch. I feel one of his hands leave my side, reaching out and flicking the lock on the door before coming to cup my ass. He pulls me into him, and I happily wrap my leg around his waist. His mouth comes down to my cleavage, licking a long line between my breasts before his eyes meet mine.

I feel my stomach physically flip as he gives me a slow smirk, gripping both my thighs and lifting me into the air. I have no choice but to wrap my other leg around him as Ronan makes quick work of walking us into the pool room and over to the bleachers. He sits down on the first row and I go with him, straddling him as my skirt bunches up around my hips.

My pussy rubs against his hard cock as he lets out an audible groan against my lips.

"Fuck, yes. Grind on me, baby."

I do as he says, his soft lips peppering my skin as his hands guide my hips. God, I've never felt anything so erotic, so intoxicating. Just a few brushes of our bodies together and I'm already prepared to explode. See, like I said? Addict.

I feel a fluttering sensation low in my belly, and my pussy begins to spasm as my clit grinds against him once more.

"Oh god. Oh no. Shit, shit, shit," I mutter through my orgasm, shuttering and shaking in his arms as he whispers into my ear.

"Just like that. You're so fucking beautiful when you fall apart for me."

I'd be embarrassed with how easily he can get me off but honestly, what is there to be embarrassed about? Sounds like a talent to me.

When my pleasure has subsided, I pull away to look at Ronan who is watching me with hungry eyes. Gently, he guides me to stand before he reaches into his pants and pulls out his cock. I physically gulp when I look at it. It's so thick. I don't think cocks are supposed to be that thick and if they are, they definitely shouldn't be this long as well.

"Get on your knees, Skyla," he commands, a soft lilt to his otherwise demanding tone.

Slowly, I sink to my knees between his legs as his hand comes to the back of my head, winding my hair around his fist as he brings me closer. My mouth begins to water as my stomach turns nervously. I do my best to remain confident, but I can't deny that I'm terrified I'll be a disappointment.

A man like this, an Olympian, has obviously been with countless women. What would he want with an inexperienced one like me? The pressure to be the best he's ever had is intimidating, though it motivates me as I slowly wrap my lips around the head of his cock. My tongue swirls around it before he gently begins pushing me down.

Inch by inch, I take his cock deeper until he's reached my throat. I gag on instinct, cringing at the sound when Ronan groans.

"Fuck, yes. Gag for me, baby. Let me hear you choke around my cock."

His words of encouragement spur me on as I do it again, able to get a little further before gagging once more. Ronan's hands cup my head as he takes over my movements, forcing me up and down over and over again. My gagging has increased, and I feel my eyes water before tears begin streaming down my face. That doesn't stop him though. He continues using my mouth for his pleasure, pushing deeper and faster until his body locks up and he lets out a strangled groan.

"That's it. Swallow all of me, baby."

In the next instant, I feel his cum hit my tongue. It's warm and slightly salty as I swallow it down. I've never tasted cum before and if I'm being honest, I thought it was going to taste a lot worse. I actually kind of like it.

Ronan slowly pulls away, leaning against the bleachers behind him before blowing out a ragged breath and closing his eyes. When he opens them, those blue orbs land on me, a satisfied smirk spread across his face.

"You did so good," he says, holding a hand out for me before pulling me back into his lap.

"Yeah?" I ask shyly, my hair falling into my face as I do.

He nods slowly, pushing my hair away from my face as he rubs the strands between his fingers.

"Oh yeah. You're my good girl, aren't you?"

I feel my cheeks flame as my teeth sink into my bottom lip and I nod. His smirk grows as he drags me in for another breathtaking kiss. His soft lips practically melting against mine before he rests his forehead against my own. I don't know what the hell we are doing, or where this is going, but I've literally never had control over anything in my life, so to hell with it. Though, I know this will all be temporary, I'll relish every second of it for as long as I can.

Chapter Seventeen
Ronan

There are a lot of things I would rather do on a Thursday than be in a meeting with the Brethren. I'd always rather do almost anything than be anywhere with the Brethren, not like I'd ever say that out loud, though.

I've been tempted half a dozen times to get up, move over to the box where they collect our phones before we enter the room. Just to check and see if Skyla has texted me. I feel a little pathetic that at thirty-two, I'm completely gone for a nineteen-year-old. Actually, when I say it like that, I feel downright disgusting.

I'm spacing out as I stare at the large ornate mirror to the side. It practically takes up the entire wall, it's so tall. It has been here for over two-hundred years, which is pretty remarkable considering its condition.

"Ronan," Christopher chastises, clearly observant of how little attention I'm paying.

It's bullshit that I'm even here. None of the other siblings from the Elders have to attend these. The oldest is the only true heir, I'm just spare parts in case someone finally takes him out.

Whoops, did I say finally? Oh well.

The only reason I'm here is because our father insisted. He was the Elder to hold the position as the head of the Brethren, for the longest period of time since its conception. He died six years ago and Christopher was practically salivating for his time to lead us. He couldn't wait for dad to pass.

My eyes are on him to show that he has my attention, but I don't speak.

"Robert and I were just discussing your betrothal to his daughter."

That grips every bit of my attention. I sit up a little higher, my back straightening as my eyes swing to Robert Williams. Annie is a nice girl. Nice enough at least, but I'm not the least bit interested in her. When she showed up to my place the other day, we had a good time until she wanted to fall into bed together. Normally that wouldn't have been a hardship, she's gorgeous with perfectly tanned skin, rich chocolate brown hair and legs that go on for miles. Since I first laid eyes on Skyla though, no one has been able to compare. Especially now that she's *mine*. Yeah, hell no.

"If I can be frank, I'm not sure we are the best match," I say carefully.

Robert's eyebrows furrow, while my brother narrows his gaze at me.

"And why is that? Do you have a better one in mind?" Christopher asks.

Yes.

"No, we've spent a little time together and we didn't have much to talk about, we don't share much in common."

"Consider yourself lucky," Will Stroughton laughs, causing several other members to chime in with their agreement.

That vein in the side of my brother's head throbs and his jaw tenses in visible irritation. He doesn't like losing the attention of a room. Our father practically beat it into his brain that if you have their attention, you have their respect. If you have their respect, you have power and if you have power…you can rule this earthly world.

"You will," Christopher says easily, claiming the spotlight once more as he levels a heavy look around the long table. "That's the point of a union. It's to grow, strengthen bonds and unite two families into one."

All hope of attempting to talk him out of this decision dies with those words. Like the others, I can read between the lines. I'm not marrying Annie because she is a good match for me. I'm marrying her because Will has something that my brother wants, whether for himself or the Brethren is inconsequential. We're all merely pawns and it's this game that he is playing.

I nod once and dip my head, an obvious sign of respect and defeat. That has his smile growing as he settles back into his chair comfortably.

"Excellent. After Asher's ceremony would be perfect. Maybe July? Enough time for us to get everything in alignment," Christopher says, though he isn't talking to me. He's looking straight at Will who nods his agreement.

My brother nods happily to himself before he goes down the table addressing a few more issues with other Elders, which I promptly tune out. Once business seems to be addressed for the day, Christopher looks at me.

"Bring them in."

I nod, standing up from my plush leather chair at the slate stone table, as I make my way to the door. When I pop it open, I find Asher and Liam standing in the waiting area pressed, polished and ready. If only they knew they'd never be ready.

They both nod at me, stepping in and depositing their phones into the box before standing beside my brother at the head of the table. Simultaneously, they bow their heads in respect and I watch the table carefully to see several nods of approval.

"Thank you for being here today," Christopher says to Asher, before his eyes dart to Liam. "As you have both been made aware, someone has been tampering with the school's security cameras. Obviously, this is not only a threat to our children but to our very foundation. So, I'm tasking you two with the job of finding who this is and finishing them."

Their faces are stoic, though even I can see the hesitancy in Liam's eyes from here. I know Christopher is testing them, mainly Asher. If he really was concerned about finding the person responsible for the outages, he could get anyone from the Hutchinson family to look into it. They are all tech geniuses, and their Legacy is still at the University.

If he wanted to have someone taken out, then Griggs would have been a much better fit. It's what his family lived and died doing; it's his destiny, to follow their footsteps in their role of the Brethren.

I'll be disappointed when they do trace it back and figure out who has been behind the outages, though I think we all know the obvious answer. I've been using them as a perfect excuse to shut down the cameras in the pool and surrounding areas when Skyla and I meet. We've been sneaking around in the Brethren's blind spots, which I know is a strategy that won't last forever. It's the best we can do, at least for now, though.

"Of course," Asher says.

Christopher nods approvingly. "Excellent, Alexander will send you the information on what we know so far. You're both dismissed. Ronan, please escort them back to their dorm."

I frown, uncomfortable with the fact that my brother is making plans or discussions and intentionally wants me out of the room for them. Still, it's not like I could refuse. So, I stand from my seat, moving over to the box where I retrieve my phone along with Liam and Asher's before we all file out of the room, through the holding room and into the tunnel.

Once we make it to the stairs and are inside the church, we all seem to exhale a sigh of relief. That's how life in this world feels, like you're always holding your breath, always waiting to see what happens next. A life on edge keeps you alert, but fuck it's exhausting.

"Man, this is bullshit. Why the fuck were we selected for this? This isn't in either of our skill sets," Liam says with a shake of his head, as we move through the three-hundred-and-fifty-year-old church.

"Because he said so," Asher shrugs, pushing open the doors before stepping out into the moonlit cemetery.

"Since when is that enough for you?" Liam challenges. "Ash, he wants us to find this person and kill them. I can't kill someone, can you?"

"If I have to," he snaps sharply, sending his best friend a withering glance before he starts typing quickly on his phone. "Your birthday isn't too far behind my own, Liam. Did you really expect to enter the Brethren without a single drop of blood on your hands?"

He pauses, looking at me as I quickly avert my gaze.

"Is that part of initiation? We have to kill for them?" he asks.

"It varies," I answer cryptically, forcing Asher to let out a derisive snort.

"Which means, yes."

Liam looks sick as he shakes his head, seemingly pushing whatever thoughts or conflictions he's feeling aside before he speaks.

"Whatever, I just want to go home. You coming?" he asks, as he begins veering right towards his dorm, while Asher is heading left.

"No, gonna go get my dick sucked real quick."

"By Skyla?" I ask irrationally, unable to hide the jealousy in my voice fast enough.

Asher doesn't think anything of it, or he doesn't notice, as he continues texting. Liam, however, is watching me with a curious gaze.

"Yeah fucking right," Asher scoffs. "That prude wouldn't know the first thing about sucking a man off."

Something in me would love nothing more than to put him in his place. Tell him how wrong he is, how she has a mouth that feels like heaven and a pussy that tastes like it too. Obviously, I don't and for good reason. He doesn't deserve to know those things about her. That's only for me to know, it's a privilege I will cherish greatly.

"Why do you hate her so much?" I bite out before I can stop myself. "She's a nice girl, she doesn't deserve your spite. She is just as much a victim in this as anybody, maybe more so. She doesn't have the advantage of growing up in this world like you two did. She was a normal girl, who has now been dropped into the middle of Brethren business during one of the most crucial and dangerous points of our history.

Asher's feet pause as he turns to face me, phone long forgotten.

"What do you mean? What's happening?"

I blow out a breath as I shake my head. "You'll be inducted soon. You'll know more than you ever cared to."

He doesn't seem to like that answer. So, he turns back around and stalks off to whatever poor girl he's basically using as a prostitute. I scoff at him, rolling my eyes before my gaze stops on Liam.

His green eyes are narrowed at me, a playful smirk tugging at his lips.

"So, you and her?"

"Me and who?" I ask, doing my best to keep my tone even.

Liam's smirk spreads into a full on grin before he giggles almost excitedly.

"No fucking way! Oh my god. Asher doesn't know, obviously. I'm assuming neither does your brother? Oh, oh, what about her dad?"

He continues his fit of giggles before I close the distance between us. Gripping his shirt in my hand, I ball it up and yank him towards me until we are nose to nose.

"Listen to me carefully, you don't know what you're talking about. If you spread bullshit rumors, I'll fucking bury you. I'm not afraid to get my hands bloody, I've done it many times before. You're just a Legacy and to your parents, you're the disappointment, the letdown. No one will mourn you for longer than a day, so before you open that cock sucking mouth of yours, think about all you're willing to lose, over a *lie*."

He looks stunned by my words. Honestly, I'm a little stunned by them. I didn't mean to be that harsh, I like the kid a lot, but to protect myself, to protect Skyla? Yeah, I'd kill him in a heartbeat, and bury him right here in this cemetery, without a single ounce of regret.

I release my hold on him, roughly shoving him away before I storm across campus towards my car. I planned on sneaking into Skyla's room tonight, something about holding her against my chest, her scent on me brings a sense of calm I haven't felt in years. I'm too pissed off right now, though. Too terrified that we've both already signed our death certificates. If I was smart enough, I'd cut all ties with her and let her go on to live her life as it was planned.

There is no fucking way that's happening, though.

Chapter Eighteen
Skyla

My arms slice through the warm water, my feet moving in perfect synchronization with my movements as I do. Nothing exists when I'm submerged in this pool of liquid dopamine. Not my father, not Salem, not Asher, not even Ronan.

Okay, to be fair, I may be overreacting a bit. He told me he might stop by last night after he had dinner with his brother. It was a maybe. I shouldn't have gotten my hopes up. Yet, there I was, laying in my bed with a brand new silk nightgown that hit just below my upper thighs and made my tits pop. I waited for hours. Trying not to be so eager, and then disappointed when he didn't show up. Once it hit one in the morning, I knew he wasn't coming. I turned off my light and rolled over, more than a little disappointed.

It's not even the fact that he didn't show up or didn't let me know that he couldn't make it. It's the fact that he has so much of a hold over me. I don't like it, not one bit. I need to try to rein in my emotions. I'm already too invested, especially for a woman in my position. I'm technically engaged, and I'd wager even the rapture wouldn't have this arrangement broken. I need to keep Ronan in a safe box, tucked away when we are able to steal a moment here or there. That is, until he gets bored of me. Which for all I know, could have been the very reason he didn't come last night.

When I finish my last lap, I come up for air, my eyes landing on the man himself. He's wearing a pair of black shorts and a black polo with the school crest on it. His hair is tousled in that perfect way and his piercing blue eyes are trained on me, shining in a way that has my stomach flipping no matter how much I beg it not to.

"Hey beautiful, how's the water?" he smiles, those perfect white teeth practically glimmering.

I give him a tight lipped smile, as I begin slowly moving towards the other side of the pool.

"It's good."

I look back over my shoulder to see his smile dim and his brows knit together.

"Is everything okay?"

I don't say anything, instead nodding my head, as I continue to push myself through the water. He doesn't speak for several moments, until I hear the water slosh. Before I can fully turn around, two strong arms wrap around me, pushing me towards the wall as I'm being spun in his arms to face him. His chest is bare, his polo abandoned on the side of the pool along with his shorts, leaving him only in his boxers.

Instinctively, my legs wrap around his torso. One of his hands slides to hold the underside of my thigh and keep me afloat. Concern is etched into his every feature as his eyes scan my face.

"What's wrong, baby?"

I shake my head and begin to tell him how fine I am, because I am. I'm totally fine. He doesn't give me the chance to do so, though. Instead, his hand pinches the fleshy part of my thigh, causing me to yelp in surprise as he speaks again.

"Never lie to me, Skyla. If this is going to work between us, we have to be one-hundred percent honest with each other."

My words pause on the tip of my tongue, hesitant to sound as insecure and rejected as I feel because I recognize how irrational I'm being.

"I just thought you were going to come over last night. When you didn't, I guess I started to wonder if you were already over this...thing between us—"

"Never," he cuts off with a shake of his head, before he reaches up, removing my goggles so he can look into my eyes as he speaks. "I could never and will never get over you, Skyla. I'm already fucking sunk. My life is literally on the line here, yours too, but I'm here. I'm thinking about you in ways I shouldn't, holding you like you're mine to keep. I can honestly say that I don't see a reality where you won't be my every moment's desire."

My chest clenches at his words, at the longing in his eyes, the desperation in his tone. We've been dealt an extremely unfair hand. That much is for sure but, despite all of the obstacles we face, and will no doubt continue to face, he still wants...me? I feel stupid for being so irrational, for assuming he could carelessly toss me to the side without a second thought. He's not like that and I know it. I just... I have abandonment issues, okay?

"I'm sorry I didn't come last night. I should have called you or at least texted. I didn't have a great end to my night, and I didn't want to bring you down with me."

I furrow my brows at that. "Is everything okay? Did you have a fight with your brother?"

He shakes his head as his hand cups my face.

"Everything is fine. I missed you," he says, before leaning forward and pressing his lips to mine. As pathetic as it sounds, one touch from his lips and everything seems to slip away. Until it's just us. Our mouths move together so flawlessly, so effortlessly, it has my body practically melting into his hold.

His lips move from my own to my cheek, peppering softly against my skin as I speak.

"I waited for you for hours. I was wearing this new silk nightgown that I wanted you to see."

He hums against my skin as I feel his tongue dart out against the sensitive flesh behind my ear.

"Tell me about it."

I swallow shakily as he begins leaving a smattering of kisses against my neck, settling at the sensitive junction, his tongue tracing patterns while his lips follow smoothly.

"It's white," I say softly, my voice raising slightly when he begins sucking at my skin. "And short," I gasp as he does it again. "A-and soft, so soft," I say at the start of a moan.

"Fuck," he grumbles against my skin. "I'm going to see you in that. Soon," he finishes, before releasing my neck with an audible pop.

I jolt at the feeling as he looks down at my neck, smirking to himself as his thumb brushes against the freshly marred skin.

"What?" I ask.

His tongue wets his lower lip as he shakes his head.

"I just love seeing you marked by me. I wish it could last forever."

"Marked by..." I trail off before my eyes widen. "Ronan! Did you give me a hickey?"

That devilish smirk spreads as he presses a soft kiss to my lips.

"Absolutely, and now that I know how beautiful you look marked by me, you'll be wearing more from now on. A lot more."

My alarm goes off, reminding me I need to get back to my dorm to shower, change and get to class. We both groan in frustration as Ronan grinds me against his hard cock through his boxers.

"What are the chances I can get you to skip your first class?" he asks as he grinds me against him again, forcing a ragged breath to escape me as he does.

"The same chances of my father coming down here, demanding why I skipped a class. It wouldn't be a good look for a Parris," I mock in my father's condescending tone.

Ronan rolls his eyes at me, and for a moment I forget how well he probably knows my father. Honestly, I'd bet anything he knows him better than me. He's certainly spent more time with him than I have, though that isn't a hard achievement to earn. Instead of feeling envy though, I just feel pity for Ronan.

I feel his hand slip behind my neck, forcing my mouth to his as he takes one more kiss before effortlessly hoisting me out of the pool and onto the edge.

"You better get to class, Miss Parris."

"And you better get dressed, Coach Ronan," I tease as I stand up.

He floats on his back, his cock comically sticking up above the surface as his hand reaches down and runs against the length of it.

"I will. Soon. Can you unlock the doors on your way out?"

I smile and nod, gathering up my things as he calls out to me once more.

"After your last class of the day, come to my office. We have unfinished business," he says with a sultry smirk that has my pussy pulsing.

I don't let him see the effect he has on me. Instead, I allow my eyes to run up and down him before I shrug my shoulders and take a backwards step towards the door.

"I don't know, by the looks of things, it seems you'll be taking matters into your own hands."

"There is always more business to finish when you're around, Skyla."

"Thank you?" I laugh.

"Oh, it's a compliment, but also a fucking curse."

Another laugh slips out of me as I shake my head and shoot him a wink before pushing through the doors. I still find myself smiling as I unlock the front door and push my way out. Unfortunately my smile is short lived when I slam into a hard body. I stumble to the side and brace myself for impact when two strong hands grip my waist, righting me before I have the chance to touch the pavement.

My thankful words and apologies die on my tongue when I see an enraged looking Vincent staring down at me. Now that I think about it, I'm not that sorry for crashing into him.

"Still going to lie to me and tell me you aren't fucking Coach, Siren?"

My face twists up, partially because of the stupid nickname but also because why the hell is he so angry all the time? Why do I seem to be the focus of his ire? To be fair, I think a lot of people are on his radar, but something tells me I irritate him on a whole other level. I honestly don't know what I did to earn that honor.

I decide he isn't worth my breath, and I roll my eyes and shake my head as I shove away from him. Surprisingly, he lets me go with ease and I take advantage of it by walking the hell away. When I go to turn around the building, I steal a look over my shoulder and catch a glimpse of Vincent still standing there, watching me. His arms are tense by his side, jaw clenched hard. The way he looks at me is unsettling, it sends a chill right down my spine that doesn't subside until the building blocks our view of one another.

Good. Fucking creep.

Maggie is excitedly telling me about her hookup from last night when a gust of wind attempts to blow my cardigan away. I quickly grab each side, wrapping it tighter around me as I try to continue listening. Since the weather is still decently warm, I would have melted if I had worn a turtleneck. Which really would have been the best choice when it came to covering up Ronan's little mark he left on me. However, a crisp white undershirt and a high collared cardigan was my next best option.

"Are you listening?" Maggie asks.

"Yes, Mags. You went down on her for twenty minutes and made her cum twice. I'm listening," I laugh.

"Good, okay," she says, as she dives back into her explicit story.

I lean forward to appear as if I'm listening more intently when her words pause and her face freezes. I look behind myself before turning back.

"What?"

Before I can stop her, her hands are at my shoulder, ripping my cardigan off my arm and pulling down my shirt. I scramble to cover myself but it's too late.

"Fuck my story, who did that and when?" she asks.

"Shhh," I hush her as my eyes dart around the courtyard, though no one is within fifty feet or so of us. "I can't say."

"Ooooh, so definitely not your fiancé. Spicy," she smirks.

I roll my eyes. "Like I'd ever let that asshole touch me."

"I don't know what to think. I'm just now finding out my innocent virgin friend has a side piece. C'mon, you have to tell me! Best friends don't keep secrets."

I shake my head in refusal, causing her to pout.

"Fine, I'm going to start rattling off names. Jeremy Stroughton?"

Shaking my head, I internally cringe. I fear blowing him off may have earned myself a forever enemy. The guy hasn't even looked at me since. I actually feel kind of bad about it.

"Oh, did you go for his bestie, Dane?"

I laugh and shake my head. "No."

"Oh, oh. What about Andrew Hutchinson? That boy is smitten over you, and I wouldn't be surprised if he's an amazing fuck."

"Jesus, Maggie. I haven't slept with anyone. I'm still a virgin."

"But you aren't as innocent as you portray. Hmmm, maybe not a student. Faculty?"

I do my best to remain composed, but something I do must give it away because she gets excited and begins rattling off all my teachers and even the headmaster.

"Fucking come on!" she says, clearly frustrated. "Coach Ronan?" she throws out.

My stomach flips at his name, but I shake my head. Unfortunately, my best friend pauses, her eyes narrowing as she cocks her head to the side.

"You're lying."

"What?" I ask.

"You're lying. Your right pupil dilated when I said his name."

I scoff. "Pfft, what do you think, you're a human lie detector or something?"

"Precisely," she says, with a satisfied smile. "You're getting more than just swim time when you go down to the pool, huh?"

I feel heat hit my face, as embarrassment from her words takes over. I quickly look around and notice a few groups of people have gathered outside. None of them are close enough to hear us, but one is my pig of a fiancé. He currently has Bridgette Brenton straddling his lap and sucking on his neck, much like his uncle was doing to me earlier.

Ironic.

"Don't worry, babe. Secrets go in the vault with me. I'll literally take them to my grave."

"Please do," I say, bringing my eyes to her. "Ronan thinks it would be really bad if people found out about us."

"Well, yeah. You both would probably be hung in the courtyard for all to see if the Elders heard about this."

"The Elders? Who are—"

"Hey pretty ladies," Liam smiles, as he hops onto the table

we're sitting at, scooting himself until he is all but sitting on top of my salad.

"Walcott," Maggie says coolly.

Since I told her how Liam was a part of the whole grave situation, she's gone out of her way to be as much of a bitch as possible. Asher is clearly untouchable, but his equally guilty partner in crime? Not at all.

Something I've noticed about Liam since meeting him, is that he's desperate for attention. He will do anything or become anyone for it. The flirt, the class clown, whatever it takes. It clearly derives from not getting enough attention at home as a child but that doesn't mean he needs to participate in straight up bullying just to stay in the inner circle. It honestly just makes him a coward.

"Please go away," I say stiffly.

"Aw, c'mon, babygirl. You can't still be mad about the bonfire. It was just a little new kid hazing. You got out didn't you?"

"No thanks to you," I snap, turning my gaze on him as I shake my head. "I could have been there for hours, Liam. All night even. I was cold and afraid and alone."

I let the hurt bleed into my voice because it did hurt. Not that he specifically owes me anything but as a human he should have reached out, he should have stopped it, he should have stayed.

Liam's signature smile falters for a moment.

"You forgave Asher," he points out lamely.

I let out a hollow laugh.

"No, I didn't. Asher and I are arranged to be married. We have to be cordial in public. Do you see us being buddy-buddy? No. He's currently sucking on his girlfriend's tongue," I say, as I point towards him and Bridgette.

Liam looks over at them and shakes his head.

"She is definitely not his girlfriend."

"I don't really care. My point is, I'm expected to behave with a certain level of respect towards Asher. I don't hold the same responsibility for you."

He frowns at that.

"So that's it? I don't get a second chance?"

"Why do you think you deserve one?" I scoff.

He opens his mouth to speak but pauses, rolling his lips together in thought before those deep green eyes come to me. There is so much raw emotion in them that they actually take me completely by surprise.

"For what it's worth, I'm truly sorry, Skyla. I shouldn't have let Asher do that to you, I should have helped you. I should have done...something. I'm sorry."

His words are drenched in sincerity, but it's not enough.

"Your apology is accepted."

He nods. "So, we're good?"

"No," I say simply. "But your apology is accepted."

Liam's head cocks to the side, a slight shake to his head.

"I don't affect you at all, do I, babygirl?"

"Affect me? How so?" I ask.

A self-deprecating laugh escapes him as he scratches at the back of his head.

"I gotta be honest, I don't think I've ever had to work so hard just for a woman to flirt with me."

"Why on earth would I flirt with you?" I ask, because genuinely, is he stupid?

"Because I'm too charming, most just can't help themselves," he grins in a cheesy way that has my mouth smirking, only a little.

"Hmm, I'm afraid I don't see the appeal."

He clutches his chest, as he pretends to faint across the table like the absolute fool that he is.

"You wound me. I guess I'll just have to turn the charm all the way up," he says as he sits up again. Leaning in close he lifts his hand to catch a single piece of my hair, slowly tucking it behind my ear. As he does, he lets his fingertips skim across my cheek in a way that sends shivers down my body. I maintain eye contact, determined not to be affected by his touch as he speaks softly.

"Your skin is so soft. I've never felt anything like it."

I'm about to tease him for the cheesy line, when I realize he didn't say it all that loud. No, instead it almost seemed like he was speaking more to himself than anything. I wait for him to break character, drop the charming enthralled act before he goes back to being his goofy all eyes on me self. He doesn't though, and his hand doesn't move away from my face. Instead it's practically cemented against me, the tips of his fingers feather-light against my cheek as they move mere centimeters back and forth .

It's as if he's trapped in this moment, and the only way he's able to be shaken from it is when a large hand drops down to his shoulder, startling us both.

"Liam, don't consort with the trash," Asher sneers as he looks down at me.

"You're engaged to trash? What does that make you?" I scoff.

Asher's eyes narrow, but he doesn't say anything for a moment.

"Go back to the girls. Felicity wants you to fuck her before your next class," Asher says coolly, clearly speaking to Liam but keeping his eyes on me.

"Aw, c'mon, Ash. I want to stay over here with the pretty girls," Liam whines, in a way that tells me he's back to being himself.

"The girls over there are the pretty ones, only the best for us, brother. Go, now," he finishes, with a sharp look at Liam that has his tail tucked between his legs.

I watch as Liam slides off the table, swaggering back over to their fan club, like Asher's little yes man. It honestly makes me lose a lot of respect for him, how he cowers to him like that.

Asher and I remain in a tense staring contest. Once he finally breaks, his eyes land on my naked ring finger before practically growling at me.

"Put your fucking ring on and keep it on. It's non-negotiable."

With that, he turns on his heel and stomps away like a toddler throwing a temper tantrum. Rolling my eyes, I turn to see Maggie watching me with wide eyes.

"Uhm, what was all of that?"

I let out a humorless laugh as I shake my head.

"I honestly couldn't tell you."

Chapter Nineteen
Skyla

I wrap my cardigan tightly around myself as the midafternoon breeze intensifies. One person seeing my hickey is bad enough. I contemplated covering it with makeup, but something tells me Ronan wouldn't like that very much. I can't help but bite back a smile at the thought of him getting upset that I would cover his mark or being proud that I didn't. Either way, I'm ridiculous. It's just a bunch of broken blood vessels, there shouldn't be anything sexy or exciting about it....and yet.

Moving through a group of students leaving the pool building, I slip through the door and down the hallway before pushing open the pool door. The comforting scent of chlorine hits me instantly, wrapping me up like a hug as I make my way to Ronan's office. Glancing around the room, I double check that no one is watching before I open the door.

My smile drops instantly when I see a gorgeous leggy brunette, in her late twenties or so, on top of his desk. She's facing him in his chair, her skirt ridden up and legs spread wide. Both of their eyes swing to me in unison, one filled with irritation and the other with panic.

I don't need to tell you whose is whose.

A numb feeling begins tingling across my skin as I take a faltering step backwards, then another before I turn and run. I run so fast I don't even remember going through the two doors needed to get outside. I run so fast that getting back to my dorm is practically a blur, so fast that I managed to outrun Ronan to the elevator of my dorm building.

He narrowly misses the closing door and beats it with a single fist, before he begins shouting out for me to 'let him explain'.

Yeah, I'll pass.

My throat begins to tighten, and tears prick my eyes as the elevator whirs up to my floor. As soon as I step inside my room though, all bets are off. My throat isn't just tight, it's practically closed off, hot and scratchy from the tears that are now free falling down my face.

I feel stupid. So fucking stupid.

Maybe I shouldn't have assumed that if we were...whatever we were, that I would be the only woman with that kind of special treatment. Maybe that was naïve or ignorant of me. As painful as it is to learn that lesson now, I guess it's better that I have all of the information now as opposed to months down the road. Where I'd, no doubt, be so in love with the man that I couldn't see straight. Guess he's a lot more like his nephew than he lets on.

I feel my phone begin to vibrate in my pocket and I pull it out to reveal Ronan's number. I couldn't decline it any faster if I tried, honestly. Unfortunately, it starts right back up again, and I hit the red button just as fast as before.

He tries calling me again and again. Eventually, I just have to turn my phone off. I don't want to hear what he has to say, and I don't want to be treated like the silly little girl I clearly am. I should have listened to him from the start. He clearly told me we could never be more than 'this'. I just didn't understand that 'this' was code for hooking up occasionally, while he pursued other women, more age-appropriate women. More beautiful women because god, I don't think I've ever seen a more stunning woman than the one who was sprawled across his desk like his next meal.

Eventually, I turn my phone on and only partially regret it when it begins buzzing like crazy. Notifications of voicemails and text after text keep coming through. I don't bother looking at a single one as I scroll through my contacts. I click on Maggie and it only rings twice before she answers.

"Hey babe! What's up?"

I try to speak but nothing comes out. Just a choppy gasping breath as I try to compose myself. Apparently, that was all Maggie needed to hear, though.

"I'm on my way. Dorm room?" she asks.

"Yeah," I finally rasp.

"Be there in fifteen."

Then, the line goes dead. I pause for a moment before I make my next call. Debating on bothering her since it's already so late in London before I decide to say fuck it, and I call my aunt Steph.

"Hello?" she answers sleepily.

"Hey," I smile sadly.

"What's wrong?" she asks, immediately sounding more alert.

"N-nothing just...stupid stuff. Guys."

She lets out a breath of relief and I can practically see her sinking back into her bed.

"They are always stupid, all the time. You'll get used to it, sweetie."

I laugh at that and nod.

"Is that why you've never bothered dating anyone?"

She hesitates for several seconds before she speaks.

"Actually, I'm sort of seeing this guy from my work. It's nothing serious but he's nice company. It's been really....lonely since you've been gone."

My heart pangs hearing that. I hate that she's been lonely, I hate that I've been lonely. I'd do almost anything to be back in London with her, especially right now.

"I'm so happy for you, Steph. You deserve every bit of happiness you can get your hands on. What's his name? How long have you guys been seeing each other? Tell me everything."

She hesitates for only a second before she begins telling me that his name is Collin, he's forty-one and extremely charming. Apparently he has a brother, Dillon, that lives in the states on the west coast. She sounds completely smitten, but slowly her voice becomes softer before she stops talking altogether. I smile to myself as I hang up the phone, just as a knock comes from my door.

My stomach flips, nerves scattering across my body, as an image of Ronan at my door flashes to the forefront of my mind. Thankfully, I hear Maggie shout through the door a second later instead.

"It's me. Open up, babe."

I push up from my bed, unlocking the door before opening it to reveal Maggie with four large bags in her hands. I quickly grab one of the slipping bags as she nods her thanks and pushes inside. Closing the door behind her, I pause. He wouldn't use his keycard to get in here...right? Suddenly, my sense of security has evaporated, and I look around before reaching for the lounge chair in the corner. It's heavier than I expect it to be, but I'm able to push it in front of the door. Hopefully it will keep him out even if he does have his master key.

When I turn around, I see Maggie watching me with concern in her eyes. She doesn't ask though, doesn't pry. Instead, she begins pulling items out of the bags, until they are scattered across my bed like a cornucopia of junk food.

I look at her curiously.

"What is all of this?"

"Nothing cures a broken heart like empty carbs and high-fructose corn syrup," she says, as she sits on the edge of the bed and digs into a bag of chips. "Oh, and this!" she says, as she hands me a coffee cup.

"What is it?" I ask.

"Apple cider," she says, through a mouthful of chips.

I wrinkle my nose. "I'm not a huge apple person."

Maggie rolls her eyes. "Just drink it."

Hesitantly, I lift it to my mouth, taking a small sip. The hot spiced cider slides down my throat easily, warming me from the inside in an instant. Oh my god. This is good. Like so good. It tastes like fall in a cup. I take another sip, and another. Maggie's smile growing with each one before I slowly sit across from her.

"I feel so dumb," I whisper.

"You're not dumb, far from. He's an idiot."

"You don't even know what happened," I point out, in a half laugh.

"Don't need to," she shrugs. "He fumbled you. Idiot."

That makes me smile, at least a tiny bit. I reach over for the TV remote, turning on the first movie I see before tossing it to the side again. Maggie turns her attention to the TV, letting me dictate the situation and pacing. Something I appreciate more than I could ever explain because I don't know what to think or feel, let alone how to express it.

"He told me to meet him in his office today and when I showed up there was a woman."

"A woman?" Maggie asks, as she turns to face me.

I nod. "A beautiful, leggy, perfectly bronzed woman."

"Okay. What was the woman doing?"

I swallow and cringe. "She was sitting on his desk, her skirt raised, legs spread and..."

Maggie waits silently before she realizes I'm not going to continue.

"I'm going to say something completely unhelpful, and I hope you won't hate me for it, but you deserve to know. That is just kind of how our world works."

I frown at that. "What do you mean?"

"I mean, that woman you saw, she's probably his fiancée or she will be."

The word is like a punch to the chest.

"Well, what am I? What was I? A distraction? A game?" I ask.

She shakes her head before shrugging. "Maybe he really does like you and was hoping you could be his mistress when he marries. It's extremely common, I actually don't know of any married men in our...circle that doesn't have a mistress."

"What? That's insane! Your dad?" I ask.

"Oh yeah. It's one of the reasons my mom left him. My stepdad has one too but he chose someone who is from a good family, so my mom overlooks it."

"That is so fucked up. Why is this okay?"

She smiles sadly and shakes her head.

"It's just the way it is, babe. 90% of the marriages are arranged, people tie themselves to smart matches while they continue pursuing love and lust discreetly. You really think I'll be happy to marry a man? Fuck no. I'll be taking a mistress or ten on my wedding night, you can trust that," she laughs hollowly.

"Why are we marrying people off anyways? This is the twenty-first century. This isn't a nobility thing where titles and provinces are on the line," I scoff.

"Isn't it, though? Sure, it's not like it was two or three-hundred years ago but that doesn't mean the game has changed, simply the pieces. We aren't battling for new land, but large estates. We aren't negotiating treaties but conducting business acquisitions and mergers. There aren't any dowries but there are the 'I scratch your back you scratch mine' methods to every arrangement. Every single one. Everything about these people is methodical, tactical, and you don't step out of line. Ever."

A heavy sinking feeling settles in my stomach as I numbly nod. It's disgusting, but apparently it's the world I now live in. Or more accurately, the one I was thrust into. Regardless, I hate everything about it.

I pick at my lunch, but I don't have any real intention of eating any of it. Maggie is rattling on about a story from high school and I'm doing my best to pay attention. Really, I am. I'm just so....lost in my own head, I guess. God, would you listen to me? How pathetic am I? I've known the man for, what? A few weeks? And I'm all torn up like this? Ridiculous.

As if my mood couldn't be soured anymore, a swaggering man with side swept blond hair and green eyes comes up to us, that smirk shining brighter than the sun.

"Hi babygirl," Liam smiles.

I stare at him blankly before turning my attention down to my food. There is a pause for several moments before he tries again, Maggie instantly becomes silent as she listens in intently.

"So, I was wondering if I could take you out tonight?" he asks.

"No," I say, as I stab my chicken with my fork and lift it to my mouth.

I glance up to see his eyes confused and his brows furrowed.

"Uh, no?"

"Yes, as in, no thank you. I decline. I refuse. I reject your proposal. Take your pick."

A choked laugh escapes him like he's trying to gauge whether I'm joking or not, before he clears his throat and attempts to lay it on even thicker. As if that were possible. He plops down into the seat beside me as he looks at me with those soft green eyes.

"Please? I have the best date planned and we will have a lot of fun."

"Is that before or after you shove me into another grave? Or maybe this time you'll pick me up, only to drop me off twenty miles away from the nearest town. Somewhere nice and secluded with no cell service," I scoff with a shake of my head. "No, you can tell Asher that whatever little plan the two of you have concocted, I'm not interested. I'm not playing your games, leave me out of everything."

His head cocks to the side slightly, like he's genuinely confused as he speaks.

"Asher doesn't know I'm trying to take you out."

I give him a dubious look, not believing him for one second but his eyes shine genuinely.

"Then why would you try?"

Liam lets out a short laugh as he pushes his hair out of his face, like it's a nervous tick or something.

"Despite what you may think, I'm not Asher's lap dog. I have a mind of my own, my own thoughts, my own desires."

"So, where does taking me out fit in?" I ask.

He smiles and shakes his head.

"Is that a yes?"

I go to correct him and say my answer stands, when two figures catch my eye across the courtyard. Ronan is walking to his car, but he isn't alone. That leggy goddess from yesterday is on his arm like an accessory as they move towards the staff parking lot. Hurt jabs inside me and before I know what I'm doing, or saying, I nod towards Liam.

"Fine. Whatever. Pick me up at seven and if you're even a second late, I'm not going with you."

A wide grin, that shines so bright it actually takes me back, spreads across his face.

"Deal, except I'll pick you up at nine. Everything doesn't start until around then."

"Everything?" I question, as he pushes up to stand and begins sauntering off.

"See you tonight, babygirl!"

Shaking my head, I look to see Maggie staring at me with wide eyes.

"Did you just agree to go out on a date, with your betrothed's best friend?"

I can't help but scoff at the word betrothed before shrugging.

"Guess so."

I'm just finishing my lipstick when my phone lights up. The contact name Asshole Fiancé displays across the screen, but I have no intention of answering it. Thankfully it goes to voicemail just as my lipstick is done. I slip it into my clutch when my phone starts up again, and again. Finally, irritation wins and I click accept.

"What?" I snap.

He's quiet for a moment, like he's taken off guard before he recovers.

"What the fuck do you think you're doing?"

"Just trying to survive this life, what about you?"

He curses under his breath before speaking.

"You know what I'm fucking talking about. You're not going on a date with Liam."

"Actually, I am. He should be here in–" I pause to check my phone before continuing, "three minutes."

"Oh, I'm sure he is. What I'm saying is, I forbid it. Take off whatever slutty clothes and botched makeup you have on and go the fuck to sleep."

I frown, looking down at my little black dress, matching black pumps and flawlessly executed makeup. Asshole.

"He's a grown man," I fire back. "He asked me out, not the other way around. You have a problem, take it up with him."

"No," Asher snarls. "I'm taking it up with you. My *fiancée*."

A humorless laugh escapes me as I toss my hand out by my side.

"Please don't act like that word actually means anything."

He's quiet for only half a second before he's back to snarling at me, like the untamed beast he is.

"Fuck it. If you're going out then so am I."

"I've quickly come to expect nothing less."

I can practically see his eyes bulging out of his head through the phone.

"You're a fucking bitch!" he snaps before ending the call.

In the next moment there's a knock at my door. Well, that was just the thing I needed to get into the spirit of the night. Thanks, Asher.

Chapter Twenty
Liam

I flatten out my shirt despite it just being a plain black t-shirt, before knocking on her door. She's always so polished and pressed to perfection, I wouldn't blame her for looking down her nose at me. Everyone else seems to.

I don't know what possessed me to push her to go out with me tonight. She's off-limits, obviously. If I hadn't ran out of my dorm room tonight, Asher would have beat my ass. He tried to when I offhandedly mentioned I was taking out his fiancée.

It's not like he likes her or anything. Honestly, he can't stand her. So, why does it matter if I spend some time with her? She's fucking hot and she has a little bit of fire in her that I'm just itching to set ablaze.

When the door opens, I put on my most charming smile. As soon as I fully see her though, I feel my smile drop and my stomach tighten. Fuck.

She's gorgeous. Her long toned legs go on for miles in those black heels, before a black dress that hugs her curves like a second skin begins at her thighs. Her hair is in loose curls, and she has a little bit of sparkly eyeshadow in the inner corners of her eyes that make them pop more than they usually do.

"What? Do I not look okay?" she asks, dropping the hand clutched around her phone to her side.

"No," I say, snapping out of the temporary daze she had me in for a minute. "You're beautiful, but I'm sorry to say, you're definitely going to have to change."

Her brows furrow at that as I gesture towards her room.

"May I?"

I watch as those beautiful green eyes narrow just a fraction, before she steps to the side. I stride across her room smoothly, my eyes taking note of every personal detail about the room as I do. I'll be honest, there isn't much. The room looks hardly lived in. Just a few pictures of her and a blonde woman. Then a blue and white bottle of perfume, a thing of lotion and a candy bar. She doesn't seem like the candy eating type, mainly because I've been watching her for weeks and all she ever eats is a salad or chicken and rice. Maybe it's a guilty pleasure of hers.

Turning my attention to her walk in closet, I step inside making myself right at home, as my fingers begin skimming through the different materials hanging on either side.

"Uhm, excuse me. What do you think you're doing?" Skyla scoffs as she comes to stand behind me.

I don't answer, instead grabbing a red shirt that seems to be the closest thing this girl owns to a casual shirt, before reaching for a black pair of jeans. I hand them both to her as I smile.

"Probably going to want more comfortable shoes too."

She blinks at me slowly, before continuing to stare at me like I've lost my mind. I just grin at her as I slip out of the closet and plop down onto one of her plush couches. I pull my phone out, pretending to scroll on it as I speak.

"Go ahead, act like I'm not even here."

She scoffs, before stomping off towards her bathroom but not before I hear her mutter.

"Entitled prick. Why the hell did I even agree to this stupid date?"

I can't help but smirk at her irritation. God, I love to wind her up. That's not why I told her to change, though. She will thank me later when she sees where we're going.

To my surprise, she actually gets changed quickly. If I thought she looked beautiful in a little black dress, seeing her in a tight pair of jeans and a casual shirt with her curls shook out does me in. There is something so fucking sexy about a woman who doesn't have to try. A woman that is just effortlessly beautiful. It's obvious Skyla has that, but she's always dressed up like a barbie doll– like she's dressing for someone else, not herself.

I clap my hands together, doing my best to swallow away this dry feeling in my throat that has suddenly set in.

"Much better," I say as I jump to my feet. "This way, milady." Offering my arm for her to take.

Her eyes look me up and down before she shakes her head. She throws her phone into a clutch, slipping her feet into a pair of socks and white tennis shoes before walking out the door. Again, I can't help but grin. That little fire in her is already smoldering, let's see if I can get her to let loose enough to burn Salem to the fucking ground tonight.

I slip out of her door and make it into the elevator just before the doors close. She looks at me unimpressed as she leans against the wall of the elevator. The doors open as we hit the first floor and I allow her to sashay her way out first. Mainly so I can admire her from back here, because *goddamn* she has a delicious ass.

She turns to look over her shoulder, catching me in the act and rolls her eyes before facing forward again. I'm not really sure where she's going, but I don't mind letting her take the driver's seat for a little while. I leisurely follow behind her, casually whistling to myself as she leads us out of her dorm, into the courtyard, and out to the parking lot before she pauses.

Spinning on her heel, she turns back to look at me with furrowed brows.

"Where are we going?"

"I was going to ask you the same thing, babygirl. You seemed so confident of your path I didn't want to interrupt."

"Okay, forget this. I'm already sick of your shit," she says, as she moves to walk past me.

I catch her hand before she can get too far, though. She jolts to a stop, attempting to free herself from my grip, but I only tighten my hold smiling down at her as I shake my head.

"Don't fight me, babygirl. I think it's cute. I love a woman who takes what she wants. You were right anyways, I parked just up here," I say, allowing my breath to fan across her cheek as I speak.

For a moment, I don't think I affect her in the slightest, which is more than aggravating for me. That is, until I see her pulse practically thundering from her neck. My mouth pulls up into a wicked grin as I inch myself closer to her, softening my words as I do.

"One night, give me one night and I guarantee you'll have the most fun you've ever had."

Her eyes are wide and hazy like a million thoughts are playing out in her head, all warring to be one to make it to the surface. I wait for her witty retort or smartass insult but neither come. Instead, she swallows once, righting her posture and agrees with a nod.

Nodding in delight, I take a step towards the parking lot forcing her to follow me, mainly because I still haven't let go of her hand. She wiggles her fingers before huffing an irritated sigh.

"Do you mind?"

"Not at all, your hands are buttery smooth." I smile, tossing her a quick wink before practically dragging her to my car. When we come up to it, I hit my key and unlock the door before holding hers open for her. Her brows furrow before she shakes her head.

"I'm not getting into that thing."

"Why not?"

"Look at the tires! They look like they are about to fall off!"

A laugh escapes me as I glance at my Nissan 350Z. With the stance tires I have on, they are definitely for performance instead of a comfy casual drive. She'll see why we need them soon, though.

"They're fine, actually just got these put on last week," I say, as I gesture to the tires with their shiny new rims to compliment the fresh rubber.

She still looks hesitant before a figure is moving across the parking lot. It takes me a moment to recognize Ronan. I give him a wave but he isn't looking at me, he's looking at her. My head swings to see Skyla staring at him like a deer caught in headlights.

Gone is her hesitation, she all but dives into the car headfirst before ripping the door out of my hand and slamming it closed. I contemplate on staying where I am as I watch Ronan pick up into a jog towards us, but then consider that this could be way more fun.

So, I slide across the hood, Dukes of Hazzard style of course, before jumping into the driver's seat. Skyla struggles with the harness until I lean over and quickly fasten her in before doing the same for myself.

"Can this thing go fast?" she asks, a hurried rasp to her usually silky voice.

I can't help but laugh as I fire up the engine, that Rb26dett swap coming to life with a throaty roar, before I dump the clutch and peel out of there. Smoke billows from my rear tires as we burn rubber all the way to the street. Glancing in my rear view mirror I see Ronan standing there, hands on his hips, surrounded in a cloud of smoke, looking absolutely fucking livid.

I drop a gear before sending us into the corner in front of us, a scream erupting from Skyla as I do. Cranking the wheel, our ass-end gives way, allowing us to seamlessly drift around the corner before I right the car. I let off the throttle, allowing us to blend in with traffic as we drive into downtown.

Skyla's screams slowly dissolve into a fit of laughter. Her smile is wide, eyes squinted and chest heaving as she giggles and squeals. It's an infectious sound, so light and carefree. It does something to me, forcing laughter to escape me as well.

I don't know how long we spend laughing like fucking fools while I maneuver us through the streets until we finally get far enough out of town.

"Okay, okay. God, I can't breathe," Skyla says softly, as her laughter dies down before she clears her throat. "Alright, where are you taking us, Mr. Walcott?" she teases.

I wince before I can help it, the sound of my father's name on her lips is like nails on a chalkboard for me.

"Just Liam, babygirl, or daddy. Whatever you're in the mood for," I say with a wink.

She doesn't seem to sense my discomfort, which I'm grateful for, as we drive up the county road before stopping at the start line.

Her mouth drops open as her eyes begin to scan the heavily crowded road.

"Welcome to the drifts, Skyla."

Before she can respond, I'm parking while undoing my harness and getting out. A crowd quickly forms around me, and I greet several people before pushing past them to reach Skyla's door. She seems to have gotten the harness off herself as she slides out the door in the next second. She has a curious smile on her face as the crowd surrounding us gets larger.

Anthony walks up to us, pulling me in for a quick bro-hug before holding out his hand. I drop the wad of cash from my pocket into his hand, and he nods his thanks before disappearing to collect the other racers buy-in for the night.

"How much was that?" Skyla asks.

More people join us, blasting music from their cars and talking amongst themselves. I wrap my arm around Skyla, dragging her against my chest to keep her away from the crowd as I speak into her ear.

"Ten k."

"Ten thousand dollars?" She asks, as she turns to face me. "For what?"

"A chance to race."

"And lose!" A heckler calls out from the side.

I roll my eyes at them before looking back at Skyla, who now has her ass pressed against me and is relaxed beneath my touch. I'm not sure if she realizes it or not, but who am I to stop her? In fact, I push things a little further to see how brave she's feeling tonight.

My hand that was resting against my car moves to her jean clad hip, gripping it in a way that she could pull away from me if she wanted, but shows that I hope she doesn't. To my pleasure, she doesn't pull away. In fact, I could swear she sinks into my touch just a little more before giving me a shy smile over her shoulder. Goddamnit, she has a beautiful smile.

The intoxicating scent of her perfume and something that is undeniably her swirls between us, forcing everything else to slowly slip away until all I see is her. Her head is still turned, eyes on me, as she moves forward first. Her eyes are practically begging with me to talk her out of what comes next. Absolutely fuck that shit, though.

When she's only half an inch from my mouth, an engine rumbles beside us until the exhaust cracks, forcing her to startle and me to curse. She pulls away from me, like she doesn't realize how she got that close to me in the first place before crossing her arms over her chest. Something like disappointment hits me in the chest, and I stand up to my full height as I open her door before gesturing inside.

She steps in without a word, and I shut it a little harder than necessary. I make eye contact with Anthony giving him a 'lets go' gesture. He gives me a thumbs up before I slip inside, doing my harness as Skyla does hers.

"You ready?" I ask.

"Should I be scared?" she laughs nervously.

I give her half of a grin as I shake my head.

"Not with me, babygirl. Never with me."

She rolls her lips together before nodding once. I gesture to the interior roll cage before pointing to the oh shit handle.

"We're about as safe as you can get. Grab onto that if you need it," I say before firing up the car.

My baby roars to life once again, and I put her into gear before creeping through the quickly dispersing crowds as all of the cars line up for the night. Usually I know everyone here, but a blacked out WRX pulls up beside me too tinted to see inside. I know I've never seen them before, though. They rap their engine, edging the starting line as Anthony comes to stand at the front. There are five of us tonight. It's only a three mile loop, but it's full of sharp S turns and even a dirt path for a quarter mile. Normally, I'd say my odds were more than fair, but tonight? I have no choice but to win. I have a hot date to impress.

When Anthony drops his arm, we all take off. I'm smashing through gears, that twin-turbo treating me real nice as we come into the first corner. Everyone is clean, keeping their distance from one another as me and the WRX maintain the lead.

On the third S turn, I glance over to check on Skyla only to find her grinning. She has an excited gleam in her eyes as her right hand holds onto the oh shit handle.

"Want to help?" I ask.

"Help?" she balks.

I grin at her, grabbing her left hand and resting it on the shifter, before dumping the clutch and laying my hand over hers. Together we grab fifth before whipping out of the turn and heading down the straight stretch. The speedometer is practically maxed as we push my baby for all she's worth.

We lose two of the cars on the dirt. Both of them spin out one after another followed by the Supra in the final stretch, effectively taking out the WRX.

"C'mon! Hurry!" Skyla squeals, as we approach the makeshift finish line.

I grin at her as I force us to shift into sixth and give us the extra push to finish. I don't bring up the fact that everyone else is miles behind us. She is too into it, why spoil the fun?

When we cross over that line the crowd erupts, bouncing and shouting wildly as bets are quickly paid. We come to a stop as Anthony jogs over to me, tossing a brown paper bag through my rolled down window. I nod my thanks before we take off again and this time, Skyla doesn't even try to take her hand out from under mine. Instead, I feel her hand grip the top of the stick shift tighter like she wants to do it all herself, and it's fucking adorable.

Before I know it, I'm pulling up to my favorite look-out point. I've actually never brought anyone here before. It's just been my place, to come and escape from the world for a little while. Something told me she'd be able to appreciate it just as much, though.

I shut the car down and before I can say anything, Skyla is out of the car and jumping up and down shouting in celebration.

"Oh my god! I can't believe that. The rush. My god, that has to be one of the most exhilarating things that I've ever done in my life!"

"It's an adrenaline high like no other, right?" I smile as I get out of the car.

She nods quickly as she spins in a circle, her arms outstretched by her sides in a carefree way that has something stirring inside me. I gotta be honest, I did not think she was going to have this much fun. I've taken a few girls drifting before, most of them are so scared shitless they never come again. Which is fine since double-dipping isn't really my thing, anyways. I wasn't expecting her to enjoy it so much, I wasn't expecting to enjoy tonight so much.

A huge piece of why I wanted to go out with her was for the challenge of it. She seems so uncrackable, and she was a challenge I happily accepted. It was a bonus that me taking her out would drive Asher crazy. He's been more of an asshole than usual lately, and one of my favorite pastimes is to fuck with him.

Though, all ulterior motives dropped, I'm having a really good time with her.

Probably too good.

Pushing away from the car, I decide to say fuck it and get out of my head. I wrap my arm around her waist and put my other hand into hers as I lead her through a very dramatic slow dance, spinning and dipping her as I do.

"How does it feel to be on a date with a winner?" I ask, as she spins in my arms.

"I'm a Parris, I wouldn't be out with you if I thought you were anything less than."

"Well, thank god I won," I laugh.

She nods her agreement, tilting her head to the side as she speaks.

"Can I ask you something?"

I nod.

"So, are you bi? Or do you label yourself? Obviously, you've been with plenty of women but I hear plenty about you being with men, and then there was that day that I walked in on you."

My eyebrows shoot up in surprise. I didn't expect her to ask that. I must take too long to answer though because she quickly scrambles to speak again.

"I'm sorry. That was really rude and invasive. Ignore me. Can we blame my lack of manners on the adrenaline rush? Lets," she cringes, as she shakes her head.

I can't help but chuckle at her panic as I shake my head.

"Don't be. I'm not exactly shy about my...proclivities," I say with a wink. "I'm not crazy about labels, but I guess I closely identify with a bisexual heteroromantic."

She gives me a confused look and I smile as I elaborate.

"I'm only interested in women romantically, but I'm sexually attracted to both men and women."

"Oh, so you wouldn't be interested in dating a man?" she hedges.

I shrug. "Sexuality is fluid and always changing so, never say never I suppose. Though, I can't see myself forming that kind of connection with a man at this time in my life, no."

Skyla nods, looking up at me shyly through her lashes.

"But you would with a woman....date that is."

I can't help but smirk at the underlying meaning in her words.

"I don't typically date, but there is always the exception," I say, allowing my eyes to roam over her, extremely purposeful in my intent.

She blushes from my gaze, nodding her head. I slowly back her up, allowing her ass to hit the hood of my car before I close in on her. She tilts her head to look up at me, but she doesn't have to for long before I'm lifting her onto the hood and stepping between her legs. Her eyes dart back and forth between my own then down to my lips, and a heavy feeling settles in the air between us as she does.

My eyes drop to her mouth, her lips so fucking full and red. They look so soft, so sweet, like a piece of goddamn fruit. I've wanted to know what she tasted like from the moment I laid eyes on her, but she needs to come to me for this. She needs to want it as bad as I do.

I do reach out, resting my hands on her hips, digging my fingers into her as I do my best to maintain my composure. Easier said than done when I have this stunner of a woman staring up at me like she's never wanted anything or anyone more.

Her neck arches up just enough and when her lips touch mine, my control snaps. I planned to be slow and gentle, let her take the lead, but I can't. One brush of her lips against mine and a zap runs through my body all the way down to my toes. It practically jolts me to life, before I'm cupping the back of her neck, decimating any distance left between us.

My tongue traces against the seam of her lips before forcing its way in. She greets me happily, tangling hers around mine as she arches into me. I press my hardening cock against her pussy and relish in the needy moan that escapes her.

Having a mind of their own, my hands begin running down her body, cupping her breasts momentarily before making their way between her thighs. I grind the heel of my palm against her, giving her just a taste of the friction I know she craves. She moans again, her mouth falling open as I rub against her faster and faster.

"Feel good, babygirl?" I murmur against her lips, as I begin peppering her neck with kisses.

"Yes," she gasps. "More."

No need to tell me twice.

Flicking the button of her jeans open I push on her chest, forcing her to sprawl out across my hood before I begin peeling her jeans down her legs. Her black silk panties stick to the material, coming off right along with them. I snatch those up quickly, pocketing them before she can argue with me.

Fucking hell.

My head drops forward for a moment before I shake it because holy fuck. I've never seen a prettier pussy in my entire life. Looking up at her through my hair, I smirk before spreading her open and revealing her perfect clit. Brushing my thumb against it, she physically shutters before letting out a breathy moan.

"Liam," she gasps.

"Fuck," I groan. "You can't say my name like that, babygirl."

"Why not?" she asks, her head lifted slightly to meet my eyes.

"Because, it makes me want to fuck you raw, right here on the hood of my car."

Hesitation flickers in her eyes, as the color nearly drains from her face. I chuckle softly as my hand taps against her thigh.

"Don't worry, I wouldn't live to see the next sunrise if I deflowered the Parris Princess."

She lets out a slow breath like she's relieved, but I don't miss the flash of disappointment that passes across her features. It's gone almost instantly, but it was there. I saw it, memorized it and will never forget it.

"But," I continue. "That doesn't mean I can't give you an orgasm or two."

Before she can speak, I slip a finger inside her. I know I shouldn't, penetration of any kind really should be off the table with her but goddamnit, I'm only human.

She's so fucking tight, if I didn't already know she was a virgin, it's guaran-fucking-teed now. Despite being tighter than a nun's pussy, she's absolutely drenched, allowing me to push a little deeper before withdrawing and repeating the motion.

I hear her breathe slowly and I look up curiously.

"You okay, babygirl?"

She nods. "It's just tight. Your fingers, they're so big. I didn't think it could hurt."

Frowning at that, I slow my motions.

"Skyla, you've been finger fucked before, right?"

Surely she has, obviously she's a virgin but it's not like all the London douchebags didn't shoot their shot with her. She's too much of a bombshell not to have a line out the door, of men desperate for her.

A slight tinge of red touches her cheeks as she shrugs softly.

"I've done it myself but—"

"Never anyone else?" I ask, way too much pleasure bleeding into my voice knowing that I'm the first person to touch her here.

She shakes her head and I feel my cock leak pre-cum in my pants at that.

"Fuck me, guess I have a high bar to set for you. Sit back and relax, babygirl. I'm gonna finger fuck you until you soak the hood of this car."

Curling my finger upwards, I go slow, rubbing her g-spot nice and easy to start. I allow her more time to adjust to the feeling as my other hand begins playing with her clit. She shutters out a satisfied moan as I continue working her over. She opens up to me surprisingly easily. Within a minute or so, I'm slipping another finger inside her, stretching her virgin pussy as wide as it's ever been. Which is so fucking hot to think about.

Her hands ball up at her sides as her breathing becomes choppy.

"Oh god. Oh god, Liam! Liam!" she shouts out, shattering apart in my arms.

Her cum begins leaking down my hand and I waste no time in removing my fingers to chase down the taste. I suck both of my fingers into my mouth, licking them clean before releasing them with a pop. The taste of her has me groaning with equal amounts of desire and frustration.

Goddamnit.

It is taking everything in me not to drop to my knees and eat her pussy until she comes down my chin before fucking her until her guts are nice and rearranged.

Unfortunately for both of us, self-preservation is in the forefront of my mind. I wasn't joking when I said that I'd probably be dead before morning if I fucked her. It would be one of four people for sure– Christopher Putnam, Henry Parris, Asher or Ronan. And all four of them would make sure it would be bloody as fuck.

She's beautiful, delicious, and honestly, pretty fucking perfect, but I'd prefer to live to see twenty-two. So I restrain myself, rearranging my cock in my pants to tuck it away, though he is definitely not on board with this plan.

"How'd I do?" I ask, with a crooked smile and a wink.

A nervous blush hits Skyla, as she covers her face with her hands for a moment before blowing out a breath and sitting up.

"Good, yeah, um. You're good. No surprise, really, I've heard you've had a lot of practice," she laughs hollowly.

I laugh at that, though I can't deny that her words hit me in the chest in an achy way that I'm not crazy about.

"Let's get you back to campus before your fiancé makes a necklace out of my balls."

She wrinkles up her nose at that.

"What an ugly necklace that would be," she says as she slides off the hood, pulling up her pants, sans panties, as she does.

I drop my mouth open in mock offense as I scoff.

"Excuse me, I'll have you know I have very pretty balls. Want me to prove it?" I tease.

She finishes buttoning her jeans as she gives me a dubious look and shakes her head.

"I'll take your word for it."

I grin as I follow her to her side of the car, opening the door before she can. She nods in thanks as I dramatically give her a bow, as if she were the Queen of England, before shutting the door behind her. I mean, I'm not far off. She's the Princess of Salem, soon to be the Queen. I just don't think she fully grasps that yet.

Chapter Twenty One
Skyla

Thankfully, we drive in silence all the way back to campus because I need space to think. I came out on this date, really, for the chance of pissing off Asher and forgetting about how much it hurt that I wasn't the only woman Ronan was entertaining. Yet, within minutes of being with Liam I forgot about both of them. In those moments, tonight, it was just him.

Yes, he's the silly, showboating, cocky man that he shows himself to be around campus, but there is another side of him. A more caring side. One that opens and closes my doors, rests his hand on my knee when we're driving as if he just wants to touch me– nothing more, nothing less. I don't know if tonight was just an act, put on by Liam, but I can't deny I found myself smiling and laughing more than I have in, I don't know how long. He's like sunshine, warm and constant, being near him is like sunbathing on a perfect day.

When we get to campus, he pulls into the parking lot right outside of my dorm before turning the car off. Spinning in his seat, he faces me, resting his head against the headrest as he smiles at me.

"I know you didn't say yes to me tonight because you really

wanted to, but whatever made you say yes, I'm fucking glad you did."

A flutter hits my chest, and I can practically feel the blush take over my cheeks as I nod.

"Me too. I wasn't expecting to have such a good time, if I'm being honest."

"I'm not so bad, huh?" he teases, with a wink that has me chuckling.

"Not at all. You're actually a pretty great guy."

His teasing smile falters for a moment, a look of earnest appreciation taking over his face before he swallows roughly, as if he was trying to push whatever emotions he's feeling away. Liam's eyes are bouncing between my own before he undoes his seatbelt, reaches his hand behind my head, and pulls me in for a kiss. Just like when he kissed me before, it's like fireworks going off through my body. A euphoric rush comes just from this man's lips being on mine.

I lean farther into him, desperate to bask in this feeling for as long as I'm allowed to as his tongue slips inside my mouth. I tangle my own with his and his hands begin running down my body. Just as fast as we started though, it's over. Liam is tearing himself away from me and forcing himself back into his seat. His breathing is labored with his fists clenched as he stares out the front windshield.

Frowning at him, I speak.

"Are you okay?"

He nods roughly before blowing out a ragged breath.

"I can't help but get a little carried away with you, and I can't afford to do that. *We* can't afford to do that."

Disappointment sinks into me, but I do my best not to let it show.

"Because I'm engaged to Asher?"

Liam scoffs. "Fuck Asher, because you deserve better. You deserve a man who is going to take his time with you, always, savor you."

His words take me by surprise as I look at him .

"Are you going to be that man?"

Now he is the one who looks surprised, though he recovers well.

"I'd love to be. Does this mean I can take you out again soon?"

I pause as if I'm weighing my options, though I already know my answer.

"Sure, I'd like that. What are we going to do next time? Go to an underground gambling ring? Fight club?"

Liam lets out a boisterous laugh, as he smiles at me and shakes his head.

"I'll start working on the plan now."

I smile and nod, feeling bold for a moment as I lean across the console and press my lips to his. He only moves his lips a little, as he lets me do the work. I appreciate the control it allows me, the power, and the smile that I can't seem to drop.

Reaching for my door, I grab the handle and push it open as I slip out of the car. When I shut it, the window rolls down and Liam is leaning over so he can look at me through it.

"I'll see you soon, babygirl."

I give him a small smile, as he gives me a wink that sends my stomach flipping. The car fires up and he takes off in the next minute, drifting out of the parking lot like the show-off he is. I can't help but chuckle to myself as I walk towards my dorm.

A figure catches my attention to my right. It's so dark out and the lighting isn't great, so it takes me a minute to figure out who is watching me. The dark sulking person is easily identifiable, though.

Vincent stares at me as if I were an insect under a microscope. The only part of him that moves are his eyes as they track me steadily. From where he is standing, it's obvious that he was watching me and Liam. I'm not sure if he was passing by, saw us and decided to people-watch for a bit, or if he's out here for more sinister reasons. Either way, I want nothing to do with the grumpy creep.

Turning away from him like there is nothing to see, I continue towards the front door, banking around the corner and thankfully, disappearing from Vincent's watchful eye. I slip inside quickly, before the elevator opens for me.

I'm already replaying tonight over and over again in my head. The adrenaline rush I got from Liam racing, the excitement, the fun. It was something so completely out of my comfort zone, yet so amazing. Though, I'm not sure if that was from the activity or the company.

God. Do I like Liam? The flirtatious womanizer, who is best friends with Satan himself?

Yes.

The answer comes immediately because, with me at least, he's not just those things. He's so much more complex than anyone gives him credit for. More complex than he gives himself credit for.

When I get to my room, I wave the keycard over the pad allowing the door to whir open. When I do, I'm only inside for a moment before I freeze. The door shuts behind me, but I'm trapped in place. There in front of me, Ronan is sitting on the edge of my bed, head hanging between his shoulders, fingers dug into the back of his hair. As soon as he hears me though, his head shoots up.

Deep dark circles encase his normally bright blue eyes, which now appear more dull and lifeless than I've ever seen. His gaze flicks over me, from head to toe, before he shoots to his feet and crosses the distance between us. I stumble back a foot or two and he doesn't miss the attempt to keep space between us. He winces, like me doing that physically hurts him, before he stops moving and speaks.

"Baby, I was so worried. It's so late. I didn't know where you were or who you were with. Are you okay?"

"What are you doing here?" I ask stiffly, he of all people does not get to barge in here and demand answers.

His frown increases as he takes half a step towards me again.

"I need you to hear me out. I need to explain and when I'm done, if you never want to speak to me again I'll leave you alone. I promise. I just want to explain, baby."

"Skyla," I correct coldly.

He swallows and nods. "Please, Skyla. Five minutes."

Despite how weak it sounds, I want to hear him out. I want to hear his excuses, no matter how inconsequential they will be. For closure's sake, I think I need this.

I nod my head once, not saying a word as I gesture for him to get on with it.

"What you saw the other day, I swear to god it wasn't what it looked like. Her name is Annie Williams. Her father is...close friends with my brother," he explains, faltering for only a moment as he continues. "They are close family friends of ours and my brother has been trying to set me up with Annie for a while. I'm not interested in her—"

"But she is in you," I finish for him, because no woman sits on a man's desk with a skirt that high up or looks up at him like he hung the moon as they walk through the courtyard if she isn't interested."

He doesn't immediately agree but, when I raise an eyebrow challenging him to lie to me, he concedes. Nodding his head as he continues.

"She showed up to my office that day unexpectedly. When there was a knock at the door I thought it was you. I tried to get her to leave, I didn't want you to walk in and get the wrong idea. That blew up in my face," he laughs bitterly.

"What about the other day? You guys looked pretty chummy walking through campus, practically hand in hand," I bite out. I can't even mask my tone for anything less than anger.

He frowns for a moment before realization hits him. Clearly he didn't see me, but I saw him.

"She dropped by again. Wanted to go to lunch. I told her no."

"Convenient," I mutter.

Ronan runs a hand through his hair before dropping it at his side.

"I don't know how to explain this, Skyla. Annie is being pushed towards me like you are being pushed towards Asher. That doesn't mean I want her, the opposite. I can't stand her. There is only one woman I want, and currently, she's effectively evaded me at every attempt to explain."

"So naturally, you use your power of authority over her and break into her room while she's gone."

He doesn't say anything for a moment, before he blows out a breath.

"I'm sorry, I should have given you space. It was fucking killing me knowing that you've assumed the worst from all of this. That you thought I didn't care about you, that I would cheat on you. That I—"

"You can't cheat on me if we aren't in a relationship, Ronan. We never were," I cut off.

His eyes fly up to mine, and what looks like hurt flashes across his face.

"Bullshit. We were together. Just because we didn't put a label on it doesn't mean you weren't mine and I wasn't yours."

He pauses for a moment, as if he is trying to find the right words.

"I'm sorry I hurt you. I'm sorry I allowed myself to be in a compromising position that made you question my loyalty to you. All I see is you, Skyla. No one else matters."

I want to believe him, so badly. That's stupid though, right? This is what any man would say if he was caught with another woman, wouldn't he? Yet, some part of me, however ignorant it may be, believes him.

"So, what do you want?" I ask, doing my best to regain control of the conversation.

"What do you mean?" Ronan asks.

"I mean, what do you want? You explained yourself, I heard you out. Five minutes is up. What do you want?"

He doesn't speak for a while, instead he just stares at me. His breathing is ragged, and the tension is so thick between us even a knife wouldn't do.

Slowly, he begins making his way towards me, closing the remaining distance between us before my back is plastered against my door and his arms are braced above me.

"You. I want you, Skyla. I'll do whatever it takes. I'll beg and plead, I'll lay at your feet and kneel before you every day. Whatever you need, whatever you want, it's yours. I would stop the earth on its axis for you."

"Why?" I ask softly, doing my best to battle the butterflies desperate to emerge at his declaration.

He shakes his head softly, lifting his hand to cup my cheek as he does.

"Because you're worth it."

Despite my best efforts, my heart swells and my stomach flips. I want to be impervious to this man, so badly. He's too old for me, he's my fiancé's uncle, and he's involved in this fucked up society that my father is wrapped up in. Nothing about him or our situation is a good idea. Yet, the feeling of his skin on mine sends all rationale out the window leaving only my fuzzy, confused, head over heels emotions.

"Do you still want me, Skyla? Do we still have a chance?"

"You hurt me," I say softly.

His face crumples as he shakes his head.

"I'm so sorry, baby. I would never betray you, ever. You have to know that. Know that right here," he says, taking one of my hands and resting it against his heart. "This belongs to you, only you. I need you more than I need air in my lungs, or the feeling of water around me on a hard day. If you don't want me though, I'll understand and I'll let you go."

Even though I think he believes his words, I don't. They seem to physically hurt him just by uttering them. He may let me go physically, but I'm not sure he would emotionally. Why do I like that? How toxic am I? Are we? That the idea of him not being able to move on from me fills me with relief, instead of panic or fear like it should?

"I want you," I say softly.

He doesn't speak like I expected. Instead, he drops my hand and cups my face with both of his hands, holding me like I'm his most prized possession as he crushes his lips to mine. It's been days since we've kissed, but it feels like years. Ronan's lips move against me seamlessly, perfectly. It's as easy as breathing, and it equally hurts and heals something inside me. God, I missed him.

His hands slide beneath my legs, lifting me into the air. I wrap my thighs around him as he carries us deeper into my room, laying me down onto the bed without breaking our kiss. His kisses pepper against my skin, across my cheek and down my neck as his hands work on the button of my jeans quickly. When he opens them, he slips a hand inside, pausing almost instantly.

"Where are your panties, baby?"

I freeze at that, guilt instantly consuming me. Do I have anything to feel guilty about? Absolutely not. Do I still feel it, because I've kissed two men within twenty minutes of each other? Most definitely.

When I don't answer, he frowns. "Where were you tonight?"

I wet my lips, doing my best to keep the guilt out of my tone. I didn't do anything wrong, though the look on Ronan's face is singing an entirely different tune.

"With Liam."

His frown morphs into an entire scowl.

"You were out with him, until one in the morning? And you came home with no panties?" he scoffs, like he can't believe what he's hearing.

"You don't get to speak to me this way," I snap. "For all I knew, you were sunk inside Anika Wilson every day since I'd seen you two. We weren't together. Don't try to shame me for trying to move on, when you practically broke my heart."

The anger in his eyes is still there, but he takes several deep breaths before speaking.

"You let him touch you?"

"Yes," I answer.

"Did he fuck you?"

"No."

He nods, breaking eye contact for a moment as he asks his next question.

"Did you enjoy it?"

I hesitate, only briefly, before being completely honest.

"Yes."

His eyes close at that, something like resignation passing across his features, as he nods his head. He leans forward, pressing a kiss against my forehead that lasts for several seconds before he speaks against my skin.

"I'm sorry, baby. I didn't mean to get upset with you. We're together now, that's what matters."

I go to respond when he stands up. My brows furrow together as I watch him move towards the door.

"Where are you going?"

He turns to look at me, a soft, not convincing at all smile on his face.

"It's late, you need to get some rest. I'll come get you for breakfast in the morning, okay?"

It takes me a second to respond as I slowly nod.

"Okay."

A tight lipped smile is what I receive in return before he opens the door.

"Sweet dreams, baby."

With that, he's gone, and I'm left feeling worse than before. Maybe I should have lied and told him I didn't enjoy it. That doesn't make me feel good either, though. I had a good time with Liam, a great one honestly, and I shouldn't have to apologize for that. Whatever, I'm sure Ronan just needs to go home and chill out. Things will be fine.

Chapter Twenty Two
Ronan

Things are not fine. Not fucking fine in the least. It's a good thing that Liam's dorm is all the way on the other side of campus from Skyla's, because two steps from the door I was ready to strangle the little fucker to death. Now, I'll just settle for beating him to a bloody pulp.

My fist beats against his door, practically rattling it off its hinges before I decide fuck it and use my master key. The door whirs open and I find Liam on his bed, cock in his hand and what I already know are Skyla's panties lifted up to his nose.

I. See. Red.

"Ronan? Get the fuck out. I—"

He can't even finish his sentence before I'm flying across the room and my fist is driving into his face. I get two good hits into him before his nose explodes, blood instantly gushing down his face as he shouts.

"What the fuck!"

Liam quickly stuffs his worthless cock back into his pants, like he's afraid I'm gonna rip it off.

Tempting.

He throws a few hits at me, but they don't deter me. I continue laying into him, attempting to land any shot I can but now that he's no longer thinking with his dick, he's hard to get a hold of. He wiggles out of my grasp and somehow manages to get my neck in a chokehold. My lungs are starved for air, but my anger fuels me as I fight and struggle against him.

"Ronan, man. Calm the fuck down! Calm down!" he snarls.

I want to seethe. I shouldn't have to calm the fuck down, but my vision is beginning to spot and the room is starting to spin. I feel my body give up long before my mind is willing to. Unfortunately, I have no choice. I go limp in his hold, and he drops me instantly, allowing me to crash to the floor as I greedily take in breath after breath.

"What the fuck was that about?" he snaps, lifting his shirt up and over his head, before using it as a makeshift rag to stop his nose from bleeding.

"Heard you touched my girl. Finger fucked her did you?"

He doesn't smirk like I expect him to, doesn't laugh or rub it in like he normally would. Instead, he almost seems pissed off, and not just because I interrupted his play time and blew up his nose.

"Your girl? Don't you mean your nephew's?" he scoffs.

"Or your best friend's. However you want to call it," I throw back.

Liam raises his eyebrows, like he can't argue with that, but he doesn't respond.

"Stay away from her, Liam. This is your only fucking warning," I say, as I push myself to my feet. I'm impressed I don't stumble a step as I head for the door.

"No," he says from behind me.

I stop on a dime, spinning to face him as I cock my head to the side.

"Excuse me? This wasn't a yes or no option. You either stay the fuck away from her, or I kill you. Simple as that."

The little shit just shakes his head, his own pissed off expression splashed across his face.

"I'm not going to stay away from her, not unless she asks me to. She's special. I like her."

Rage ignites inside me once more, as I close the distance between us, coming up until our foreheads are practically smashed together.

"Of course she's special. She's my fucking girlfriend."

"And Asher's fiancée," Liam challenges.

I narrow my eyes at him.

"What the fuck are you trying to say?"

"I'm saying, in this world, our world, labels don't mean shit. You don't give a fuck about sneaking around with your nephew's fianceé behind his back, so why the fuck should I care about openly pursuing your girlfriend," he says, air quoting girlfriend in a way that personally fucking offends me.

"And by openly you mean, for one hour before you'll be buried in the Gallows Hill cemetery?"

"That's the one," he agrees easily, as if we weren't casually speaking about his impending murder.

"What the fuck are you playing at? She isn't one of your whores that you can play with and toss to the side."

"I know."

"Then what the fuck do you want with her?" I ask, fisting his shirt in my hands as I shake him.

"The same thing you do," he says simply. "This life we were born into is hard, all innocence, kindness and compassion was practically beaten out of us from birth. Not her though. She's like a goddamn unicorn in our world, and everywhere around us there are people ready to slaughter her. I won't let that happen."

My breathing is ragged and uneven, but I don't speak as I mull over his words.

"So, what? You're telling me you don't want her for yourself? You just want her wellbeing?" I ask.

"Oh fuck no. I want her all to myself. If I thought I could get away with it, she'd already be in my car, and we'd be hundreds of miles away by morning. Unfortunately, that isn't the reality we exist in. So, I'll settle for stealing kisses when no one is looking and protecting her every time she turns her back."

"You won't be stealing shit from her!" I seethe.

He nods. "You're right, because she would willingly give them to me."

That signature goading smirk is back, and *fuck* I want to beat his ass. Again. Dumb motherfucker. It's like he wants to get the shit kicked out of him.

Before I can tear into him anymore, the door is thrown open, and a stumbling Asher barrels his way inside. He snickers to himself, before crashing onto Liam's king sized bed and rolling onto his back. Bright red lipstick is smeared across his lips and down his neck. It's an orangey red that looks like it should only belong to strippers or prostitutes, not a daughter of the Brethren, whichever one Asher was with tonight.

"Dids youz have fun with *my* virgin cunt?" Asher cackles, slurring so heavily we can barely understand him.

Liam doesn't respond as Asher continues.

"Fuckk you, man. That's was my cunt, my only reward for this shits life iz given," he grumbles as his head moves to the side.

"I didn't fuck her," Liam says evenly, while I watch my nephew in disappointment and a little bit of sadness.

Those bloodshot brown eyes come to Liam, surprise is about the only emotion he's probably able to display right now.

"No shits? Youz never don't fuck bitches when you go outs."

"It's not like that, man. She was just trying to piss you off and you know how I like to rile you up," Liam downplays, lamely.

"Pfttt, tell her I don't gives a fuck. You coulda fucked her for alls I care."

Liam and I share a *yeah fucking right* look, before we both move over to him. We wrap Asher's arms around either of our shoulders before lifting him to stand, steadily walking him out of Liam's room and across the hall to his own.

Asher continues to mutter some incoherent shit as we get him into his room, rolling him onto his stomach so he doesn't fucking choke on his own vomit. When he's as good as a blacked out drunk person can be, we both make our way out of his room pausing in the hallway as we look at each other.

"You lied," I say simply.

I don't need to specify what he lied about, he knows and there are too many prying ears. Too many bugs in the halls, feral for any amount of information they could get on any of us. It's hard enough keeping up on the sweeps around Skyla's dorm and my own place. Hopefully Liam and Asher do their bug checks regularly like I taught them, otherwise we both won't live to spend another day with her.

"He doesn't need to know," he shrugs.

"Why not?" I challenge.

Liam gives a disappointed smile as he shakes his head.

"Because no matter what happens, the outcome will remain the same."

His words are like a punch to the gut. I don't want to believe him, but fuck, he's got a point. No matter what I feel for Skyla, or her for me, the likelihood that I will have to sit back and watch her marry Asher is strong. Now, the chance of her having to watch me marry Annie could be just as likely, and somehow that's worse. I can bury my feelings, be brave for the both of us, but if I have to marry another woman while she sits in the front row, her heart hurting on full display for me? Nah, that will fuck me up.

"Just...keep her safe when I can't. Okay?" I ask, sharing a look with him as I dare not to look around the hall and raise suspicion.

Liam nods and I turn on my heel heading for the door. The only good thing that came out of this night is that Skyla is talking to me again. That we are together again, and this time, I'm not letting her go. Not until she's pried from my cold severed fingers.

Chapter Twenty Three
Skyla

I'm walking to my Introduction to Business class the next day. My new favorite morning drink is firmly in my hand when a pair of arms grab me, pulling me into a supply closet. Apple cider splashes across my arm before I lose my grip on it entirely, watching as it spills on the floor.

I look up to see how huge this closet is. It's bigger than you'd expect a closet to be, much like everything at this university, but it's still only about six feet deep and four feet wide. There are shelves of cleaning supplies and maintenance tools as well as Liam and Ronan.

Liam unwinds his arms from around my waist before pressing a chaste kiss against my lips. For half a second, I lean into the gesture before I remember where we are, who is in front of us and everything that came with last night. Ripping myself away from him, my eyes come up to Ronan, waiting for his anger or chastising. Instead, he is stoic, his watchful eyes on the two of us.

"What's going on?" I ask softly, as my eyes bounce between the two of them.

I look up at Ronan to see some red marks around his neck.

"Oh my god! What happened?"

"You like him," Ronan says stiffly, dodging my question completely.

It doesn't sound like a question, though I'm not sure it's a statement either. Maybe a verification of sorts? Maybe it is his way of asking, but he's so damn direct it's hard to tell.

"I—"

The words die on my tongue. To be honest, Liam is kind of obnoxious, and half the time he's practically Asher's little lap dog. He's slept with half the population of this university, and I'm not so sure that would stop just because I confessed that I may have felt a spark there last night. Liam seems to be able to understand my hesitancy as he gains my attention.

"I like you, babygirl. I want more nights like last night, I want your days too. I want you."

A rush of butterflies take flight inside me as his light green eyes latch onto mine, not letting me go for seemingly anything.

"What about Asher?" I find myself asking.

Liam's smile doesn't budge, even for a second as he lifts a hand up, his thumb brushing against the outline of my mouth.

"What about him? If he's not going to recognize what a perfect diamond was laid before his feet, I'm certainly not going to pass it up. You deserve to be taken care of, treasured. He's so unworthy of you, it's unreal. I just hope that my dumbass hasn't earned the same fate," he says, with a slight crook of his head. As if he were testing the waters with that last part.

My eyes come to Ronan, who apparently hasn't looked away since I was pulled into this closet. My eyes are asking him a million questions and thankfully, he speaks.

"It's okay, if you want to be with him. It would be easier, at least for the time being."

I frown at that, taking a step away from Liam until I'm pressed against Ronan. I have to look up to maintain eye contact as I shake my head.

"I want you, Ronan. I...we..."

I'm tongue tied, and amazed at how I got myself into this situation in the first place.

"What if you didn't have to choose?" Liam says.

"What?" I ask, turning to face him fully.

He takes a step closer, pinning me in against Ronan's chest while he plasters himself against my front.

"What if we didn't make you choose? What if you could be with both of us?"

I blink at him, waiting for this jester to deliver the punchline. It doesn't seem to come, though. Instead, he's watching me with rapt attention as Ronan's hand comes to my hip, squeezing gently.

"I...what?" I ask breathlessly.

They can't be serious....can they?"

"Things are...messy right now," Ronan continues. "I can't be with you the way I want to, the way you deserve. Though, you would still need a level of...discretion with Liam since you are engaged. He can be with you in a lot of ways and places that I can't."

I frown at that as I look up at him.

"So, what? He's going to keep me warm for you? Am I just a plaything that you want to keep satisfied, while you handle Amber whatever while I—"

I don't get to finish my sentence. Ronan's lips are pressed against my own in an instant, and all irritation, confliction and sadness die right then and there. His hold on my hip tightens to the point of near pain, but I'd never ask him to stop. His tongue strokes against my own briefly before he pulls away, resting his forehead against mine as he speaks just above a whisper.

"You're everything, Skyla. Absolutely fucking everything. No one matters to me more than you, do you understand me?"

My stomach flips at the sincerity in his words. Surely he can't actually mean that, right? We've only known each other for about a month. There is no way feelings can develop that quickly. But...

"It took Liam three hours of begging this morning for me to even semi agree to this. You think I want to share my girl? That I like the thought of his hands, his lips, on you? Fuck. No."

I shake my head. "Then, why even offer?"

His eyes cut away from mine to meet Liam's before coming back to me.

"Because he made some excellent points and if I'm honest, I've never seen the kid work so hard for anything in his life. He wants you, almost as much as I do and that's saying a lot. If he is willing to risk severe bodily harm, again," he says, as he gestures to the bruising on Liam's face and his nose that look a little swollen now that I stare at it. "By coming to me with this and knowing you want him too... he's the only man that would be barely worthy of you."

"Apart from you, of course," I fill in.

He gives me a barely there smile and shrugs.

"I'm not so sure I'm even there."

I roll my eyes at his dramatics and slip my hand behind his neck, pulling him down to my lips before speaking against him.

"You're more than there, Ronan."

His stoic mask cracks at the seams, and a small soft smile shines through.

"So, what do you say babygirl?" Liam asks, his voice honey smooth, though I can sense a hint of impatience beneath it. As if he were anxious. It's kind of cute.

Looking between them I shake my head.

"How would this work?"

"Well, we haven't exactly written out a visitation schedule," Liam teases.

I scoff and smack his arm as he chuckles and Ronan intervenes.

"We can take it day by day, and if you ever feel overwhelmed or don't want to be with one or even both of us, open communication. You call the shots here, baby."

"What if you guys want to be done? If you don't want to be with me or—"

"Not gonna happen," they say in unison.

I can't stop the smile that spreads across my face at their unwavering insistence. Could I really date two men at the same time? To make matters worse, while I'm technically engaged? To make it even worse, when one of those men is my fiancé's best friend while the other is his uncle...Yeah, I don't see that blowing up in any of our faces in the future.

Still, I'm not a stupid woman. What they are offering me here is many women's dream. Mine especially, because I like both of them for very different reasons.

"Okay," I say.

"Yeah?" Liam asks, his eagerness bleeding through immediately.

I smile at him, and he practically pounces on me. His mouth on mine, tongue tangling with my own as Ronan makes a sound in the back of his throat before clearing it.

"I have a meeting with the Headmaster. You keep her safe or I'll fucking gut you," Ronan says, though his words don't hold that much heat. Maybe it's because he trusts Liam with me, or maybe it's because he's not that worried and is trying to flex his authoritative muscle. Either way, it's sexy as hell to hear a man demand your safety like that. Though, I've gotta wonder, what is he supposed to be protecting me from? Asher?

Likely.

Liam pulls away from me, giving Ronan a mock salute that has him rolling his eyes before he pulls me in for a kiss. When he releases my hip and backs away, he slips past us as he turns to Liam once more.

"Be discreet, please. Make sure there are no...prying eyes."

"Ronan, I've got this," Liam says, as he loops an arm around my waist.

Ronan's face tenses slightly, almost in displeasure before he gives a terse nod and slips out of the closet, shutting the door behind him.

"So, now that the grown up is gone. You sure you're in, babygirl? You seem hesitant."

I turn my head slightly as I try to verbalize the array of emotions racing through me.

"I just...I like you. I didn't expect to when I said yes to our date, trust me," I laugh lightly before smiling. "You're different than you portray. There is more to you than you let on, and I'd like to get to know that Liam more, but I also really care for Ronan and—"

"Say less, babygirl. I'd love to show you the real me. This world...sometimes you have to hide pieces of yourself, for preservation and survival."

I nod, understanding that if everyone in this town is like my father, then it makes complete sense.

"However I will say, your fiancé will kick my front teeth in when he finds out about us."

I laugh at his words as I tilt my head back.

"Didn't Ronan just say that we need to keep a low profile? Away from prying eyes?" I remind.

"Of course, but he wasn't talking about Asher."

"Who was he talking about then?"

He doesn't respond at first, then he simply shrugs and gives me that signature smile that sends my heart racing as he cups the back of my head and pulls me in.

"Who cares," he says, before crashing his lips against me.

Something feels different in this kiss than before. There is so much need, so much unquenched desire. Suddenly his hands are everywhere, setting my body on fire with every inch he touches.

I feel his hands come to the hem of my skirt before bunching it up around my hips. It's a warmer day today so I skipped the stockings, and god I couldn't be more grateful when Liam is able to easily slide down my panties before dropping to his knees.

"Fuck, have I told you how pretty your pussy is, babygirl?"

I make a strangled noise in my throat because honestly, how does he expect me to think, let alone speak when his mouth is inches from me?

Before I can even try to formulate a response his tongue is out, flattening against my slit before running it through me in one long delicious lick that has me shuddering. He repeats the move again and again, his eyes on me the entire time. I feel one of his hands come to my left thigh, before lifting it up and out, resting it over his shoulder to allow him better access.

God, does he make use of that access too. Liam begins devouring me like he was a starved man, and I was a feast he couldn't resist. His tongue expertly twirls around my clit, licking me from top to bottom, until I'm a writhing panting mess.

I lean my back against the wall to help stabilize me, because my legs are all but gelatin at this point, but he seems to have a better idea. Once my back is against the wall, Liam takes my right leg, lifting it up and resting it against his other shoulder. I almost lose my balance until his large hands come to my waist, holding me perfectly in place as he slowly begins to stand.

There is something to be said about a man that can pick you up. There is something entirely different about a man that can lift you into the air while your thighs are wrapped around his shoulders, and his face buried in your pussy.

He doesn't skip a beat. Rising to his full height before he presses me all the way against the wall, his tongue stroking and licking me as his hands hold me in place. I bury my fingers into his blond, almost wavy hair. At first, I think I do it to balance myself but really, it's so that I can grind myself against him better because I'm so close to my release I can practically taste it.

Liam must be able to tell too because he moans against me, vibrating my clit just enough to throw me right over the edge. I come hard and the first moan that comes out of me is so loud, I have to release his hair and slap my hand over my mouth so that no one thinks a person is being murdered in here. I feel wave after wave of my orgasm hit me, and Liam doesn't stop eating me until he's licked every inch of me clean.

Once the euphoric typhoon subsides, he slowly lowers himself back down to his knees allowing my feet to hit the ground before he stands up again, once again pocketing my panties as he does. His hands reach out, pulling down my skirt and even smoothing a few lines out as he does before he gives me that dopey smile that I love.

He runs a hand through his now messy hair, before opening the closet door and letting me step out first. He follows closely behind me, wrapping his arms around me as he whispers into my ear.

"Thank you, babygirl. I almost skipped breakfast. Most important meal of the day!"

I scoff, shoving him away before he reels me back in. He presses a kiss to my nose and then to my cheek before burying his face into my neck, making a growling sound that has me squealing. When he finally lets up, we are both laughing and smiling like a couple of fools. A light feeling wrapping us up into a perfect cocoon. At least for two-point-five seconds before a pair of dark brown eyes catch my attention.

He's standing there glaring at us with a woman on each arm but honestly, he's not paying them any attention. Honestly, he's not paying any attention to me either. Instead, his eyes are set firmly on his best friend. Liam doesn't shy away from his glare either. Rather, he returns it with a goading edge.

For a moment I wonder if the only reason Liam is interested in me at all is just to get under Asher's skin. That thought disappears in the next moment though when Liam wraps his arm around my shoulder, casually letting it drape around me as he presses a kiss to the side of my head and begins guiding me towards the class that I'm already late for.

Asher all but stomps off in the opposite direction, his groupies quickly in tow as he leaves them in the dust. We don't pay them any attention, though. I'm happy, we're happy, at least I think so and for once, I won't be letting Asher fucking Putnam ruin that.

Chapter Twenty Four
Asher

I don't cause a scene in front of others. That would make me look weak, make it look like I care. Which I don't. At least not for the reasons people would assume. I don't give a fuck that someone has no doubt deflowered my promised virgin. If she's confirmed not to be a virgin before our wedding they will kill her on sight, and I'll be on to the next of whomever my father lines up for me.

No, I don't give a fuck what Skyla Parris does. What I give a fuck about, is that my own best friend, my fucking Bond Brother of all people would try to humiliate me like that.

He doesn't see me coming, which is really a fault to him. He's getting sloppy, he's barely cut out for this life as it is. The only thing holding him together and out of the Brethren's focus, is me. See if I save his fucking ass now.

I barrel into him through his opened bedroom door, before throwing him to the ground. He lands with a hard thud, and I waste no time delivering a punch straight to his temple. He grunts out in pain, his eyes blinking like he's in a daze from my hit before I give him another to the stomach.

Liam gains his bearings enough to understand that he's under attack, before he begins fighting back. His body begins to buck in an attempt to lift me off of him and he starts sending out his own defensive blows. A few of them land, and soon we are in easily the worst scrap of our lives with one another before he speaks in between punches.

"Asher! What the fuck. Use your words you fucking toddler."

I laugh maniacally at that, my eyes no doubt looking crazed, as I sneer down at him.

"Use my words? Okay. Despicable, deplorable, atrocious, piece of fucking shit friend!" I roar into his face.

He hits me in the jaw once, hard. I have no choice but to stumble off of him and he wastes no time scrambling out from underneath me. Liam jumps to his feet and crosses his room, waiting on the other side as he watches me carefully. I rub my hand against my jaw as I work it back and forth.

Not broken.

"Why does it make you so angry?" Liam asks.

I let out a bitter laugh as I look at him.

"You're serious?"

He shrugs, his face full of confusion.

"Yeah, actually. You hate her, you talk about the Brethren killing her literally all the time. What's the big deal if I date her? You don't think she'll live to your wedding anyways."

"Date?" I ask sharply. "You don't date anyone."

Liam pockets his hands into his jeans and shrugs again.

"She's pretty fucking amazing dude. You'd see that if you weren't so deep in your head."

"She's a piece of forbidden fruit. You've always wanted what you can't have and because of you, I could now face backlash. This isn't about you dating her, I don't give a fuck about that. I give a fuck when my dad will, no doubt, call me into his office and ask why my fiancée is seen fucking my bond brother!"

He rolls his eyes. "We've never fucked, nor would I ever fuck her. I'm not going to put her in danger like that."

Fury practically blinds me as I stare at him.

"Her? What about me motherfucker! You know what he's like, you know what he could do if he thinks I'm embarrassing the family, the Brethren. I've been your best friend for twenty one years and this is it? This is the treatment I receive?"

To my surprise, Liam doesn't immediately back down. He doesn't profusely apologize or promise to never see her again, which pisses me the fuck off. Instead, he stands a little taller, rolling his shoulders back as he speaks.

"There is a difference between loyalty and submission, Asher. I'm beginning to think you don't give a fuck about my loyalty, only my submission. It doesn't bother you that I like her. It bothers you that you've told me I'm not allowed to like her, and I date her anyways. It bothers you that I'm not your little bitch. That you can't say to jump, and I'll beg to suck your dick in thanks."

My eyebrows pull together, caught off guard from the heat of his words as he continues.

"I haven't gone along with you all these years because I thought you could do no wrong, or that you were the kind of god that you clearly think you are. I went along with you because I thought that's what friendship was about, supporting one another, even when we don't like what they're doing."

"Maybe I was wrong, and that's on me, but I'm going to cut the shit with you. I like her a lot, and I'm not the only one. You can hate her all you want. You can hate me all you want, but don't you dare act like me, choosing my happiness for once has anything to do with betrayal."

I mull over his words, unsure what to say or how to respond, when a piece of his words stand out to me.

"Who else?"

"What?" he asks.

"You said you're not the only one. Is she seeing others? You is bad enough, but if she's out there slutting it up—"

"Watch your fucking mouth," Liam practically snarls, a sound I don't think I've ever heard come from him before.

He closes the distance between us, nose to nose as he lowers his voice to a deathly low sound.

"One more word about her, and I'll break your goddamn jaw this time. I mean it. The shit talking is over. You want to bitch, you do it elsewhere. I'm not going to stand here and let you talk about my girl like that."

"Your girl?" I scoff.

"That's right. My. Fucking. Girl," he doubles down, the lethality in his tone is so unlike him it makes my head spin.

I stand there speechless for several seconds, unable to process this fucked up situation. Saved or burned by the bell, however you want to look at it, my phone begins ringing. I fish it out of my pocket and check the ID before cursing under my breath. I answer it as I keep my eyes on Liam.

"Hello, Father."

I expect concern or unease to flash in Liam's eyes, but they hold steady, unyielding and looking straight pissed off.

"You and your fiancée's presence is required at the manor. Wednesday, seven o'clock."

To my surprise, that's all he has to say before the call ends. Maybe Liam's debauchery with my fiancée hasn't made it to my father's ears yet. Though, it's only a matter of time.

"Looks like I'm taking *your* girl out Wednesday night. A nice little cozy dinner at the manor. Can't wait to see what we will talk about," I say, as I turn on my heel and storm out of his room, barreling into mine before slamming the door shut behind me.

Chapter Twenty Five
Skyla

Ronan had texted me a little after leaving me and Liam, to tell me he wouldn't be able to see me tonight despite us trying to make plans. He said something came up that he couldn't get out of and that he hoped Liam and I had a good night together.

This is weird, right? It's only been about twelve hours, but my brain is struggling to comprehend such a foreign concept. I'm dating two men...at the same time...and they know about it...and are at least, moderately okay with it? I swear I'm not complaining, I'm living millions of women's dreams, it's just unfamiliar territory. Despite not knowing how long it will last, I'm going to enjoy every second of it for now.

Liam took me to dinner at an amazing little sushi restaurant across town before he said he had to get home. He told me Asher was no doubt waiting for him so that he could throw his fit about us being together. I told Liam he shouldn't bother entertaining his temper tantrum, but he told me it was more complicated than that as he peppered my face with kisses and ate my pussy before he walked me to my door.

Such a gentleman.

I wave my keycard over my door, and it clicks open with ease, however as soon as I step inside the room something immediately feels off. I can't put my finger on it, it's just...different.

"Hello?" I call out stupidly. Even if someone was in here, do I really think they would shout out, 'yeah, it's just me!'.

My eyes dance around my room before pausing on my bed. The comforter is rumpled and there are a pair of my panties in the middle of the bed, as well as a piece of paper. I swallow shakily, taking slow steps towards my bed, before I pick up the paper.

To my light,
You shine so bright, like the sun on a summer's day
Your creamy colored skin aching to be touched
Your delicate sensitive soul longing to be held
I'll care for you and love you deeper than anyone could
Just open your eyes my light, shine on me

A chill runs down my spine as goosebumps scatter across my arms. My eyes flick down to see a pair of panties that I know for a fact were in my laundry hamper. I put them in there this morning when I got ready. Lifting them up slowly, I notice that the majority of them are wet. Only one guess as to what the liquid is.

Revulsion, embarrassment and terror all rage through me simultaneously. This is getting fucking ridiculous. A few little notes and gifts were easy enough to explain away before but this? This is too far. It can't be Asher. He would be too proud of something like this, much like he was with the pillow incident. He'd have signed his name on the letter, that is if he was the kind of man that would write poetry, even ironically so. No, this is definitely not Asher.

My mind races with potential suspects, before one person in particular comes to mind.

Son of a bitch.

I grab the only dry end of my white panties before I storm back out the door and into the elevator. It doesn't take me long to get to the pool and once I do, my target is right where I'd expect him to be.

I burst through the doors, coming up to the side of the pool as Vincent passes by, finishing his lap. I, however, don't have the patience to wait for him to finish. I ball the panties up, throwing them directly at his head. It's not like it hurts, though I wish it would. It is enough to grab his attention.

His head pops up out of water, his black hair soaked and wild without a swim cap on as he rips his goggles off his head and reaches for my panties that are now floating away from him in the water.

"What the fuck?" he practically snarls. "Why the hell are you throwing your panties at me?"

"Oh, I figured you'd want them back. You were so well acquainted with them, why don't you just fucking keep them!" I shout.

His face screws up as he looks at me.

"What the fuck are you talking about?"

"I'm talking about you! You fucking pervert. It's so obvious, it has to be you. You're everywhere I turn, watching me, and I'm fucking sick of it! Stop with the creepy love notes, stop with the gifts and if you ever break into my room again I will have your ass locked up so fast it will make your head spin!" I seethe.

He stares at me for several seconds before he pushes himself out of the pool, dripping wet panties in hand as he looks down at them before up to me.

"Show me."

"What? No. Didn't you just hear me?" I scoff. "Stay the fuck away from me. I don't know what you—"

I'm silenced almost immediately when he drops his goggles and the panties to the floor, his dripping wet hands cupping either side of my cheeks as those piercing silver eyes stab straight through me.

"Siren, whatever is going on, it wasn't me. I'm always watching you because I don't know how not to, but do you really think I'm the type to send you love notes and gifts?"

I open my mouth, ready to spit that I absolutely think he would, when I pause. When he puts it like that, I'm not as confident. I don't know if he's just trying to manipulate me. Something about the raw honesty in his tone, the fierceness in his silver bullet eyes and the way he's holding me so tenderly, as if I were a piece of glass about to shatter apart at any moment, has me believing him.

A million thoughts race through my mind as I look up at him, unsure how to proceed when a useless piece of information sticks out to me above all else.

"What do you mean you don't know how not to watch me?"

He blinks several times, that emotionless face giving absolutely nothing away as he speaks again, his voice low and gravelly.

"Show me your room."

I watch him hesitantly, not sure what to do or say. I was so sure if it wasn't Asher, it had to be him. Unless he's the world's most convincing liar though, which is possible I suppose. It's not him.

Despite the little voice in my head screaming to run far from this man, I slowly nod, turning to walk back towards the door. I hear some rustling sounds and when I turn back, Vincent has a pair of sweats pulled on as well as a Black Sabbath t-shirt and a pair of slides. His hair is still dripping wet as he packs his goggles back into his bag before lifting my panties up. He inspects them carefully as if there was something to inspect before he slips them into his pocket and throws his bag over his shoulder.

I lead the way out of the building and into the crisp night air. I'd feel cold if it wasn't for the 6'4 shadow that has practically attached itself to me. Vincent walks so closely, it's as if he's attempting to wrap himself around every inch of me without touching. I'd never admit it, but it makes me feel safe. If it really isn't him who has been breaking in, he's ready to protect me should they jump out of the bushes or something. God, would you listen to me? I'm losing it.

When we step into the elevator together, his presence practically swallows the small space whole, leaving no room to think or even breathe. I'm extremely aware of how close Vincent is to me.

The scent of him is overwhelming, the strong smell of chlorine that is like my own personal aromatherapy combined with something muskier that has to be entirely him. I'm not sure I've ever been this close to him, for this long, to notice. He smells amazing though.

As soon as the elevator doors open, I step out, needing a little bit of distance between us as I shake my head and open my door. I'm about to step inside my room when Vincent steps around me, gently pushing me behind him as he does. His eyes scan the room from top to bottom before he takes a step inside.

He moves deeper into my room, heading for the bathroom. He looks inside the glass shower and behind the door before heading to my closet where he looks behind the door, through the racks of clothes and even on the ground. I didn't think about checking out the room more. Is it possible that there could have been someone in my room when I came in? That they hadn't left yet? The very thought rolls my stomach.

"Explain everything to me in detail," Vincent says, as he turns to face me.

I nod, starting from my first day here. I explained the notes and the gifts as best as I could. He asked if I still had anything, but apart from the letter on the bed, I had thrown them all away. He looked so disheartened by that and I won't lie, it kind of stung. Being a disappointment is very obviously a trigger of mine.

I watch as he steps over to my bed, his eyes calculated as they roam over the rumpled comforter.

"And you're sure it wasn't one of your boyfriends?" he asks.

"What?" I nearly choke out.

He turns to look at me over his shoulder.

"Coach? Walcott? No?"

"They aren't my," I begin to say. "How did you…"

"You're not subtle, Siren. You wear your emotions clear as day. You should work on that, it's a dangerous habit."

My stomach clenches as I swallow roughly and nod.

"It wasn't them, they wouldn't…what do I do?" I ask, hating how much my voice shakes.

"Be on alert, keep your eye out for absolutely anything that could clue you in to whoever this is," he says as he turns to face me. "They seem to be infatuated with you which is good."

I let out a hollow laugh as I shake my head.

"I have a stalker, how is that good?"

His eyes look straight at mine, nearly sucking the breath out of my lungs as he speaks.

"It's better than them being violent."

Oh god, I can't handle this. Maybe I should call my dad. Not sure what he could, or even would be willing to do, but this is his school. I haven't done anything wrong. It's not like it's my fault some creep has become interested in me.

"Why does part of me wish it just would have been you?" I groan, running a hand through my hair as I do.

He takes a step closer to me, his eyes never wavering from mine as his chest brushes against me.

"You don't, trust me. Once I set my sights on something, I'll stop at nothing to have it. You couldn't handle what all that would entail, Siren."

I feel my pulse quickening under his stare and I'm not sure if it's out of fear or anticipation. I couldn't tell you what I'm anticipating. I suppose that's the point. I have no idea what to expect from him. Yesterday I thought he hated me on a cellular level for zero reason, an hour ago I thought that he was stalking me and now...I'm not sure what to think about Vincent Griggs.

Chapter Twenty Six
Vincent

Her silky blonde hair falls at her sides as she runs her fingers through it. She's walking through the courtyard with Bartlett as always. They are discussing something that forces my Siren to toss her head back and laugh, that melodic sound running through my entire body. As usual, I'm ten steps behind her and even more usual, she has no idea.

I don't know what it was about her that caught my eye. It could have been those wildly bright green eyes, her porcelain doll-like face or her curves that make me want to sink my teeth into every single inch of her. Or it could be something deeper, more poetic, like my soul recognizing hers and demanding I claim her.

It wasn't an accident that I happened to stumble upon her in the cemetery, when Putnam pushed her into that hole. I overheard her promising Walcott that she would go to the bonfire, so I followed them to the party. I paid even closer attention to her when Bartlett fucked off to get laid, leaving her vulnerable and for the taking.

Of course, I had to follow her when I saw where she was being led. When I watched Putnam lay his hands on her, I wanted to gut him right then and there, bury him right beside all the scorned bodies rotting in the earth beneath our feet. I didn't though, I sat back, and I watched. Observed.

I watched on as she screamed and begged. I saw how, for a moment, Walcott almost defied his future leader before heeling like the good little bitch he is. I studied how she panicked and fought, trying everything she could think of. I'll be honest, I was disappointed she gave up so quickly. I thought she had more of a fighting spirit. Then again, my Siren doesn't belong on land, she belongs in the water, right alongside me.

Meeting her came at an unexpected time, and I've all but abandoned my prior goals and duties, even to the Brethren, to keep my eyes on her. Hence, why this stalker situation is so frustrating.

I can't blame her for assuming that I was the one stalking her, in her defense, I am. Just not in the noticeable way that makes her afraid and fearful of her safety, which she should be. From what she has told me, I anticipate their efforts will only increase. Which means I don't have long to figure out who it is and eliminate them from the equation. Hopefully I can utilize the skills the Brethren so graciously gifted me, to finish the task as quickly and efficiently as possible.

It's already been a week since the dead man walking broke into my Siren's room and violated her privacy. One week, since he officially signed his death certificate and one week of me going down the list to figure out who the fuck it is. I have a few leads to look into this afternoon, a few guys from the football team that were discussing her in the locker room the other day. It could be nothing, but it could be everything and there is only one way for me to find out.

For a moment, I'm so wrapped up in my thoughts that I almost miss him. Almost miss when a hand darts out from the wall of thick boxwood bushes and latches onto her arm, dragging her into the covered hide away. My steps quicken and I'm about to reach for my gun tucked in the back of my pants when my footsteps freeze, and a familiar voice hits my ears.

"I missed you, baby," Coach Ronan says, followed by the sound of kissing.

My lip curls up at that, anger pulsing through my body at the thought of him touching her, kissing her. Doesn't everyone understand that she is clearly mine? She's not ready for me yet but she will be, soon, and when she is, I'll hack off every limb belonging to anyone that's ever touched her.

Stepping away, I find a causal spot to the side of the bushes to lean against the wall, pulling out a cigarette and lighting it between my lips while I listen.

"What are you doing tonight?" he asks.

"Nothing, why?" my Siren responds.

"I want to spend some time with you, away from here. Do you want to come to my place tonight?"

"Oh, sure. Of course! When?"

"Now," he says, before their feet shuffle slightly.

"Is it safe? You know, you said we had to be careful when we're seen together and—"

"Why do you think we're talking in the bushes, baby?" he chuckles softly, a giggle coming from her that has my eyes rolling.

"I've taken care of everything. It's safe. Meet me in the south parking lot in ten minutes, yeah?"

"Okay," she says, a soft mewling sound escaping her that I can only assume is from him kissing what's mine. Again.

I take another drag, allowing the nicotine to fill my lungs before breathing out the puff of smoke. In the next moment, Ronan emerges, casually walking towards the staff parking lot as if he wasn't pulling students into the bushes to plan a secret rendezvous. I knew leaving a tip for the headmaster, that Coach Ronan wasn't behaving appropriately with some intended students wouldn't do much. He's a Putnam after all, but I figured it would make him be a little more discreet, so I didn't have to see him blatantly touch her in broad daylight. Seems to have worked, after their little chat the other day.

Ronan is an idiot. I don't give a fuck how bad he wants her, how bad he craves her. Every time he touches her, looks at her for too long or makes plans to take her off campus, he puts her life in danger. Either he doesn't give a fuck about her life or he's just reckless with it. Either way, he's a danger to her and a threat to me.

Wanting her is not an excuse. If it was, I'd have taken her for myself the very first night, Asher Putnam be damned. I would have placed a bullet right between the piece of shit's eyes the first day he spoke disrespectfully to her, and whisked her away where even the Brethren could never find us. Fortunately for her, and him I suppose, I have more self-control than that. I know better than to give in to my desires, my cravings and I do a fine fucking job of putting on a show.

For all my Siren knows, I practically despise her. She no doubt assumes that I couldn't care less about her or her wellbeing. As if I wasn't ready to burn the world around us to a crisp, so she wouldn't be burdened with having to deal with another living person apart from me. As if I'm not prepared to beat, gut and kill anyone who breathes in her direction. I've already made a list and believe me, when the moment is right I'll begin working down that list. Starting with Asher fucking Putnam.

My phone buzzes in my pocket as my Siren emerges from the bushes, brushing her hair down so it doesn't look like her fiancé's uncle was just mauling her on the other side of this foliage. I let her get far enough ahead of me before I pull it out, a sour feeling settling in my stomach when I read the message.

Unknown: 1247 Carey Dr Cambridge, MA. 51(M). Self-care.

The messages come from burner phones to burner phones. I get a new one each week and it's never been clear to me which members send out the requests. I only know who sanctions them, and of course he's the same son of a bitch who sanctions everything in this wicked fucking world we're trapped in.

When the messages come through, they are intended to be vague for obvious reasons. An address, age and identified gender along with the task. Some of the tasks are as simple as a little rough up, what they code as playtime. Others are, a quick in and out kill, like 'one and done'. Then, there are more detailed requests like this one. It's not enough for me to take care of them, I have to make it look like a suicide, which honestly isn't as hard as it sounds.

Most of the Legacies haven't assumed their position yet. That part usually comes after graduation. Due to the lack of eliminators we currently have though, I was inducted early. I still am kept in the dark about most things, just like the other Legacies and I don't have my ring or privileges yet as an official Elder. Yet, I'm still required to perform the duties of such.

Similar to rushing into a fraternity, before you can join, you must prove your dedication and worthiness. So far I've yet to disappoint, and will continue that way until it suits me otherwise.

Looks like I'll have a late night tonight. I don't like knowing that Skyla will be away from campus for an extended period without me there to keep an eye on her. Ronan better keep her from harm, or I'll be disposing of two bodies tonight.

Chapter Twenty Seven
Skyla

Ronan's large hand cups my knee as he easily maneuvers us through the streets of Salem. There is a nervousness inside me, that I couldn't put into words if I tried. He's never taken me to his house before. This is the first time we will be spending an extended period of time away from...well, everything.

I've thought about this moment, thousands of times through my life and hundreds since meeting Ronan, but the fact that it's finally here? My anxiety is currently running wild.

Turning to face him, I smile, which he returns with a swoony one of his own. I have nothing to be nervous about. If there was anyone I was going to give my virginity to, I'd want it to be him. He's so kind and gentle with me. I know I'm in good hands and even more so, I want him to have it.

I have no doubt Liam will be upset that he wasn't the one, but things with us are new. They don't feel like they are in the same place as me and Ronan. That's not a bad thing either. New is fun and exciting. New is...different.

A notification from my phone pulls me out of my thoughts as I grab my phone and glance at the screen. Irritation instantly rises in me as I see who it is.

Asshole Fiancé: Dinner at my father's house tomorrow. Be ready by six. Wear something he will like.

Oh, fucking great.

I must make a displeased noise, because Ronan's brows furrow as he looks at me.

"What's wrong?"

I wave my phone at him and grimace.

"Looks like I'm having dinner with Asher and your brother tomorrow night."

Instantly, he tenses. His hand on the wheel becomes stiff, and the hand that is cupping my knee tightens. I understand feeling on edge about Christopher, but Ronan is his brother. Surely, he can't feel the same level of intimidation that I do, or even that Asher clearly does but won't admit.

"Did he say why?" Ronan asks carefully.

"No, why?"

He presses his lips together in a firm line and doesn't speak for a few moments.

"I'll see if I can attend, don't worry."

I frown at that.

"Why should I worry? Is there something that I should be worried about?"

His icy blue eyes find mine as we come up to a stop light.

"When it comes to my brother? Always."

A foreboding feeling settles low in my stomach. Well, great. I wasn't worried before, just irritated that I'd have to spend an entire evening with Asher. Now I'm really worried as to what the night could be about.

"Do you think he knows? About you and me? Or me and Liam? Or, well, both?"

Ronan shakes his head immediately, giving me at least a semblance of relief.

"If he did, Liam and I would be rotting deep in the earth already."

My face pinches at that.

"But, you're his brother."

"And if he finds out I plan on desecrating a match made by the Brethren, he'll likely pull the trigger himself," Ronan finishes.

I'm quiet for several seconds before I speak.

"You plan on desecrating our match?"

Ronan turns into a long road, mansions on either side of us as we cruise to the very end.

"Yes."

"How?"

He lets out a heavy breath as we pull up to the house at the very end. A wrought iron gate swings open, allowing us inside before revealing a beautiful house. It's not over the top and pretentious like my father's home or Putnam manor. It's elegant, without being ostentatious. The large pillars encasing the front porch are black, and as my eyes skate over the entirety of the house I realize that the entire thing is black. Such a stark comparison to all the typical crisp white homes I've seen so far. It's beautiful in a gothic kind of way.

My admiration for the home is cut short, when he continues speaking.

"I don't fucking know," he says, with a shake of a head before leaning over and cupping my jaw with his hand.

"But I won't stop until I find a way. I can't stand back while you marry him. I refuse. The only person you'll be marrying in this lifetime is me, that's a fucking promise."

I can't help but smile into his hand.

"You want to marry me?"

"Fuck yes I do," he says, a smile of his own playing at his lips.

"Think we could get your brother to approve a slight substitu-tion? You're still a Putnam," I tease, though I'm really not teasing all that much.

His smile turns sad as his thumb runs over my lower lip.

"I wish, baby. We'll find a way around all of this, though. I promise."

I nod, believing he means every single word, before he pulls me in for a soft kiss. I try to deepen it, but he pulls away before I can.

"You ready?"

I smile and nod before he opens his door and makes his way around the car, getting my door for me.

"Thank you," I smile.

He looks over his shoulder, as if to make sure no one followed us, before he slips his arm around my shoulders and guides me towards the front door.

When we step inside, the foyer is large and pristine, though that same gothic theme carries on in here. Onyx marble floors carry throughout the house, accompanied by charcoal gray walls. Some-how, there is still warmth to the place. It shouldn't work, but it just...does.

Ronan moves into the kitchen, pulling me along with him before stopping at the island where a variety of ingredients are sprawled out.

"I didn't have enough time to call my cook in, but I did have some ingredients delivered. I figured I could make you dinner."

My eyes scan the ingredients before I smile.

"Spaghetti and meatballs?"

"One of your favorites," he confirms with a soft smirk. "And extra garlic bread, of course."

"Of course," I tease. "Can I help?"

His brows dip a little as he cocks his head to the side.

"Do you want to?"

I nod and he laughs before shrugging his shoulders.

"I'd love that."

Aunt Steph and I always made dinner together, okay not always. We always had our meals delivered or meal-prepped, but sometimes we made dinner together and when we did, it was always a good time.

Step by step, Ronan and I work in perfect unison as we make dinner. When I'm stirring the sauce, he cages me in from behind, wrapping his giant frame around me as I cook. Then, when he was bending over to put the bread into the oven, I obviously had to smack his biteable ass with a towel. To which, he chased me through the house and into the living room before pinning me to the couch and covering my face with kisses. The bread burned but neither of us cared.

Now that dinner is done and our dishes are clean, Ronan turns to me, leaning against the dishwasher. His sleeves are rolled up, showcasing his corded forearms and his dark hair is pushed to the side just enough to keep it out of his face.

"What do you think, baby? Want to watch a movie?"

Before I can stop myself, I blurt out my thoughts.

"Not really."

He looks a little surprised, but smiles at me regardless.

"Okay, what do you want to do?"

My mouth dries a little, as the nervousness from earlier creeps back in.

"I want..." I trail off for a moment, before attempting to appear a whole lot more confident than I feel suddenly. "I want to see your bedroom."

His eyes flash with surprise again, but a satisfied grin quickly covers the emotion as he prowls towards me like a hunter.

"Yeah?" he asks. "Whatever you want, baby."

Slipping my hand into his, he begins guiding me through the house and up the grand staircase. My heart is practically jack hammering out of my chest, which is stupid because I've never felt so sure about anything in my life. Honestly, I think it's just more about the idea of the moment finally being here. About it not living up to expectation. About it blowing all of my expectations out of the water, and the consequences of us never leaving these four walls again.

He leads us into a room on the top floor, pushing the door open and revealing a grand master bedroom. If I'm honest, I'm not the least bit interested in how his balcony overlooks the property or what I can see is a large en suite. I'm far more enamored by the way Ronan looks at me. The way he turns to me like a hungry predator before backing me up to the bed, forcing me to fall with a soft bounce.

His body covers mine before I even have a chance to breathe, as his mouth presses to mine. Our tongues battle in a fight for dominance, a fight I lose remarkably fast. His hands are everywhere, roaming up and down my body before his mouth moves across my face and down to my neck. I feel his cock harden as he begins grinding himself against me through our clothes.

"There is a condom in my purse," I gasp out, as he sucks on the sensitive flesh where my collarbone meets my neck. "It's downstairs. Or if you have any up here," I continue, before his entire body stills.

Slowly, he lifts himself up enough to make eye contact with me, his face practically devoid of all emotion.

"Come again?"

"A condom," I say on an exhale. "You know, protection? I mean, I guess it's not one hundred percent necessary. The school did force me to get the shot and an STD panel. I'm assuming the same happens for faculty so maybe—"

"We're not having sex tonight, baby," he says, cutting me off shortly.

All other words die on my tongue as I look at him, disappointment and confusion warring inside of me.

"Wait...why not? I thought..." I trail off, too humiliated to verbalize what I thought tonight was about.

"I asked you to come tonight because I wanted us to get some space from Gallows Hill, from the Brethren. I wanted to have a night of just you and me, where we didn't have to constantly look over our shoulders. You thought I brought you here for sex?"

"I don't know. I just...assumed. We've been seeing each other for a while and...I mean, don't you want to?"

He pushes up from me completely, sitting at the edge of the bed as he blows out a breath and runs his fingers through his hair. Ronan sits there for several seconds as I sit up, watching him closely until he finally seems to settle on a singular thought.

"I want to, of course. I want you in every earthly way possible, but I can't. We can't."

"But why?" I ask, the sting of rejection ebbing slightly, but not all the way.

His hand reaches up, gently brushing against my face as he speaks.

"If I can't find a way to get you out of this marriage to Asher, if I can't get my brother to reconsider...if you have to go through with everything, and they found out you weren't a virgin?"

Ronan literally shutters, as if whatever he is thinking is so horrible he can't even utter the words.

"We can't let that happen, and the only way to make sure it doesn't happen is to not have sex. Really, no penetration at all, if we can help it."

I frown at that. "Liam fingered me, that's penetration."

Ronan's teeth clench together, his jaw ticking as he speaks.

"Yes, and he was fucking stupid for that, something I've made him abundantly aware of."

His hand grips the back of my neck, holding me in place as he presses his forehead to mine.

"I want to make love to you so fucking bad, but not at the potential risk to you. I'd sacrifice everything before you, Skyla."

My heart flip flops in my chest at his words, and I find myself nodding against his hold despite how unfair this feels.

His lips press against mine, gently kissing me. Slowly, easily. Like we have all the time in the world. Well, if we can't have sex, I know there is at least one thing he won't deny me.

I don't break our kiss as I move to slide in between his legs. He lets me move freely before I lower myself, peppering his neck and clothed chest with kisses. I pause when I come to his slacks, undoing them before pulling them and his boxers down revealing his hard cock.

There is a bead of pre-cum on the tip and when I flatten my tongue against it, Ronan lets out a sharp hiss through his teeth before he's pushing my head down. He forces me to take him so fast that I can't help but gag. Breathing through my nose, I allow him to do it again and again. I'm embarrassed that I can't keep the gagging under control, but he doesn't seem to mind.

"Fuck yes, baby. Such a good girl. Gag on my cock. Gag on daddy's cock."

Something completely fucked up in me practically melts at his praise, and I do my best to take him deeper. I moan around his cock before gagging once again. I feel Ronan's fingers dig into my hair as he begins fucking my face, using me for every ounce of pleasure he can wring out of me. It's an intense feeling, one I've become addicted to with him.

"Oh fuck, baby. Yes. God, yes. You're daddy's perfect girl, you know that? You know how perfect you are for me?" he asks as he pulls me back by my hair, looking down at me in a sort of reverence that has my pussy absolutely soaked.

"Tell me you want daddy's cock," Ronan says, lust completely covering his bright blue eyes.

I don't hesitate for even a moment.

"I want daddy's cock."

Ronan forces himself back down my throat, causing tears to instantly spring to my eyes as he begins fucking my face again.

"Fuck yes you do. It's because you're such a good girl. Daddy's girl. You gonna take my cum, baby?"

I nod the best I can when I have virtually no control over my face.

"Play with your pussy. I want you to come with me."

I do as he says, slipping my hand inside my skirt, my fingers instantly finding my clit. I'm tempted to slip a finger inside, but I wonder if Ronan considers that penetration. I've done it before, and nothing has happened, so surely it wouldn't be the worst thing. My thumb continues circling my clit as I slip a finger inside myself, groaning at the feeling of at least something being in me.

"There you go, baby. I love to hear you moaning on my cock. Does that feel good? Are you touching yourself just right?"

"Mhmm," I moan around his thick cock as my pussy begins to tremble.

I push my finger in and out of me as Ronan's grip on my hair tightens.

"Are you finger fucking yourself, baby?"

My watering eyes look up to see him staring down at me. I nod my head, and he snaps his hips against me hard, forcing me to gag and cough around him before he returns to his steady pace."

"That's so goddamn hot and unfair. Your tiny little fingers can play with that pussy all day long without risking you. If I slipped my fucking pinky in you I'd tear your fucking hymen in two."

My thumb rubs against my clit faster and faster, my breathing becoming choppy before a blinding white light hits me. I come hard, moaning and groaning around his cock as my pussy pulses in pleasure. Just as my orgasm begins to subside, though, Ronan is reaching down, gripping my hand and sucking my finger into his mouth.

He lets out a feral sound around my finger as his cock swells, emptying his cum down my throat. I suck him harder than before, using my tongue to catch any spare drop I may have missed as his cock continues throbbing inside my mouth, his tongue tangled around my finger before he releases it with a pop.

Slowly, I pull away from him, releasing his cock as I stand up. I'm only on my feet for a second at most before Ronan is pulling me down.

"Let's go again," he smirks, before dropping to my thighs.

Four orgasms later, my head is resting on Ronan's chest, some horror movie playing on the TV as his fingers tangle in my hair. We just got out of the shower, where he washed and rinsed my hair before dressing me in one of his shirts that looks more like a dress than a shirt on me. My eyes are just beginning to flutter closed when my phone buzzes.

Blindly, I reach over to see it's a text from Liam.

Liam: Where are you?

I tap out my reply quickly.

Me: With Ronan.

Liam: Where?

Looking up at Ronan, I show him the text, silently asking if I can tell him. Ronan gives me a soft nod before pressing a kiss to my head.

Me: His house.

Liam: What the hell! You guys are having a sleep-over without me?

I chuckle.

Me: Something like that.

Liam: Can I come over? Please, please, please? I'll suck Ronan's dick if that's what it takes.

A scoff comes from above me, and I glance up to see Ronan roll his eyes and shake his head.

"I take it that's a no to his generous offer?" I snicker.

"Yeah, that's a fuck no. There is only one person I want sucking my dick, and she's already here."

"And her jaw is sore as hell," I say, stretching out my jaw dramatically.

We both burst out laughing, allowing it to slowly subside until we are left in a comfortable silence, smiles on both of our faces.

"Do you want him to come over?" Ronan asks.

I pause for a moment before looking up at him.

"I like this right now. I don't want him to feel left out but this feels good. Does that make me a bad person?"

"Not at all, baby. I'm sure there will be times you'll just want to spend time with him and...that's okay too."

I smirk at him. "You said that a little begrudgingly."

An irritated look passes across his face before he smirks.

"I'm trying. You're lucky I agreed to share my woman at all."

My smile fades a little, but before I can spiral or over think he's right there.

"I'm just kidding. I...well, if I'm going to be honest, I'd share you with as many men as it took. Whatever you want or need to be happy, you can have it, as long as I get an equal piece of your heart at the end of the day."

"I don't want you to think you're not enough. You are. You're so much, you're everything. I just—"

"Have feelings for Liam too. I know, baby. I've made peace with it, or I'm trying to. You might have to deal with a few more asshole comments here and there. I get it, though. This life we were all born into," he says, gesturing around the room. "There are very few moments where we are allotted true happiness. When we find them, we have to grab on with both hands."

My eyes flicker back and forth between his, so much care, so much adoration practically drowning them. My mouth moves before my brain can tell it no, this moment being too perfect, too pure.

"I love you, Ronan."

I expect him to stiffen beneath me, look a little shocked or maybe even terrified. Instead of any of those, the opposite happens. He practically relaxes against me, sinking into the bed further than he was before as a heart melting smile spreads across his face. He cups my cheek with one of his hands, as he rests our foreheads together.

"I'm so fucking in love with you, baby."

Chapter Twenty Eight
Skyla

I flatten the hem of my black dress against my lower thigh as Asher drives down the road in silence. He didn't say anything to me when I came out to the car, didn't make any snide remarks about my outfit, my attitude or the fact that I'm dating his best friend. Instead, he has remained completely stoic which is fine with me.

My phone buzzes in my clutch and I pull it out quickly, unable to stop the smile that comes to my face.

Liam: Is he treating my girl alright?

Me: Surprisingly, he's been mute.

Liam: Good. Just keep your head down tonight, and come home to me. I'll be in your room waiting.

Shaking my head, I scoff as I reply.

Me: You need a key to get into my room, remember?

Liam: Babygirl, the fact that you assume I haven't already duplicated your key is adorable.

What a little shit. I'm typing out my reply when my phone is ripped from my hands and tossed onto the floorboard.

"Fuck around with my best friend all you want, but if my father finds out, you're gonna get all three of us fucking buried. Use your last remaining brain cells, and have some goddamn common sense!" Asher snaps, before pushing his way out his door.

He storms around to my side, ripping the door open just as I unbuckle my seat belt before his hand is wrapped around my bicep, yanking me to my feet.

His dark brown eyes are practically on fire as he sneers down at me, his grip on me beginning to shake as if he were barely restraining himself.

"We are going to walk through those doors, and you're not going to say a goddamn word unless you are directly asked. Do you understand me? You will be silent. You will be demure. You will be a fucking wallflower."

"The fact that you think I need a reminder of how to behave in front of men like our fathers is astounding. You're not the only one who grew up like this. I'm not some ill-mannered degenerate. I believe that title goes to the man who is currently leaving bruises on his fiancée's arm," I grit out, as my arm begins to ache in pain.

Surprisingly, he releases me in an instant, those molten eyes coming down to the reddening area before coming back to my eyes. He doesn't apologize and I don't expect him to. Instead, he gives me a terse nod, offers his arm and we begin walking up the front steps of Putnam Manor together.

We don't even make it to the front door before a butler is opening it for us, bowing slightly, as if we were royalty while we step in. Asher doesn't even make eye contact, but I give him a small smile of appreciation as he ushers us through the foyer and into the grand dining room.

My father and Asher's are seated at the table, amber colored drinks in crystal glasses before them. Their eyes snap to us, like lions stalking their prey, and a sudden urge to flee takes over me.

However, I push that fear away and proceed to put on the song and dance Asher and I have agreed upon.

Christopher is seated at the head of the table, with my father on his left. Asher pulls out my seat beside him while he takes the seat on his father's right. Gently taking my seat, I make eye contact with my father and give him a soft smile and submissive head dip that always seems to please him. He nods approvingly before my eyes meet Christopher's.

He is watching me with a barely there smile, his eyes full of intrigue as he stares at me.

"She really is a spitting image of Giselle, isn't she?" he asks, assumingly speaking to my father but his eyes never leave mine.

My father hums his agreement, but doesn't speak. I have the urge to ask him how well he knew my mother. I'd assume very well, since they obviously went to school together. Aunt Steph told me as much as she could about her, but that's only one person's perception of her. I want the whole image, the whole person. I do the smart thing though and bite my tongue, staying still and silent as Asher is handed a glass of the same scotch our fathers are drinking.

"How have things been?" Christopher asks after a heavy moment, finally looking away from me and turning to face his son.

Asher is stiff and rigid, though his words are as smooth as honey.

"Very well. I've been making excellent headway in my studies as well as fortifying new friendships that will be beneficial to us all."

The cryptic meaning behind his words are plain as day, I just don't have a clue what it is yet. That's the point though, I'm sure. Nothing about these men, this society, screams subtle. They are very proud of themselves and whatever business they conduct, they just simply won't give you the exact details.

A small garden salad is placed before each of us, and I practically jump out of my seat with excitement to focus on anything other than the stiff conversation the three of them begin to make. Happily busying myself with my food, I take small delicate bites, intending on stretching out my attention over each course to avoid my father's permanent disapproving stare or Christopher's wolfish gaze that sends chills down my spine.

I'm disappointed Ronan couldn't be here tonight. He told me he tried to casually receive an invitation, to which he was promptly rejected. It would have looked weird if he insisted but I could really use him right now. He always knows how to put me at ease, make me feel comforted and supported. It's as if he can sense what I need before even I do. God, I wish he would unexpectedly walk in here right now.

Unfortunately, I know that isn't an option considering he had to head to New York on an errand for the Brethren. That's what he told me, at least, and obviously I didn't pry. I haven't heard from him since he left this morning, and he told me that he wouldn't be back for a few days. He did promise to facetime with me tonight once I'm home, so at least I can look forward to that.

My thigh is squeezed suddenly, sharply, and my head whips up from my empty salad plate to find Asher's eyes on me, his jaw tense as he flicks his eyes to his father who is already watching me. Placing my fork down quickly, I give him all my attention no matter how it rolls my stomach.

"My apologies."

"No apologies needed, my dear," Christopher says, with a patient smile that looks anything but. "Your father and I have been discussing wedding plans and seeing as you and Asher have gotten along so well, we thought it would be best to move up the nuptials."

Yeah, Asher and I get along so well. We—

"I beg your pardon?" I ask before I can help myself, earning another harsh squeeze from Asher as I correct my next words. "When were you thinking?"

"October 31st," he nods, as if it were set in stone.

I frown at that. "Halloween?"

The table goes still, and I can't help but feel as if I've said the wrong thing, but I'm not the one suggesting a Halloween wedding. What, are we giving away candy as wedding favors? Everyone has to dress up in a costume?

"That's a month from now," Asher states, taking control of the conversation.

"Correct," Christopher answers as his eyes come to him. "We still intend to have the wedding celebrations in the spring, but we felt that the ceremony itself could occur sooner."

"Why?" I blurt out, practically choking on my words when I realize that I said that out loud.

Christopher's easy going smile slips away, an angered glare rivaling my father's taking over.

"Because I deemed it so. I set the plans, I give the instructions and you both would do well to follow them," he snaps, before he gestures to the wait staff and turns his ire to Asher.

"Son, tell me, why isn't your fiancée over the moon to become a Putnam? Have you been mistreating her? Disrespecting her?"

"Of course not," Asher defends, as one of the staff hands Christopher a yellow envelope.

Christopher nods like he believes Asher, before dropping the envelope onto his untouched plate. Wordlessly, Asher opens it, pulling out picture after picture of him. It's not just him, though. It's him and Bridgette Brenton, it's him and Marcy Kravitz. It's the picture of my pillow and the note that was sent out to the entire school. There is even a picture of him, shoving me mid-frame, into that empty grave in the cemetery.

If I allowed it, my mouth would be unhinged on the floor. I force my lips closed though and stare on in shock. The only indicator of fear is in the slight shake of Asher's hands, as he thumbs through picture after picture.

He swallows once, roughly, before setting the photos down and looking between my father and his.

"I have been discreet."

In a flash, Christopher's hand is behind Asher's head, smashing it against the table, the glass of his drink and plate shattering from the impact. I startle at the crash, but don't move a muscle as I watch on with horror.

Christopher digs his fingers into Asher's hair, rearing his face back up to look at him. Blood instantly begins seeping out of the multiple cuts on his face, and his nose is bent in a way that has to be broken.

My eyes are wide, and my breath stalled in my lungs as I watch Christopher unleash his fury.

"You have been everything but!" he sneers. "You have disrespected your fiancée, your match, my own Bond Brother. Your insolence and defiance is not only noted, it is deplorable. If I even hear a whisper of you in a room alone with another woman, apart from your fiancée, until your ceremony, I will personally break every bone in your face while Henry handles your arms and your legs."

I risk a glance over to my father, surprised to see such a satisfied grin across his features. He stares at Asher like he is eager for the chance to hurt him, blood thirsty even. It's a look I've never seen on him before. One I didn't even think he would be capable of.

Asher doesn't make a sound, he's completely silent, as he stares at his father.

"Understood," Asher says numbly, not a hint of hurt or emotion behind his words.

Christopher lets go of his hair, nodding once, before rearing back and delivering a punch so vicious it literally knocks Asher out of his chair and onto his back.

"Son or not, everyone will fall into line or find themselves dispensed. Get out of my sight."

Asher shakes his head, blinking the no doubt stars away before he pushes himself up to stand. My eyes cautiously come to Christopher who takes his seat again, reaching his hand out for a staff member to hand him a towel. He easily wipes the blood off of his knuckles, as he gives me an empathetic smile that truly speaks to how much of a psychopath he is.

"My deepest apologies, Skyla. Normally, I would handle such messy matters in private, but I thought it important that you witness his punishment since it is you and your father who are truly the victims here. The relationship between the Putnam's and the Parris' mean absolutely everything to me, as well as my son," he says, cutting Asher a sharp look who is now standing.

"Should he ever misbehave again, I want you to come directly to me. Do you understand?"

I hesitate, glancing at Asher's bloodied face as he looks down at me, softly nodding his head. I mimic the movement, giving Christopher a tight smile.

"Thank you."

He nods in approval, before giving me a dismissive hand wave. I practically scramble to my feet and Asher is right beside me, gently cupping my arm as we briskly make our exit. We don't say a word as we leave the manor. Asher opens my door quietly before closing it and slipping inside his own. He fires up the car and we are gone in the next second.

We drive for a few miles in silence, him wiping at his eyes every few seconds. It's clear he can't see with the way the blood is pouring into his eyes, and not only is it sad, it's dangerous. A drugstore is up on our right, and I point to it as I speak.

"Pull over."

"You can get your boyfriend to get you tampons later," he grouches lowly.

I roll my eyes, surprised he even has any fight left in him tonight.

"Pull over so I can get some stuff to clean up your face, idiot. You can't see and I'd like to make it home in one piece."

To my surprise, he doesn't argue. He hits his blinker and whips into the parking lot without a single complaint. I slip out of the car, fully aware of the possibility that he may just leave me here. I don't have much to work with, since I don't really know the extent of his injuries, but I do grab some tweezers, rubbing alcohol, bandages and gauze.

Once I've checked out, I'm back at the car, more than a little relieved that he didn't take off on me. Instead of going to my side, I open his door, crouching down beside him.

"Face me," I say.

He sneers at me. "Why?"

I roll my eyes. "Because, that way I know what is glass and what is your arrogant fucking mouth," I snap.

Begrudgingly, he faces me, and I instantly notice one piece of glass embedded just below his eyebrow. Pulling out the tweezers, I sterilize them with a little bit of alcohol before I pause.

"This might not feel very good."

"Whatever," he says numbly.

I nod as I grip the glass shard, carefully pulling it out and repulsed to see the size of it. He doesn't grimace or flinch as I pull piece by piece out of his face, until there is nothing left that I can see. Taking some of the gauze, I soak it in alcohol before applying it to his open cuts. His left eye twitches just slightly, but that's the only indication he gives that he isn't a robot and does feel some pain. As I work on cleaning him up as best as I can, his eyes track me, slowly following my every move.

Once his wounds are clean, I'm actually impressed that the damage isn't near as bad as I expected. The cuts don't seem too deep, so I don't think he will need any stitches. I unpeel a band aid and go to put it on the deepest cut on his cheek, when his hand catches my wrist midair.

"What are you doing?" he practically growls.

I wave the band aid dramatically, causing him to roll his eyes and shake his head.

"I'm fine."

Whatever. I point towards his nose that is slightly bent to the side now.

"What about that? It looks like it might be broken."

He looks into the rear view mirror and assesses his nose before he pinches it between both hands and jerks. I gasp at the horrific cracking noise it makes, as he scrunches his nose up and down a few times and inhales deeply.

"Good as new."

I stare at him in shock for several seconds, before I begin gathering up all the supplies, putting them back into the bag and making my way around the car. As soon as I slip inside, Asher fires up the car and we are pulling back onto the road.

We're almost back to campus when he speaks, his eyes remaining on the road as he does.

"Thanks."

It's so low, almost a grumble. Honestly, it was so quiet that I think for a moment that I imagined it, until he looks at me from the corner of his eyes.

"You didn't have to."

"I know," I say.

"Then why did you?" he fires back, as he turns into the parking lot.

I don't answer when he parks the car, not even when he turns the engine off and turns in his seat to face me. His head is angled to the side curiously, his eyes narrowed as if he was on guard. If what I saw tonight was just a glimpse of his childhood, then it makes a lot more sense why Asher is the way he is. It's not an excuse by any means, but all the pieces are starting to fit together.

"Because, despite this villainized image you have of me in your head, I'm a good person, Asher. I'm not my father's daughter, just like you're not your father's son."

His brows cave in as he speaks.

"If you tell anyone about what you saw tonight—"

"Trust me, I have far more interesting things to discuss than you," I say on a scoff, though I don't miss the way his shoulders relax, and he eases back into the seat.

This piece of him I really get. Christopher must be exactly like my dad. Image is everything.

Without another word, I grab my clutch and my phone and push my door open, shutting it without a backwards glance as I make my way to my dorm. My head is reeling with everything that happened tonight. From the way Asher's father treated him, to being told I'm getting married in a little over thirty days. To a man that can hardly stand me, to top it off. I feel myself visibly frowning until I open my bedroom door, revealing a smiley golden retriever of a human laying on my bed watching a movie.

When his eyes lock on mine, he smiles so wide that I can't help but return it.

"Babygirl! You're back early."

He closes the distance between us, cupping my face and dragging me in for a kiss that I lean into, all too willingly. When we break apart, he grins at me, making my heart flip flop as he reaches for my hand.

"C'mon, the movie just started."

I chuckle at him as I stand in place.

"I want to change and take a shower first."

"Great idea. I could use a shower too," he says, with a waggle of his eyebrows.

I roll my eyes and shake my head as I move to the bathroom, shooting off a quick text to Ronan that I'm home safe, before setting my phone onto the bathroom vanity.

"That wasn't a no!" Liam shouts, before walking into the bathroom.

He's behind me in a flash, his hand on my dress zipper while the other rests on my hip.

"What are you doing?" I laugh.

"Shhh, I've always wanted to do this move," he smirks as he slowly pulls the zipper down, chasing the newly exposed skin with his finger as he does.

It sends a shiver down my spine and forces a deep chuckle to escape him.

"Am I supposed to believe you've never done that before?" I ask breathlessly.

"Doesn't it sound better if I say yes?" he asks.

I snicker.

"You're such a manwhore."

"Was," he says, reaching around to cup my jaw and force my eyes to him over my shoulder. "Abso-fucking-lutely was before you. Now, I'm just your whore."

My pulse quickens and I feel my chest tighten. That isn't sweet. Is it? I don't know. Maybe it is.

I'm about to speak when my phone starts ringing. It startles us both for a moment before Liam turns to look at it, smirking when he accepts the facetime call.

Chapter Twenty Nine
Liam

"Well, hey there, hot stuff," I smirk into the camera.

Ronan's face goes from a dopey love struck smile, to irritation in half a second when he realizes that it's just me.

"Why the fuck didn't I assume that as soon as I left town, you'd swoop in and monopolize my girl?" he gripes.

"Our girl," I correct. "And to be fair, Asher has been the one monopolizing her all night. I just got her and you're interrupting sooo."

Ronan scoffs as he calls out for her.

"Baby, is this little shit head bothering you?"

"He's fine," she giggles sweetly. "But I do need to take a shower."

"And I was just about to help her with that," I add on.

"The fuck you are," Ronan snaps.

I roll my eyes at him.

"Now, now, Ronan. That's not very good sharing," I chastise, doing my best to hold in my laughter as his irritation builds.

"Liam," Skyla asks, in that tone that brings me to my fucking knees.

"Yes, babygirl?"

"Can you please step out into the room?"

She asks with such a pretty smile there is no way I could deny her, but I do pout the entire way, taking the phone with me as I do.

"She's kicking us out," I complain, as I close the bathroom door behind me.

"Technically, she just kicked you out."

"If I don't get sexy shower time, neither do you," I huff, as I flop back onto her bed, resting one of my arms behind my head as I hold the phone with the other.

"So, how did tonight go?" Ronan asks.

My eyes darting over to the bathroom door before coming back to him.

"With my stuff or hers?"

"Both."

"Mine is fine. I need Asher to pull his head out of his ass and lift his weight, so we have at least something to present to the Elders next week. She literally just walked in the door, though, so I'm not sure on her end. She looked sad when she walked in the door, but I haven't had time to pry."

"Well, pry away and then let me know what she says."

"Shouldn't you be a good and patient boyfriend and ask her yourself?" I say.

"I am a good boyfriend, not a patient one. Not when it comes to my brother."

I nod my head. "Agreed. I'll talk to her."

"Or Asher," Ronan suggests, forcing me to choke out a laugh.

"You're joking, right? We've hardly made eye contact since the other night, let alone talked. I tell you what, man. For a guy that claims to hate his fiancée, he sure is possessive over her."

Ronan scoffs. "He sees her like a possession, a prize he's earned, and his best friend is holding it before he's even had a chance. You can't really blame him."

"Yeah, well wait until he finds out his uncle licked it first, I mean held," I say, with a forced smile.

He scowls at that. "Yeah, can't imagine that's going to go over too well."

"Nope," I say, popping the p when the bathroom door opens and Skyla steps out in nothing but a towel.

I feel myself practically swallow my tongue as I watch her timidly scurry her way over to her dresser.

"Fuck, babygirl. You should wear that all the time."

"I'm only wearing a towel," she frowns.

"I know," I wink. "Ronan, look how sexy our girl is," I say, as I turn the phone to face her.

She takes a few steps forward and waves shyly, her wet hair falling against her bronze shoulders.

"Hi."

"Hi, baby. You look so fucking beautiful."

I stand up, moving over to her dresser that is across from her bed and prop her phone up.

"Because I'm super good at sharing, give us a spin, babygirl. Show Ronan the full effect of what he's missing out on right now."

She looks between the phone and me shyly as Ronan nods encouragingly before she takes my outstretched hand. I raise it above her head and twirl her in place, her towel unfortunately staying put as she does.

"You're perfect," Ronan whispers, causing Skyla to blush.

"Thank you."

"What do you think, babygirl? Think we should give Coach a little show?"

She looks between Ronan and I several times before she slowly drops her towel. My mouth parts in surprise and when I look at Ronan, he's wearing a similar expression. Fuck yes!

I wrap my arm around her waist lifting her up and over my shoulder before I take her down to her bed. We land with a bounce, and she giggles as I begin covering her body with kisses. Holy shit could she be any more perfect? Her skin is smooth like silk, not a single imperfection. Her breasts are just the right size, perky with nipples the softest shade of pink and her pussy is easily the eighth wonder of the world.

"Move fucker, I don't want to see you. I want to see her," Ronan barks through the phone.

An amused chuckle bellows from me as I lift myself off Skyla and onto my back. I reach for her hips and drag her over to me, forcing her to straddle me.

"Ride my face, babygirl," I say, as I grip each hip in my hand.

"What?" she asks, as she looks down at me.

"Sit on my face," I smile, as I attempt to pull her down to me.

"No way, I'll crush you!"

"If I die, I die. Ronan, you'll make sure to tell everyone I died a legend at my funeral, right?"

"You got it," he chuckles.

"It's settled," I say, before yanking her down onto me.

She loses her balance and has no choice but to fall onto my face. Fucking hell. This is one thousand percent the closest I'll ever get to heaven and fuck if I'm not going to enjoy every single fucking second.

I feel her try to lift her weight off me, but I wrap an arm around her waist, pinning her into place as my tongue begins running through her pussy. She lets out a breathy gasp that has my cock instantly hard as a steel fucking pipe. Her plump ass is resting on my head, and I honestly feel like a kid in a candy store. I want to lick, suck and fuck every single inch of her. Unfortunately, that last one is off the table, so the first two will have to do.

"Oh my god!" Skyla gasps, as one of her hands reaches for the wall in an attempt to balance herself.

"Fuck, baby. You're so beautiful like this. Does that feel good?" Ronan asks.

"Uh huh," she pants, as I run my tongue from her clit to her asshole.

She tenses up at first, but the more I lick her the more relaxed she gets.

"What's he doing, baby? Is he eating your pussy?" Ronan asks, as the sound of a zipper being undone comes through the phone.

"N-no."

"No?" he questions before a lighter tone takes over his voice. "Is he eating that delectable ass, baby?"

"Y-yeah," she answers, as she squirms on my face.

"Do you like it?" Ronan continues.

"I think so," she groans, pressing herself against me, harder this time.

I smirk against her soft flesh. Oh, she fucking likes it, alright.

"Can I touch you?" Skyla asks, assumingly talking to me.

I lift her off of me just an inch or two so I can talk.

"Babygirl, you never have to ask. The answer is always going to be a fuck yes."

I lower her back down and continue dining on my girl as I feel her begin to push down my sweats. I lift my hips up, helping her push them down until they are to my knees.

In the next second, she gasps and Ronan curses.

"Jesus Christ, how many fucking piercings do you have?"

"Eight," I murmur against Skyla's pussy.

"Eight?! Didn't that hurt?" she squeals.

I nod my head, but continue eating her, not willing to waste any more time talking. I feel her hesitation and honestly, she doesn't have to do anything. I'm more than happy to have my girl sitting on my face until the end of time. Out of nowhere, though, I feel her hand wrap around my shaft, causing a rush of pleasure to run up my spine.

Carefully, she drags her hand up my cock, rubbing my precum across the tip before going back down again.

"I don't want to hurt you," she says softly.

I shake my head, trying to tell her that she couldn't possibly do that. I mean, she could but I'd take any pain she'd give me as a blessing. I want anything she is willing to give me.

"Nice and slow strokes, baby," Ronan guides.

She begins doing as he says and my cock twitches in her hand from it.

"Just like that. Good girl," he praises. "Now, I want you to wrap those pretty little lips around his head. Just like you do for me, okay?"

"Okay," she says, a twinge of nervousness beneath her words, as I feel her warm mouth suck my tip in.

My eyes roll back into my fucking head as her tongue twirls around me, forcing me to groan against her pussy lips as I flick my tongue faster against her clit. She lets out a moan of her own as she slowly starts taking me deeper and deeper.

"That's a good girl. You're taking his cock fucking beautifully. Go a little deeper, you can do it. There you go," Ronan encourages, his voice becoming more strained by the second.

I can't see him, but he'd have to be insane not to jerk off to us. We're hot as fuck together.

Slowly, Skyla pushes herself deeper and deeper until she's practically taking all of me. I'm already so fucking close, because this goddess is just too perfect not to nut immediately. Her tongue runs along my piercings in a perfect stroke that has my vision blurring. I pinch her clit with my teeth as euphoria slams into me. I feel my cock throb before I shoot my load down her throat.

She groans around my cock, either out of pain from my little love bite or pleasure, not too sure. Maybe it's both because just as I'm coming down from my orgasm, she's soaking my tongue. I lap up every drop of her as she pulls herself off my cock and begins screaming her release. She moans and groans, grinding her pussy into me as she rides out her orgasm. I'm desperate to wring every ounce of pleasure out of her, and I hear Ronan follow closely behind us with a feral sounding growl and a chant of 'fuck' over and over again.

The room is silent for a few moments before Skyla slowly eases off my face and I sit up, hair mussed, face covered in my girl's juices and a winning smile on my face.

"Fuck, Ronan. You should call more often."

He scoffs and flips me off, while Skyla giggles and pushes my shoulder.

"You did so good, baby. I'm so proud of you," Ronan says to Skyla, but I can't help but fuck with him as I bounce up from the bed, pulling my pants back up as I do.

"Aw, thanks, daddy. Well, it's been fun but I gotta snuggle with my girl. Byeeee," I say as I hang up the phone, only barely hearing him say something about me being a little fucker.

Turning to face Skyla, she's watching me with a tired smile and a shake of her head.

"That wasn't very nice, Liam."

Dropping onto the bed beside her, I look up at her and smile.

"I'm not a very nice man, Skyla."

"Yes you are," she says, with that same smile and a shake of her head.

"I love that you think that," I say genuinely, as I reach up and brush her hair out of her face. She sinks into my touch and somehow, that gesture alone feels even better than the orgasm I just had.

Okay, no it doesn't. I think that was the best orgasm of my life, but still.

I scooch up to the top of the bed, laying on the edge as I lift up my arm for her in invitation. She smiles, standing up before grabbing a black silk nightgown from her closet. I pout that she's not rubbing her naked body against me as she lays in my arms, but when I feel her press a soft kiss to my chest, I guess I can live with it.

Reaching for the remote, I begin scrolling through shows before I give her an option between a horror movie or a romantic comedy. To my surprise, she picks the horror and I turn it on before pulling the blankets over us.

We watch the movie in perfect silence, me running my fingers through her hair and her drawing lazy designs with her fingertip against my skin before she speaks.

"I like you too much, I think."

I press a kiss to the top of her head as I look down at her, despite her eyes still on the TV.

"Yeah? How come?"

"I don't know. You didn't give me much of a choice. I love Ronan but I..."

Her words trail off, and my chest clenches in anticipation before I speak for her.

"I'm falling for you, Skyla. Hard. There is no choice for me anymore. It's you, babygirl."

She looks up at me, gem colored eyes full of emotion.

"Really?"

I nod, as I lean down and press my lips to hers.

"Really," I whisper against her skin.

It feels fucking crazy that I could be this out of my mind for a girl I literally just started dating. I've been with plenty of women, had tons of repeats and I never felt a tenth of what I feel for Skyla, with any of them. I knew from the first moment I saw her that she was fucking special, and I know even more in this moment, I'll never let her go.

Chapter Thirty
Skyla

The cold night air pricks at my skin, the damp midnight dew of the grass chilling my feet to the bone. I'm moving through the old graveyard of the school, desperate for a way out, but I keep looping back to the same place. I look down at the headstones surrounding me, trying to make sense of where I am so I don't keep going in circles but, they are the same three over and over again.

Bridgette Bishop, Sarah Osbourne and Elizabeth Proctor.

I turn left, running down the row through the clouded mist, glancing at the next three graves.

Bridgette Bishop, Sarah Osbourne and Elizabeth Proctor.

Whipping around, I look at the row in front of me to read the names.

Bridgette Bishop, Sarah Osbourne and Elizabeth Proctor.

They are everywhere, surrounding me. My pulse begins to race as my eyes flick around the graveyard when a hand cups my shoulder, and I let out a blood curdling scream.

I throw myself upright, panting and blinking rapidly as my mind struggles to comprehend that I'm in my room. My heart is practically beating out of my chest when the door is thrown open, a shadowed figure standing in the doorway. He lowers his foot, and I'm about to let out another scream when I recognize the figure.

"Vincent?" I breathe out roughly, before running my hands through my hair.

He takes several steps in, and for the first time I notice a gun in his hand. He points it towards Liam, and I practically jump on top of my comatose boyfriend.

"It's Liam, it's Liam!" I say quickly.

He looks down at him before his eyes come back up to me.

"I heard you scream."

"Yeah," I pant. "It was a nightmare. I—"

I pause.

"Wait, were you outside my door?"

Vincent stands up a little taller, tucking his gun behind his back as he nods.

"Why?"

"Your stalker...I haven't found anything. It's driving me fucking nuts," he says, his eyes becoming wild for a moment before he closes them and shakes his head. "I wanted to make sure you were safe."

Shooting a snarled look at Liam, he scoffs. "Clearly he's not going to protect you if there is danger."

I look down at him. His mouth is slightly parted, a soft snore coming from him as he appears to be having the best sleep of his life. He's not wrong. I'm not sure an earthquake would wake Liam right now, or ever.

"How long have you been outside my room?" I ask.

Vincent looks down at me, rolling his lips together as if he were contemplating how much to share before he speaks.

"Since the day you told me about your stalker."

My eyes widen. "Every night?"

He nods.

"When do you sleep?" I ask.

He shrugs.

"When I can."

I frown at that. "You need to go get some sleep. I'll be okay."

Vincent shakes his head.

"I'm fine. Sorry I scared you. Go back to sleep, Siren."

He takes a step towards the door when I call out to him.

"Wait."

Carefully, I crawl over Liam, scooting off the bed before I stand in front of Vincent.

"Stay?" I ask softly, looking at the plush couch pushed to my back wall.

He swallows roughly but doesn't say a word before he looks down at me, those slate grey eyes illuminated by the night sky. Slowly, he nods before shutting my door and engaging the lock that Liam and I definitely didn't use before bed. Oops.

When Vincent comes to stand beside me again, I tentatively reach for his hand. I'm surprised when he doesn't swat me away or brush me off, but instead, laces our fingers together. My stomach flips at the feeling, as I look up to see him staring at me intently.

I pull him towards me as I slowly walk us to my couch, before gesturing for him to lay down. He releases my hand, shrugging off his jacket and setting his gun on the floor beside him before laying flat on his back. I smile softly at him when his hand reaches up, catching my hip and gently pulling me towards him. I don't know why I let him pull me. I'm even more unsure why when I get to the edge of the couch, I crawl on top of him, settling my body to lay on his.

My head rests against his chest, where I can hear his heart beating like a drum as I feel his arms wrap around me like a cocoon. The feeling of safety that washes over me is indescribable. I've never felt anything like it in my entire life. Like absolutely nothing could hurt me. Like I'm invincible.

I feel his chest heave up as he inhales the top of my head,

releasing that same breath with a content sounding sigh that sounds very uncharacteristic for this broody, grumpy man.

"How did you get into my room?" I ask softly.

"Made a duplicate of the one Liam made," he answers easily.

I frown, turning my head up to find him already watching me.

"How did you know he made one?"

"I study people, Siren. I watch them. I follow them. It's what I do."

"Why?" I ask.

"No better way to beat your opponent than to memorize their every move."

"Liam is your opponent?" I laugh lightly, though my laughter dies at the seriousness of his voice.

"Yes."

Those piercing eyes are staring at me so heavily, his sharp features painting him more like a warrior in this midnight lighting. I've never realized just how gorgeous he is before now. I knew he was good looking, obviously, but god. He's seriously beautiful.

I want to ask him why Liam is his opponent. What they would even be fighting over. What the prize would be. Before I can though, he leans down and presses his lips against my forehead, sending a flurry of confusing butterflies rushing through me as he does.

"Sleep, Siren. I've got you."

I feel my eyes shut of their own accord, as if they answer only to him and I fall asleep to the rhythmic beat of his heart beneath my head.

Sunlight warms my face and like a sunflower, I smile into it. Slowly, I blink my eyes open disoriented at first when I realize I'm not in my bed. I'm even more confused when I see Liam standing over me shirtless, with just his sweats on, smiling at me with a mischievous smirk. The thing that throws me completely though, is when I hear a voice I was definitely not expecting come from beneath me.

"Good morning, Siren."

My head turns to find Vincent staring at me, that same impassive look on his face, though I could swear his eyes look lighter today somehow. His arms are still wrapped around me, and my body is on top of his.

Turning to face Liam again, he's still watching me with that damn smirk.

"I've got to be honest, this is not what I expected to wake up to," he says.

I push away from Vincent quickly, standing to my feet before faltering for a moment. Vincent's large hand reaches out to my hip, stabilizing me until I'm balanced. Liam's eyes flick down at the move, intrigue filling his green gaze as he looks back up to me.

"Vincent heard me yell last night. I was having a nightmare, and you didn't wake up and I didn't want him to sleep in the hall or anything so I told him he could stay and—"

"And you thought you'd be a good host and snuggle up with him instead of offering a blanket?" Liam asks, his amusement clear in his tone.

I frown as Vincent sits up on the couch, shrugging his leather jacket back on and tucking his gun into his pants. When he stands up I can practically feel him tower over me and the same feeling of safety cloaks me as he steps forward, resting a hand on my hip and pressing a kiss to the top of my head.

"See you soon, Siren," he says, before he's moving through the room and slipping out the door.

My mouth is parted in surprise, but not as much as Liam's is. He turns back to face me with wide eyes and a laugh.

"Lucy, you got some explaining to do!" he says, in a terrible Ricky accent from I Love Lucy.

When I don't laugh, he shakes his head.

"I'm not mad, baby. A little confused to wake up and find my girlfriend snuggled up with another man. The meanest, coldest man on campus, of all people, honestly. What's going on with all that?" he says, as he gestures towards the couch.

"I don't know. I was kinda freaked out from my dream and he made me feel...safe. Nothing happened. I swear," I assure quickly, to which he pulls me into his arms and shakes his head.

"I know, baby. Even if it did, I'm cool. I'm already sharing you with Ronan. Why not Griggs too?"

I scoff, attempting to push him away as I shake my head.

"Me and Vincent? Yeah, right. The guy hates me and he's an ass. There is no way. Us? Ha!" I laugh sarcastically, knowing how defensive and ridiculous I sound to my own ears.

Liam's smile only grows, as he shakes his head and gives me a quick peck. "Whatever you say, babygirl. I'm just saying, I wouldn't mind adding another man to this little thing we have going. You guys would be hot as fuck together."

Something unfamiliar runs through me at his words and I can feel his eyes watching me carefully, as if he were testing me. I don't respond and thankfully he doesn't push it anymore. Vincent and me? The most ridiculous thing I've ever heard of. I'm taken, happily. I don't have just one boyfriend, I have two! And an asshole fiancé. I'm so good. Yeah, no. Hard pass.

Right?

Chapter Thirty One
Vincent

I'm sitting outside of Skyla's door, disassembling and reassembling my gun over and over again as I pass the time. My eyes are continually tracking the hallways, waiting, watching.

One of the reasons I'm so excellent at my position within the Brethren is my patience. I could stake out a job for days, my attention never wavering. I wasn't lying to Skyla that once I set my eyes on something, I don't stop until it's mine. Whether that be a dead body, a stalker or her.

I don't give a fuck about her 'boyfriends', I don't even give a damn about her 'fiancé'. I want her and no matter how impossibly difficult it will be, I will have her. One day. When she's ready.

A breathy moan sounds through the door that has my hands pausing. I listen again, some muffled words that have me frowning. I quickly reassemble my gun, loading one in the chamber before standing. Swiping the key card I made for her room, her door opens easily, and I push inside, my eyes scanning the empty still room.

I know for a fact that Asher, Liam and Ronan are all out of town. I couldn't get the specifics for what, just that they are in New

York for a job. Which is interesting because I was supposed to be in New York for a job this week that was suddenly canceled. There is no way the two could be connected. Then again, maybe they could be.

Moving lightly on my feet, I'm able to clear both the bathroom and her closet before coming to her bed. She's alone, laying perfectly in the middle of it, the straps of her white tank top a beautiful contrast to her sun kissed skin. Goddamnit, she's so perfect.

Her hair is fanned out across her pillow like it would be in the water, like the perfect sea temptress she is. Her rosy red lips are begging for my cock to slide in between, her hard nipples straining against the thin shirt aching for my mouth latched around them.

"Liam," she moans, her voice soft and sleep drenched. "Oh, Liam. Please, touch me," she begs.

I can't tell if she's asleep or only semi-conscious. Either way, it doesn't matter to me. I find myself closing the distance between us, coming to her side as my fingers skate against her cheek.

"I'm here, Siren," I murmur, not giving a shit that it's not my name on her lips, it's not me filling her dreams. It will be when I'm done with her.

"More," she whimpers. "Give me more," she begs, as her back arches and her legs seem to rub together beneath the sheets.

I feel my cock stiffen, and before I know what I'm doing, I'm peeling back her blankets, exposing her bare legs in nothing but a tiny pair of sleep shorts. Kneeling onto the bed, I crawl between her legs, tucking my gun into my waistband before resting my hands on her knees. My tattooed fingers are such a stark contrast to her blank skin. It feels forbidden, like I'm about to soil her with my blood stained hands. Like they are too keen to violence for her precious body.

Not precious enough to stop me when the next moan flutters from her mouth. My hands force her knees apart, allowing her to open up to me so that I can take in the view. She's fucking perfect. Just like I knew she would be. My face is only a foot or so away, I can smell her arousal from whatever fantasy she is dreaming about right now, and I don't even attempt to hold myself back.

Sticking my tongue out, I run a long line through her, her taste instantly spreading across my tongue. I grumble my pleasure against her. Goddamnit, she's fucking delicious too. What isn't perfect about my Siren?

She gasps at the touch, and I do it again and again, allowing moan after moan to fall from her lips.

"Yes, Liam," she groans. "You feel so good. Don't stop," her sleepy voice murmurs.

It only slightly irks me that she continues to call me Walcott. Can't she tell that it's me? That he could never make her feel the way I can? He wasn't made for her. I was.

Proving to her that it couldn't possibly be Liam, I continue licking and sucking her before my teeth graze against her clit. She rewards me with a sweet sounding groan before I do it again and again. I feel her body begin to shake beneath me and with one well timed nip against her clit, she comes hard.

I'm not sure how she's able to still be sleeping or if she's trapped in some type of half dream, half sentient haze. She's able to orgasm beautifully though, moaning and wiggling in the sheets as I continue eating her through her release until her body is still and breathing heavy. She doesn't speak after that and I try to continue, but she doesn't respond to my touch.

I could try waking her. It's clear that her body wants me, even if her mind isn't ready to admit it yet. Then again, she came to me so easily yesterday, crawling on top of me and falling asleep like I was her safeguard. It was easily the best night of my life, and I didn't even get a wink of sleep.

Deciding that she needs her rest, I place a gentle kiss to her inner thigh, a promise of more to come and soon. I slide out of her bed, tucking the blankets over her and resuming my position outside her door, reinvigorated and ready to shoot any motherfucker that even steps foot on this floor.

Chapter Thirty Two
Skyla

The next day went by fairly uneventfully, despite the embarrassingly large wet spot on my panties. That dream with Liam was so realistic I could practically feel him.

Liam walked me to all my classes, and we had lunch together. Asher avoided my gaze entirely, which is better than being glared at everywhere I go. Aunt Steph and I chatted for a little while before Maggie and I went to the mall after my last lecture of the day. Still haven't really told her about the whole me, Ronan and Liam thing. Is it so bad that I don't want to? Not yet at least.

Liam texted me a few hours ago saying that he had to go meet up with Ronan in New York. I guess whatever he's doing there he needs Asher and Liam's help. I wish I could ask questions, but I've already caught on to the fact that if it has to do with the Brethren, I won't be getting any answers.

I texted both Liam and Ronan and told them I missed them, that I couldn't wait for them to be back. Which prompted Liam to create a group chat. It's almost midnight and I'm ready to pass out, but I shoot off a text to the chat after Liam asked Ronan and I if we were stranded on a desert island, what are the three things we would bring. As soon as I hit send, I hear a soft thunk against my door.

Frowning, I stand up slowly, reaching around for any kind of weapon I can. Unplugging the bedside lamp, I grip it in my hand and raise it like a bat, slowly opening the door in anticipation of whatever is on the other side.

As soon as those grey eyes collide with my own, relief floods me and I lower my makeshift weapon as I blow out a breath. His eyes flick between the lamp and me before a small grin spreads across his face. Honest to god, a grin, and god, it's glorious.

"What were you going to do with that, Siren? Club me to death?"

"If you were trying to hurt me, yes."

His grin stays in place as he nods approvingly.

"You could have chosen worse weapons on the spot."

"Thanks," I huff.

He doesn't say anything, continuing to stare up at me from his post against the wall.

"Are you going to camp out here every night?"

Vincent nods.

"He hasn't bothered me at night, though," I point out. "And I haven't heard anything from him since that note."

"Probably because he knows I've been watching you like a hawk. As soon as you drop your guard, he'll be back. That's a guarantee."

"So, what? You're just going to keep patrol outside my room and watch me until the end of time?"

"If that's what it takes," he answers immediately.

"Why?" I ask, with a shake of my head.

He pushes off the wall, crowding me against the door jamb, before resting one hand on the wall above me. I watch in fascination as his black hair hangs in his face slightly, and his hand reaches up to brush a piece of hair behind my ear.

"You're a smart woman, Siren. You already know the answer to that."

My heart is thumping wildly in my chest as this unnamed pull seems to hum between us while my eyes flick back and forth between his.

"Tell me anyways," I practically whisper.

He leans forward, his face so close to mine it barely grazes against my cheek as his lips rest on the shell of my ear. I wait with bated breath for his words as I feel his lips move against my skin.

"No."

It's a defiant word, not sexy or swoony at all. Tell that to my body, though. Chills breakout across my skin, from my arms to my toes. Slowly, he pulls away, just enough to meet my eyes again as he turns his head to the side.

"Are you going to invite me in again?" he asks curiously.

"Will you say yes if I do?" I question.

His hand runs through my hair again, tangling through the strands before winding around them and making a fist. He pulls my head back just slightly, so that he can tower over me that much more.

"Ask and find out."

Vincent's lips are so close to mine, I'm practically dizzy. The power he exudes is overwhelming. I can barely keep myself upright as I get lost in his metallic gaze.

"Will you come in?"

That same grin returns, and it nearly takes my breath away being this close to it.

"Sure, Siren. Whatever you want."

In the next moment, he releases his hold on my hair, taking a step back and gesturing for me to step inside. Blinking quickly, I nod to myself and step back in, tugging down my sleep shorts slightly as if that were going to hide the wet spot that has soaked through.

Vincent steps through the door before shutting it behind him, but he doesn't move apart from that. I make my way over to my bed, pausing before speaking.

"If you're going to be my acting guardian angel, I want you to at least get some sleep. Wherever you're most comfortable," I say, as I crawl back into bed.

He nods, slipping off his jacket, setting his gun on the table and kicking off his combat boots. Then he practically prowls over to me, slipping beneath my covers before gripping my hips and dragging me up and on top of him. I open my mouth to say something when he speaks.

"This. This is the most comfortable I've been in my entire life."

Something in his words melts me and I find my body relaxing against his, though my eyes still remain on him.

"You can't be comfortable sleeping in your jeans."

"I'm harnessing every ounce of self-control I currently possess, Siren," he says. "If I took them off, terrible things would happen."

Frowning, I turn my head to the side.

"Like what?"

I watch as his eyes dilate, and his arms tighten around me.

"I'd tear through your precious virginity so fast, you wouldn't get the chance to breathe the word no."

Choking on my breath, I stare at him with wide eyes, unsure of how to respond.

"So, yeah. The jeans stay on," he says simply, before pressing a kiss against my forehead. Something he clearly enjoys doing.

"I have a boyfriend," I say softly, my mind still reeling that he would even say something like that.

"You have two last time I checked."

"Yeah, I do. I...probably shouldn't be lying in bed with you."

"Probably not," he agrees.

I stare at him, waiting for him to move but he just continues to watch me.

"Are you going to let me go?"

"No."

"No?" I question.

"Yeah, no."

"But I don't think Liam and Ronan—"

"Aren't here right now. They are off doing fuck knows what for the Brethren, while there is a predator out there harassing you. Their priorities are fucked."

I push up from him as much as he allows while I glare daggers at him.

"Fuck you. They don't even know about any of it."

This seems to take him by surprise for a moment.

"You haven't told them?"

I shake my head.

"But you told me."

"Well, technically, I accused you."

He nods. "But when you found out it wasn't me...you still didn't tell them? Why?"

I shrug. "I guess, I didn't want them to worry over nothing. I'm hoping everything will just go away, then nothing there is to be concerned about, you know?"

"That's stupid," Vincent chastises with a shake of his head.

"If you're going to continue to insult me and my boyfriends you can leave. Go obsess over someone else, and leave me the hell—"

His lips smash against mine before I can stop it, before I can register it. My words are cut off mid-sentence as his pillowy soft mouth silences my own. He doesn't try to deepen the kiss, doesn't even slip his tongue in. It's as if he was using this merely as a tool to shut me up, but regardless of the minimal effort, my body is practically on fire from the touch alone.

When we break apart, I notice my chest isn't the only one heaving. His eyes sear straight into my own, but he doesn't say a word. Neither of us do. Instead, he pushes against my head, forcing it back down onto his chest before his arms wrap tightly around me and his fingers tangle into my hair until my eyelids slowly droop shut.

Chapter Thirty Three
Ronan

We're finally driving down the road on our way back to the hotel. It's been a long fucking day and I'm exhausted. Not more so than Asher and Liam, though. This isn't their area of expertise, nor will it be. I think Christopher just gave them this job to test their mettle. Asher did better than I expected, honestly. Liam...not so much.

Turning in my seat, I glance to the back to see him staring out the window blankly, his face carrying a haunted look to it. I tap his knee with my hand, forcing him to look at me.

"You good, man?"

He nods, but doesn't speak as he returns his gaze out the window. I give him a sympathetic grimace as I nod and turn back around. I remember my first kill. It never gets easier, and it's something that will probably live with both of them for the rest of their lives.

Do I feel bad that I put a relatively innocent man on the chopping block to take the fall for my own meddling with the school cameras? Not really. I say that because being relatively innocent is a stretch. The man was a crook, who beat on his wife and kids and embezzled millions from a children's charity in New York. The world is better off without him, My brother will be satiated that the boys did as they were told and took care of the camera 'outages'. Three birds, one stone.

Since I know cutting the feed is no longer an option, I have to be smart about when and where I see or interact with Skyla. So will Liam.

Liam wasn't able to get out of Skyla what the dinner at my brother's was about. He said he asked her about it, and she shut down immediately, so he dropped it. I haven't even attempted to try and pry with Asher because honestly, he's had a bad fucking day. Maybe when we get back to the hotel I can bring it up in passing. Not knowing is driving me fucking batshit.

My phone buzzes in my pocket, shaking me out of my thoughts, and I can't help but smile when Skyla's name comes across my screen. She replied to the stupid group chat that Liam created for us. He asked what three things you would bring to a desert island.

Skyla: You, Ronan and a forever replenishing magic buffet. That way I could have my guys with me, and we would never run out of food. We could live fat and happy forever.

My smile grows as I read her text and type out my reply.

Me: Your guys, baby? I like that. I'd happily be stuck on an island with you for the rest of my life. Liam can come too, I guess.

As soon as I hit send my phone is snatched out of my hand. I go to grab it back as Asher holds it away from me, pressed up against his window as he begins reading the messages.

Oh fuck.

His eyes fly across the screen, scrolling up to the beginning of the chat where Liam announced that this was the official 'Skyla's boyfriends' chat. Asher's eyes are instantly wild and filled with fury.

"What the FUCK is this?!" he shouts, ripping the wheel in the middle of the street and heading in the opposite direction of the hotel. "You're fucking shitting me, right? She got to you too?" Asher practically screams.

"Technically, he got to her first," Liam provides, extremely unhelpfully. I liked it better when he was traumatized and silent.

Asher's eyes fly to him in the rear view mirror as he lets out a hollow laugh.

"Un-fucking-believable. You know what, I could expect it from Liam, he will fuck anything that moves, but YOU!?" he snaps, his eyes colliding with mine, showing for just a second the betrayal deep within them.

He turns back to the road, shaking his head with a disparaging laugh.

"Out of all people, I never would have thought that you could do this to me."

"What exactly have I done to you, Asher? You don't care for Skyla. You can't stand her. I'm sorry I fell in love with her, really. I am. How do you think I feel? I'm in love with a woman who I will never be able to fully have. I have this piece with her now, but she's marrying my fucking nephew. I'll lose her one day, we both will," I say, as I glance back to Liam before continuing.

"How do you think we feel, knowing that we will have to stand there and watch you take the woman we love as your wife while we don't get a goddamn say or choice in the matter?"

Asher fumes, as the car begins picking up speed.

"I don't give a fuck! You could have had anyone but my fiancée. Do you know what will happen if my dad finds out? He'll kill us all, your precious little fucking whore included."

My jaw tenses immediately, and my fists clench.

"Don't call her that, Asher. That's your only warning."

He scoffs and shakes his head.

"What would you call a woman dating two men at the same

fucking time? Hell, I'm sure there are more. With you two out of town, I'm sure she has the next one on the roster warming her bed."

"Fuck you," Liam chimes in, with a shake of his head as he pulls out his phone, assumingly texting Skyla to give her a heads up that Asher knows.

"Where are you going?" I finally ask, as he weaves in and out of traffic.

"Salem. Should be there in a few hours. I need to have a little talk with my *fiancée*."

We drive the rest of the way in heavy silence. Liam and I share a few worried glances here and there, as Asher seems to be a ticking fucking time bomb, but none of us say a word. When we get to campus, Asher doesn't waste time with the parking lot. No, he drives straight up onto the sidewalk and down the walkway before parking literally in front of the Parris Dorm doors.

He's out of the car in a flash and Liam and I are hot on his heels. We barely make it inside the elevator with him and when he gets to her door he holds out his hand, assumingly waiting for a keycard. I go to reach for my own when Liam passes one to him. I give him a sideways look to which he shakes his head.

I wish we could have warned her, given her a heads up that we would be ambushing her at two in the morning. Unfortunately, she's no doubt asleep and any chance of a good night's rest is officially over when Asher swipes the card against the reader, forcing the lock to give free.

When we step inside, my brain takes a moment to understand what I'm looking at. Skyla is in her bed but she's not alone. There is someone beneath her. A man. And she's asleep on his chest.

"Oh fuck," Liam whispers under his breath.

In the next moment, the man beneath Skyla grabs a gun from

the bedside table and aims it at us. In a surprisingly quick draw, Asher has his own gun pulled and pointed at the man, a gun that is freshly worn in by now.

"Whoa, whoa, whoa," Liam says, as he steps around me, waking Skyla in the process.

The room is dark, but the moonlight streaming in and the hallway light allows us to see just enough. Her eyes blink open softly, shock and fear splashing across her face as she first sees Asher, or more precisely, Asher's gun. She whips her head down to see who I now can tell is Vincent Griggs holding a gun to us, his arm around her tightening in protection.

Skyla and Griggs?

What the fuck.

"What's going on?" she asks shakily.

"What's going on is I'm engaged to a stupid fucking whore!" Asher spits out, refusing to lower the gun.

I hear the flick of the safety from Vincent's gun before he speaks.

"Say that again, Putnam. I dare you."

Asher lets out a hollow laugh as he shakes his head.

"Fucking hell. I was just joking in the car about her having another man on the side. I didn't think she actually would. You get around pretty well for a little virgin, Princess. Though, I'm sure after a night with Griggs, you're the furthest thing from one now."

She pushes out of his hold and surprisingly, he lets her. She stands to her feet, as her eyes come to me and Liam. Regret splashes across her features while this led ball that has dropped into my gut only seems to sink lower.

"It's not what you're thinking. He's only trying to protect me."

"Oh, he looked like he was guarding your pussy real well from where I'm standing," Asher snarks.

"Baby..." I trail off with a shake of my head, as I try to give her the benefit of the doubt.

"Did he touch you, babygirl?" Liam asks in a tone that doesn't sound all that upset. More so curious.

"No!" she says quickly. "Of course not. Well, he did kiss me, but it ended there. I swear."

Asher lets out an annoying as fuck laugh as he shakes his head.

"Aw, did you hear that guys? She swears," he says, imitating her voice.

She ignores him, looking straight at me as she takes several steps to me.

"Ronan, please. He's just been watching over me for a little while, that's it."

"Why?" I ask, doing my best to reign in my temper and allow her a chance to explain.

She hesitates, sharing a look with Griggs that pisses me the fuck off before he stands, coming too close to her. He isn't touching her, but he might as well be with the way he seems to wrap himself around her.

"She has a stalker. They've been leaving her poems and gifts since her first day here. I've been watching her for weeks and I haven't been able to track them down."

"Are you fucking kidding me?" Asher scoffs, as he tosses his hands out at his sides. "There is your fucking stalker!" he says, pointing to Griggs with the gun. "Can I just kill him and be done with it?"

Liam steps beside Asher, forcing the gun down and sharing a look that clearly says, 'no more bloodshed tonight'. Surprisingly, Asher concedes and tucks his gun into his waistband as I turn to face Skyla.

"Why didn't you tell me?"

She shrugs. "I didn't want to worry you guys. At first I thought it was Asher being a prick, nothing out of the norm," she says with a sneer, to which he flips her off before she continues. "Then I thought maybe it was Vincent. He's always...watching me," she trails off, stealing a look at him. He stares down at her...I don't want to say adoringly, because that's not it. More like, possessively. Like she is property. Like she is *his* property.

"When it wasn't him I guess I got a little scared and I wanted to pretend it wasn't happening," she says as she runs a hand through her hair. "I haven't gotten anything since Vincent started watching my room. It's probably just someone trying to mess with me, right?"

My feelings about walking in to find my girlfriend laying on top of another man are pushed to the side, my sole focus of her safety is at the forefront of my mind as it begins racing.

"So, yesterday morning, he was outside watching over you? That's why he heard your nightmare?" Liam asks.

"You slept with her last night?" Asher scoffs in disbelief.

Liam rolls his eyes as I turn to him.

"You knew about this?" I say, gesturing to Griggs.

"No. I mean, I woke up and they were snuggling on the couch. She said she had a nightmare. I don't know, I didn't think much of it."

"You didn't think much about your girlfriend sliding out of bed with you and crawling on top of another man? Fuck, Liam. How pathetic is that dick you're laying down," Asher jabs.

"Do us all a favor and shut the fuck up for once," Liam sneers, spinning on his heel until he's nose to nose with Asher. A fire that I've never quite seen from Liam consumes his typical go with the flow personality. Asher doesn't move an inch, their foreheads practically glued to each other as they proceed to have some kind of dick measuring contest. I don't have time for this shit, though.

"What do you think, Griggs?" I ask, choosing my words carefully.

He glances down at Skyla, before looking at me.

"I think the exact same thing that you're thinking."

"Fuck," Liam whispers under his breath, now several feet away from Asher.

Skyla's eyes bounce around the room, concern heavy in her features, as she seems to be searching for an answer.

"What? What are you guys thinking?"

No one says anything before Asher laughs and takes a step towards her.

"You know what we are thinking? That one piece of ass is not worth all this fucking drama. You're a waste of goddamn space!" he barks, closing the distance between them as he raises one of his hands.

In an instant, Griggs pushes her behind him and holds Asher back with a forearm to his chest.

"Jesus, I wasn't gonna fucking hit her," Asher grouches.

"Don't really know what you Putnam men are capable of," Vincent shoots back.

Asher's eyes narrow at him.

"What's that supposed to mean?"

"Okay, can we just keep our shit together for five seconds?" I ask. Vincent and Asher keep glaring at each other before I continue. "Griggs?"

His eyes come to mine, a short nod following.

"It's the only reasonable conclusion. If it was anyone else but her, maybe not, but she is too valuable to not be a target."

I nod my agreement as Skyla tosses her hands in the air.

"Is someone going to tell me what the fuck is going on?"

Taking a step towards her, I cup the side of her face as I shake my head.

"There are other...societies out there. Other...groups. Ones that may want to get to you."

She frowns. "Why?"

"Because you're marrying me, Princess," Asher gnashes.

I ignore him, focusing on my beautiful, terrified girl.

"Because you're important to the Brethren. Your marriage to Asher is the start of the next generation. Your pure bloodline makes you the perfect bride, and the perfect target to those wishing to weaken our bonds and traditions."

She frowns at that. "I thought the Brethren weren't a cult, this is feeling very cultish."

"It's not," Asher, Liam and I say simultaneously, while Griggs says, "It is."

We all shoot a look at him, at which he doesn't even flinch. I turn back to her and shake my head.

"It's complicated."

"And you can't uncomplicate it," she guesses.

I nod in agreement, and she shakes her head.

"Okay, so what do I do? Who is doing this? It doesn't seem so bad right now, they are acting like they are in love with me. Right, Vincent?"

He nods, pulling out his wallet and unfolding a piece of paper. He hands it to me and my eyes skim over it, stomach turning at the clear infatuation of the letter.

"I dusted for fingerprints. Couldn't pull anything but hers. He also left...remnants on her panties," he grits through clenched teeth before shaking his head. "She threw them into the pool, though and I wasn't able to pull a viable DNA sample from it."

Skyla looks at him like he has two heads as Asher and Liam read the letter in my hands.

"Dusted for fingerprints? DNA samples? Who are you?"

He doesn't answer, looking to me for my response or reaction, maybe.

"What the fuck?" Asher grumbles under his breath. If he's pissed about Liam and I...and apparently Griggs having a romantic interest in his fiancé, he will be downright furious if one of *them* has an interest in her.

We've been trained to despise them from birth, literally. For over three-hundred-years. No matter how much he hates Skyla, he hates them more. We all do.

"You're never to be alone again, one of us will be with you at all times," I say, as I look at her before looking at the other guys.

"I can protect her," Vincent argues.

I turn my narrowed eyes on him.

"I'm not risking her safety for your ego. You can't be everywhere at once. You have...responsibilities," I say, casting a wary look to Liam and Asher who look puzzled by that piece of information. Legacies don't typically have dedicated positions within the Brethren until after graduation. Griggs is a special case, and that's a fact that no one outside the Elders and himself know.

His jaw tenses several times, before he gives a terse nod.

"Agreed? Everyone takes a shift from now on."

They all nod, even Asher.

"And then what?" she asks.

"And then...we wait for them to make a move," I say, as I scratch the back of my head.

I hope we're wrong. I hope it is just some punk kid fucking with her. I hope it's as simple as someone having a crush and being too shy to come forward. Though, there is a sinking feeling in my stomach that screams otherwise.

Chapter Thirty Four
Vincent

The next night, I watch in fascination as she types away on her laptop, finishing up her assignment that is due tomorrow for her history class. I'm sitting on the edge of the bed, while she's at her desk. The bottom left corner of her mouth is slightly pulled in, those beautiful white teeth holding that plump lip hostage. I want nothing more than to brush my thumb along that lip to free it from her hold and sink my own teeth into it. It takes everything in me not to.

Me, Ronan, Liam and even Asher have been using all of the resources at our disposal, quietly, to keep our ears to the ground. We don't want to start asking the wrong questions to the wrong people, that would no doubt sign her death certificate faster than doing nothing.

Everyone knows that the Parris Princess has an expiration date on her head. They always do. Women rarely last in the inner circle, hence why, almost none of the Elders are still married. They get married out of tradition, have a kid or two, and then poof. They are gone.

Anger begins to burn beneath my skin as I think about that

happening to my Siren. Fuck if I'll let that happen. I'll be there, ready and waiting. As soon as Putnam looks like he will even breathe on her wrong, Asher or his father really, I'll fucking blow their brains out and take her away from all this.

I'll no doubt have her two boyfriends to deal with in the fallout. That is, if they keep their interest in her after she's married to Asher. I'd be shocked if they didn't. They both seem quite taken with her, and in part, I can't blame them. She's fucking perfect. As long as they remember that, at the end of the day, it won't be one of them holding her at night. It will be me.

"You know, it's really hard to work when you just stare at me like that," Skyla says, not taking her eyes off her screen as she continues to type.

"I'm supposed to watch you," I respond.

She scoffs and turns to face me with a small smile that makes my empty chest tighten, just a bit.

"I don't think Ronan meant literally."

"Don't give a fuck what Ronan meant. I'm keeping you safe. You just do your thing, pretend I'm not here."

An airy laugh escapes her, and I want nothing more than to bottle the sound, keep it trapped forever and only pull it out on my darkest nights.

"That's impossible. It's fine, I just finished," she says, as she closes her laptop, nodding to herself before turning to face me.

"So, what are we doing tonight?" she asks.

"Is there something you want to do?"

She shrugs. "Get out of this place," she smiles sadly. "That's probably off limits for now, though, huh?"

Technically, yes. We all agreed we would keep her on campus, but if my Siren wants to leave, then we'll leave.

"Grab your shoes and a jacket," I say, as I stand and move towards the door.

"Really?" she asks, practically bouncing out of her chair.

"Quickly. Before I change my mind."

She slips on the first pair of shoes she sees in her closet, before pulling on a black jacket. I encourage her to step through her door first and she does so as I come to walk behind her, always just a half an inch apart. Close enough to almost be touching, but far enough that I won't be tempted into grabbing her, hauling her over my shoulder and fucking ruining her.

She continues looking back at me, checking to see if we are going the right way as we make our way out of her dorm and to the closest parking lot. She goes to walk past my ride when I reach out and squeeze her hip, stopping her on a dime. Her eyes come down to my bike, surprise and a bit of intimidation in those deep green gems.

"You drive a motorcycle?" she asks, crossing her arms over her chest as a gust of wind picks up.

Her jacket is skintight and thin, it won't be nearly warm enough for her. Peeling my leather jacket off, I hold it out for her, helping each arm in before zipping it closed. When it's zipped to the top, I can't help but smirk. The thing is five sizes too big for her and it's practically swallowing her whole, I fucking love it. Seeing her in my clothes provokes something carnal inside of me. The urge to keep her dressed in *me* forever is suddenly an overwhelming need.

Forcing myself to turn away from her, I grab the helmet I have but rarely use, handing it to her before swinging my leg over the bike and firing it up. She purrs to life, that throaty exhaust taking up the night air around us.

Skyla tries and fails to get the helmet fastened, as I gesture for her to come closer. When she does, my fingers quickly move against the straps, tightening it just enough before tapping the helmet in a 'you're good' gesture.

She's wearing a pair of leggings and white tennis shoes that she looks like fucking heaven in, before she lifts one leg, tossing it over the bike behind me. To my surprise, she doesn't hesitate to wrap her arms around my torso, laying her head against my back.

My own little backpack.

I pop the bike into gear and take off slowly at first, enjoying the way her muscles tense around me, plastering herself against my back. I find myself pushing my bike a little faster and harder than I normally would for a leisurely drive. The more I do, the tighter she holds me, and her body wrapped around me like this gives me an adrenaline high like no other.

We drive for over an hour, weaving through the backroads, before coming up to a dirt road. I turn onto it, slowing down in preservation of my paintjob. After a mile or so, we make a sharp left turn down a small trail that could barely fit a bicycle, let alone a motorcycle. We just barely fit, I've been here enough to make sure of it.

When we get to our destination, I shut the bike off and climb to my feet. I help Skyla with her helmet, pulling it off her head and resting it on the handlebar, before offering a hand. She slips her slim fingers through mine as I pull her to her feet. She tries to wiggle her fingers free, but I have no intention of letting her go, gripping her tighter until she gives up her struggle.

"What is this place?" she asks, her eyes taking in the hidden meadow.

"Hot spring," I say, gesturing towards the body of water in front of us.

She looks back at me in surprise before she steps towards it. I go with her, insistent on not letting go of her hand as she bends down, dipping her fingers into the water.

"Oh my god! It's like a hot tub. How did you find this place?" she asks as she stands up.

"Found it a couple years ago on a drive. Want to go in?"

Her brows knit together.

"We don't have bathing suits."

I raise one of my brows in question, waiting for her to come up with a viable excuse. Her mind seems to race for several seconds, her eyes bouncing back and forth between mine before she reaches for the zipper of my leather jacket that she has on. I stop her in place, though, dropping the hand I was holding hostage as my fingers come to the zipper, slowly lowering it for her.

Her breathing upticks when I push the material off her shoulders and down her arms before my fingers come to the hemline of her shirt. My thumbs graze the bare skin beneath and a chill runs through my body at the brush of her skin against mine. I clench my jaw, doing my best to remain composed as I carefully peel the shirt up and over her head.

I watch with rapt attention as her thumbs hook into the waistline of her leggings, kicking her shoes off and peeling them down before removing her socks as well. Suddenly, it's as if every fantasy I've had of her has been shattered to pieces, because nothing is as beautiful as the real thing.

She's wearing a nearly sheer white bra, her hardened nipples straining against the thin fabric with a pair of matching white panties. I can see just the outline of her slit and the sheer top part of the panties allow me a quick view of her bald pussy. Fuck!

"Your turn," she says breathily, a sound that goes straight to my cock, making it hard to a painful extent.

I grab the back of my shirt with one hand, pulling it up and over my head before tossing it to the ground. My hands move to my belt then, undoing it with the other as I unbutton my jeans and push them down. I'm left in just my black boxers but to my dismay, that's not where she's looking. No, her eyes are focused on the extensive tattoos littering my torso and arms. They are hidden just enough with a suit, per the Brethren's requirements but every other inch of my skin? Covered.

"This isn't the first time you've seen my tattoos, Siren," I remind her.

She shakes her head.

"They're just so...pretty."

An amused huff escapes me as I close the distance between us. Normally, I try to keep a little space but not right now, I'm only fucking human and I need to know what it feels like to hold her bare flesh in my hands.

My hands travel down her back, before resting on her hips as I tilt my head down to meet her eyes.

"You think I'm pretty, Siren?"

"Why do you call me that?" she asks softly.

I don't respond, just continue to stare at her as she asks again.

"Why?"

Swallowing roughly, I allow my hands to skim down her body, pausing when I reach her thighs before I lift her into the air. She panics for a moment, plastering herself against my chest as she wraps her arms around my neck. When she can tell that I've got her, she relaxes a little and looks down at me. I easily walk us to the edge of the spring, slowly sinking myself in before the tips of her toes graze against the surface.

"Oh my god," she practically moans in my arms, as I sink us lower and lower.

Once we are immersed enough to swim, I begin kicking my feet, pushing us to the far end where I know there is a perfect makeshift seat. I press my back up against the wall, the water hitting just above my pecs as I sit down, Skyla still wrapped up in my lap. Her eyes are closed, body leaning back slightly into the water. I hold onto her like that for several moments, enjoying the soft sway of her body against mine.

She looks so free, so perfect. Like she was always meant to be here. With me.

Her eyes slowly flutter open as she draws herself up to sit, our faces now only inches apart as those full pink lips speak.

"Why do you call me, Siren?"

I take a deep inhale before I exhale words too true for her to hear.

"You're entrancing. Like a mythical creature dwelling in bodies of water, luring men to their death just for a look at you."

Her mouth parts slightly, and I feel her breathing stall for a moment.

"That's how you see me?"

"That's how *everyone* sees you," I say, tightening my hold on her as I do.

She shakes her head as if she doesn't believe me.

"I thought you despised me. You acted like you *hated* me."

I lift one of my hands out of the water, using my thumb and forefinger to trace the outline of her jaw before coming to her lips. The water from my thumb wets her lip, making them all the more tantalizing as I speak.

"Don't you know the line between hatred and obsession is extremely thin?"

Her eyes widen, but she doesn't speak, instead she moves closer. I'm not sure if she can tell that she's doing it or not but either way, I wait for her. I let her come to me until she is a hair's breadth away.

My hand falls to the back of her neck, cupping it tightly to make sure she won't try to flee from me. Letting her go was never an option, but now? With her straddled in my lap, her breath mingling with mine and lust and desire for me drowning those pretty little eyes. No, now she's tied to me forever.

She leans forward just a little bit more, forcing the water to move around us and our lips to gently bump together. That bump is all it takes for my self-restraint to snap in two. Much like last night, I smash my lips against hers, having no time or patience to be soft or gentle. Not with her. I want to break her in half and then kiss the pieces back together. I want to force tears to pour down her face from choking on my cock, and then I want to lick them clean. Pain and pleasure, blending together in an addictive combination that will intertwine our souls for all eternity.

Her lips move against mine, all too willingly, all too giving. I have no choice but to take it all. Take absolutely everything I can, after all, it's mine. Every inch of her. Mine.

Our tongues tangle, though she is easily subdued. Her head tilting back, granting me the pleasure of tongue fucking her mouth as she begins grinding that soft pussy against my cock. I lift my hips, giving her the friction she needs as she continues humping and grinding against me. Her breathy moans spilling into my mouth as I continue to devour her.

Every movement of her body against mine, every whimper and tremor. It fuels something inside of me, something dark and unruly. Something fucking feral for her.

I feel her begin to shake in my hands and her movements stutter before she begins to scream. I tear my mouth away from hers, sinking my teeth into her shoulder as her screams ricochet through the woods around us. It only intensifies the harder I bite, and it makes my cock ache and twitch that she enjoys the pain I give her.

Her screams and moans slowly dissipate, and I release my hold on her shoulder before I begin covering it with kisses. Softly, I kiss and lick away the pain I gave her, giving her a new feeling to hold onto. A new one to associate this mark with. My teeth indented perfectly into her creamy skin, it's no question what that bruise will look like in the coming days.

Good.

I want her to bear my mark. I want the world to know that she is mine and I am hers.

The logical side of my brain is screaming at what a terrible plan that is. About how discretion and patience are the only way I'll be able to save her from the impending fate she is awaiting. The primal side of me beats its chest in pride, ready to mirror the action to the other shoulder and every square inch of her fleshy body.

Amazingly so, I restrain myself, my eyes coming to hers. She lets out a shaky breath, but she doesn't say a word, her brain working a million miles a minute as she begins to overthink and spiral before me.

Not allowing her to do so, I press a tender kiss against her lips, one I'm even impressed I could deliver. When I pull away, a little bit of that panic ebbs.

It's a start.

"I'm with Ronan and Liam. I can't....we can't...I—"

"Do you want me, Siren?" I ask, rubbing soft circles against her skin beneath the water.

"I can't," she practically whimpers, like it pains her to say it as she closes her eyes.

I tighten my hold on the back of her neck, squeezing the sides and forcing her eyes to flash open.

"Do. You. Want. Me?" I repeat.

Her chest is practically heaving, her eyes racing across my face.

"Yes," she breathes out softly.

It's music to my fucking ears and for the first time in years, I feel a thud come from inside my chest. I thought the organ in there had died long ago, with no chance of revival. Apparently, all it took was a perfect Siren to bring it back to life.

"Then that's it," I say simply, like nothing else matters.

"I won't leave Liam and Ronan."

"I didn't expect you would," I say, though I had hoped. "I understand you need to explore your feelings with them. As long as I'm the one inked into your soul when all is said and done."

She looks hesitant, like she doesn't want to promise me that. I don't like what it does to me inside. I want her to agree, to profess her love for me and at least agree that when she tires of them we can go on and live our perfect life together. She doesn't though, and it takes everything in me not to blow the fuck up.

"I need to talk to them...I don't know if they will be okay with this," she says, worrying her lip between her teeth much like she was earlier tonight.

My thumb pulls it free, sucking the abused lip into my mouth before releasing it with a pop.

"The part where you were grinding against my cock and came, or the part where you never want to stop?" I ask with a tilt of my head.

"Both," she rasps.

That forces some of my temper to ease and a smirk to pull at the corner of my mouth.

"Good."

Chapter Thirty Five
Skyla

Liam is on babysitting duty today, and I texted Ronan to ask him to meet us back at my room. It was obvious that Liam could tell something was up, I've hardly spoken all day. The guilt of last night has been eating at me, and I honestly have no one to blame but myself.

I've never done any of this before, and I already know I'm messing it all up. Honestly, Asher is right. I'm being a fucking whore. Maybe, if I would have been allowed to have a boyfriend or two growing up, I wouldn't be falling on my face for every man that shows me attention.

Okay, that's harsh. It hasn't been every man, but still. Three men, two of which are my boyfriends, one of which wants to be and none of which are my fiancé. It's fair to say I'm a *little* whorish.

When the sound of the lock whirs and the door is pushed open, I look up from where I'm sitting on my bed to see Ronan step inside. Concern is etched across his face, a look mirroring Liam's. They are both standing in front of me, arms crossed, brows furrowed.

"What's going on?" Ronan asks me before turning to face Liam.

He shrugs his shoulders helplessly, but doesn't speak as both of their eyes land on me.

"I need to talk to you guys about something and I really don't want to," I laugh bitterly, before shaking my head.

I decide there is no gentle way to tell them that I basically cheated on them last night, so I decide to just spit out.

"Vincent and I kissed again. And I sat in his lap and...he made me come."

My heart is jackhammering in my chest as I wait for them to explode, to come unglued. I wait for them to call me every name in the book before slamming the door in my face.

"That's it?" Liam asks.

I frown.

"Well, yeah...I figured you would be furious."

Liam shakes his head as he crouches down in front of me, taking my hand in his and pressing it against his chest. I feel his heart beating so hard it's about to break free of his chest.

"Babygirl, you scared the shit out of me. I thought you were going to break up with us or something."

"Never!" I say with a shake of my head. "Alhough, I wouldn't blame you if you wanted it to be over. I'm so sorry. I don't know what came over me. I just—"

"You like him," Ronan inserts.

My eyes come to him and I see that he is standing in the same place, still as a statue and a frown across his beautiful face.

"I-I do. Not in the same way I feel for you two," I say, glancing at Liam before looking back up to Ronan. "But I do...and I'm so sorry."

"Stop saying sorry," Liam says. "I've been waiting for this since I found you guys together that first morning. It was obvious he made you feel safe, and I've never seen him down bad for anyone before you. I'm cool with it, babygirl, but maybe three boyfriends will be enough?" he says with a teasing smirk.

My gaze comes up to Ronan, a softer expression as he nods.

"He treats you well?"

"He's done nothing but protect and look after me," I shrug nervously.

"You know what I've said. I'll share you with whoever you need, as long as I get an equal piece of your heart."

I'm not sure what to think or do at this moment, so I just stare. When neither of them speak, my mind begins to race even faster.

"So...that's it? You're just okay with it? Okay with Vincent and I having a relationship as well?"

"If he makes you happy then I'll tolerate him, for you," Ronan answers with a simple nod.

My eyes come to Liam who throws his hands up in defense.

"Don't look at me for the jealous boyfriend thing, you won't find it. I think it's hot as fuck and we needed a third guy anyways."

"Why?" I ask with furrowed brows.

"Because we were a throuple, now it's a full blown harem. I can't wait for us to all have sexy time together," Liam says with a waggle of his eyebrows.

Ronan smacks the back of his head and curses.

"We're her boyfriends, not yours."

"You say that now," Liam winks, in a way that doesn't seem to impress Ronan but certainly has filthy fantasies running through my mind. Why does the thought of my boyfriends being boyfriends sound so hot?

"Try your luck with Griggs, I'm all pussy," Ronan says, as he closes the distance between us, leaning down and pressing his lips to mine.

My heart clenches and butterflies fill me, when he pulls back and looks into my eyes.

"So, are we...okay?" I ask.

"Fucking perfect, baby," he says, before practically shoving Liam to the floor.

He falls on his ass but quickly scrambles to his feet as Ronan covers my body with his, peppering my face and neck with kisses.

"Hey! You have to share," Liam pouts like a toddler, forcing a chuckle out of me as Ronan grumbles under his breath.

He rolls over onto his back but pulls me with him. His hands snake beneath my skirt, pushing it up and over my hips before pulling my panties to the side.

"Mmm there is my wet little pussy. I've missed you," he says as his hands grip my upper thighs, dragging me up to his face before his mouth latches onto my clit.

I let out a surprised gasp as he forces me to sit on his face. His tongue flicks against my clit several times before drawing a lazy line through my pussy. My hand reaches down, digging into his hair as I force him closer to me.

Fuck, that feels way too good.

"Holy shit. Is this how hot it was when you watched her ride my face?" Liam groans and I look over to see his pants already around his ankles, that pretty decorated cock being stroked by his hand.

Ronan lifts me off his face for a moment as he growls.

"Fucking hotter. She was totally naked when she rode your face."

"Well, we can solve that," Liam says as he lets go of his cock, grabbing the hem of my shirt and pulling it up and over my head.

With a single flick of his other hand, he unclasps my bra, forcing my breasts to spill free. Ronan's eyes collide with my own, his mouth still eating me like a starved man as one of his hands comes up to cup my right breast. Liam reaches over and grabs the left as he continues stroking his cock again. Leaning down, Liam presses his lips to mine, his fingers flicking against my nipple as his tongue twirls with my own.

The stimulation is overwhelming, and yet I'm desperate for more at the same time. Ronan flattens out his tongue and runs it through me, forcing a moan to escape me as Liam smiles against my lips.

"Feel good, babygirl?" he murmurs.

I let out a breathy nod as he takes a step away, pressing his cock against my lips.

"Open."

I do as he says as he pushes his cock into my mouth, going all the way until he bottoms out in my throat. I gag around him but breathe through my nose to keep my composure.

"Fuck yes," Liam grits through clenched teeth. "You know I love it when you choke on me."

His hips pull out before thrusting into me again and again. Ronan increases his efforts as I feel one of his hands slide between us, going to his cock where he begins stroking himself. Liam pulls back for a moment, forcing my head to the side as he pushes me back.

"Be a good girl and spit on Ronan's cock, baby."

I gather up all of the saliva in my mouth and spit onto Ronan's tip, forcing him to groan in appreciation as his hand grips his cock tightly. I watch in fascination as he begins jerking his cock faster and faster, before Liam buries his fingers into my hair and drags me back to him.

"All the way, babygirl," he says, as he pushes himself back down my throat.

Somehow we seem to find a rhythm that suits us all perfectly. Me sucking Liam while he face fucks me and Ronan eating my pussy while he strokes himself. All that can be heard is the sloppy sounds of Ronan and my mouths and Liam's pleasure fueled moans.

I feel Liam's cock begin to throb in my throat and that familiar building feeling in my lower stomach. One more swipe of Ronan's tongue against my clit, and I'm a goner. I scream out my release, muffled by Liam's cock stuffed in my mouth as my pussy spasms and pulses, leaking my release all over Ronan's face. His tongue greedily laps up all I have to give him, and Liam lets out a savage curse as his cock swells, his hot cum running right down my throat.

I do my best to swallow it all, sucking him a little harder to get that much more out of him. I feel Ronan tense beneath me, his own muffled groan shaking the walls of the room as he finds his release.

We all attempt to catch our breaths as Liam slowly pulls away from me, caressing my jaw in a loving way, as he bends down and presses a sweet kiss to my lips before moving to the bathroom. The sound of the shower echoes through the room before Liam is back, shirt and pants now discarded as he offers me his hand.

Carefully, I climb off Ronan and watch as he pulls his clothes off with one hand as Liam offers him a washcloth. He dips his head in thanks, as he quickly cleans himself up before getting undressed as well.

"What are we doing now?" I ask as Liam does the zipper of my skirt, pulling it and my panties to the floor before guiding me to the bathroom.

All three of us step into the warm water, sandwiching me in the middle, with Liam in front of me and Ronan behind me. Liam's hands rest on the small of my waist, while Ronan's settle on my hips.

"Now," Ronan says, "We worship you."

Was what we did not worship? Because that's what it felt like to me. Maybe I'm wrong, because when Liam's mouth captures my own at the same time Ronan's comes to my neck, I understand what the word truly means.

Together, their mouths and hands touch every inch of me, washing my hair and my body, turning my head back and forth to share kisses between the two. All I can do is keep myself upright at this point, they are handling everything else, turning me into a giant pile of pliable goo.

Once our shower is over, Liam dries me off while Ronan grabs my favorite pajamas for me. The boys just slide on their boxers, before Ronan climbs into my bed first, followed by me and then Liam. It's not even close to nighttime, but that doesn't stop me from crashing hard, cuddled between my boyfriends. God, I really should be ashamed of that statement, but ask me if I care.

I'm woken up by a loud pounding sound. I jolt awake at the same time as Ronan, while Liam, per usual, is dead to the world. In the next moment, Vincent blows into the room, pausing in his steps only for a moment before he shuts the door behind him.

The blankets are covering us, but it's very easy to tell that we are naked under here. Vincent has basically seen me naked, but there is something in me that suddenly feels shy. I give him a nervous smile as he stares at me blankly.

My smile begins to fade, anger clearly etching into his features when he closes the distance between us, leaning over Liam to cup the back of my neck and bring his lips to mine. It's a reassuring kiss, one that tells me he isn't mad about what he walked into, at least I assume that's what it means.

"They know about us, I take it?" Vincent asks, as he pulls back just an inch from my face.

"Yeah, we know. Welcome to the club. We're gonna get t-shirts," Liam yawns.

Vincent rolls his eyes, but doesn't respond as he looks straight into my soul.

"We have a problem, Siren."

I frown.

"What happened?" Ronan asks.

Vincent presses his lips against mine one more time, this time in a harsher way, one that almost feels like punishment before he takes a step back and stands up.

"I was just...mingling and overheard an interesting piece of information," he says, as his eyes come to me before moving to Liam and Ronan. "Apparently, the ceremony of Asher and Skyla's union has been moved up."

"What?" Ronan asks, the single word as sharp as a dagger.

"October 31st is what I hear," Vincent says to him before looking down at me again. "Care to elaborate on that, Siren?"

I grimace and nod my head.

"Yep. That's what the dinner at Christopher's was about. He knows about Asher whoring around campus and the hazing shit he did to me. He told him that he had to respect me from here on out, and that our ceremony would be moved up. We're still having the wedding, but I assume we are going to the courthouse or something to make it official, on Halloween of all days. Ridiculous, right?"

Everyone is silent, all sharing heavy looks between each other, but not bothering to share whatever they are thinking out loud. I look over to see Liam's brows practically knitted together, Vincent's eyes dark and hostile, while Ronan is fuming mad beside me.

"That's less than a month away. We need more time," he says more to himself.

"She's out of time. Preparations are being made. You and I both know exactly why he chose that day," Vincent says to Ronan.

"Wait, why?" I ask.

No one speaks and it pisses me off.

"Okay, that's it. One of you needs to start talking, immediately!"

"Babygirl, we want to...we just...can't."

"Yes you can. It's called communication, Liam."

"It's called sacred secrets, Siren," Vincent says.

I frown, looking at all of them desperately before my eyes stop on Ronan. He's staring at the ceiling before slowly turning his head to me.

"What do you know about the Salem witch trials?"

Chapter Thirty Six
Skyla

"What? The witch trials? I don't know. Some kids claimed that women in the town were witches and possessed them or something. It started a mad hunt for witches and a bunch of innocent people died. What about it?" I ask.

All the guys share uneasy looks between each other, Liam silently shaking his head at Ronan like he's begging him not to share anything with me. My eyes stay on Ronan as I lift a waiting eyebrow.

Ronan rubs his hand against his jaw, staring at the ground before looking back to me.

"The history books got most of it right...but not all. Yes, many died unnecessarily, but there were witches in Salem, still are too."

"What? Witches? Like cauldrons, spells and all that?" I scoff.

"No, you're thinking of the dramatized Hollywood version of witches, but people who practice various forms of magic, harnessing energy from nature and darker forces, yes," Vincent corrects.

My brows furrow, a disbelieving look on my face as Ronan continues.

"No one truly knows what happened with the trials. Some say the women were wrongfully accused, others say they really were practitioners of magic. Either way, the town turned to chaos. Once the trials had ended, it didn't stop there."

"Our ancestors knew that there were remaining witches, furious ones," Liam intervenes. "And even those that had been executed, most of them had families. Children, spouses, siblings. Some in Salem, others in nearby towns and states."

"And, rightfully so, they wanted revenge," Vincent adds on.

"So, what were the townsfolk of Salem to do?" Ronan asks. "They decided there was safety and power in numbers and thus—"

"The Brethren was born," I guess, causing all three to nod their heads in agreement.

"Holy shit. So it's not a society, it really is a cult. It's an anti-witch culty protection group," I guffaw, unbelieving of my own words.

"To put it simply," Vincent agrees.

"You guys don't actually believe this shit, though, right?" I ask.

They all have uneasy looks, even Vincent as he continues.

"I've seen a lot over the last two years, enough to know that as much as the Brethren lie to us, there is an equal amount of truth to our practices, to our protection. They are very much out there, active and waiting."

My mind is reeling as I do my best to comprehend all of this.

"I don't understand. Is that who my stalker is? One of them?"

"We suspect," Ronan says.

"Why me? What did I do?"

"You're important to the Brethren, which means you're a perfect target. No better day than to form a union of strength, than on one of their most sacred days. They believe the veil between this world and the spirit world is lowered on that day, giving them more strength and connection to cause more damage and chaos."

"I still don't get it. It's not like Asher and I getting married is all of a sudden going to make us untouchable. What's the point?"

Liam winces as he shakes his head from side to side.

"That's where the practices and beliefs get...muddled. As a part of the newest generation, I agree with you. Though the older generation, like Asher's father and yours...."

"They believe it is a key element to maintaining our lineage and power," Ronan fills in.

"But that's fucking crazy."

Vincent nods. "We didn't claim them to be sane, Siren."

"Well, what am I supposed to do? Do I just marry Asher and hope for the best? Hope this cult or coven or whatever doesn't come for me? What about after we're married? Will they lose interest?"

"Not likely," Vincent says.

A sinking feeling settles in my stomach as I nod.

"So, do I just live my life always on edge until one day they do catch up and kill me?"

"That will not happen," Vincent says vehemently, while Liam and Ronan mimic the same sentiments.

"We will protect you, Skyla, trust that. Things are...shifting and for now, we all have to play our part in this song and dance. I just...I thought I had more time," he says with a shake of his head.

Yeah, well it sounds like if these crazy witches, or at least descendants of witches, get a hold of me, my time is literally up, so same here.

Chapter Thirty Seven
Asher

I glance down at my phone to see we are ten minutes late for our first class. I don't know about her, but I don't want my dad getting told shit about my attendance, so she better hurry the fuck up.

Her door swings open and I kick off the wall across the hall, stopping in my tracks as I watch Liam step out of the room with her. His arm is wrapped around her shoulder, and she is tucked into his side as they smile at each other like the other hung the fucking moon. My lip curls up at them as I sneer.

"You're off Princess Patrol. Now stop touching her in public, before someone sees."

Liam shrugs his shoulder off her, shaking his head and rolling his eyes before turning to face her.

"See you soon, babygirl," he says, leaning forward and brushing a kiss to her cheek that has me looking over my shoulder to make sure no one can see.

When he pulls away, he levels me with a heated look but doesn't say anything before shaking his head and walking off.

"Give me one second," Skyla says as she steps back into her room, grabbing her laptop and her purse.

"So, are you seriously seeing them all?" I ask, as my eyes trace the room.

"Yes," she answers hesitantly.

"How does that even work? They take turns on who gets to fuck around with you each night?" I ask as I look down at her.

She rolls her eyes at me and shakes her head.

"Is that how it works with you and your groupies?"

I scoff. "No. I call them when I want to fuck. No expectations."

"Well, basically the same, except we have communication skills and care for one another."

I lift a disbelieving eyebrow at her, because she can't be this naïve. She seriously thinks Liam is dating her for her personality? Or Griggs. Everyone knows that guys humps and dumps. The few women that have slept with him said they were terrified the entire fucking time, and then he never looked them in the eye again. And don't even get me started on Ronan.

Yeah, sounds like the perfect group of guys to share and *love* one woman.

Without another word, she steps out of her room as I follow after her, shutting the door behind me. We make our way into the elevator, out into the courtyard and to her first class without a single word spoken.

You know, my fiancée isn't too bad when she's silent. Maybe this marriage won't be the worst thing in the world. She can do her thing, I'll do mine. My father will be pleased. Everyone wins.

"See ya," she says as she steps into the class, not sticking around for me to say anything, which I wasn't planning on anyways, so it's whatever.

I turn on my heel, heading in the direction of my class when I see Griggs cornering Jeremy Stroughton. He has him pinned against the side of a building, his forearm against his throat as he looms over him menacingly. Intrigue gets the better of me and I switch directions, heading straight for them as I do.

"What's going on here?" I ask when I'm only a few feet away.

Jeremy's eyes come to me in a panic, begging and pleading for help.

"Asher, man. Thank fuck you're here. Get this psycho off of me," he stutters, as Vincent pushes more of his weight against his throat.

I tip my head to the side like I'm contemplating it when I turn to Griggs.

"What did he do?"

He doesn't take those creepy grey eyes off his target, as he speaks through clenched teeth.

"Him and Dane Lewis were having a little bet about who could fuck Parris first."

"Oh really?" I say with an interested raise of my brows, as I face the man about to shit his pants on the spot.

"Overheard them talking about how they were going to pull her into the gym after class and they'd hold her down. Take her at the same time."

My head whips over to Griggs, unable to hide the anger that instantly consumes me. It comes on so fast and so intense, I've never felt anything like it. I'm shaking with rage, as I wind my arm back and deliver a punch straight to his nose. Jeremy's nose explodes, gushing down his face as I hit him again and again, all the while Griggs holds him perfectly in place for me.

Teamwork.

I shake my hand out as I take a step back.

"I wonder what we're gonna do with a piece of shit like you now," I say out loud as I look at Griggs.

It takes me a moment to see it but honestly, I can't believe that I missed it before. He has his gun out, pressed against Jeremys dick, his finger on the trigger. Fuck, that's a good way to go about it. If you're going to actively plot to rape a woman, you deserve to have your dick shot off.

"W-why do you even care!?" Jeremy blubbers, tears and blood leaking down his face as he looks to Griggs.

He doesn't say a word, instead, he pulls the trigger. It makes a light pop sound and when he pulls the gun away I notice he put a silencer on the end.

Nicely done.

I lean forward, covering my hand over his mouth as he lets out a blood curdling scream. Vincent and I look at each other, communicating silently before I nod. I wrap my arms under Jeremy's, somehow still able to keep his screams covered, as Vincent tucks his gun into his pants and grabs his legs. Together, we carry him down the side of the building and out to a car that has a popped trunk, already pre-lined with plastic.

I give him a sideways look, but he doesn't meet my eye, casually tossing Jeremy's legs inside like he's a bag of groceries. I haven't been privy to some of the darker sides of the Brethren. I've been mostly kept in the face of it all. It's interesting to see just how different others have been raised. What killing machines the Brethren can turn someone into.

"He's a Legacy," I remind him. "Same with Lewis. You can't kill them."

"I know. Accidental castration happens though, and with that double femur break that Lewis is suffering from, he's going to be wheelchair bound for a long time," he says hollowly.

I blink at him, letting out a choked laugh.

"You crazy son of a bitch. Where the fuck is Dane?"

"At the hospital. He took a nasty fall down the stairs this morning."

A wicked smile curves my face.

"You've been a busy bee this morning, haven't you?"

He doesn't respond, instead, moving to the driver's seat.

"Need any loose ends tied up?" I ask.

Griggs shakes his head.

"Just go keep her safe."

"Looks like you've got it covered, what do you need me for?" I scoff.

To my utter shock, he smirks, like a smile kind of smirk. I don't think I've seen this guy smile in his twenty-one years of life. Don't get me wrong, it is the evil unhinged kind of smirk, but still. Fucking wild.

Griggs takes off and is blending into morning traffic in the next minute. I turn to head back to campus, irritation still gnawing at me inside. Why the fuck is everyone intent on stalking or hurting my fiancée? I have enough shit on my plate, and if she got hurt on my watch, my father would likely shoot *my* dick off.

Looking down at my phone, I realize that my lecture is already more than half over, so I decide to just post up outside of Skyla's class until she gets out. I choose to inform my father of my little delay this morning, one to excuse my tardiness from my class and two, proving that I can be the protective fiancé he expects me to be. To no one's surprise, he responds back quickly with a 'well done' and nothing more. Yes, I took credit for Grigg's handywork. No, I don't feel bad about it.

I answer a few texts while I wait for Skyla, mainly mass deleting the unhinged ones coming from Bridgette. The sex is good, but when she doesn't get all of my attention she goes full psycho. Since the dinner at my father's I haven't so much as looked at her, and it's sending her into a full neurotic meltdown.

Crazy bitch.

When the class door opens, people begin pouring out of the room. I don't make eye contact with any of them, a sense of anxiety hitting me for a moment when I don't immediately spot Skyla. Fucking hell, if I've lost her on day one of Princess Patrol. I am so fucked.

Thankfully, she's one of the last people to emerge from the room. She is sandwiched between Bartlett and Liam as he says something that makes both girls laugh. Something about seeing her laugh irks me, and I'm all too happy to interrupt their little giggle sesh.

"C'mon, you're gonna be late," I say as I reach down, cupping her elbow and pulling her away.

Liam reaches out, grabbing my bicep and squeezing.

"Hey, don't be manhandling my woman like that, bro. She can walk beside you, like an equal. You don't need to drag her around like a doll."

I'm still not used to this version of Liam. The one that talks back, the one that thinks he has any right to tell me what I can or can't do. I don't like it one fucking bit, honestly.

"My fiancée, my call," I say simply.

"My girlfriend, my rules. Show her respect or I'll knock your front teeth in," Liam says, intentionally keeping his voice low from all the eavesdroppers. Like Bartlett.

I cast her a sideways glance that has her practically shriveling up on the spot. When my eyes come back to Liam, he hasn't budged an inch, his jaw clenched like he's gearing up for a fight.

I dramatically drop her arm, holding out my hands in a placating way. His eyes track the movement, before I see his shoulders loosen softly. Resting his hand on Skyla's lower back, he ushers her past me as they continue on their way. I follow after silently, just close enough to hear her whisper to him.

"That whole caveman, 'don't touch my woman like that' thing? Hot," she says with a giggle at the end.

Liam gives her a crooked smile, and leans in to kiss her when I shove his back roughly. He stumbles a step or two before shooting a narrowed gaze at me. I give him a deadpanned look that hopefully he reads as, 'don't be stupid and kiss my fiancée in the middle of campus'. Thankfully, he doesn't argue with me. Instead he turns around and pretends like I'm not here. Meanwhile every step they take, his fingers intentionally brush against the back of her hand. It's a small move the untrained eye would never spot. It's so obviously intentional to me, though.

This pattern repeats itself after each class, until Liam has to stay behind during lunch and explain why he wasn't in class the other day to his econ professor. He better come up with something good, because Professor Reynolds plays golf with his dad and Liam is no doubt a constant topic on that front. Mainly, how much of a disappointment he is, I'm sure.

Skyla and Bartlett are eating lunch at their usual table while I sit across from them, fucking around on my phone. I'm sure my father's spies will love all the shots they are getting with Skyla and I today. To make things better, I've hardly looked at another woman for longer than two seconds. It will pacify my father, but my cock is feeling neglected as fuck. For the next month it looks like I'll be jerking it, because I'm not risking shit for some half assed blowjob or stretched out pussy.

Nah, I'll wait until after the ceremony, when all eyes are no longer solely on me.

I still don't get why all of this is happening. Having the ceremony on October 31st makes sense. It's a powerful day for *them*, and what better way to undermine and form a stronger bond for the Brethren than completing a union like ours on that day? But why not an entire wedding? I haven't been able to figure that part out yet, and I've been trying to stay out of my father's way as much as possible lately.

I'm lost in my thoughts, and I don't see what happens next before it's already in progress. Bridgette, very pathetically and clearly fake-falls behind Skyla, falling forward with her China plate. Before Bridgette 'falls' she raises her arms, forcing the thick plate to hit Skyla in the back of the head, the material shattering apart against her, before all of the broken pieces fall to the ground.

A collective hush falls over the room and before I know what I'm doing, I'm on my feet. Rounding the table, I bend down to where Bridgette is smiling like the evil fucking cunt that she is. My hand wraps around her throat, as I easily lift her up into the air before pinning her against the wall. Her eyes are wide and limbs flailing,as her toes just barely scrape the floor.

Her hands are clawing at my wrist, desperate to get me off of her but I can fucking promise, she will lose that fight.

"Now that I've got your attention, this is a reminder for you and anyone who is smart enough to listen," I bellow, turning my head to make eye contact with as many people as possible, before bringing my eyes back to the worm before me. "My fiancée is off-limits. If you look at her, I'll gouge your fucking eyes out. If you talk to her, I'll cut out your tongue. And if you touch her," I say, allowing a feral growl to rip through my chest as I chuckle. "I'll fucking kill you," I say lowly, allowing the ferocity of my words to melt into this thick woman's skull."

Her face is beginning to turn blue, and I know I have a choice to make. Will I get shit for killing a member's daughter? No doubt about it, but she doesn't even belong to an Elder family. So does it really matter?

"Shit, hold still," I hear from behind me, as I turn to see Bartlett attempting to pull pieces of plate from Skyla's head. A head that has a decent sized red spot soaking her blonde hair. Rage ignites inside of me once more, but I don't allow myself to give any more of it to Bridgette. She's not worth it.

Tossing her to the floor, I release her as I turn back to Skyla and practically shove Bartlett away.

"Hey!" she gripes.

I ignore her, inspecting the wound and seeing that it is deep enough that she will need stitches. Kneeling down to her side, I see Skyla hiding her face. I try to pull her hands free, but she holds on tighter.

"Is your face hurt too? Let me see."

She shakes her head as her words come out muffled.

"I just want to leave."

I nod at that and slip my arm beneath her knees, wrapping my other around her back as I lift her up. She comes to me easily, as I carry her bridal style out of the dining hall. I kick the door open, walking through easily as Skyla buries her face into my chest. I feel the occasional drop of blood land on my arm from her head, but I don't give a shit. I hold her a little tighter, allowing her as much privacy from all the prying eyes as I can.

I don't even realize that she's crying until we're stepping inside the nurse's area. She's silent about it, but tears are pouring down her face and leaving mascara tracks in their wake. It makes my chest fucking burn, to see someone I know to be a very strong woman broken down by someone so insignificant.

I'm not sure Skyla understands what will be happening in the next month, at least not fully. She doesn't see this place like a king-dom, but it is– Gallows Hill, Salem, the country, really. It is all one large kingdom of the Brethren, and I'm first in line for the throne, which means so is Skyla. I will rule over all like I am their king, and she is my queen. She can't cry over commoners like Bridgette when she was raised from birth to rule.

Walking us through the room, I choose the first empty bed I see, closing the curtain around us as I set her on the edge. Slowly, she loosens her grip on me before pulling away all together. Forcing away the small tug that pulls on me when she does, I force her chin up to me. Those bright green eyes meet mine, red and watery as she attempts to turn away. I don't let her, though.

"You're right to never let them see you cry. I'm not them, though."

"No, you're worse," she says hollowly, her voice slightly rasping like she's doing her best to choke back more tears.

"You got that right," I agree. "But I'll never take your moment of weakness and turn it against you like they would."

Her brows furrow as she looks up at me. "Why?"

"Because you didn't to me."

She stares up at me, blinking for several seconds before she nods her understanding. My mind has played that night over and over again. My father lashing out, normal. Him doing it in front of Skyla, surprising. Her tenderly caring for me and then not telling a soul after, fucking mind boggling.

Her eyes blink slowly and fear tears through me for half a second. I rip past the curtain as I shout out into the room.

"Someone get the fuck over here and help her!"

In a rush, two nurses appear from out of nowhere, gasping in surprise when they see the back of her head.

"What happened?" one asks.

"Someone tripped," I say flatly, as I come around to the front of Skyla.

I snap my fingers in her face causing her eyes to look up at me, hazy and dilated.

"Shit. I think she has a concussion."

The other nurse comes around, looking in her eyes before she nods.

"How do you feel, Princess?" I ask.

"Like I'm gonna puke," she mumbles, before her stomach heaves.

I just barely grab the trash can beside me in time, holding it up as she wretches what small amount of contents were in there. She pukes again and again, and I softly rub her back while I hold the can for her.

"Ow," she complains softly. The two nurses are pulling out the few pieces of the plate remaining, wiping away the blood and sterilizing the wounds.

I set the puke can to the side, before grabbing a tissue and handing it to her. She takes it gratefully, wiping her face before tossing it into the can as well.

"That was gross," she grumbles.

"I've seen worse. You should have seen Liam when we were eight, and he was convinced he was ready to watch scary movies. We watched one of the Saw movies and he literally pissed his pants. The couch had to be thrown away; it reeked so bad," I laugh.

Skyla chuckles once before she softens.

"Aw, that's sad. He was probably so embarrassed. I'm sure your dad loved dealing with that."

I scoff. "I handled it. I had the cleaner try to take care of the couch, but when they couldn't I just had a new one brought in."

"Your dad never knew?" she asks, as the nurses grab the suture kit.

I shake my head as I continue trying to distract her while they give her a numbing shot. She winces from it, but doesn't say anything as I speak.

"Can you imagine what he would have done to Liam had he known? Believe it or not, I think his temper has ebbed over the years," I laugh hollowly. "Liam's parents suck, but they aren't as... strict as my father," I say.

Skyla watches me carefully as she nods.

"You're a good friend when you want to be."

I choose not to respond, because I don't know about that. Skyla's fingers twist together in her lap, a nervous tick I've noticed, as the nurses begin stitching her up. I don't think anything of it, reaching out and stopping her hands, before taking one of them in mine. I squeeze it gently. Her eyes don't meet mine, and I look away before they do. We sit there for fifteen minutes or so, allowing the nurses to patch her up in silence.

They give us the run-down on keeping it clean and all that kind of stuff. They gave her dissolvable stitches, so she won't need them removed, and they explained all the steps to watch over someone with a concussion. Then I was asked if I was going to be the one to watch over Skyla tonight. She said no while I said yes, causing the nurses to look uneasily at me before they gave me all the instructions anyways.

We don't even make it five steps out of the medical building before all of Skyla's 'men' rush us.

Oh joy.

Chapter Thirty Eight
Skyla

"Babygirl, what happened? Are you okay?" Liam asks, voice raised in panic.

"Where are you hurt?" Ronan demands, concern etched deep in his eyes as they trace over me from head to toe.

"I told you to keep her fucking safe, Putnam," Vincent gnashes at Asher, who gives him a bored expression.

"What would you have liked me to do, Griggs? Shoot Brenton before she even approached the table? Just to be safe?" Asher snarks.

"Yes," Vincent says seriously, not a hint of remorse in his words.

Asher rolls his eyes, but doesn't say anything as all the guys start up on him.

"Seriously, what the fuck, man? You couldn't have done anything to stop her? This is your crazy fucking ex we are talking about," Liam says.

"She's not my ex. She was a regular thing, that's it."

"Well, your regular *thing* just assaulted my *everything*. So I'm gonna need you to handle your shit before I do," Ronan fills in.

Shaking his head, Asher tries to storm off when I catch his arm.

He looks back in surprise, his eyes curious as he stays silent. His tense body softly relaxes as I speak.

"Thank you," I say.

It's like it takes his brain a few extra seconds to process the words before he blinks and nods, shifting his stance so he is no longer walking away. His eyes stay on mine the entire time he speaks to the guys. No matter how much I want to look away, I can't because there are three golden flecks in his left eye that I've never noticed until now. How have I not noticed them before?

"Brenton 'tripped' with her plate, and it hit Skyla in the back of the head. She has six stitches, and a concussion."

"I'll kill the fucking bitch," Vincent seethes.

That has my eyes pulling away from Asher's as I release my hold on his arm to reach for Vincent.

"Please don't. She's not worth it. Can someone just take me home? Please?" I ask.

"I will," all four of them say at once, forcing my eyes to meet each one of them.

"The more the merrier, I guess," I say with a small smile, as I begin walking.

As a unit, they all surround me like some sort of private protection detail. Ronan is in front of me, Vincent on my left, Liam on my right and Asher behind me. It's almost amusing how all of their heads seem to swivel at different times, scanning their surroundings thoroughly, like we are about to be attacked any minute.

When we get to my room we all spill inside before they form a straight line, all staring at me. Okay, this whole unified front thing is starting to unnerve me a bit. I wonder if this is what they practice at their Brethren meetings.

"What do you want to do, babygirl? Hot shower?" Liam asks.

Asher shoves his shoulder hard.

"No dumbass. She needs to keep her stitches dry for at least a day."

Liam frowns like he's disappointed for not knowing that and it hurts my heart a little bit. I take a few steps towards him, brushing my lips against his cheek before giving him a soft smile. He returns it, the sadness still there in his eyes but easing by the second.

"How about a movie?" Ronan offers.

"Not good for her with the concussion," Asher interrupts.

Ronan cuts him an irritated look before Vincent steps up beside me.

"How about you fuckers get lost. It's my night to watch her anyways."

"You watch her every night regardless," Liam scoffs.

"Exactly."

"I told the nurses that I'd stay up with her and make sure she doesn't sleep for too long. So I'm staying," Asher says, as he plops down on the loveseat beside my bed.

I'm surprised that he wants to stay. The nurse just said I needed someone, it didn't have to be him. When I have three other eager volunteers, you'd think he'd take the out and run. Something warms inside of my chest that he doesn't want to.

"Well, if Asher is staying I'm not going anywhere," Liam says, as he comes to stand by me and Vincent. "What do you say, Griggs? I'll be the little spoon tonight," he smirks playfully.

"Touch me and I'll chop your fucking hands off."

Liam makes an offended noise, as he shakes his head and slides into my bed first.

"I swear, you guys don't know what you're missing. The way men have begged me for just a touch would blow your minds."

"Oh, we're sure," Asher draws sarcastically.

"It's true! You know how much ass I get!" Liam says as he points at him.

"Unfortunately so, I've walked in on you in far too many compromising positions for my liking."

Liam shrugs casually, like he couldn't give a shit before Ronan stretches out on the couch, wordlessly claiming it.

"You should get some sleep," Asher says. "I'll wake you up in two hours."

"It's like one in the afternoon?" I laugh.

Asher stands up from the chair, closing the curtains until it is practically pitch black in here.

"Rest," he says.

Vincent moves to my dresser, handing me a pair of sleep shorts and a tank top. I begin to pull down my skirt since everyone in this room has already seen me at least mostly naked, before I pause. My eyes land on Asher who is watching me with an expression that I can only label as animalistic. I can't tell if it's hunger or something more dangerous. He looks ready to pounce on me, but I'm not sure it's in a good way. Not that there would be a good way for Asher to do anything to me.

Swallowing roughly, I decide to just get changed. It's not that big of a deal. Slipping off my skirt and peeling down my leggings, I glance to see his eyes chasing each inch of newly exposed skin before settling on my panties. I slip my shorts on, removing the sight in the next moment, before grabbing the hem of my shirt.

When I pull the material up and over my head, Vincent comes to me. Positioning himself against me, and in a not so subtle move, that blocks Asher's view before he reaches for the clasp of my bra. My breasts spill free as he undoes it, and I half expect Vincent to touch them. Instead, he keeps his eyes on mine, body blocking me as he pulls my tank top on for me.

Vincent presses a kiss to my forehead, before guiding me towards the bed where Liam is waiting with open arms.

"C'mon, babygirl. Let's snuggle," he says, with a waggle of his eyebrows.

I smirk and shake my head as I crawl into his arms, laying on my side when I feel Vincent wrap himself around my back. His fingers gently examine the bandage covering my cut, before he presses featherlight kisses around the area.

"Sleep, Siren. We got you."

After the third time being woken up, I decided I wanted to be up for a while. It's better than the feeling of just starting to fall into a good dream, only to be interrupted by Asher's annoying as hell alarm. Unfortunately it's now ten at night and I've already gotten six, albeit interrupted, hours of sleep.

My stomach grumbles, and I look over to see Asher is the only person that is still awake.

"You hungry?" Asher asks.

"How'd you know? You a mind reader or something?" I ask.

"I can hear your stomach from over here, Princess. What do you want?"

"What's open at this time of night?" I counter.

"Well the dining hall should have late night snacks and things like that made. If you want something a little more substantial, I'll call in the chef to make you whatever you want," he says as he begins thumbing through his phone.

"Are you crazy? No. We aren't going to wake someone up to come into work and be at my beck and call," I laugh quietly.

"Why not?"

I stare at him for a moment before shaking my head.

"Because that's not respectful, nor kind to do. They are trying to sleep, let them. I think I have some extra protein shakes if you could hand me one," I say as I point towards my fridge.

Asher frowns and shakes his head.

"You've hardly eaten today and what you did eat, you puked out. You need real food."

I feel a hand touch my hips, a sleepy voice murmuring in my ear.

"Just let him get you food, Siren," Vincent says softly.

Slowly I concede, nodding my head. Though, it's not like Asher needed my permission. He's already busy assumingly ordering food or calling the chef to come in.

It doesn't take long for the food to get here. Actually, it's kind of amazing how fast it gets here. Asher meets whoever the delivery person is at the door, making sure not to allow them a peek inside. I assume, seeing his fiancée tangled in bed with two other men and a third on the couch would come across a tad taboo.

When he steps back in, he has four large bags that he's somehow managing to hold with his two hands as he kicks the door shut. Surprisingly, Ronan, Liam and even Vincent stay asleep. Asher sets out the food across my desk, before pulling up the loveseat next to my desk chair.

He leans over Vincent, offering me a hand out of bed. I slip my hand in his as he pulls me up and out. My feet almost kick Vincent and I tuck them quickly, somehow wrapping myself around Asher in the process.

Asher looks down at me in surprise, before the smallest smirk touches his face.

"Looks like you're more of a koala bear than princess."

I give him a dry laugh as I shake my head, while he essentially carries me over to the desk. He sets me down on the loveseat while he takes the desk chair, before he begins unpacking bag after bag.

There is a pizza, supreme with no mushrooms and extra bacon, my all-time favorite way. Along with spaghetti, bacon cheese-burgers with chili cheese fries, and the biggest surprise, scratch made fish and chips. I haven't been able to find any decent fish and chips since coming to America. All of the batter is heavy and greasy, while the fish is very clearly frozen. Just from appearance alone I can tell this is good quality. The breading is light and flaky, and the fries look to be that perfect combination of crispy and soft.

All manners forgotten in the name of food, I dig in, trying a little bit of everything as I do. I eat and leave no crumbs behind.

"So," I say as I finish my second piece of pizza, god I'm really on a roll. I don't think I've eaten this much in the last three months. "Is it a coincidence you were able to guess all of my favorite foods without asking me a thing?"

Asher shrugs, busying himself with a burger in front of him.

"It was in your file."

I frown. "What file?"

"The one my dad gave me on you, before you came to Salem. It had pictures of you, your favorite foods, hobbies, friends. All of that stuff."

"Why would you need that?"

He swallows his food and takes a sip of one of the water bottles before speaking.

"It's designed to get the relationship on the right foot– establish common ground, shared interests."

"You clearly had no interest in that," I say with a hollow laugh.

He scoffs and nods before taking another bite, chewing it thoughtfully before taking another drink.

"I'm sorry. I don't think I apologized for the shit I pulled, did I?"

"Have you ever even apologized for anything in your life?"

Asher chuckles and nods his agreement.

"Fair point. Well, I am. I feel like shit, honestly. It wasn't too hard to explain away any guilt, blaming my actions on the thought of you being a calculated bitch but...you're not."

I don't respond, because while this isn't the best apology I've ever received in my life, it feels like this is a lot for him and I don't want to ruin it.

"When I saw those pictures at dinner," he says as he looks at me, trailing off with a shake of his head as he continues.

"It was like a lead ball had dropped into my stomach. I didn't think too much about how scared you would be in that hole. Looking at the pictures where you were desperately climbing the dirt wall, fear so deeply etched across your face," he winces. "I didn't like that I did that. I didn't like that I had become someone I always swore I wouldn't."

"Who is that?" I ask.

"My father," he says, his eyes locking on mine. "He's a man who enjoys others' misery, relishes in it. If he can flex his power and teach you a lesson in the same move, it's an extra good day in his eyes. The way I've treated you is only a tenth of what he did to my own mother, but I swore nonetheless that if I ever got married, I'd never lay a hand on my wife or disrespect her like that. And look at me now," he laughs, in a self-deprecating way that hurts my heart.

Images of a young Asher, watching the horrors of his childhood, flit through my mind. Seeing his father hurt and abuse his mother, before no doubt coming for him. I can practically hear his small voice vowing to never be like Christopher, and he's not, not yet at least.

"If it helps, you treated me like that when I was just your fiancée. There is still hope you'll treat your wife better," I tease, trying to lighten the mood.

Asher doesn't smile, though. Instead he turns to face me fully, his hand covering my own. My first instinct is to pull away from his touch. When I don't, something light settles inside me as Asher wraps his fingers around my hand at the same time.

"I'm sorry, Skyla. Truly. The way I've behaved and treated you opened yourself up to be hurt like you were today. I lead by example, and for over a month I've been setting the example that it's okay to hurt you, to disrespect you. I promise, moving forward no one will even dare touch a hair on your head," he says, his other hand coming to smooth down part of my hair.

My throat is suddenly thick and scratchy. I do my best to clear it as I nod.

"Thank you, I appreciate that."

He runs his tongue along his lower lip, like he's thinking over his next words.

"And as for the ceremony coming up...I know it's fast. I know there are a handful of people you'd rather be marrying," he says, his eyes tracing over the men in the room with us before coming back to me. "But I promise as your husband, to treat you with all the respect you deserve. It's not a perfect situation, but I'm going to try to at least make it a good one."

My heart squeezes at that, and a sense of relief washes over me. I've been so sad and so scared about what the future held with Asher. I wasn't sure what to expect honestly, the common denominator in all scenarios I envisioned was misery, though. So, to hear him say he's going to try. Even if he doesn't always succeed, at least he's going to try. It's worth more than I could ever express.

"When we move into our home after the wedding and everything...as far as them," he says, nodding his head to the guys. "Well...they are always welcome in our home...discreetly, of course."

I'm surprised by his words. Is he saying that I can still be with them even after Asher and I marry? I don't know what I expected for all of us after we did, I guess I didn't want to think about it, and honestly maybe they won't want me by that point. Feelings change, it's not like they'd want to share one woman forever, right? Still, the feeling of knowing that if we break up, it won't be by Asher's hands gives me a small sense of peace that I treasure greatly.

"And your...uhm, groupies too," I say, not sure what the appropriate word is for sluts. "Maybe besides Bridgette. I'd be okay if I never saw her again," I grimace.

A dark look passes across Asher's face as he shakes his head.

"You won't have to worry about her. She will never be around again."

I nod, thankful at that.

"Honestly, you won't need to worry about any women. I won't be bringing anyone to our home. I'm not going to disrespect you like that."

Frowning, I turn my head to the side.

"Isn't it the same thing?" I say, gesturing to the guys.

He shakes his head.

"Why not?"

Those chocolate brown eyes come up to me, his voice low and serious.

"Because, I don't love them."

My stomach flips and my heart stutters out of rhythm for a moment. Ronan and I have told each other that we loved one another. Liam and I have come close several times, and if what Vincent and I have isn't love, I don't know what to call it. Do I seriously love three men? At the same time?

Yeah...I guess I do.

"You might meet someone that you do," I offer. "Everyone deserves the freedom to love and be loved by someone. Everyone deserves that gift. So, when she comes along one day, I'll support you however I can," I say with a small encouraging smile.

Asher's brows knit together slightly, before a half smile lifts his face.

"Thank you, Skyla."

A rustling in the sheets catches our attention, snapping us out of this intense moment as we look to see Liam assumingly searching for me. He doesn't find me, but he does find himself nuzzled into Vincent. Vincent's arms reach out in his sleep, tucking Liam against his chest as he wraps his arms around him. Liam wiggles his ass into him, fully taking on the little spoon roll.

Asher and I look at each other with matching expressions before we begin laughing softly.

"How mad do you think Vincent will be when he wakes up?" I ask.

"So fucking pissed," Asher says as he stands up, snapping a picture of them cuddling together.

I give a warning look and he rolls his eyes.

"I'm not gonna share it. Just a little friendly blackmail."

Smiling, I shake my head as a yawn works its way out of me.

"Should we leave this out for them?" I ask, as I gesture to the food.

Asher nods. "They can have our scraps. Want to try to sleep a little more?"

I shrug and nod. He pulls out his phone to set another alarm as I stand up and my eyes go from the bed to the couch. I don't want to be caught up in the middle of whatever fight will happen when the guys wake up, so I tip toe over to Ronan, lifting the blanket he laid over himself before sliding under.

He wakes only for a moment as I lay on top of his chest. He presses a kiss to the top of my head before wrapping his arms around me. My head is sideways on his chest, looking out at the room and I see Asher situating himself in the loveseat once more. His eyes are on me, but he doesn't say anything. I give him a small smile as I mouth 'night'. He does the same before breaking eye contact, looking up at the ceiling and closing his eyes.

Chapter Thirty Nine
Liam

I rub at my sore bicep. Fuck. It's been three days and I swear to god the bruise from Vincent's fist is only getting worse. I was just as surprised as he was when I woke up to find that the person cuddling me was not my girlfriend, but one of the most intimidating men on campus. Griggs didn't even think twice, his eyelids fluttered open, looked at my face and bam, right to the arm. I'm glad Asher was there to pull him off me because he was going for my face next, and god knows I can't risk any damage to my money maker.

I'm making my way through the courtyard with some guys that I consider acquaintances. They are guys that started hanging around me when we all started at Gallows Hill University. Suckling at the power teat, I suppose. No one really cared about who was a Legacy and who was just a child of a member in high school and younger but here? Everything changed. A new food chain was built. The only thing that has stayed the same, is Asher still rules above all. Putnam's wouldn't allow it to be any other way.

One of the guys is going on and on about his new watch, that none of us give a shit about, before my eyes catch a glimpse of her.

Her hair moves in the breeze, an olive green cardigan draped over her shoulders, complimented by a pair of leggings that look especially delicious on her. I find myself veering in her direction before I can help myself, the group of guys mindlessly following after me.

I pause, frowning at them before shaking my head.

"I'll see you around," I say dismissively.

Thankfully they all get the hint, as they scatter like roaches in the next moment. Casually, I look around to see if anyone is watching me and to my eye, I don't think so.

I make my way towards her, my eyes scanning the rooms she's obliviously passing before one catches my eye.

Perfect.

Picking up my pace a little, I have to jog to reach her in time, but she still doesn't hear me coming. My left hand reaches for the door of an empty lecture hall while my right goes to her hip. Before she can think or even speak, I'm pushing her inside and shutting the door behind us. She stumbles a few steps and when she rights herself. She looks ready to fight, until she sees that it's me.

"Liam! You scared the shit out of me," she breathes out raggedly.

"Sorry," I smile, as I move from the door to her. "I saw an opportunity and had to take it."

"Yeah, well, I thought you were the stalker or something!"

"I said I was sorry," I say as I close the distance between us, my hands on her hips and my neck bending down to begin kissing her neck. She arches into my touch, extending her neck a little more as she huffs.

"Well, it's fine I guess. As long as you keep doing that."

I smile against the curve of her collarbone before nodding, wordlessly obeying her every wish. My tongue draws lazy circles across her chest, moving down further and further until I'm stopped by her shirt. Pulling the neckline of her tank top down to rest beneath her breasts. I pull them out of her bra, groaning at the sight before me.

My cock hardens instantly. Fuck, I need her so goddamn bad.

"Lay down, babygirl," I say, as I gesture towards the long skinny table before us.

She doesn't hesitate, pulling away from me and laying on her back with her feet planted on the table and knees bent. I grin as I run my hands up and down her body, before coming back to her breasts. One hand begins rolling her nipple between my thumb and forefinger, as I pull out my cock with the other.

"Open up, babygirl. I need that sweet little mouth."

"What about the door?" she asks anxiously, casting a glance at the door with no lock.

I shake my head. "No one ever uses this room. We're good."

She looks hesitant but nods regardless, popping her mouth open as I rest the tip of my cock on her lips. Her tongue flicks out first, swirling around the head before she sucks it deeper into her mouth. My head tips back with pleasure as she takes me deeper and deeper until she gags, forcing my cock to jerk with pleasure.

Her tongue begins making this S-like pattern on the underside of my cock with every bob of her head. It sends a tingling sensation straight to my balls, and I find myself fucking her face more than she's sucking my dick.

"Touch yourself," I grit out. "Play with that pretty pussy, just how you like it."

I watch as Skyla hooks her fingers into her leggings, pulling her underwear down with them, revealing her porcelain smooth skin and perfect little pussy.

Her fingers don't hesitate, clearly knowing exactly what she's doing and needing. They start with soft circles around her clit, picking up speed the harder I fuck her face.

"Dip a finger inside. Not too deep. I want to taste you," I groan as my fist winds around a handful of her hair, using it for better leverage.

She does as I say, slipping her middle finger inside just an inch or so. She does a swirling motion, pulling out the glistening finger and offering it up to me. Like the fine delicacy she is, I wrap my mouth around her in an instant, moaning at the taste that has me so fucking addicted.

When I release her finger, I grit my teeth as I attempt to control my orgasm.

"Rub that clit, babygirl. Make yourself come all over this table."

Her eyes squint closed and she nods before her hand begins rapidly rubbing herself. She's whimpering around my cock, her body practically vibrating with anticipation as the door opens.

I don't stop fucking her mouth, mainly because I don't know how to, but she sure as hell stops rubbing herself. As if her not playing with her pussy would make this situation look better for anyone.

My eyes connect with a familiar pair of brown ones and relief settles in me that it's no one who would expose our secret. However, now a new thrill runs through me. We've got a voyeur.

I say that because he is halfway in the door, eyebrows to his hairline, mouth parted in shock as he takes in the sight before him. I mean, it's a pretty fucking beautiful sight. Skyla is spread out on the table, tits out, mouth stuffed with cock and her bare legs spread, giving him a perfect view of that pussy that his eyes have been glued to for several seconds now.

"Joining us, brother?" I tease, though that thrill amplifies in me at the idea.

Fuck. That would be so goddamn hot to share her with Asher. Say what you want, but I love sharing my woman. Something about seeing her completely satisfied, doted on and adored like she deserves with a whole lot of orgasms all around makes for a good ass time.

He doesn't say anything but to my surprise he shuts the door behind him, pushing a chair in front of the handle to stop anyone else from coming in. When he's done he remains in place, just watching. I can see from here his chest is rising and falling quickly, but he doesn't say anything, and he hardly moves a muscle.

"This okay with you, babygirl?" I ask as I cup her jaw, slowing down my thrusts for a moment.

Her eyes connect with Asher's, probably giving him one sexy as hell view. Those pretty green eyes on him, mouth stretched open with a cock inside. Goddamn, I might come from looking at her myself.

Slowly, her gaze comes back to mine and she nods softly. I'm surprised by her answer if I'm honest. Until a few days ago, they could hardly stand to be in the same room as each other. Not sure what happened for this flip in dynamics, but hey, I'm not going to turn down a hot threesome with my best friend and my girlfriend.

Asher's eyes remain solely on her as he takes several steps towards her. I'm not even sure if he realizes he's moving towards us or not. He seems entranced, in a daze until he stops just near her thighs. Skyla wiggles her pussy in anticipation and Asher's eyes fly down to it, desire practically drowning his features as he stares at her.

Her clit is so pink and swollen, pussy practically soaking the table beneath her as she whimpers and groans.

"You want to be touched, babygirl?" I ask, as that tingling in the base of my spine begins, my balls tightening as she nods her head.

"You want Asher to touch you?" I ask again, everyone in the room needing her full consent before we cross any boundaries.

She doesn't nod immediately this time, first her head swiveling back and forth between Asher and I several times before she nods at Asher. My cock pulses in her mouth at that, and I feel a bead of pre-cum drop hit her tongue.

Asher exhales a slow heavy breath before his hands come away from his sides, each gripping Skyla's hips tightly. So tight, his knuckles begin to turn white. His entire body is vibrating as he slowly lowers his face down to her pussy. I can hear him slightly inhale, as if he were savoring the scent of her before he blows on her clit once.

Somehow, that small move of touching her but not is enough to send us both over the edge. Skyla's mouth tightens around me, her back bowing off the table as she moans and screams her release around my cock. I can't stop myself as my cum practically shoots into the back of her throat. She swallows every drop like a good girl, her tongue tracing around me from top to bottom to make sure she hasn't missed a bit of it before those pouty lips release me.

Leaning down I steal a kiss from her, my tongue tangling with hers as I do. I've never minded the taste of myself on someone. I actually really enjoy giving head, and the taste just doesn't bother me like it bothers some. I find it fucking hot actually, when you can taste yourself on your partners lips or their body. Like proof that you were there. Fuck. My cock is already getting hard again.

My eyes pull away from my babygirl to see Asher still in the same position. His hands grip Skyla's hips mercilessly, eyes on her pussy like he's trying to figure out if he should run like hell or devour her whole. The devious part of me is practically fucking feral for him to devour her whole. I'm ready to shove his head between her legs myself, because I know once he has a single taste of her he'll be a goner like the rest of us.

In the next moment his gaze snaps to hers, what looks like regret filling his eyes as he releases her and pulls away. He crosses the room, kicking the chair out of the way before practically ripping the door off its hinges on his way out.

I frown as he goes, turning back to Skyla who is wearing a matching frown. Determination to not let him ruin this for us, I smile down at her. brushing some hair away from her face as I help her sit up.

"You did so good, babygirl. I'm so proud of you."

She smiles softly at me, as I begin putting her back together. I tuck her breasts back into her bra, pulling her shirt up before dropping to my knees. I steal a quick kiss to her pussy that makes her giggle before pulling her panties and leggings up.

She's laughing lightly as I cup her jaw.

"I love you, Liam," she says with a shake of her head, her eyes widening as she does.

My heart beats out of rhythm, what I can only describe as butterflies rushing through me, as my entire body begins to thrum.

"You do?" I ask, doing my best to keep the overeagerness out of my voice.

"Oh, I. Uh. I...I do," she says, tripping over her words before saying that last part hesitantly.

If I wasn't so fucking happy right now, I might fuck with her, tease her a little bit but I just can't. Smashing my lips against hers, I hold her against me for several seconds before pulling her away smiling down at her as I do.

"I love you too, babygirl."

"Really?" she asks with a relieved smile.

"Oh, fuck yes."

We grin at each other, pressing our lips together once more before I help her off the table. There is a little wet spot beneath her and it makes me proud as fuck. We make our way out of the room casually, when we run right into Vincent.

His face is stoic but when his eyes roam Skyla from head to toe, something like annoyance flickers across them. I can tell that out of everyone, he will have the hardest time sharing her. He seems very much like the obsessive 'I don't share with anyone' type. Lucky that our girl can practically convince a fish to tap dance with just a quick smile.

"Looks like your escort is here, Miss Parris. It has been an absolute pleasure," I say with a dramatic bow.

She laughs and rolls her eyes, nodding at me the way a royal would.

"Good day, Mr. Walcott."

Vincent grunts as they walk past me, though I think that's the equivalent of a 'hey' for him, so I'll take it. I head towards my last class of the day when I see Asher on the phone. He's talking quietly, before he gives a solemn nod and hangs up. His eyes meet mine and he walks towards me. We have the next class together, so we begin walking in silence.

When I realize he isn't going to bring it up, I decide to rip the band aid off.

"That shit was hot, huh?"

"What shit?" Asher asks robotically, keeping his eyes forward as he does.

"You know, the sight of her pussy glistening, clit swollen begging to be touched, pretty pink nipples so hard they could cut diamonds. Ring a bell?"

His jaw tenses in response, but that's all I get out of him. We take a left and are almost to class when I stop him in his path with a fist to his chest. He looks down at it before meeting my eyes.

"All I'm trying to say is that, I know you're catching feelings for her and it's okay. We're great at sharing in case you can't tell. If anyone is going to fall for her, I'd want it to be her soon to be husband. She deserves the best of everything in life, and when you're not being an entitled prick that includes you too, man."

He doesn't respond and I don't expect him to. Asher will over-think and overanalyze every second of this conversation until he's near a mental breakdown. Then, and only then, will he make a decision about choosing to admit his developing feelings for Skyla, or ignore them all together.

Tune in next week, for another exciting episode of Asher Putnam and his emotional constipation!

Chapter Forty
Skyla

My mind is so wrapped up in yesterday that I hate to say, I have no idea what Maggie has been talking about for the last ten minutes. All I can think about is us in that classroom. Not just Liam and I. Liam, Asher and I– us.

I was so lust drunk, so caught up in the moment, that my brain wasn't even functioning properly. I was excited the second my eyes landed on Asher's, his shocked expression only fueling that excitement. Then, when he shut the door and blocked it, signifying he was staying, I was practically ready to come from that alone.

It's no secret that Asher Putnam is gorgeous. He's easily one of the sexiest men that I've ever laid my eyes on, and to have his eyes on me? His attention on me? It was an overwhelming sense of gratification. I wanted to keep his eyes on me forever. Which wasn't that hard of a task because he seemed unable to look away, no matter how hard I could tell he was trying to.

When Liam asked me if I wanted him to touch me, I only paused because I surprised myself with how fast I wanted to say yes. I wanted him to touch me, more than I wanted my next breath.

I honestly don't know who I've become in all this. Isn't it bad enough asking three men to share me with each other? Now, dizzying thoughts of adding a fourth to our dynamics is equally tempting and terrifying.

How would the others react? How would Asher react? My assumption is both would not be good. But if anyone was going to be added to this...thing, why shouldn't it be Asher? I know that he said the guys would be welcome anytime, and that he would be discreet when he would see women once we are married, but I don't want that. At all. The very topic turned my stomach, if I'm being honest.

Oh god. I think I have feelings for him. Not just lusty you're hot and I bet we would have amazing hook-ups together, feelings. Me not wanting him to see other people, to sleep with them. I think that counts as the real deal 'I want you for myself' feelings....shit.

"So, I don't know what to do. She's nice but she literally told me she was wanting to experiment. If I'm being honest, being the straight girls one night 'experience' has gotten really old. I want someone to want me for me, not for the thrill or taboo factor, you know? I thought I had that this summer, but she was just like all the rest," Maggie says, with a frustrated sigh.

I frown, feeling like total crap that she was bearing her heart and soul to me while I was daydreaming about what it would be like to have a fourth boyfriend. I'm the worst.

"What happened to her? The girl this summer?" I ask.

Maggie looks at me as we ride the elevator up to my room.

"Nothing, really. One day we were wrapped around each other in bed, admitting heavy feelings, the next we were here, and she was pretending I never existed outside of these walls," she laughs, though it's a sad bitter sound.

I pull her in for a hug, rubbing her back soothingly.

"I'm sorry, Mags."

She sniffs once, before clearing her throat and shaking her head as she pulls away.

"It's whatever. I'd just like to get over her by getting under someone that would actually be interested in dating me, not just fucking me, you know?"

I go to respond when she cuts me off.

"Oh wait, you don't know because you have three boyfriends. You don't know about such issues, when everyone and their mother is desperate to be a part of your little harem."

I roll my eyes, shushing her as I look around the halls.

"Ears everywhere, remember?" I scold, as we step out of the elevator.

"Relax. You're golden for now. You're not getting married until June. The heat will really come right before then. All eyes on you."

"Actually," I say. "It's been moved up. October."

Maggie stops in her tracks, eyes wide as she leans forward.

"Excuse me?"

"I think it's supposed to be a secret, but Asher and I are legally getting married in October. On Halloween of all days," I laugh bitterly. "We are still going to have the wedding in June, but no, eyes are very much on Asher and me, right now."

"Wow, uh. Are you ready for that?" she asks.

I laugh and shake my head. "Not in the slightest," I say, as I swipe my key card and step inside, a heavy feeling of dread sinking in instantly.

There is a white piece of paper resting on my bed, along with three pictures. Shakily, I step forward taking care not to touch anything this time as I read the letter.

My jealousy is bitter and unwavering
Do you enjoy seeing the way you have me shaking?
You have always and will always be mine

So I have to ask, why waste their time?
The clock will strike twelve and along will they go
Off to their duties, other women, they'll leave you all alone
I'll always be here to pick up your pieces and lick away the pain
Just let me in, my love, scream out my name

Beneath the poem is something new. Two scribbled sentences that look a lot less thought out than this creepy rhymey poem.

Are you trying to make me jealous? Because it's working.

My stomach bottoms out when I see that the three pictures are of me and each of my guys. There is a picture of Ronan and I in his car, his hand resting high up on my bare thigh. Then there is Liam and I walking to class, his pinky hooking with mine as we walk. The last is Vincent and I. He has me pinned against a wall down the side of a building he swore no cameras could see. His hand is on my throat, other hand buried in my hair and his lips on mine.

Fuck.

Suddenly, my breathing becomes ragged. I'm unable to catch my breath, to think, to stand. The world becomes dizzy and hazy, and I stumble to the ground, laying on my side as I tuck my legs to my chest.

"Oh my god! Skyla! Are you okay?" Maggie says as she drops beside me, looking me over as if she can find something physically wrong with me.

"Can't," I heave. "Breathe," I rasp. In and out. In and out. I'm desperate for an ounce of oxygen but coming up short with each attempt. "Call," I gasp. "Guys."

The more I focus on how much I can't breathe, the worse I get until I'm full on hyperventilating. I can't do this. I can't take this. I've tried to brush it all off, tried to forget it. There is no forgetting it, though. Someone has been actively stalking me for weeks now and I'm officially terrified.

He can slip in and out of my room with no issues, he can follow me and my guys around and none of us are any wiser. He has to be on campus. He's near me, close enough to touch me. And that thought alone, sends me spiraling into another panic attack.

I don't know how much time goes by before I hear the sound of heavy footsteps thunder across the floor. Ronan steps into the room first, his panicked eyes flicking around the room. I didn't hear Maggie call him, but she must have. His eyes take in the bed, before he drops to the floor beside me.

"Baby, are you hurt? What happened?"

My breathing is loud and erratic as I try to speak.

"H-he," I huff. "Is b-back," I say, as a choked sob tears through me.

Ronan instantly gathers me into his arms, rocking me like a child as I sob and choke on the air around me. My head is so light, it feels like I'm practically floating. I feel so close to passing out, and all I can do is suffer in this strange space between consciousness and unconsciousness.

The door gets thrown open again a few moments later, a drop of sweat falling down the side of Vincent's face as his eyes scan the room, gun in his hand.

He's always the one to pull a gun first, and ask questions later. Which, I guess when your girlfriend has a deranged stalker isn't the worst motto to have. His eyes run over the note quickly, before he is in front of me.

"Siren," he says steadily, reaching a hand to my cheek. "Can you feel this?"

I shake my head, feeling numb. His eyes are patient but his face is thunderous as he nods.

"Okay, what do you see? Name five things you can see."

"I-I c-can'tttt," I whine, in between labored breaths.

"She can't breathe, let alone talk," Ronan snaps.

Vincent ignores him, keeping his eyes on me.

"It's okay, Siren. I'm here. Deep breath in through your nose," he says, demonstrating it like I'm an idiot or something. "Deep breath out through your mouth," he breathes out.

He continues doing this over and over again, until I find myself trying to follow along. I take a choppy breath in, blowing out shakily.

"Good, that was good. Again. In and out," he says, breathing on pace as he does.

Soon I'm able to get a breath or two in before he nods.

"Now tell me three things you can see."

"Y-you, the c-couch and my b-bed," I say as I begin to panic again.

"Shhh, shhh," Vincent says, as Liam and Asher rush into the room.

"What happened?"

"What's going on?"

"Shut the fuck up!" Ronan practically snarls as he holds me tighter.

"Eyes on me, Siren. Two things you can feel," Vincent says, reaching out to rest his hand on my cheek again.

I feel my eyes close, sinking into his touch.

"Y-your hand and...and...Ronan's-s arms wrapped around me-e," I say, only having a few stutters this time.

"That's so good. Almost there. One thing you can smell."

I try to inhale through my nose as best as I can.

"Ronan's cologne," I answer.

Earning a tighter squeeze from Ronan and an encouraging nod from Vincent. He doesn't smile but he rarely does so that's no surprise. His hand does cup my face tenderly though, his thumb rubbing against my cheek as he presses his lips to my forehead.

"You did so good, Siren. I love you so much, don't ever scare me like that again, okay?"

I hear Maggie softly 'aw' in the background, but I ignore her and everyone else around us.

"I... I love you too." I say, thankfully not stuttering for lack of oxygen, but out of shock. I don't know. I had hoped he loved me, but it feels...different to hear him say it out loud. Reassuring.

Vincent leans forward, capturing my lips with his as rustling happens over my shoulder. He can tell the moment I hear it because I tense up at the reminder. He deepens the kiss, allowing his tongue to tangle with mine as his arm makes some kind of motion. I feel the air shift like people have stepped out, but I'm too wrapped up in this kiss to care.

When he pulls away I feel a tug come from my jaw, my head tilted back for Ronan who bends down to meet me. The kiss is so vastly different from Vincent's or even Liam's, but it's addicting all the same.

As we break apart, Ronan smiles down at me lovingly and it forces a smile out of me as well.

"There's my beautiful baby's smile."

I smile wider as I feel Vincent's hand in my hair, slowly massaging my head as Ronan's fingers dance along my jawline .

"Okay, you guys are so cute I want to barf. I'm also seriously considering switching teams, because I want someone to look at me like that," Maggie says from the corner. Ronan and Vincent both shoot her irritated looks, but that doesn't stop her. "Seriously babe, you've gotta be able to spare a boyfriend or two for a night, right? Think any of them will let me peg them?"

A laugh bubbles out of me. "Probably Liam," I say.

"I heard my name," my adorable goof says, with a smile as he pops his head in the door.

"Maggie asked if any of my boyfriend's would like to get pegged and I said probably you."

"Fuck yes," he smirks, "but only by my girl, sorry, Bartlett."

Maggie gives him an exaggerated 'oh shoot' snap as she shakes her head.

"Dang, almost had you too."

The air in the room lifts lightly, for a moment I forget about the stalker, the pictures, and everything to focus on the most important piece of information. Liam would want me to peg him? I don't know how I feel about that...it could be pretty hot, I guess. Nope, scratch that. I think it would be really hot. Shit. Maybe one day.

Liam comes to crouch beside me, taking one of my hands into his as he gives me a concerned smile.

"You okay, babygirl?"

Having all three of their hands on me is like the best kind of drug. It numbs and soothes me simultaneously. My body instantly relaxes, melting into all of their touch as I nod my head softly.

"I'm sorry."

"Don't be," Ronan says. "We all let down our guard."

My eyes come to Vincent who has his jaw clenched and his eyes turned away.

"Vincent? Are you okay?"

Slowly he turns to me, his eyes so sad they break my damn heart and his mouth smashed into a firm line as he shakes his head.

"I'm so sorry, Siren. I usually check your room every day before you get back. I thought you and Bartlett were going to her place. I should have checked."

I frown at that.

"It's not your fault. It's not like you could have known that he was going to choose today to leave something."

All three guys share an uneasy look as Asher steps in through the door, a gloved hand holding the piece of paper as he nods.

"He's left you something every day this week. We've just been able to intercept it before you could see."

"What?" I ask, as I whip around in Ronan's lap so that I can face Asher head on.

His posture is rigid, jaw set like he's prepared for me to come unglued.

"So, you guys have been lying to me? What else has he left?"

"Just pictures of you, more of your ruined panties," Liam grits out with a disgusted shake of his head.

"And more poems, all adoring and loving," Ronan finishes.

My eyes come to Vincent's first, before moving to Liam, Ronan and finally landing on Asher.

"I can't believe you guys kept this from me! How am I supposed to trust any of you if you're keeping things from me? It's my life that could be in danger. Does that not mean anything, to any of you?" I scoff.

"It means everything, to all of us," Vincent says fiercely.

"Then, why the fuck would you think it was a safer plan to have me let my guard down? How is it better for me to think the situation is getting better, instead of keeping my defenses up to protect myself?"

"We didn't want you to worry, babygirl," Liam says.

"We just wanted you to have a little bit of a normal life. For just a bit," Ronan finishes.

I let out a bitter laugh.

"Whose brilliant plan was that?" I practically snarl.

Liam begins to speak. "We—"

"It was me," Asher says.

All eyes swing to him as he remains unmoving.

"I decided it was best to keep you in the dark. I didn't want your messy emotions getting in the way of things," he says, as he gestures to where I sit on the floor.

That jab felt especially painful, poking at a tender part of my walls that were slowly coming down for him.

"I forced them not to tell you, it's on me. I'd do it all over again, because you've smiled more in this last week than I bet you have in your whole life."

I open my mouth to argue that fact before I nod in agreement.

"See? You're welcome," Asher says, in a way that raises my hackles.

"Shut the fuck up, man," Liam grumbles. "What can we do for you?" he asks as he faces me again.

"This. Can I just have more of this?" I ask, gesturing to the fact that they are all touching me.

They all nod as Ronan stands up, keeping me in his arms as he does before laying on my bed and setting me in the middle. Vincent takes up the other side while Liam crawls between my legs, resting his head on my upper thigh.,

"Thank you," I whisper softly, allowing my body to relax into the feel of them all.

I look around the room to find that Maggie is gone. She probably wanted to make a quiet escape in the heat of everything, and I don't blame her. I'm grateful she was here, because I don't know how I would have been able to call the guys otherwise.

The only person still standing is Asher. The letter in his hand is clenched tightly by his side, his eyes flicking between the four of us before settling on me. There are so many emotions in his gaze and yet I struggle to name any of them. I feel like I'm crazy, like I'm seeing what I want to see, not what's actually there.

I want to see desire deep in those melted chocolate eyes. I want to see envy and lust, wishing he was with us right now. I want to see pure desperation for me and only me.

How fucking selfish am I?

If any of those emotions were there, they are gone in a flash before he straightens up and nods.

"I'm gonna go try to lift some prints. Keep your eyes on her," he says before turning and heading out the door, closing it behind him as he does.

Despite it being the middle of the day, I feel my eyes begin to flutter closed, the exhaustion of the panic attack taking full control of my body as I drift off to sleep surrounded by the three men who hold my heart, and I theirs.

Chapter Forty One
Asher

I move through campus briskly, not paying attention to anyone or anything. I'm heading to my dorm building but only going one floor up to Andrew Hutchinson's room. His dad owns the largest tech security company on the east coast and his son is his little protégé. I know how to lift fingerprints, we're taught basic things like that in our training, but I don't have the time, patience or energy for that. I'll leave it to the geek.

My fist pounds on the door, some scrambling sounds coming from inside before Andrew peeks his head out. He seems to almost relax when he sees that it's me, which is usually not the reaction that I get. Most people around here fear me just as much as they fear my father. He tells me it's a good thing. I've just never really known any different.

"Hey, Asher. What's up?"

"I need you to lift some prints for me and run them. No one has touched it but me with my glove on so whoever comes up, I want the name. Got it?"

"Sure. No problem," he says as his eyes begin scanning over the paper."

"I said lift it, don't fucking read it," I snap, causing himself to straighten up and push his door open.

"Come in, set it right there," he says, pointing to a blank desk with a myriad of tools and tech gadgets. I won't even begin to guess what they do.

Three expensive looking cameras sit on the shelf above as well as several photographs hung up on the walls. They are landscape photos like the forest, the beach and stuff like that. They are clearly amateur but not half bad.

"How long?" I ask as I turn to face him as he begins collecting his supplies.

"Uh, half an hour? Maybe more?" he says.

"Make it less," I say as I move past him, shutting his door behind me as I turn towards the elevators.

I don't feel like waiting around, hovering over his shoulder so I decide to head up to my room. It isn't where I really want to be right now, but where I really want to be isn't an option for me. Not now, not ever.

I don't know when it happened. I'm not sure if it happened slowly or seemingly overnight. All I know is that for longer than I'd care to admit, things have been feeling...different. And I don't know how to stop it. I don't know how to shut my mind off, to not think about her, to not want her.

Sure, she's always been a smoke show. I knew that from the moment my father handed me her file, with a 'meet your future wife' speech. I was so pissed off that my time as a bachelor was getting cut short. As the most powerful man on campus, I wasn't even included in the decision of who would be my wife.

I was so furious and angry that this woman was getting thrust upon me, and I took it out on her. For weeks, I thought of idea after idea on how to make her life hell. How to force her to call this thing off herself. I knew there was no way it could come from my side, but I had hoped maybe she had more say in this than me. I should have known better.

One moment spent with her and her father, and I knew that the man had more disdain for her than my father did for me, I really didn't think that was possible. Two moments spent with her after she witnessed my father's rage firsthand and treated me with kindness I didn't deserve, and I knew that I had so wrongly misjudged her. Three moments of seeing her mostly naked and wanting, watching her beg and whine and moan around Liam's cock while being desperate for my touch, and I knew I was fucking done for.

As I step inside my room, I kick the door shut, burying my fingers into my hair as I pull hard.

FUCK!

This wasn't the plan. I wasn't supposed to fall for her. Even when I decided hating her would be futile, I thought we could be amicable. Have a friendship of sorts and I was even willing to allow her to see the guys, even if saying the words out loud tasted like ash on my tongue. The truth is, I think realization hit me at that very moment. The one where a small voice in my head jumped out and asked, 'What if you could be enough? What if having you and you having her was all you two needed?'

I squashed that inner voice to dust, because we both know that's not how that would go down. I want to be selfish. I want to steal her away from all of them, keep her tucked away and safe. It's obvious that currently, there isn't any room in her heart for me. There's no room left.

If I ban her from ever seeing them again, if I kept her locked away in a cage, she would only hate me, not love them less. As much of a monster as I'm sometimes portrayed to be, I'm not completely heartless. I know me being selfish would hurt Ronan and Liam...I don't really give a fuck about Vincent to be honest, but most of all I'd be hurting her. I've already hurt her enough. I don't want to inflict more pain. She doesn't deserve it.

So, I'll be the one that suffers. Once we're married, she will be able to live at least, for the most part, happily ever after with her boyfriends. I'll go out, get black out drunk and lose myself in whatever wet and willing hole is up for the taking that night. It won't really matter in the end, none of them will be her, so none of them will be worth a fucking damn.

My phone buzzes in my hand, and despite it only being ten minutes I had hoped it was Hutchinson. Unfortunately, it's the devil incarnate himself.

"Hello, father," I greet.

"Asher, how are things coming along?"

"Things are going well. How about with you?"

"All good here. You staying out of trouble?" he asks, a heavy warning lacing his words. I'm actually thankful that I'm able to be honest at the moment. Lying to him is always a tossup, he is too well versed at bullshitting. It only works maybe forty percent of the time.

"Actually, I am. Skyla and I have been spending more time together. She's actually pretty great, I see why you selected her for me."

"Really?" he says, surprise evident in his tone. "Well, isn't that delightful to hear. She's such a good girl, isn't she? So pretty and polite. Just watch that you conceal that fire. Her mother had it, just the same and look how that ended for her."

I nod, hating that Skyla has revealed that side of herself to him already. He sees her as a threat. Not outright, but a potential wild card which is almost worse.

"Whatever Henry did seems to have stuck, she's extremely obedient once you break her down a little. Like a wild mustang," I compare, my stomach turning at the bullshit comment.

My father barks out a laugh.

"Aren't they all."

"I've been wanting to ask, why are we moving up the ceremony? I can make my assumptions, but why hold off on the actual wedding itself? Isn't the ceremony usually held in conjunction with the wedding?"

The phone goes silent. It extends for so long I almost think we lost connection when he speaks. There's no humor in his voice, no emotion. Just careful calculation.

"Because, I deemed it so."

I struggle to come up with just the right response when he continues.

"Who the hell do you think you are? If I tell you to slit that girl's pretty little neck in the middle of the courtyard, you'll do it with a goddamn smile on your face!" he snarls. "I am your king! I am your god! If I command it, it is done. End of discussion."

"Of course, father," I concede quickly, doing my best to de-escalate the situation. "My apologies. I was merely curious."

"It is not your job to be curious," he continues. "Your job is to keep things in order at the university, staff and students included. Your job is to keep yourself and your fiancée out of trouble. Your job is to do as you're fucking told! I'm gifting you a virgin bride, one of the finest you could ever dream of, before your actual wedding. All that should be coming out of your ungrateful mouth is 'Thank you'."

I hold my tongue, waiting for him to finish his tirade before he blows out a ragged breath.

"I thought I raised you better than this. Maybe I've given you too much power too soon. Maybe this is too great of a reward."

"I apologize, father. I know, you only have myself and the Brethren's best interests in mind."

"Hmm," he hums, like he isn't sure if I'm bullshitting him or not.

Honestly, maybe it works fifty percent of the time because I think I'm getting better at it.

"Thank you," I add on. "For Skyla. She really is better than I could have imagined."

Shit. I definitely shouldn't have included that last piece.

"Is she now?" my father asks, interest officially piqued.

Fuck.

"Yes, she is," I say smoothly, despite my racing heart. "She's stunning and has been quite cooperative as I establish the rules and protocols of our future relationship."

He pauses like he doesn't quite believe me but lets it slide.

"Well, that is certainly good to hear. I will pass on the good news to Henry as well. Talk soon," he says, before abruptly hanging up.

I hold the phone in my hand for a moment or two, re-thinking every word that I said. I meant every one about her, the nice ones, at least. Something in my gut tells me that was the wrong move with my father.

As I begin pacing the room, I'm filled with more conflict, more panic, more frustration than I've felt in a long time. The only thing I can bring myself to focus on currently, is getting Hutchinson to hurry the fuck up with those fingerprints.

Chapter Forty Two
Skyla

Soft lips rouse me awake, beginning at my inner thigh before peppering my pussy. I feel the lips brush against the lacy material and realize that I'm naked. Or at least my pants are gone. Blinking my eyes open, I look down to see Liam with his face pressed against me, assaulting my skin with a smattering of kisses, as his pretty green eyes come up to mine.

"Sleep well, babygirl?"

"Mhmm," I hum before chuckling. "What exactly do you think you're doing?" I ask.

"Giving you the best wakeup call ever," he smirks with a wink, before he continues.

"We told him not to," Ronan defends from my side, startling me for a moment.

Oh my god. I forgot I fell asleep between all three of them. No wonder I'm so freaking hot. Glancing to my left, I see Vincent watching me, his eyes intent and focused as he brushes some hair out of my face.

"You've had a hard day. Is this what you want? Or do you need some space?"

Liam pauses, waiting for my response. I reach one hand out, threading it in Liam's hair before forcing his head back down. He goes happily, pulling my panties to the side as he begins pressing soft kisses up and down my slit.

"I want you," I say to Vincent before turning to face Ronan. "All of you."

Ronan and Vincent share a look over my head before both glancing down to me. I hear a rip and look down to see that Liam has ripped my panties, pushing the useless scraps to the side as he settles himself further between my legs.

"That's more like it," he says, before his tongue glides through my pussy.

The move takes my breath away and before I can catch it, Ronan is there.He presses his lips to mine, placing a hand on my hip as his tongue gently strokes against my own. In the next moment, I feel a hand at my jaw, pulling me away from him and towards another waiting mouth.

Vincent's kiss is much harsher than Ronan's. Where Ronan's makes me feel safe and cherished, Vincent's makes me feel like I'm his obsession, like I'm treasured. He treats me like I'm the most precious thing in the world, and he doesn't know if he wants to keep me safe or break all my pieces apart just so he can memorize each individual fragment.

As Vincent deepens the kiss, Ronan begins placing kisses against my shoulder, running up and down my neck as he starts to grind his cock against my ass. Liam's tongue meanwhile, is swirling around my clit, forcing me to gasp and whimper into Vincent's mouth.

If I thought it was intense being with Liam and Ronan at the same time, having all three of them like this is practically mind blowing. I don't know where to focus, where I should allow myself to feel the most pleasure. So, I turn my brain off and simply feel. I alternate between kissing Ronan and Vincent, while running my fingers through Liam's hair as I grind my hips against his face.

Before I can stop myself, I feel that familiar pressure building in my lower belly and before I know it I'm coming– hard. Screaming against Ronan's lips, he silences me with his hand, as Liam continues feasting on me like he never wants to stop. It's intoxicating, erotic and I only want more.

When my orgasm has eased, Liam pops up from his place between my legs, his lips glistening with my release before he crawls over my body pulling me in for a kiss. My taste is the first thing I notice and on him, it's so fucking delicious. My tongue chases him down for more of it, and we fall into a messy heap of tangled hands and mouths. I don't know who I'm kissing or touching at any given moment. All I know is this right here, feels like the closest thing to heaven.

A cock is pushed into my face, and I take it in my mouth happily hearing the deep guttural groan of Ronan as I do. Looking to my left I see Liam laying where I was, stroking his pierced cock. I move from Ronan to Liam, taking him into my mouth as well. He winds his fist into my hair and uses that leverage to face fuck me, much like he did in the empty classroom the other day.

I gag and choke on him. I take him to the back of my throat before releasing him, forcing a whiney moan to slip past his lips as I come to Vincent. His eyes are pitch black with lust, and he wastes no time shoving me down onto his cock. I can't help but moan at the ferocity of his thrusts, when I start to feel a mouth trailing down my ass cheeks. Though my shirt is still on, my bottom half is completely bare, as I'm practically bent over Liam in an effort to reach Vincent. He doesn't seem to mind though as he positions himself right behind me, his tongue licking from my pussy to my ass.

Suddenly the sensation is ripped away, and the bed bounces as

I look back to see Ronan shove Liam out of the way before taking his spot.

"Greedy fucking bastard," Ronan grumbles, before spearing me with his tongue.

I gasp at the way his tongue feels so different inside of me than Liam's, and I arch my back to give him better access. Ronan's hands come to my hips as I continue taking Vincent into my mouth, his encouraging thrusts only egging me on to make him come, and hard.

My eyes flick to the side to see Liam standing in front of us, stroking his cock quickly. Guilt flickers inside of me that I can't touch him in this position, but he just smiles and shakes his head like he can read my mind.

"Don't you fucking feel sorry for me. I'm trying everything I can to not blow my load at the sight of you right now. You're so goddamn perfect," he groans as he jerks his hips. "I can't wait for us to take you the way you deserve. One for each hole. How does that sound, boys?" he asks, earning approving groans from Ronan and Vincent as I smile around Vincent's cock.

"Go ahead, baby. Make Griggs come. You've got a fucking line," he smirks, like the cheeky asshole he is.

I take Vincent deeper than before and I reach a hand up to cup his balls.

"Fuck yes," he hisses as I begin massaging them, while he takes control of his thrusts.

"That's it, babygirl. He loves that. Swirl your tongue around his head," Liam encourages.

I do as he says and Vincent groans in approval.

"You're welcome," Liam smirks.

I roll my eyes at him before I continue, flicking my tongue against his head once more when Ronan's tongue hits me in just the right spot, sending my second orgasm crashing into me like a tidal wave. I squirm and moan which seems to be the push Vincent needs, because his orgasm comes out of nowhere. His cum pours down my throat as he pushes himself deeper. I gag around him and do my best to swallow every drop, but he just keeps coming. He rips away with a savage growl before tapping my cheek.

"Swallow it all like a good girl."

I do as he says, swallowing what was left in my mouth, causing pride to shine in his eyes as he crawls out from beneath me and moves to the other side of the room. We all switch positions, Ronan coming to stand beside Liam as they both stroke their cocks.

Moving back and forth between the two of them, I take turns sucking their cocks. As I'm sucking on Ronan, Liam lets a string of curse words out before grabbing my hair and ripping me over to him.

"C'mere, my pretty little cum slut," he says, before shoving himself into me and coming down my throat.

I run my tongue along his piercings and he moans, cursing out his release before he slowly eases back. There is a relaxed smile on his face when my chin is pinched and I'm pulled back over to Ronan.

"Open your mouth," he grits between clenched teeth.

I just barely open in time before he's shooting his cum into my mouth. It doesn't go as deep as Liam or Vincent, instead coating my tongue with his release as he jerks off into my mouth. His movements slow and he lets out a heavy breath before a smile emerges.

"Goddamnit, you are so fucking perfect, baby."

"Isn't she?" Liam smiles. "So perfect for us."

"Agreed," Vincent says from his relaxed position on the couch, what can be considered a Vincent version of a smirk on his face, as I look around at my guys with a shy smile.

"Aw c'mon, babygirl. You can't act that shy when you just took three cocks in your mouth, back to back," Liam smirks.

Ronan smacks the back of his head and scolds him.

"You're embarrassing her."

"I'm not trying to! It was a compliment," Liam defends, with tossed out arms and that has me chuckling.

All three of them seem to soften when I do, each holding an adoring look for me in their eyes. Wow. I'm totally in love with all three of them.

Chapter Forty Three
Vincent

It's officially October, and I fucking hate it. I don't think I've ever hated a month so much in my life, but this one? This one can burn in fucking hell. It's the time of the year, when every annoying as fuck tourist comes to Salem, trying to see or do what, I don't really know. The streets are crowded, businesses jack up their prices and stupid as fuck events and carnivals go on every goddamn weekend.

I think the worst part about this October though, is what will come at the end of the month. Skyla doesn't know the extent of what will happen. Truthfully, none of us know except for Ronan. Despite all of our threats, he hasn't revealed what the ceremony will consist of. He said that if he revealed the secrets before the day of, he could risk banishment, but he said it was not good for any of us. So obviously, I've been freaking the fuck out. And how do I deal with freaking out? Bloodshed of course.

I'm currently sitting on top of some stinky piece of shit, that tried to steal millions from one of the Brethren's investment businesses. Real estate or stock market, shit? I don't really know, and I don't really care. When I got the mark, I was more than happy to relieve a little anxiety. It's just this poor fucker's fault that he is the one paying the price.

The text said freestyle, which means I get to kill him however the fuck I want. If I make too much of a mess I'll call in a cleanup crew. Looking around at his blood soaked office, I'd say a cleanup crew will definitely be necessary. He's stuck to the floor, two twelve inch rods impaling each thigh and effectively nailing him to the ground. It only took two swings from my sledgehammer on both to get him nice and locked down to the ground.

This is the side of me that few have seen. Many speculate, but only a handful have ever witnessed it, and those that have usually aren't around to tell the tale. It's a side I'm desperate to hide from my Siren. I'm not sure she'd ever look at me the same. If she couldn't look at me, couldn't love me? Fuck bloodshed. I'd kill every motherfucker on this earth including her before ending myself. Without her, I'm fucking nothing. I'm barely even anything with her. So, I have to keep this part of me hidden, private, tucked away for the right moment.

I don't want to say that I enjoy taking lives, that would make me a psychopath. On second thought, maybe I am one actually because I really do enjoy it. Only to those that deserve it. Only to those that the world is better off without.

This piece of shit? The one who hits his wife, ignores his children and steals from one of the most well-known and feared secret societies in the country. Yeah, no one is going to lose a wink of sleep over him.

Tired of dragging this out, I settle for a simple beheading. Reaching for the hatchet I always bring with me in my bag of goodies, I lift it up. He squirms beneath me, fear in his eyes as I allow gravity to do a majority of the work, slicing straight through his fatty flesh before the loose head flops to the side.

Standing up, I reach for the expensive handkerchief in his pocket. I wipe away the blood splattered across my face before tossing the cloth back onto his now decapitated body. Stripping off my gloves, I pull out my phone and shoot off a quick text requesting a cleanup crew with very vague details.

Once I get the confirmation, I'm free to leave. I strip off all of my clothes and shoes, leaving them beside the body for disposal before changing into the new shirt, pants and shoes that I brought with me.

A quick run of a comb through my tousled black hair and I'm good to go. I'm on my way home for the night when my phone buzzes in my pocket. I smash the elevator button, stepping inside as it takes me down to the parking garage.

Siren: Up for a late night swim?

My heart clenches just from her name on my screen, let alone her wanting to see me.

Me: I'll be there in ten.

I know damn well it's at least a twenty minute drive back to Gallows Hill, but see if that stops me from getting to my girl. When I step out of the elevator I make my way over to my bike, tossing my leg over the blacked out beast before firing it up. Slipping on the helmet, I kick it into gear and take off, zipping in and out of traffic as I leave the city and head back to Salem.

We've still been taking shifts watching over Skyla, her stalker is still very much out there. Just because he hasn't made a move since the day with the pictures, means nothing to me. The others slowly seem to be letting their guards down again, but I won't make that mistake twice. It's infuriating that Asher wasn't able to pull any fingerprints from the letter. He used Hutchinson to run it which I think was his first mistake. If you want something done right, you do it yourself.

Fingerprints are such a long shot a majority of the time. Someone like this is careful, calculated and smart as hell. They'd know better when writing and delivering these letters. They'd wear fresh gloves and come and go at times and places when there is no surveillance. I've installed some cameras in the hallway outside Skyla's door but besides that, I have no idea what to do except wait for the piece of shit to fuck up. And when he does, I'll skin him alive like the worthless worm deserves.

I get there in nine minutes, which even I'm impressed by. Parking right outside the pool building, I toss my helmet onto the handlebar and head inside, intent on getting to my Siren as fast as possible.

When I get there she's already doing laps, though she's clearly going at a leisurely pace. Her body glides through the water like it was born to do so, and when she flips around to go the other way I notice she's not wearing a normal swimsuit. No, she's wearing a red and white polka dot bikini that her tits are practically spilling out of.

Jesus.

As she makes her way back towards my side of the pool I move to the edge, crouching down and waiting for her. When she reaches the edge and goes to turn around, I stop her, gripping her throat and lifting her several feet out of the water.

She gasps at the action before I crush my lips against hers, desperate to taste her. I've been fucking itching to touch her again and I only said goodbye to her not four hours ago. I'm so fucking in love with this girl, and I don't give a damn. She makes this shitty life worth living, makes my formerly worthless heart beat for the first time in years, just for her.

When I pull away I release her, allowing her to sink back into the water. She smiles up at me softly, removing her goggles as she brushes her hair back.

"No cap and inappropriate swim attire," I tsk. "Coach is going to be furious with you if he finds out."

"So, let's not tell him," she smirks at me.

I cross my arms over my chest, looking down at her seriously.

"What exactly do you think you're doing out here, all alone at night, Siren? Especially looking like that."

She shrugs, floating on her back as she speaks.

"Ronan is here, in his office."

Irritation passes through me for only a moment. I've gotten more used to the sharing thing, and sometimes it's hot as hell, but my mind hasn't changed. One day, eventually, a choice will come whether she wants it to or not. When it does, I'll be the one holding her in my arms or I'll fucking gut the others until I am.

"Why isn't he here with you then?" I ask, allowing my voice to carry towards his office.

"I wanted some time just you and me...is that okay?"

I scoff as I grab the back of my shirt, pulling it up and over my head before I kick off my shoes and undo my pants.

"Anytime you need me, Siren, I'm here."

When I'm down to my boxers I slip into the pool, my arms winding around her quickly as she wraps her legs around my torso. Pushing us through the water, we slowly bob and float together, enjoying the peace that comes from our shared space.

She pulls back for a moment, a smile on her face that slowly begins to morph.

"What's that?" she asks.

"What's what?"

She touches my neck, forcing it sideways as her finger rubs against me, her wet finger coming back with a tinge of red.

"Is that blood?" she asks. "Are you bleeding?"

Her eyes begin quickly scanning over me, assessing me for injuries when she comes up short.

"It's not mine," I say, hoping that will be enough to ease her mind because it's not exactly like I can give her any more details other than that.

She frowns at that, pulling away slightly. If she thinks physical distance can get in between us at this point, she's crazy. I allow her to take her space, still floating in place as she speaks.

"Are you dangerous? Should I...should I be afraid of you?"

"Yes," I answer honestly. "To both."

My Siren doesn't outwardly react to that, instead she seems to process the information, mulling over her words carefully.

"Would you ever hurt me?"

"Never," I say immediately.

"Would you ever let anyone else hurt me?"

"I'll be cold and rotting in the ground before I let that happen."

She nods consideringly at that, before slowly coming back into my arms. Like the last piece of a puzzle clicking into place, my body physically reacts to her touch.

"That's kind of romantic, in a crazy way."

"That's the only way I know how to be romantic, Siren."

Rolling her eyes, she smiles.

"That's not true. That hot spring you took me to? Very romantic."

"If you think that's romance, you seriously need your bar raised."

Her head cocks to the side, a daring smile on her face as she practically taunts me.

"Oh yeah? Show me, how high should it go?"

"I'm not the man for the job, but I promise to try and be worthy of you every second of this lifetime."

I slip my hand beneath her jaw, bringing her lips to mine as I take it slow, savoring her touch, her scent, her taste. I'm obsessed with her. Off the rails. I want nothing more than to bottle her up and keep her near me always, forever.

She lets out a breathy moan when I move from her mouth to her cheek, kissing the chlorine off her skin as my tongue traces over the pulse point on her neck. I keep her pinned to my chest with one arm. My other hand begins trailing against her mostly bare skin, forcing goosebumps to erupt in my path before I slip beneath her bottoms.

My fingers dance over her clit, teasing her as I continue kissing her skin.

"Vincent," she gasps.

"Yes, Siren. Tell me what you want, what you crave."

"You, I-I want you."

The beast inside of me beats his chest in victory, her words the sweetest sound I've ever heard as I quicken my pace. Her breathing is noticeably quicker, her nails digging into my shoulders as I continue.

"Oh my god. Oh that feels good," she moans.

"Tell me you love me, Siren."

"I love you," she answers immediately, like admitting it is as easy as breathing for her.

"I love you," I say, nipping at her neck softly. "I want to take you away, from all of this evil, from all this pain. Just you and me, Siren."

She whimpers but doesn't say anything. My hand moves faster, practically as fast as it can underwater, forcing her eyes to fly open and land on me.

"Run away with me, Skyla. Be mine, forever. I'll always protect you, always keep you safe."

A love drunk haze covers her beautiful face, but conflict is heavy in her eyes.

"It's not just us, Vincent. You know that."

My jaw tenses before I blow out a ragged breath and nod, pinching her clit in a way that has her shattering apart in my arms despite how displeased she just made me. I can't share her forever, I can't.

A thought comes to mind though, one that I'd never even considered before. If I force her to leave them, to only be with me, could she ever really love me after that? Do I care as long as I have her? Warring thoughts rage inside my mind as my perfect sea goddess rests her head on my shoulder, holding me tightly as she sighs.

"We all run or we all stay. We're in this together," she says, unknowingly settling several debates inside my head.

I don't like the outcome of this logic, but is sharing her with two others that would gladly lay their lives down for her worse than losing her? Absolutely not. No matter what it takes, I'm keeping her. Hell itself couldn't keep me from my Siren.

Chapter Forty Four
Skyla

Maggie and I are currently strolling through downtown Salem during their fall festival. Okay, to be fair the entire month of October so far has been a fall festival. The guys all came with me, but one-by-one, they all got pulled away for other things. Now the only one left with us is Asher, following from a few feet back and looking absolutely miserable to be here.

My eyes catch on a treat stand, and I turn a sharp left and hurry over to it. Once I've procured the goodie, I make my way back to Asher with a megawatt smile that's only a tiny bit fake. I hold it out to him and his brows furrow.

"What?" he asks.

"Take it. I got it for you," I say as he slowly lifts his hand, gripping the stick.

"Why?"

"Because, you look like death warmed over back here. A little sugar should perk you right up!" I smile brightly, taking a little fun in the way irritation amplifies in his eyes.

"It's a caramel apple," he says flatly.

I nod. "Practically dopamine on a stick. You have natural sugars and artificial sugars."

He shakes his head as he holds it out for me.

"C'mon, please? One bite," I ask with big eyes, they seem to be getting me everything that I want with my guys lately.

Not that Asher is one of my guys or anything.

Asher stares at me for a little bit before he lifts the apple to his mouth, keeping his eyes on me as he takes a huge bite. I want to grin in triumph, but I find myself focusing on his mouth. He savagely chews the apple, and when he took a bite some of the juices got onto his lips and chin. In a move I can only describe as witchcraft, his tongue flicks out licking his lips and upper chin clean.

My eyes track that tongue for longer than I'd care to admit. Memories of that lecture hall, his mouth mere inches from my naked flesh, his eyes full of heat and that tongue. God, I wanted that tongue more in that moment than I wanted anything else. I was curious, surprised, and so incredibly turned on. I never expected to care for Asher, let alone like him, but over the last few weeks or so, he's been slowly tearing through my walls. Dare I say we are even friends now, as good of friends as he knows how to be at least.

Still, it feels better to know that in two weeks I'm not marrying someone I hate, but at least someone I kind of care for.

When Asher swallows the apple I track the movement, watching his throat work in a way that shouldn't be nearly as sexy as it is. I feel Maggie pinch my arm and I jolt in place, forcing myself to be the first one to break eye contact with Asher as I turn away.

We begin walking again and I can feel her eyes on me, a teasing smile as I level her with a sideways look.

"Shut up."

She's been giving me shit about Asher ever since I told her

about me and the guys. She obviously knew about Ronan and she assumed there was something with Liam. Then she noticed Vincent hanging around me more but didn't say anything. That is until she opened my door one day, a door I very much thought I locked but apparently didn't, while Vincent's head was buried between my thighs. Ever since, she's been asking me when Asher will join the harem and if I have a spot on my list for her.

She snickers, looping our arms together but doesn't say anything as we make our way over to the carnival games. I've never been to a carnival before, so everything I know about them is from the TV. I'm not sure why Steph never let me go when I was younger. I remember a few carnival-like events happening around town, but she always came up with something better to do at home. I didn't care very much in the end, but now it has me wondering why I had to miss out. It's a little chaotic and noisy, and absolutely packed, but I kind of love the energy that is buzzing around here. It feels like joy and happiness. I wish I could trap this moment in a container and look back at it on the harder days.

We sit down on a couple of swivel bar stools as we hold this gun thing in our hands.

"See the circle?" Maggie says, as she points to the target in front of me.

I nod.

"You want to make sure you hit it right on the dot, it will make your balloon blow up faster."

"My balloon?" I question as my gun starts squirting water.

Yanking it over the several inches that it's off I hit the target, but the balloon blows up so slow it's no comparison to Maggie's. When her balloon pops, I'm assuming that means she's won. She gets up and begins shaking her ass in my face, before the carnival guy hands her a little stuffed owl.

Asher steps forward, handing the guy some cash before crouching down behind me. His arms wrap around me, hands gripping the handles just below my own as he levels the thing out. I can feel his breath dancing against my neck as his head leans over my shoulder, his deep voice doing something to me it never has before.

"You hit the circle last time, but you want it to hit the little black dot in the circle."

I turn to look up at him, our faces inches apart as I nod softly.

"C'mon, Bartlett. Double or nothing," he says to Maggie, to which she happily accepts.

As soon as the water kicks on we are slightly off, but Asher adjusts us slightly and it's a guaranteed win from there. Our balloon blows up huge and fast before it pops. Excitement rushes through me as I jump off my stool and into Asher's arms. He catches me easily as he spins me around a few times, meanwhile I'm cheering like I just won the Olympics.

When he lets me down, my body slides against his slowly, my chest brushing against nearly every inch of him until my feet hit the ground. Those three golden flecks are on full display in this lighting, when a stuffed bear with a witch's broom and a witch hat is shoved in between us.

Maggie gives us a knowing smile but doesn't say anything as she casually strolls away.

"Do you want it?" I ask, offering the bear to Asher.

He gives a half laugh and shakes his head.

"All yours, Princess. You can cuddle it at night when you're missing me," he says with a quick wink.

It's so fast I almost feel like I made it up, but his quick steps away from me tell me he's embarrassed and doesn't want to look me in the eye right now. Asher Putnam doesn't get embarrassed, and he definitely doesn't flirt with me. Maybe this whole celibacy thing is getting to him. What the hell is happening to us?

He keeps his distance for the rest of the night, following no more than five steps behind Maggie and me the whole time. Things are about to start winding down and despite being in canvas shoes, my feet are killing me.

"One last thing!" Maggie says as she points to the ferris wheel.

I let out a bitter laugh as I shake my head.

"Absolutely not."

She pouts, practically dragging my arm out of its socket as she pulls us in line.

"Maggie, seriously. Stop. I hate heights. This thing doesn't look safe."

"Oh, don't be such a baby. It's fine!"

Before I can respond, she hands the ride attendant our tickets and suddenly we are brushing past him moving to the available chair in front of us. It's the metal kind. The one that moves a lot and squeaks and moans when you sit on it. Also known as the super dangerous kind. Maggie all but shoves me into the seat before she pauses.

"Oh no," she says with fake disappointment. "I forgot. I have dinner plans with my parents. I have to go. Asher! Will you ride with my girl?" Maggie says.

He looks at her for several seconds, before he hops up and over the ride's fence as he comes up to pass Maggie. She whispers something to him, but I can't quite hear it as she scurries off, heading in the direction where we parked. Oh my god, the little bitch is actually ditching me.

Asher plops down into the seat, consuming three quarters of the bench with how large he is. He pulls down what seems to be a safety bar before it clicks into place. My hands wrap around it, clinging to it for dear life, as a cold sweat begins to break out starting at my forehead and moving all the way to my toes.

The ride jerks forward, forcing us to begin raising as my stomach starts to churn. God, I hate heights.

"Hey, open your eyes," Asher says gently.

I don't realize that my eyes are closed until I slowly blink them open, the first thing I see being him. He watches me with a patient look as he nods.

"You're okay. We're safe. If this thing was gonna kill someone, it would have killed the hundreds of others that have ridden it today."

The ride stops with an abrupt jerk, forcing our seat to rock. I do everything in my power to hold in the scream that's begging to be set free. Looking around I see that they stopped us at the top. Fabulous.

"Or everything was loosening up from the hundreds of others, just in time for us to fall to our deaths," I grimace.

"What's the worst that could come of that?" Asher asks.

I look at him like he's crazy.

"Uhm, dying?"

He nods. "But after that. Say you fell from here," he says looking over the edge. "You'd no doubt have a quick and painless death. So, what is the worst that can happen? You get that free fall sensation for maybe five seconds and then nothing. Lights out."

"Is this supposed to be making me feel better?" I scoff.

"It helps me," he shrugs, as he looks away from me and out to the sunsetting sky before us. "I like to think that when I die, I'll get to see my mom again. She was perfect, and there's no doubt she is in heaven. I'll definitely be on the fast track for the other side," he says, pointing to the ground. "But, maybe I'll get a few moments with her before I'm damned for all eternity."

Blinking slowly, I tilt my head to the side.

"I didn't know you were religious."

He shakes his head, like he's shaking himself out of a memory.

"I'm not. Not really. We're all raised Puritan by faith, obviously, but times have changed. We aren't forcibly bound by all of the things that our ancestors were. At least mostly."

"Wow, you guys take family lineage really seriously around here."

Asher faces me. "Everyone in Salem does, and beyond. It's everything to the Brethren."

I open my mouth to ask a question but he shakes his head, intercepting me before continuing.

"The point I'm trying to make is, what's the worst thing about dying? Not living on earth anymore? You'd be reunited with your mom too, and you will definitely be going to heaven, so you'll get to actually spend forever with her."

The thought is nice in theory. I've craved to meet her, truly know her, my whole life. The older I get, the hazier the few memories I have of her become. I'd love to replace the muddled remnants of the past with some that are fresh and new, but not at the risk of dying. Not yet.

"As soon as you stop fearing death, no fear will ever have the ability to take hold of you," Asher says, his eyes focused on the setting sun before he turns to me.

"Is that what you've done? You don't fear anything?" I ask.

I'm suddenly acutely aware of his thigh pressed against mine, his arm in his lap that is practically on my leg. His shoulders are several inches taller than my own, but they are touching every inch of my arm as he looks down at me.

His eyes flick from my left eye, to the right and down to my mouth before back up again. He does this two or three times, his chest rising and falling steadily as he does.

I'm not sure who moves first, I don't think it matters either. With our eyes on each other, we both lean in slowly, cautiously, giving the other plenty of time to stop. Neither of us seem interested in that, though. Our lips are less than two inches from each other, my heart hammering inside of my chest as I abandon all reason for this moment, allowing myself to just be.

The sound of the ferris wheel starting up again forces us both forward, and I tense immediately. I feel Asher's arms wrap around me, tucking me safely against his chest as he shushes me softly.

"Shh, it's okay. We're heading down now. Almost done."

I nod, burying my face further into his chest having no shame as I take a slow inhale of his cologne. It's fresh and clean, with a hint of something oaky beneath it. I find myself wanting to get lost in the scent, who needs fresh air when I can have this?

The ride jerks to a stop and the attendant lifts the bar for us. Neither Asher nor I move for several seconds, though. Instead, we cling to each other, like we're the only people in this world, in this moment. Okay, it's really that I'm clinging to him and he's holding me, but same thing.

Eventually, he's the first to cave, a featherlight press of his lips against the crown of my head as he squeezes me encouragingly.

"C'mon, let's get you home."

I nod, slowly pulling away as Asher steps off first offering his hand to me. I take it as I step off the ride. When we're out of the fenced part and joining the leaving crowd, I expect him to drop my hand. He doesn't, though. In fact, when I try to pull my hand free, his fingers intertwine with mine, giving me no choice but to accept it.

Looking up at him, I'm desperate to read his face, to see what he's thinking...what he's feeling. He gives nothing away, though. That stoic look and rigid posture perfectly in place as he keeps his eyes forward.

I'm disappointed, as I slowly turn away and we walk word-lessly, hand in hand, the entire way back to the car.

Chapter Forty Five
Ronan

I'd much rather be at the carnival with Skyla, or in bed with Skyla. Really anything to do with Skyla, than where I am right now. Instead, I'm in my brother's home, our childhood home, in his office.

I hate coming here. It's filled with more horrors than any home should ever possess. The things these walls have witnessed are nothing short of undiluted evil. Growing up I swore I would never carry on the dark habits of our family's Legacy. Christopher, though? He always had it in him, dare I say, he may even rival our father.

"How were the boys in your opinion? Who needed the most guidance? Who took charge? I need more details than this piss-poor excuse of a report," he snaps, slapping down the folder I gave him after Asher and Liam had handled their assignment, with my assistance.

I hate having to get into details. The truth is, if he knew how hard of a time Liam had with everything before, during and after, he'd kill him without hesitation. There is no room for weak men in the Brethren, let alone in the Elders. Don't get me wrong, I really like Liam, he's a good guy but...he doesn't have what it takes. Not on the level he'll be expected to perform.

Despite him being a good kid, my girl loves him and there is no way I'm risking her going through that kind of heartache. So I lie, easily, casually, and with all the right words to satiate my blood thirsty brother.

"They did well for their first time, they clearly need more practice. Something we already knew," I say, with an exaggerated eye roll. "Asher most definitely took charge, not that I'm surprised. Liam has followed in his shadow his whole life. It was all too predictable that the same dynamic would apply in the field."

Christopher watches me carefully, as if he were trying to discern if I'm lying or hiding anything from him. Shit, at this point, what am I not lying about or hiding from him?

"Do you think he should be removed?" Christopher asks, with a tilt of his head.

I don't answer immediately, showing I'm giving this idea some real thought before I look at him and fold my arms over my chest.

"I think it's too early to say. I'd need to see more, maybe him without Asher and forced to take the lead. He has potential, and as the Walcott's only heir, I think it would be in the Brethren's best interest to see if he can prove himself."

Christopher thinks over my words carefully before nodding.

"I agree. I'll have something arranged for him shortly after the ceremony. You'll oversee him," he says, making it clear that if I had any protests, they're a moot point. This is non-negotiable.

This may be a mis-step, but I can't resist the door he has unknowingly cracked open for me.

Gesturing to the black leather bound book with the sacred B crest stamped onto the front, I ask, "Why are we having the ceremony moved up, brother? It breaks tradition. You of all people are dedicated to upholding all traditions and laws that are written there."

It was our ancestors' journal, Thomas Putnam. The man who founded it all. The creator of the Brethren and more famously known as 'the father of Ann Putnam' one of the largest accusers from the trials. Because of her mouth, Thomas's hands and the help of the Parris family, over sixty people were accused and tried. A fact that Thomas brags about often throughout the journal.

My brother places a possessive hand on the journal, his and the Brethren's most sacred possession.

"I do what I do, because I must."

"For what purpose?" I push. "On Hallows Eve of all nights?"

To my surprise, he doesn't snap into a blinding rage. Instead, his eyes trace around the room, verifying it's empty before continuing.

"There are rumors of an attack that night– on the girl. It is believed they will harness enough power to not only harm the girl, but all of us, all at once."

I remain unblinking as I stare at him. We've all grown up with the legends, the stories. Of how the Brethren was formed as a way of protection from the witches they didn't catch, the ones who remained hidden and the descendants of the ones who were executed. I'm open minded to the idea of them and their descendants being capable of witchcraft of sorts, though I don't think I believe in it as wholly as my brother or the other Elders.

My mind cannot fathom a group of people practicing black magic, just to continuously attack and torture a group of descendants from an event that occurred more than three-hundred-years-ago. Maybe I'm wrong, but maybe I'm not. Maybe this is one giant game of the trials yet again, with two sides of the same coin fighting against one another for centuries. It's no longer hunting witches down, and hanging them from the gallows. Now it's forcing their businesses to collapse, their inheritance ruined and a handful of them thrown in jail or 'mysteriously' disappearing.

The same could be said for them, I suppose. We have lost many members over the years, even members of several Elder families. I suppose my brother has some merit for being overly cautious. The hate is very clear on both sides. I just wonder, if either truly knows what they're fighting over in this day and age.

Regardless of my skepticism, the idea of an attack on Skyla turns my stomach. Though only slightly more than the idea of her going through the archaic and revolting ceremony. With this new information in mind, I know there is no way to stop it. No way to save her, and I fucking hate myself for not being able to act sooner.

"Have you informed Asher of what the night will require of him?" I ask.

Christopher shakes his head.

"I can hardly stand the sight of that boy," he sneers. "You will apprise him of his responsibilities. The girl as well, only what she needs to know."

I nod solemnly as I receive a dismissive gesture from my brother. Happily standing up and getting the hell away from this house, I almost make it to the door before he calls out.

"I'm trusting you with this brother. Should either act out of turn, I will know who to blame," he says, his threat clear, intent known.

Nodding my agreement, I step all the way through the doorway before I'm making my way to my car.

Fuck me.

I head straight to campus, feeling the need to rip the band aid off. Though I know it's going to fucking suck. When I get to the Parris dorm, I find Asher in the hallway, sitting on the floor with his arms braced on his knees and his head against the wall. He doesn't see me because his eyes are on the ceiling and I'm about to ask him what he's doing, when understanding hits me.

"Liam!" Skyla practically screams out, followed by a loud smack and another moan.

Asher's eyes shutter, closed so tightly it looks like he's in pain.

Poor fucking bastard. He's so gone for her, and he won't even admit it to himself. Not that I'm sure he'd even have a chance if he did. He's treated her like shit and Skyla isn't just going to forget of all that. In the same breath though, they've been getting along a lot better lately, spending more time together. Maybe he would have a chance.

It would be a little odd for me to be sharing my girlfriend with my nephew...I just want to see her happy though, him too. What kind of man does that make me, that I'm fine with sharing her with the whole fucking school if that's what she needs? As long as she won't stop loving me. A lucky one I'd say, because I still hold her heart and she holds mine.

"Hey," I say, as I come to stand in front of Asher.

His eyes pop open as he looks at me, standing up to his feet.

"Hey."

My head gestures to the door.

"Liam?"

"And Griggs," he hmphs.

"Why aren't you in there?" I test.

He scoffs like that's a crazy idea before he scrambles a little, picking up a takeout bag.

"She was hungry, and delivery was gonna take too long, so I ran out for a bit."

"That was nice of you," I say.

Asher shrugs. "Except when I got back they were all...busy."

I nod my understanding, staying quiet for a few moments.

"How was the carnival?"

He huffs out a short laugh and shakes his head.

"Lame and crowded."

"Did Skyla have a good time?" I ask, watching with intrigue as his eyes dilate slightly when I say her name.

Interesting.

"Yeah," he nods coolly, though he's already given himself away.

"Good."

"You gonna go in there too?" Asher asks, a hint of bitterness to his voice.

For a moment I contemplate it, but another pleasure filled moan sounds through the door and I'm suddenly second guessing it. She's having a good night, a great one from the sounds of it. I'm not going to ruin it with heavy shit like this.

I look at Asher, wondering if I should tell him before I think better of it. He's not going to like this anymore than she will, none of us will, honestly. So I'll let them have a little longer, I'll wait until it's absolutely necessary.

"Nah, I just wanted to check on her. I'll see her tomorrow. You staying?" I ask with a curious brow.

He shrugs, leaning against the wall with his foot kicked up on it, like he's more than happy hanging out in the hallway.

"Yeah, gotta get the princess her food when she's done," he says, rolling his eyes in irritation that I feel is only partially authentic.

I nod, clapping his shoulder as I turn on my heels and head home. I'm not sure how I'll be able to look my baby in the eye until that conversation comes. This is so fucked.

Chapter Forty Six
Skyla

Ronan has been distant lately. I've tried to get him to come over, or to let me come to him. Instead, he dodges me at every turn. The last few times I went to the pool he wasn't even there, some substitute swim coach in his place. I've asked all the guys, wondering if they know what has been going on, but they're as clueless as me.

The worst case scenarios come to mind, and they taunt me daily. Has he gotten sick of this arrangement? Does he want me to himself, or not at all? Has he found someone else? Someone who is more 'appropriate', given our situation? My stomach works itself into knots when a text lights up my phone, forcing me to spring out of bed.

Liam and Vincent stir beside me, Vincent obviously much more alert than Liam as he reaches for me.

"What's wrong, Siren?"

"Ronan texted me," I say as I read it over as fast as I can manage.

"Bout time," he grumbles.

Ronan: Will you meet me at my place in an hour? Bring the guys. I love you.

My heart flutters at that simple I love you, but when it comes after nearly two weeks of hardly any contact, I can't deny I'm more than slightly irritated. Okay, so he definitely still loves me, unless of course he's only saying that to get me over there, so he can break my heart properly, in person. Though, if he was planning that, why would he tell me to bring the guys? He has to know that if he breaks my heart, the guys will lose their shit on him, Asher included.

He's been surprisingly protective of me over the last few weeks. Ever since the carnival. We are definitely friends at this point, maybe more? I don't know. I tried to bring up the almost kiss the next day, but he brushed it off like he didn't know what I was talking about.

Is it bad that a small part of me hoped that when he came back from getting takeout he'd walk in, see me and the guys together and get jealous? Want to join? Or watch? Something?

Instead, he just sat outside and waited for us to be done before giving me my food and leaving at the same moment. After that though, things were semi-normal. Except anytime one of his little groupies would give me a dirty look or a whispered remark, he'd practically charge them. It took Liam and I both to hold him back from Bridgette one day when she called me a two-cent whore. After he nearly crushed her trachea in the dining hall, you'd think she'd be a little more careful. Or maybe she's just dumb, probably the latter.

Regardless, it made my heart swell each and every time he defended me. Jeremy and Dane just glanced at me the other day, and Asher wrapped his arm around my shoulder protectively, giving them both a murderous glare that shouldn't have been as sweet as it was. They scrambled out of there, despite Dane being in a wheelchair. Vincent said he fell down a flight of stairs or something, but the twinkle in his eye told me he had something to do with it. I should probably be way more concerned that one of my boyfriends is clearly a dangerous man. Tell that to my love-struck dumb little heart, though.

"He said that we need to come over to his place in an hour," I say.

Liam groans as he wraps his arm around my stomach.

"Fuck him. Tell him we'll go when we're good and ready," his sleepy voice grumbles.

I laugh lightly, but honestly I need to get out of this bed. The anxiety rising inside of me wouldn't allow me to sit still and wait around even if I tried. Slipping out of bed and onto my feet, I make my way into the bathroom where I take a quick shower, skipping my hair this morning before getting ready.

When I come out of the bathroom, Vincent is already gathering up his new clothes for the day and passes me to the bathroom with a stolen kiss from my lips, while Liam is still in bed. The guys have been keeping clothes and toiletries here lately because honestly, they are here more than they are in their own rooms these days.

A few kisses and promises of head later rouses Liam awake, and he practically springs out of bed, running for the bathroom.

"Hope you're nice and sudsy, Vinny!" Liam shouts as he runs into the bathroom, promptly followed by him shouting out a loud "Ow!"

I smile and shake my head as I slide on a pair of leggings and an oversized sweatshirt. Since it's Saturday and we're just going to Ronan's, I don't bother putting hours into my appearance. The guys have slowly broken me of the idea that I have to look completely put together, all of the time. When three gorgeous sexy men tell you over and over again that you look just as beautiful with or without makeup or fancy clothes, you can't help it, you start to believe them.

A knock comes from my door, and I frown in confusion as I

open it. I'm surprised when I see Asher standing there, hair damp and tousled like he just got out of the shower himself.

"Hey," he says, his eyes running over me appreciatively as if I was wearing a skintight mini dress.

"Hi," I smile shyly.

I can't believe we're getting married tomorrow. It's such a weird feeling. I'm in love with someone, several someone's, and none of them are my fiancé. I don't exactly hate my fiancé though, not anymore. I...I actually think I like him, but the fear of rejection far outweighs my desire to know how he feels about me in return.

"Ronan texted me," he says.

I nod. "Me too."

"Can I drive you?" he asks.

I can't help but smirk.

"Since when do you ever ask? What happened to the demanding, 'be ready at this time or I'm leaving you' texts?"

He rolls his eyes, but a breathtaking smile takes over his face.

"I never said that."

I choke on a laugh and nod. "You practically did, every single time. You could hardly stand to breathe the same air as me."

His arm lifts to rest on the door frame as he leans down, until we're practically at eye level.

"Things can change."

My breathing stalls as my heart flips.

"Yeah, they can," I say cryptically, causing him to lift a curious eyebrow as his smile shifts into a soft smirk.

"Yeah?"

I swallow roughly, my teeth catching the inside of my lip as I nod. His eyes lock on the movement, tracking me slowly before coming back to meet my gaze.

For the love of god just kiss me already! I think I'm going to die from the buildup of all this sexual tension.

He can't actually read my mind, which is stupid if you ask me. I think things would be a lot simpler if he could or vice versa. Vincent comes out of the bathroom, drying his jet black hair with a towel, dressed in his black jeans and shirt that I'm sorry to say, look exactly like what he wore yesterday and the day before. My boyfriend is simple in his 'I don't have to try' goth style. He's still hot as hell, though, so I don't mind.

"Little close to my girl, don't you think, Putnam?" Vincent says as he steps behind me, slipping an arm around my waist as he pulls my ass back to him.

I scoff, smacking his chest but he doesn't take his eyes off Asher. Vincent has been like this ever since Asher and I started getting along. I think he can sense things shifting between us and he doesn't like it. He already hates sharing me with Liam and Ronan, I fear Asher would be his breaking point.

Asher being the arrogant asshole he is doesn't budge an inch, in fact, I think he moves in just a hair closer as his eyes remain on me.

"I'm not hearing any complaints from her."

The way his mischievous smile curves his face has a rush of butterflies fluttering through my stomach as I do my best to bite back a smile in return.

Vincent doesn't say anything as Asher continues staring at me, that smile still in place when Liam steps into the room. His footsteps pause, as he no doubt takes in the scene before him.

"Oh shit, what did I just walk in on? The tension in here could choke a fucking horse."

I wrinkle my nose at that and turn to face him.

"What?" I ask.

Liam laughs and shrugs his shoulders.

"Ha! I don't know. Shit was feeling a little too heavy for my liking, though."

Vincent scoffs and I shake my head as I steal one more glance at Asher. He's dropped his arm from the doorframe, but his eyes are still on me before he finally breaks eye contact.

"I'm driving the princess," he says to the room.

"Like fuck," Vincent laughs hollowly.

Asher gives him an unimpressed look.

"Down boy. You guys can ride with me too."

"I don't want to squeeze into the Maserati's tiny as fuck backseat, Ash," Liam whines.

"I brought the Rolls. Will everyone just shut the hell up and get in the fucking car?" Asher snaps, before blowing out a slow breath and looking at me.

"You ready, Princess?"

Nodding, I reach for my purse, but Vincent is already there, handing it to me with an appraising look.

"What?" I ask him.

He stares for several more seconds before he leans forward, pressing his lips against mine. I sink into the kiss, never getting tired of the overwhelming feeling that consumes me with each kiss.

When I open my eyes to pull away, I see that his eyes are wide open and firmly trained on Asher in a taunting way. Pulling away from him, I smack his chest as I shake my head.

Before I can say anything, Asher is gone, storming off down the hall.

"That was really shitty, Vincent," I say with a frown, before I start after Asher.

The elevator doors begin to shut, and I have to squeeze myself inside, my sweatshirt getting trapped between the doors as I do.

"Oh shit!" I gasp before Asher's hands wrap around the material, yanking hard and freeing me.

I tumble a few steps and he's there as well.

He's everywhere. All the time.

His hands are resting on my forearms, head tilted down to look at me in concern.

"I'm sorry," I say softly.

Asher's eyes scan mine like he's confused about why I'm apologizing, as if he forgot why he stormed away for a moment. He shrugs it off, releasing his hold on me as he leans against the back wall of the elevator.

"You're my fiancé, Asher. Soon to be my husband, tomorrow soon. That wasn't okay. Vincent needs to respect you, at least enough not to pull petty shit like that," I continue, despite his eyes being now closed and his head tilted up.

When the elevator stops, the doors pop open, and he pushes away from the wall.

"It's whatever," he says as he brushes past me, stepping into the hall before taking a right and making his way outside.

"It's not whatever. I'm trying to apologize and validate your feelings here! The least you could do is stop walking for two seconds," I huff as I follow after him.

A bitter sounding laugh escapes his chest as he shakes his head, his eyes still forward.

"What feelings?"

I blink at that, before hurt and irritation flicker inside me. I jog the remaining distance between us, catching him by the arm before I force him to face me.

"For me! Don't lie and say that you don't have them, I'm not stupid."

He looks down at me, assessingly, before trying to walk away again.

"Asher!" I snap, yanking on his arm and refusing to let go as he turns, throwing his arms out and screaming at the top of his lungs in the middle of the empty courtyard.

"FINE! You want me to admit that I have feelings for you? That I've fallen so fucking hard for you and I don't know how to get up? You want me to sit here, and tell you how I haven't been able to stop thinking about you from the moment I met you? How you have always occupied a majority of my headspace, but now..." he takes a long pause as he laughs hollowly.

"Now, I'm absolutely FUCKED. There is no room for anything except you. Skyla Parris, is practically inked into my DNA, there forever, and I can't have her," he shakes his head, taking several deep breaths before those chocolate brown eyes come back to me.

"You know what the worst part is?" he smiles angrily. "We're going to be married tomorrow, you're going to be my wife and I *still* won't have you. Not in the way that counts, not in the way I want you."

I blink at him several times but I don't speak. How can I when my mind is racing a million miles a second. I was hoping he'd admit that he's been having some feelings for me, but I didn't expect all of...that.

Asher watches me carefully, his body language rigid and guarded but his eyes so expressive and so sad. Hesitantly, I take a small step towards him, softening my voice to match the emotion behind my words.

"What if...you could? What if...we could?"

His brows pinch together, not in confusion but almost like he is in pain.

Shaking his head he looks away as I take another step forward.

"Your roster is full, Princess. There is no room for me, and I wouldn't exactly be welcomed by your little fan club."

I reach a hand up to his face, forcing his cheek to look at me. Surprisingly he lets me, his jaw tight and those three golden flecks practically shining in the October morning.

"What if none of that mattered?"

He frowns but doesn't respond.

"What if both of those excuses were gone, then what would you say?"

"They aren't excuses, Skyla. It's the facts. It's—"

"Answer the question, Asher," I snap.

His eyes roam over my face before he shakes his head.

"Then nothing could stop me from having you."

My heart beats out of rhythm, the air practically buzzing around us as someone comes to stand between us.

"Everything okay? I heard yelling." Liam asks cautiously.

Asher's eyes close, as if he were to say, 'See?'.

He pulls away from my touch and a stupid part of me hurts because of it. Asher faces Liam nods his head.

"It's all good. We're fine. Right, Skyla?"

I know it started out as a sarcastic nickname, but I can't lie, I like it so much better when he calls me Princess. Maybe that makes me a little fucked up. I honestly don't really care.

"Sure. We're fine," I say slowly, giving him the opportunity to speak up. Not that I'd really expect him to.

Asher gives me a tight lipped smile, as he nods and moves to where a black Rolls Royce is parked slipping into the driver's seat. Liam follows after him and I'm about to as well when a hand comes to my back.

I turn to see Vincent there, his black hair falling into his face. I'm about to walk away because I can't deal with him right now when he stops me, gripping my cheeks together and squishing them with one hand as he speaks through clenched teeth.

"If you're gonna be pissed at me, be pissed at me, but never fucking walk away from me again. Do you understand?" he asks, giving my head a small shake as he emphasizes his seriousness.

"I'm gonna do shit that pisses you off and maybe even makes you hate me at times, but that doesn't mean you go off on your own when there is someone out there watching you, Siren. So next time, just punch me or slap me or something, but don't you fucking run away from me."

He releases his hold on my face slightly so I can speak.

"It's not like I was alone. I was with Asher."

Vincent scoffs. "Yeah, I trust *that* Putnam with your safety about as far as I could throw a goddamn elephant."

I frown at that. "Well, maybe you should. He's going to be my husband."

Vincent bristles at that, dropping his hold on me altogether.

"Don't fucking remind me."

He storms away, but not without taking me with him. His hand is wrapped around my bicep as he practically drags me to the car, opening the back door before ragdoll tossing me inside. Liam is in the seat beside me waiting and thankfully helps break my fall.

"What the fuck!" Liam snaps as Vincent sits in the passenger seat, shutting the door with a hard thunk.

Liam's fingers are featherlight, dancing over my cheeks that are no doubt red. Anger transforms his features, a look I don't often see on him as he reaches between the front seats and hits Vincent right in the face.

Vincent whips around, ready to leap for him as Liam speaks.

"Piece of shit! You hurt her!"

His attack on Liam pauses as his eyes come to me assessingly. He reaches out to touch me and I pull back slightly, causing his fingers to hang in the air. Regret splashes across his face, a look I've really never seen on his face before. He slowly turns around, speaking only to Asher.

"Drive," he rasps.

Asher's eyes come to mine in the mirror. Anger and frustration in them, before he puts the car into gear and pulls out of the parking lot. Liam lifts his arm up, allowing me to lean closer to him and I take every opportunity for his comfort. It's not like I'm some battered woman who is terrified of Vincent. I know it was an acci-dent, he was just trying to get my attention and keep his anger in check. He needs to do a better job of that, though.

Chapter Forty Seven
Asher

My knuckles turn white from the grip I have on the steering wheel. It's taking everything in me not to shoot Griggs right in the head. Blow his brains all over this fucking car, because the world would be much better off without him in it. Fuck knows Skyla would be.

Liam had to physically pin me against the seat to hold me back. From the instant I saw him pinch her face like that, I was ready to kill him. Coming from the man that is so goddamn concerned about her safety, so protective, he sure is fucking rough with her.

No doubt, that comes from the double life he leads. It must be hard to murder people in cold blood, literally rip them to pieces then take a quick shower and be forced to obey normal social constructs.

Oh, did you think I was being sympathetic? Fuck no, I'm being sarcastic as fuck. Develop a split personality disorder if he has to, go to therapy, fucking whatever it takes, but something I will not tolerate is him letting that side seep over into *my* fiancée's life. *Absolutely* the fuck not.

We ride the rest of the way in silence and thankfully, we get to

Ronan's in no time. I throw my door open first, stepping out as everyone else does the same.

"Siren, can we talk?" Griggs asks, his tone surprisingly gentle.

"I don't think that's a good idea," Liam says.

"I agree, fuck that," I add in.

He shoots us both a dirty look, before softening and looking back at her. She bites the inside of her lip and nods, pressing a kiss to Liam's cheek before moving over to the front yard of Ronan's for some semblance of privacy.

Liam and I seem to be on the same page, neither of us wanting to give them privacy, though, and Skyla turns to us with a tired huff.

"Go inside. We'll be there in a minute."

We share a 'hell no' look with each other before she adds on an exasperated, "Please."

Liam blows out a frustrated breath as he claps my shoulder.

"Come on, let's let her and her boyfriend figure this out while we drill her other boyfriend as to why the fuck he's been avoiding my girlfriend."

I give him a sideways glance as we make our way up Ronan's front steps.

"You realize how fucking weird that sentence is, right?"

He shrugs as he pushes his way through the front door, not bothering to knock. I steal one more glance at Skyla only to find Griggs on his knees before her, his head hung in shame as she looks down at him, before I shut the door behind us.

Good. Little fucker.

Ronan is in the living room, a glass of scotch already in his hand as he nods in greeting.

"Hey. How you guys doing?" he asks.

Liam scoffs. "We're fine. Skyla is the one that's been fucking spiraling."

"Why?" Ronan asks, as concern instantly takes over.

"Because of you, dumbass," I scoff as Liam continues.

"You practically ghosted her, with no reason or explanation. She was freaking out, man."

He frowns, nodding as he looks down at his drink.

"Where is she?"

"Making up with Griggs," I answer.

Ronan lifts an eyebrow.

"What did he do?"

I shake my head, not feeling like getting into it.

"What's up with this cryptic shit of 'meet me at my house'," I ask.

He sets his drink down, scratching at the back of his head as he looks at us.

"I have to tell you guys some shit and I've been trying to keep it to myself. I just...needed some space."

My eyebrows pinch together, and my mouth screws up at that.

"You've got less than two minutes to polish up that apology, because that shit isn't going to fly with Skyla."

Nodding, Ronan looks up at the ceiling and shakes his head when the door opens, Griggs and Skyla walking hand in hand.

That was fast. Times up, Ronan.

They shut the door before she pauses, and Ronan stands. He moves to her but stops about a foot shy.

"Hi, baby."

She stares at him, slowly blinking for several seconds.

"Hi, baby? Hi, baby. Is that really all you have to say to me? Ronan, what the fuck! One minute you were by my side, the next you were gone. I couldn't reach you. I couldn't see you. I was convinced you didn't want to be with me, or you fell in love with someone else. Something! Anything, to explain why the fuck my boyfriend who professes his love daily would disappear on me like that?"

Shit. She's torn into Griggs, me, and now Ronan all before ten in the morning. Liam better watch his back, the princess is on a warpath.

"Never, baby. You're my everything. I just, I need to tell you some things and I've been fucking dreading it. I wanted to wait until the last possible minute because I didn't want you to sit here and waste away worrying, but I couldn't continue not being honest with you..." he says, trailing off with a shake of his head.

"Can you sit down?" he asks.

She nods, taking a seat on the couch opposite of him. Vincent takes his seat beside her, a possessive hand latched around her thigh as Ronan takes a seat on the coffee table. I sit in the armchair, in perfect view of Skyla and Ronan while Liam plops down onto the other couch.

"So, tomorrow," Ronan begins, "Is your commitment ceremony. None of you have ever attended one, though, right?"

We all shake our heads as Ronan runs a hand through his hair.

"Traditionally, it occurs after the wedding, at midnight specifically. Though, yours has been moved up to before the wedding."

"Yeah, we know. Get to the point," I say.

Ronan cuts me an irritated look before turning back to Skyla.

"It's so important that you're a virgin on your wedding night, or in this case on your ceremony night, because there will be a doctor to verify before the ritual."

"Ritual?" Skyla echoes.

He nods.

"It's custom that when an Elder or Legacy takes a bride, he... deflowers her before all the Elders."

"Deflowers?" Liam asks with a screwed up face, as Skyla's face pales and my stomach twists.

"L-like sex?" she stutters. "In front of everyone?"

Ronan nods as she shakes her head.

"I can't do that. I won't do that. That's so...disgusting! Humiliating. Embarrassing. In front of my dad?! In front of Asher's?" she asks, her panicked eyes coming to me as if to ask, 'Did you know about this?'. I shake my head as I continue staring at Ronan in disbelief.

"Once the...task," he grits between clenched teeth, "has been performed, Asher will take the bloodied sheet before completing the next step. You'll be able to go home after that. The next day you'll be expected to move into your home, together."

"We don't have a home yet," Skyla says.

"Actually, we do," I say.

She whips around to look at me with a confused gaze.

"My father gifted it to me when he announced our official engagement," I say, pulling out my keys and lifting up the one that goes to our new house.

"It's not decorated yet, I wanted to leave it blank for you, so that you could make it your own," I say with a shrug.

At least that's the version that I go with. Truth is, it was fully decorated. I paid someone to furnish it when school began. Since that night at my father's, the night she took care of me, I had every single piece removed and returned. She has lost so much freedom, so much say, even more than me. I wanted her to be able to control one piece of her life, at the very least.

"That was nice of you," she says, though her voice is devoid of any emotion as she stares at her hands.

Her throat swallows roughly as she looks up to Ronan, tears brimming her eyes in a way that aches my fucking heart.

"I have to do this? There isn't another way?"

Ronan shakes his head sadly.

"I'm sorry, baby."

"W-what if I refuse?" she chokes softly.

Vincent's hand squeezes her leg tightly before he shares a look with me, Liam and then finally Ronan.

We know what will happen if she refuses, and we all know that the task of removing her would be left to the man that is currently holding onto her like she is his life raft.

"You can't, Skyla," I say, speaking for everyone. "They'll kill you."

A strangled sob escapes her as she buries her face in her hands.

"Why does everyone have to be there? If we have to do it, why can't we do it in private?" she asks, blinking back some of her tears as she does.

"To ensure the ritual is completed properly," Ronan says diplomatically.

"No, it's so a bunch of fucking perverts can watch!" she snaps.

Ronan doesn't disagree, and it makes my blood boil. This is fucking bullshit. I knew there was going to be an expectation for our wedding night, obviously. You're not gifted a virgin bride and told you can handle her however you see fit. But no one ever told me I'd have to take her virginity in a room full of people. It's going to feel uncomfortable enough for me, but her being the only woman in the room, no doubt naked. My stomach rolls at the thought.

"There's more," Ronan continues.

Of fucking course there is.

"You all will be there as well," he says, looking at Liam and Vincent.

"What?" Liam asks.

Ronan turns around to look at him as he nods.

"All Elders and Legacies of appropriate age. The last ceremony was over six years ago when you all were too young to attend. Now...you're not."

"All Legacies of age?" Vincent clarifies.

Ronan nods and Vincent stands.

"Where are you going?" Skyla asks as he heads for the door.

"No one can watch you if their eyes are plucked from their fucking heads."

"That's a fucking stupid idea!" I call out as Skyla shouts for him.

"Vincent! Please! Get over here."

His name on her lips forces him to pause, his hand gripping the door handle tightly before he spins to face the room. His chest is heaving, his eyes wild and crazed. I'd imagine this is what one of the best eliminators for the Brethren looks like when he's on the verge of a kill. Like a wild blood thirsty animal ready to be let loose.

"This is the shit that cannot happen," Ronan says as he gestures to all of us. "You cannot allow your emotions to get the better of you. Too many eyes will be in that room. One move like that," he says, as he points to Vincent, "and all of our lives could be at risk. Most of all hers. So, you lock it down, you space out. You sing fucking show tunes in your head. I don't give a fuck, but you cannot react."

Liam, Vincent and I all share looks of frustration and concern as we nod.

"You think this is going to be easy for me?" Ronan laughs bitterly. "Do you think I enjoyed keeping this from you? It's been fucking killing me, but I knew you would all freak out, most of all you, baby," he says to Skyla. "And I knew there was nothing any of us could do. I've talked to my brother and...it didn't go well. This is happening or people are dying. And if you die, I die," he says as he reaches for Skyla's hand.

She lets him take it as she stares at him and shakes her head.

"I can't believe this."

"I know and I'm sorry. I'm so fucking sorry, baby. If there was anything I could do, I would. I've already tried and failed," he says on a pained rasp.

Skyla nods numbly, but doesn't say anything, none of us do apart from Ronan. He goes into detail about what tomorrow will look like for her, and what she will be expected to do once she's in the room. When he's finished, she stands up, her face looking pale if not a little green.

"Excuse me," she says, as she makes her way to the bathroom. Liam and Vincent both stand but she waves them off as Ronan hangs his head.

Once Skyla is out of the room, he turns to me.

"There is more you need to know. For your ears only."

I stand, gesturing for him to take the lead as he stands. We weave through his house before coming to one of the rooms on the other end of the house. When we're inside, he begins walking me through the expectations from my end for the ceremony and what will occur after. I know I need to pay attention, but honestly, I'd rather not.

Chapter Forty Eight
Skyla

I'm quiet as Asher drives. My mind is racing, and it's taking everything within me not to have another full blown panic attack. Forget the stalker, this, in front of me, happening tomorrow...it feels like a lead ball has been dropped into my stomach.

I don't care that Ronan kept it to himself in order to not let me worry over it for weeks. That wasn't his decision to make. I had a right to know what has been decided for me, what will be...done to me.

My eyes flick over to Asher, watching him out of the corner of my eye. From the beginning, it's basically been heavily implied that Asher would have to be the one to take my virginity. At first I couldn't imagine anything more awful, then I sort of started to come around to the idea. I mean, it could be worse. He could be much worse.

But like that? On display, like some kind of disgusting song and dance...my stomach threatens to empty its contents at the mere thought of it.

I do take a small amount of comfort that Asher was in the dark just as much as I was. I'm not just taking his word for it either. The look of shock on his face when Ronan began said it all. He was blindsided and didn't know what to do or think.

Before I know it, we're pulling up to a large pair of wrought iron gates. Asher enters in a code, and the heavy gates swing open revealing a long winding driveway with a perfectly manicured lawn on either side. Huge bushy trees adorning the sides, every fifty feet, in perfect line with the driveway.

When we pull up to the house, I'm pleasantly surprised. It's not nearly as grand as Asher's dads or as ostentatious as my father's. Sure, it's still a mansion but it's clean from the outside, simple and it has a porch swing on the front. I don't know why, but I've always found them to be so charming. I always told myself one day I would have a house with one.

I suppose the manifesting really paid off.

Asher parks the car, glancing over to me.

"What do you think? From the outside?"

I nod, as my eyes continue to roam the grounds.

"It's beautiful. I love the land and that swing," I say with a small smile.

Asher grins and nods.

"That's why I picked this house out of all of the others. I could have put one on any of the houses, but this one just felt...right, you know?"

I nod my agreement as he opens his door, coming around to get mine as well. I smile in thanks as he slips his hand behind my back, ushering me up the front steps.

"I'm sorry you weren't a part of the selection process. Whatever you want changed, consider it done. Money or time is no object," he says in a way that drips sincerity.

Smiling again, I nod as Asher pulls out his key, unlocking the front door before stepping inside, quickly disarming the alarm and turning to face me. I take a small step inside, my shoes echoing against the hardwood floors. He wasn't kidding when he said the place isn't decorated. There isn't a single picture, rug or piece of furniture in sight. The place is basically a blank canvas, but something in me kind of likes that.

The foyer is huge, unnecessarily so. There is so much empty space it almost feels awkward.

"What if we got a round table to go right here," I say, as I gesture to the center of the room. "We could put a vase of flowers on it or something. I don't know, it would eat up the space while still making it feel aesthetically clean."

Asher nods, pulling out his phone, his fingers flying across the keyboard.

"What else?"

I frown. "What? Just like that?"

"Just like that, Princess," he nods. "What else?"

My eyes skim around the house, landing on an empty space that I assume is intended as a formal living room. There is a large bay window in the corner that has a smile touching my lips as I imagine it.

"Can we have a piano? Right over there," I say, as I point to the right of the window.

"Do you play?" Asher asks in surprise.

I nod. I haven't, obviously, since I left London. Honestly, even before that. I was pretty good in school, though.

"What, didn't you read that in your file about me?" I tease lightly.

He shakes his head, typing out his notes.

"That file didn't tell me shit when it came to you. Not the things that matter, at least."

"I'm an open book," I shrug, as we step into the formal living room.

"Are you?" he asks dubiously.

"Not particularly, but I'd be willing to answer some questions if you have any."

He thinks on it for a second before he shakes his head. "Can I save them for another time?"

"Sure," I laugh, as we step into the dining room. It is about the size of the one at my father's, and it's even painted the same soft cream. My nose wrinkles at the color, an action that isn't lost on Asher.

"What's wrong?"

"Nothing," I shake my head quickly.

"C'mon, Princess. Out with it."

I shrug as I move through the space.

"I just don't love the color."

Asher nods. "What color would you want?"

"Maybe a nice soft grey? Still neutral but a little ...different, I guess."

He doesn't ask different from what, nor does he try to argue. Instead, he continues furiously taking notes before giving me a smile and a nod. We continue this through the kitchen, living room, and bathrooms until we are upstairs in the bedrooms.

Asher pauses outside a set of double doors.

"This could be your room, if you want. Obviously you'll need the larger room, what with your...company," he says, his pace slowing on the word company.

"Are we going to have separate rooms?" I ask as I step inside, impressed by the sheer size of the room. The en suite attached looks just as massive, and I see two walk in closets. It's a master bedroom dream.

"Well, I assumed. Not sure how much they'd love the idea of us sharing a bed every night," Asher laughs sarcastically.

"You'd be surprised, they seem to not mind sharing. In fact Liam downright loves it," I tease with a wink.

Instead of laughter, I'm met with silence. My gaze comes up to see Asher's eyes have darkened, quite literally smoldering straight through me as my words hang in the air between us. Clearing my throat, I step out of the bedroom, finding another one and another and another.

"Oh my gosh, how many bedrooms does this place have?"

"Seven bedrooms, five and a half baths," he says, as he follows close behind.

"Wow, seven? What are we going to do with all of them."

"My father's hope is that we'd fill them with children," he chuckles, but when I turn to him with alarmed eyes he puts his hands up placatingly.

"I'm kidding. I mean, I'm not, but I didn't mean we were going to start having kids right now or anything. I just meant down the road, maybe, if things go okay...I'll need an heir eventually and—"

"Asher, it's fine. I get what you mean. Calm down."

He huffs out a breath as he nods. I peek into the bedroom beside the master and smile as I envision it before me.

"The crib could go over there, and the dresser there. What do you think about one of those really soft fluffy rugs in the middle of the room?" I ask as I point to the carpeted floor.

"Yeah," he says slowly. "That would be nice."

I continue smiling as I envision it. I'm only nineteen. The idea of children should terrify me, and it does to an extent, absolutely, but one day, maybe.

We finish with all the rooms inside of the house before making our way out back. It already has an inground pool, with a really cool waterfall built around it and a hot tub, so I couldn't be happier.

Asher says that he'd like to get some type of a gazebo back here and I nod my agreement. Eventually, we find our way back to the front of the house where we take a seat on the porch swing. We're slowly swaying on it, when I turn to face him.

"We're going to have a happy life, right?"

He falters for a moment, like that was the last thing he expected me to ask before he reaches out, covering my hand with his as he squeezes.

"As happy as we're allowed."

I can feel my mouth tip down at that, it wasn't really the words I was looking for, but it's honest. Can't fault him for that. Us getting married isn't going to magically pull any of us out from under anyone's thumb. We're as trapped today, as we were yesterday, and the day before that. Right now, we aren't trying to progress, we are trying to survive.

"I'm scared," I admit, on a soft whisper while staring out at the porch.

I feel Asher's eyes on me, and I turn, giving him a watery smile.

"About tomorrow," I explain. "I've had the experience built up in my head for a while, and this wasn't how I pictured it going."

He nods as he scoots a little closer to me, our thighs touching one another and our clasped hands now in his lap.

"I know. It wasn't what I had planned for us either."

"You had something planned?" I ask, my mouth lifting slightly.

Asher runs a hand through his deep brown hair, forcing it out of his face as he does.

"I mean, not set in stone or anything, but I'd thought about it. Thought about how it would go."

"How did it look?" I ask softly, my eyes locking onto his, my face closer than I intended. I don't pull away, though, and neither does he.

"You, me, this house. I pictured bringing you home after the wedding, and getting you out of that white dress that will no doubt drive me fucking wild all night. I would have kissed you, before making sure my lips touched every single inch of your skin. I'd have given you a minimum of two orgasms before I even tried to fuck you, intent on easing you into it."

"And then?" I practically beg.

His hand reaches out to me cupping my jaw as he brings us so close together, our lips brush against one another as he speaks.

"And then I would have made love to you for hours. Over and

over again, knowing that I could never have my fill of you but trying nonetheless."

I feel a shiver run up my spine at the way his deep voice rumbles each word.

"Tomorrow will easily be one of the hardest things we will both ever face, I won't lie," he admits as he continues. "But today...right now, I want to take something, just for us. No one interfering, no one demanding. Something they will never be able to take away," he says, his lower lip brushing against my own every other word. I'm practically shaking with need, the tension, the desperation so overwhelming I fear I'm ready to combust.

"Give me something that's just for us, Asher. Please."

The whimper in my please seems to snap any resistance he had. His lips close the distance, pressing fully against my own. A tingling rush starts at where our mouths meet and runs all the way to my toes. A light feeling overtaking me, as I melt into his touch.

He's surprisingly a gentle kisser. I expected him to be harsh and demanding like Vincent, and maybe he is occasionally but right now, with me, he's just...perfect.

Never thought I'd think that about Asher Putnam.

I feel his fingers weave through my hair, curling around my strands against my scalp and pulling slightly. The sensation forces a moan out of me, and that gives him the perfect access to slip his tongue in before tangling with my own. I don't even try to battle him for dominance. Instead, I sit here pliant, willing and ready to take anything and everything he's willing to give me.

He pulls away roughly, a ragged breath escaping him like it was a difficult thing to do. Like he could have gotten lost in me for hours, the way I want to get lost in him. His eyes are bouncing across my face, over and over again before settling on my eyes.

A slow smile lifts his face as he shakes his head.

"Of course you're an amazing kisser, is there anything about you that isn't goddamn perfect?"

"According to you? Absolutely," I laugh.

He lets out a humorless laugh as he looks up at the sky, before coming back down to me.

"Princess, I've been full of shit this entire time. I wanted you from the very moment I saw your pictures in that file."

That surprises me. I tilt my head to the side, leaning into the hold he still has on me.

"Then why did you treat me like shit?"

I watch as his tongue darts out, wetting his lower lip before he shakes his head again.

"Because I'm a fucking idiot," he says as he drops his head back down, pressing his lips to mine once more.

We stay on that porch swing for hours, wasting time like we have all of it in the world. Eventually, when the sun starts to set, we decide to head back to campus for the night. We're currently pulling into the parking lot, Asher's hand intertwined with my own since he fired the car up. I even tried to free my hand a few times to grab something out of my purse, but he wasn't having it. I suppose I can't complain all that much.

He shuts off the car and unbuckles his seat belt. I look at him with a confused look and smile.

"What are you doing?" I ask.

"Walking you to your room?" he asks, as if he doesn't understand why I would ask.

I let out a short laugh. "Since when?"

"Since I realized how goddamn precious those lips were. They need to be protected at all costs," he smirks as he leans across the center console.

Smiling to myself, I only lean forward a few inches letting him do most of the work, which he seems to have no problem doing. His hand cups my jaw, holding me close to him as he deepens the kiss when a sharp knock catches our attention.

We both jolt apart, turning to see Liam at my window with a

goofy smile. Asher makes an irritated noise in the back of his throat before he grumbles.

"One of your guard dogs is here."

"Didn't you just say that you're basically one of them?" I scoff with a smirk.

His eyes search mine, his words hesitant.

"I don't know...am I?"

The air is so thick, it's suddenly hard to breathe. We both know what he's really asking, and I don't really know if I have an answer for him. Thankfully, the comedic relief is here, so I don't have to give him a response right this second.

My door swings open and Liam leans in, planting a slobbery kiss on my cheek before he looks at both of us smiling.

"Soooo, when did this happen?" he asks with a waggle of his eyebrows.

"None of your fucking business," Asher grouches as he leans his head back against his seat, a smile playing at his lips as he squeezes my hand tighter, like he can't find it in him to be mad right now.

Liam's mouth drops open.

"Is that a smile? Did you just smile?! For a girl? Oh my god! And you're holding hands? Who are you and what have you done with my best friend?"

His excited eyes flick to me as he shakes his head.

"Babygirl, you have magic love powers or something. All you have to do is look at a man and he's head over heels for you."

"Speak for yourself," Asher scoffs.

"Oh no, lover boy. No going back now. I know what I saw. You're into my girlfriend. It's a good thing I love to share," Liam smirks.

Asher rolls his head to Liam, a dubious look on his face.

"Or are you dating my soon to be wife?"

Liam frowns at that before shaking his head.

"I don't like the sound of that. I had her first. Dibs."

I can't help but let out a laugh.

"You're ridiculous," I say as I push Liam out of the way. He quickly steps back, and I turn to Asher.

"I need my hand back if I'm gonna go inside."

He looks down at it, as if he were contemplating how he could hold onto it for the night without chopping it off. Lifting our joined hands to his lips, he presses a featherlight kiss against the back of my hand.

I smile at the tender gesture.

"You don't want to come in, do you? Stay for a while?"

His eyes darken, and I honestly think he's about to say yes when his phone begins buzzing in the center console. I watch as his eyes shutter closed and when they open again, all desire seems to be drained right out of them.

"I'll see you tomorrow."

I nod, trying and failing to hide my disappointment when he frees my hand and picks up his phone. I slide out of the car without another word, giving him a half a wave that he returns before I close the door and he answers.

"C'mon, I can't wait to see the look on Vincent's face when he finds out he has to share you with Asher too!" Liam practically giggles.

"You're such a little pot stirrer," I laugh with a shake of my head.

"Oh absolutely."

Chapter Forty Nine
Skyla

Turns out, Vincent wasn't as upset as Liam or I thought he would be. Vincent and Ronan were waiting for me in my room when I got back, and before I could even sit them down and explain my feelings for Asher or what happened, Liam word vomited it to them.

"Guess who I just found making out with our girl in the parking lot?"

It took half a second for Ronan and Vincent to simultaneously say, "Asher."

Apparently, they saw it coming even before I did. We all talked about it, Ronan said it didn't matter to him and Vincent said that as long as he is the one who gets to kill him if he hurts me, then he's fine with it. Which is very on brand for him but sweet, nonetheless.

The next morning, Liam and Vincent got called away early. Assumingly, to be summoned for tonight. Ronan spent the entire day with me, though, and his watchful eyes tracked every move I made.

I've been trying to keep it together, to not picture how absolutely embarrassing and humiliating it will be to be so vulnerable in front of so many people, a bunch of strange men no less. A knock on the door sends my body jolting, which Ronan takes note of before standing up and answering the door.

Waiting for me on the floor is a white box. He carries it inside, setting it onto the desk for me. The way he's looking at it, it's like he already knows what's inside.

Peeling back the top, I reach inside and hold up the white silky material. It's a nightgown, so smooth and sheer it's practically see through, with at least fifty buttons going down from the neck to the floor. There is a card at the bottom. I lift it up to read the perfect scrawled penmanship across it.

This and nothing more.
Looking forward to seeing you.
Christopher

I frown, and Ronan plucks the card from my hand, giving a frown of his own.

"That's kind of creepy, right?" I ask.

Ronan just swallows, tilting his head to the side consideringly before shaking it.

"He's just trying to get into your head. Don't let him."

"Well, do I have to wear this thing?"

He nods and I frown. I mean, I suppose if I can keep it on during the ceremony, though I doubt I will be able to, it'll be something. It's better than them ordering me to march in completely naked, right?

We spend hours inside my room, mainly because I'm terrified to leave. Ronan said that we would have to leave at eleven thirty, but ever since it turned eleven, I haven't been able to stop shaking.

My stomach has been tight and ready to upturn all of its contents from the day but at eleven fifteen, I let it win and rush into the bathroom.

I heave and heave but to my disappointment, nothing is coming out. Instead, I'm left a panicked, shaking and sick mess. I don't even feel the tears pouring down my face until they begin splashing against my arms. A knock comes from the door, Ronan's voice soft and concerned.

"Are you okay, baby?"

"N-no," I laugh self-deprecatingly.

"Asher is here. Do you want me to send him away?"

I think about it for a moment before I reach for some toilet paper, drying my face as best as I can before answering.

"Let him in."

The bathroom door opens in the next moment, Asher's face filled with sympathy as he crouches down beside me.

"Princess," he says softly, as he wipes my tears away with his thumbs.

"Hi," I say with a pathetic smile, as another tear drops.

"It's gonna be okay. It's one night. One night that I'll spend the rest of my life trying to help you forget, okay?"

I nod, leaning into his touch as he cups my face.

"I wanted to check on you before I head out. Just keep your eyes on me the whole time, okay? Did Ronan explain everything to you?"

Nodding again, he blows out a soft breath.

"Good. I'm so sorry about this," he says, pressing a lingering kiss to my forehead as he shakes his head and pulls away. "So sorry," he whispers under his breath as he stands.

"I'll see you soon," I say with a watery smile.

He gives me a sad, tight lipped smile in response before stepping out of the bathroom. Ronan comes in right after him, dropping to the floor and pulling me into his lap. He cradles me like a wounded child, tucking me against his chest as he rocks me slightly. It's calming, forcing me to relax for the first time since I woke up this morning.

"It's almost time," he murmurs against the crown of my head.

"I know," I rasp, before slowly pulling myself to stand.

Ronan helps me, and I move to the counter to wash my face. Thankfully I knew I'd need to save makeup for last as I make sure to grab my waterproof mascara in case any more tears pop up. I do a half assed job that I'm sure I'll be hearing about from my father later, but ask me if I care right now.

Once my makeup is done and my hair is brushed, I begin stripping out of my clothes until I'm completely naked. I undo the top, twenty or so buttons before slipping on the dress. Ronan steps forward, redoing them for me as I stand there like a doll for him to dress.

"Can I wear shoes?" I ask.

He looks at me consideringly before nodding.

"You'll have to take them off once we are inside but for now, yes."

My nose wrinkles. "Do you guys get to wear shoes?"

"Yes."

"Then why can't I?" I ask, defiance rippling through me.

Ronan instantly senses it and his fingers stall on the buttons, holding my shoulders tightly.

"Look at me."

I do as he says, to find a serious expression on his face.

"I could not be more serious when I say this, Skyla. Do not talk back. Do not ask questions. Do. Not. Speak. The entire time we are there."

Slowly, I nod. It's not a hard concept. My father has always emphasized the importance of women being seen and not heard. An ideal that Aunt Steph undermined every chance she could. When we weren't in my father's presence, of course.

I slip on a pair of flats as the clock strikes eleven twenty and Ronan opens the door. I leave my key and phone here, since he said they wouldn't be allowed wherever we are going anyways. As soon as we step outside the building, Ronan stops me in my tracks, tying a blindfold on my face.

"Seriously?" I ask.

"Sorry, baby. Rules."

I scoff but let him tie the white satin material around my eyes as he begins guiding me. When we get to his car, he opens the door, helping me in before we begin driving. We drive for probably five minutes before we park, though I swear we just drove in a bunch of circles.

My flats thunk against the hard pavement before it soon changes to something different. My steps are more echoed, and a chill erupts over my spine as we carefully go down a set of stairs.

"Almost there," Ronan says.

A musty smell fills my nose, and I do my best to breathe through my mouth as we walk. After a little ways, Ronan stops me, pulling my shoes off before setting them to the side.

"We have to go in here first. Keep your blindfold on," he whispers, as he takes me into a room where a chilling voice greets us.

"Ah, welcome, Miss Parris," a man says from my left.

I don't say anything, giving a polite smile and a nod. Ronan lifts me up and onto a table before pushing me to lay down. I do as he guides, while I prepare for the examination.

Thankfully, Ronan gave me a heads up.

"Feet together and let your legs fall open please."

My stomach rolling at the request, I do as he says, an appreciative guffaw falling from his lips that makes me sick.

"Mr. Putnam is a very lucky man. You're so beautiful."

"Is she a virgin or not?" Ronan grits through clenched teeth.

I can practically hear him working his jaw over and over again, so he doesn't break this guy's.

"It certainly appears so. Allow me to confirm," he says before he slips a finger inside me, feeling around and pressing on me in a way that's painful before I whimper.

"Most definitely. A prize indeed," the doctor says, his smile audible in his tone. Ronan's rough hands pull down my dress, helping me sit up before sliding off the bed.

"Thanks, Doc," Ronan says briskly, as he begins walking us out.

"Oh, the pleasure is all mine!" he says before I hear a door shut.

"Fucking piece of shit," Ronan grumbles under his breath, lowering it to a whisper as he speaks. "You okay?"

I nod, not speaking as we come to a stop.

"Okay. We're here. We will wait until someone comes to get us. Are you ready?"

Shaking my head no, I do my best to hold down the nerves buzzing inside me. God, part of me wishes I could keep my blindfold on the whole time. It would be easier to disassociate at least.

Unfortunately for me, the sound of a door snicks open, before a voice I don't recognize says, "They are ready for her."

Chapter Fifty
Skyla

Following Ronan's steps I pause when he stops me, his fingers going to the back of the blindfold. As soon as he unties it, it's like I can finally see for the first time in years. The room is dimly lit, only by torches lining the cobblestone walls. Men surround the perimeter, the older ones in deep burgundy cloaked robes, while the guys who attend Gallows Hill wear crisp white dress shirts and black dress pants.

It only takes me half a second to find Vincent and then Liam just a little further down. Liam is standing in front of his father, as Vincent is standing alone. Dane and Jeremy are here as well as Andrew Hutchinson and a few others. Andrew's face in particular twists up in sadness and sympathy as he looks at me. I'm not sure what he's doing in the Brethren, he seems much too soft, too kind.

Liam is watching me with a blank face, but his eyes are filled with pain. I flick my gaze to Vincent as casually as I can manage, to see his stoic face looking more murderous than anything. I look away from them quickly, trying not to gain any unnecessary attention as my eyes find my father and Asher's father next.

Christopher smiles as he holds out his hands, the robe sleeves hanging off his arms by several inches.

"Welcome, Skyla. What a glorious night it is."

I do my best to give him a convincing smile, dipping my head down in obedience. A few approving murmurs sound through the room, and that at least helps make me feel like I'm doing something right.

"Please, lie down," Christopher says as he gestures towards a stone slab in the middle of the room.

How did I not notice this first?

With shaky steps, I make my way to the stone, slowly laying down on top of it as I do. My head looks behind me and notices a large golden mirror. The frame is ornate and large, going almost all the way to the ceiling and being at least six-feet-wide. It's positioned so me and the slab are perfectly centered.

Wouldn't want anyone to miss the view, I suppose.

Revulsion rolls through me as the doors open once more. This time, Asher is the one to step inside. As opposed to the rest of them, he is wearing a white robe. His face is blank, posture stiff as he comes to stand before me. He doesn't look at me, though. His eyes are on his father, and I do my best to fix my eyes on the ceiling. There are so many cobblestone bricks, maybe I could count them and when I'm done, it'll hopefully be over.

"Asher Putnam, you are brought here today to solidify your place in the Brethren and strengthen your family's legacy. In taking a bride, you secure the ability for an heir and strengthen our bonds. Stronger together, immeasurable as one."

"Maleficis esse mori," Asher responds.

What is that? Latin? He speaks Latin?

"Maleficis esse mori," all the other men in the room chant as one.

It startles me, but I don't let it show before Asher turns to me, someone stepping forward with a wooden box. He lifts up my right hand, pulling out an old looking dagger from the box before dragging the tip against my palm. His eyes don't meet mine which somehow makes this worse. If he'd just look at me, maybe I wouldn't feel as terrified. I knew this part was coming, Ronan told me it would. Doesn't make it any less painful.

My eyes squint softly, as I try to hold in my pain while another man steps forward with a large book, smearing my bloody handprint across it before setting my hand by my side. It's still bleeding heavily, but no one seems to be too concerned with it as a third man steps forward, a red hot iron brand in hand. He hands the material covered handle to Asher and finally, he meets my eyes.

His face is hard and emotionless, but his eyes give me an apologetic gleam before he's pressing the brand into my other palm. I can't hold back my screams for this one. My lips are smashed together to muffle the sound, but it doesn't make it quieter.

"Mmmmhmmm aghhhh!" I grumble and shout, my head turning to see Vincent take a step forward. I didn't notice until now that Ronan has taken up a place behind him, his hand on Vincent's shoulder in a casual way, though I can tell that it's really so he can hold him in place.

The searing pain doesn't ebb unfortunately, the smell of my flesh burning fills the room, a smell so foul I want nothing more than to gag. Amazingly, I keep it together, as both palms are now screaming at me in displeasure.

Asher pulls the brand away, handing it back to the man before his fingers grip my dress. I expect him to get to work on the buttons, but he wastes no time, grabbing the top hemline and ripping hard. The buttons give free easily, scattering all around me, and falling to the ground until the robe is completely ripped open. My breasts spill free, and my eyes flick to see Liam's jaw set painfully tight, while Vincent looks on the edge of losing it. Ronan leans down to whisper something into his ear that seems to calm him down.

God, I wish they didn't have to see this. I wish I didn't have to live it.

Asher drops his robe, revealing that he is also completely naked as he spreads my legs and climbs on top of me. His hands rest on either side of my head as he lines his cock up to my entrance. His eyes meet mine, a sense of ease settling in me when I see those three golden flecks. He mouths something, so soft I almost think I'm imagining it. When he does it again, though, I know it was intentional.

"Eyes on me."

I do as he says, watching him intently as he snaps his hips forward, hard. My mouth opens as pain rips through me. Asher's thrusts are rushed and savage, only leaving room for results, not pleasure. The combined pain from my hands to my vagina getting literally ripped open has me whimpering and lightly sobbing. Tears roll down my face, but I don't outwardly cry. I attempt to take every thrust he gives me, his face serious and intent and his hips snap faster and faster.

He drops to his forearms, letting out a pleasure filled growl as he buries his face into my hair.

"Almost done" he grits into my ear.

I nod, not knowing what I'm doing until it's too late.

"It's okay, baby. I love you," I sob, only realizing that not only did I just expose what he told me in my ear to the entire room, I called him baby, I told him that I loved him.

Where the hell did that come from?

My eyes do a quick look around the room, surprise on each and every face. Apart from Christopher who looks downright furious. Asher pulls back his hand, letting it fly through the air so fast I don't even see it coming.

The slap makes my eyes water even more, the sting of my cheek just another body part added to the long list of things Asher has hurt tonight. He gathers up spit in the next moment, spitting into my face before an evil laugh rips through him, his thrusts quickening.

"Stupid bitch. So fucking gullible. Love?" he laughs. "I'll never love you," he says as his face contorts, and his body tightens.

My heart shatters at the same moment his body releases. I feel his cum flood me, his curses and moans loud in the otherwise silent room before he gives me a wicked smile.

"That was almost too easy," he smirks.

"What was?" I ask just above a whisper.

The smile curves up higher and higher, nothing but black visible in his eyes.

"Everything."

Thank you

I know, I know. You probably kind of hate me for ending it like that. Do you see the size of this thing, though? We had to stop at some point, and what better point to stop than when the asshole MMC we were *just* starting to fall for turns back into the asshat we've known throughout this book. Go ahead, hate me a little. Just know that Descent will make up for it in all the ways the count (and the HEAVY spice in it helps.) After all, our girl is no longer a virgin... let the fun begin.

Once you're finished with Descent, you might as well jump into Demise! Then when that is all said and done, why not finish off with Deliverance, am I right? Or step back in time to see how the Brethren all began with Damnation!

If you're looking to check out some of my other work outside of Gallows Hill, then you are in luck! I have included a shameless plug list below!

Stand Alones –

Graves – An MFM stalker romance

Gratify – Forbidden age gap romance

Jagged Harts – Enemies to lovers MMA romance.

Graves & Griggs: A Very Bloody Christmas

The Alphaletes Series –

The Loyalties We Break – Ex-boyfriend's best friend sports romance

The Walls We Break – Single mom sports romance

The Hearts We Break – Friends to lovers sports romance

The Rules We Break – Enemies to lovers sports romance

The ONS Series –

One Night Seduction

One Night Scandal

One Night Surrender

Acknowledgments

There are so many thank you's for this story! This was a work in progress for almost a year and a half and now that book one is done, it's a bittersweet feeling.

Thank you to Sara, my PA/Alpha/Poor person that has to field my every question, comment and insecurity while writing a book. There is no doubt that this book would not have hit its deadline had it not been for you and your dedication to not only me but this world. I love you so much!

Thank you to my Betas, Kreature, Brittany, Elena & Jennifer. Your insight was invaluable and every second that you spent with me and this story I'm incredibly grateful for. I love you all and am so happy to have such amazing people on my team!

Thank you to my editor, Lyndsey. Phew, girl. This book put us both through the wringer! Thank you so much for your high level of attention to detail, your understanding and your extremely hard work. Those 3AM nights are not unnoticed and I'm forever grateful to have met you, become friends with you, and have you on my team!

Thank you to all of my ARC readers. Every review you leave, every post you make, every comment you create helps in ways you can't even imagine. I'm so grateful to have such a fantastic group, reading, promoting and supporting my book!

Last but of course not least, thank you to my amazing readers. You all are the reason that on even the hard days, I keep pushing.

The amount of love and kindness you all have shown and continue to show me have changed in ways I can't even describe. Thank you for taking the time to read my books and following me along this journey. I love you all so incredibly deeply.